ATAN

THE REVOLUTIONARY

by

ROBERT SEAN LEWIS

Atan the Revolutionary/Robert Sean Lewis
ISBN 978-1-955018-37-1 (paperback)
ISBN 978-1-955018-43-2 (large print)
ISBN 978-1-955018-33-3 (eBook)
ISBN 978-1-955018-36-4 (hardback)

FIRST EDITION

"A speculative dystopian tale written in an engaging literary style, *Atan the Revolutionary* could become a classic. A revolution needs a cultural leader, not a political one. Lewis might be him."

~ V.N. Alexander, author of *Locus Amoenus*

"*Atan the Revolutionary* is a masterful and engaging story about getting back to our roots—a way of being in the world that revels in the beauty, adventure, and interconnectedness that life is meant to provide. Such a literary undertaking testifies to the author's many years of radical reflection and passionate activism. His main character, Atan, struggles with the dynamics of two worldviews, as do many Indigenous leaders today. Atan, the way that Lewis presents him, could be any one of us who has glimpsed truth and magic amidst the systems that stifle both. Young and old alike will want to resist pausing to reflect but will be unable to do so."

~ Four Arrows (aka Don Trent Jacobs), co-author of *Restoring the Kinship Worldview: Indigenous Voices Introduce 28 Precepts for Balancing Life on Planet Earth*

"A story for our time. Lewis skilfully weaves a tale about awakening, revolution, and moral responsibility as we learn about the life and times of Atan the revolutionary. Contrasting Indigenous wisdom with the corrupted political systems of late modernity and keeping a steady eye on the greatest hidden truths of our time, Lewis captures beautifully the struggle to find the courage to stand up and fight for justice. In a world still plagued with deception and corruption, Lewis's storytelling can help lead us toward truth, justice, and accountability.

~ Piers Robinson, co-author of *Pockets of Resistance: British News Media, War and Theory in the 2003 Invasion of Iraq*

"*Atan the Revolutionary* traces the spiritual quest of its hero as he strives to recapture the key to the re-enchantment of a world that is descending into a materialistic dystopia. As the reader follows the tortuous path of Atan's struggle, love and spirit battle to break through and reset the world."

~ Richard Pope, author of *Flight from Grace: A Cultural History of Humans and Birds*

Acknowledgments

The Times They Are A-Changin'
Words and Music by Bob Dylan
Copyright © 1963, 1964 UNIVERSAL TUNES
Copyright Renewed
All Rights Reserved Used by Permission
Reprinted by Permission of Hal Leonard LLC

Dress Rehearsal Rag
Words and Music by Leonard Cohen
Copyright © 1967 Sony Music Publishing (US) LLC
Copyright Renewed
All Rights Administered by Sony Music Publishing (US) LLC, 424 Church Street, Suite 1200, Nashville, TN 37219
International Copyright Secured All Rights Reserved
Reprinted by Permission of Hal Leonard LLC

Chelsea Hotel #2
Words and Music by Leonard Cohen
Copyright © 1974 Sony Music Publishing (US) LLC
Copyright Renewed
All Rights Administered by Sony Music Publishing (US) LLC, 424 Church Street, Suite 1200, Nashville, TN 37219
International Copyright Secured All Rights Reserved
Reprinted by Permission of Hal Leonard LLC

Tower of Song
Words and Music by Leonard Cohen
Copyright © 1988 Sony Music Publishing (US) LLC
All Rights Administered by Sony Music Publishing (US) LLC, 424 Church Street, Suite 1200, Nashville, TN 37219
International Copyright Secured All Rights Reserved
Reprinted by Permission of Hal Leonard LLC

Anthem
Words and Music by Leonard Cohen
Copyright © 1992 Sony Music Publishing (US) LLC
All Rights Administered by Sony Music Publishing (US) LLC, 424 Church Street, Suite 1200, Nashville, TN 37219
International Copyright Secured All Rights Reserved
Reprinted by Permission of Hal Leonard LLC

PSYCHO KILLER
Words by DAVID BYRNE, CHRIS FRANTZ and TINA WEYMOUTH
Music by DAVID BYRNE
© 1976 (Renewed) WC MUSIC CORP. and INDEX MUSIC, INC.
All Rights Administered by WC MUSIC CORP.
All Rights Reserved
Used by Permission of ALFRED MUSIC

For my father,

Ronald Ernest Lewis (1936–2022),
who admonished me to look for fertilizer in the valleys
and leave the mountaintops to the saints

Table of Contents

ONE

1969

Just before the Easter break, with the bay still frozen over and the students restless for winter to end, the teacher didn't know what to think when Rachel brought her grandfather to class one morning without warning. He'd come to tell the children a story, and Rachel was going to translate, the girl informed her. Fourteen that year, Rachel struggled to read English and had been kept back so many times that she was still in the fourth grade. But she could speak the language well enough, thanks to her fondness for radio broadcasts, especially *The Northern Messenger*, whose host at the CBC studios in Montreal read letters addressed to listeners in Inuit settlements scattered across the north.

Standing before the teacher, the old man paused to look at her, perhaps taken aback by her size, what with her plump cheeks, her double chin, her heavy breasts resting atop a belly rounded by the baby burrowed inside her, full-grown now and past due. But in his eyes, she saw only delight.

Rachel slipped a hand under her grandfather's arm and led him along an aisle of desks to the front of the room, where they sat down together on the floor, cross-legged. Without waiting to be asked, the students wiggled out of their desks and went to the front of the room too, jostling each other until all of them had found a spot on the floor at the old man's knees.

Perched behind her students on a desktop, the teacher crossed her nyloned calves at the ankles and let her patent-leather Mary Janes—in sensible beige, without too much of a heel—dangle just above the floor, marveling that even their incessant coughing had ceased. Having stayed up late to prepare a quiz on the winter term's spelling, math, and geography, she was at first put off by the old man's unexpected visit, but her students seemed in thrall of him. For two long years, she had failed to spark anything like excitement in their passive faces. The more animated she became, the less they responded. Encouraged to try new things, they withdrew. The old man's arrival had transformed them into eager learners.

As he looked at the children one by one, some of them squirmed. Studying a solemn boy seated behind the others, the old man spoke to him in Inuktitut, and the boy nodded. When the old man responded, the children laughed as one of the girls reached over and poked the boy in the ribs.

"What did your grandfather say?" the teacher asked Rachel.

"Nothing," the girl answered.

Pointing a finger at his granddaughter, the old man clucked his tongue. Chastened, Rachel explained to the teacher that her grandfather had asked the boy if his family name was Pudloo, which it was. In reply, her grandfather had told him, "You have your father's frown," making the children laugh.

At that, without any words of introduction, as if he needed no gestures of formality to lend his story significance, the old man cleared his throat and began to speak, nodding as he listened to Rachel interpret his words, the girl barely missing a beat.

"Before I came to this world and was still inside my mother's tummy, the people had grown hungry because the caribou hadn't come to feed them. Then, one night, when my mother was as round as an igloo,

I visited my father in a dream. He saw me swimming inside my mother like a fish, and then I grew into a youngster who was little Pudloo's age.

"Antlers sprouted from my head, and I had hooves for feet. Behind me, my father could see the northern ocean and the beach where the caribou went into the water before swimming out to an island offshore to eat good food. 'The caribou are coming,' I told him.

"So my parents went to that place to wait for the herd.

"When a month passed, and the caribou didn't come, my parents argued about what to do. They had used up the last of the whale oil trying to stay warm, and my father hadn't caught any fish for three days. Hungry, my mother nagged him to take her back to her family. They had stayed too long, she said, and if they weren't careful, I would be born before they could get home. But my father wouldn't leave.

"The next night, a whaling ship anchored in the bay, and my father set out to get some oil from the crew. Outside my parents' tent, he saw two puffs of ice hanging in the air in front of him. In the dim light of the nighttime sun, he could make out the wet, quivering nostrils of a big bull caribou. Standing nose to nose with the animal, he suddenly heard hooves thundering past as the first of the caribou headed toward the shore.

"At that moment, my mother let out a terrible cry. When my father ran back inside, he found her on the floor, down on her hands and knees, straining with all her might as she tried to push me out. 'We have to name the child, or he won't come,' he told my mother. But she wanted to see me first so she could decide what I was like.

"'Wait,' she said.

"'The caribou are here,' my father said. 'This child knows things. He is wise. We will call him Ataninnuaq.'"

As Rachel translated this part of the story, the teacher struggled to catch the old man's name.

"Atan-innu-aq," Rachel repeated.

"Atan-innu-aq," the teacher said.

"It means wise counselor," Rachel added.

The girl sounded boastful, apparently certain of her grandfather's standing in a greater order. For her part, the teacher couldn't decide if the old man was wise or not. What he'd said about his father's dream seemed like a family legend, something exaggerated over time until it became a myth. She would have to remember to talk to her students about this kind of story another day.

Right then, the old man looked at the teacher and said to Rachel, "Tell her this is all true. It was 1889."

When Rachel translated what her grandfather had said, the teacher recoiled in surprise. It was as if he had read her thoughts.

"My grandfather is an *angakkuq*," Rachel added. "An-ga-kkuq."

"What is that?" the teacher asked when she had regained her balance.

"Like a doctor."

"Really ... a doctor?"

"But not like your doctors, who heal only bodies. He's a spirit doctor."

"Oh, a medicine man."

Rachel shook her head. "No, an *angakkuq*," she repeated. "We're not Indians."

The old man coughed.

"My mother didn't want to name me Ataninnuaq," he explained. "She told my father it would bring them trouble if they chose a strong name. 'What if the baby is a numbskull like my brother?' she asked him."

The children giggled.

"'Or what if he is hard-headed like yours? People will tease him and mock us.'

"But my father wouldn't change his mind. He put his hand on my mother's back and said, 'Ataninnuaq, come out.'

"And I came out. My father had to catch me. He wrapped me in skins and placed me in my mother's lap. Then he heated the blade of his knife in the flame of the oil lamp and used it to cut the birth cord.

"Spitting on her thumb, my mother wiped the mucus from my eyes and looked at me. What she saw surprised her. It was true, she told my father. I knew things.

"'Ataninnuaq,' she said, no longer worried.

"That is how I got my name," the old man said, his gaze fixed on the teacher. "A name is one of our spirits."

The teacher was intrigued. "How many spirits do you have?" she asked Rachel.

"Three," the girl said.

"What are the other two?"

"The breath and the soul. The breath dies with your body, but the soul goes to live with our ancestors."

"I see," the teacher said, not wanting to admit she didn't understand at all.

"My younger brother never moved inside my mother's tummy, not even a little kick," the old man said. "She thought he was dead, but my father said the baby was waiting, like a good hunter. So they called him Ujarak."

"Ujarak means rock," Rachel added.

"Oh," the teacher said, feeling strangely like a student in her own classroom.

"My brother would not be an *angakkuq* like me," the old man went on. "He would be a hunter because he could stay still for a long time.

"As a boy, Ujarak would show the bravery of a hunter, too, like the time a wolf skulked into our winter camp, angling toward the sled dogs our father kept tied up next to our snow house. Howling and yanking at their chains, the dogs alerted Ujarak, who ran toward the pack, pumping his little legs as hard as he could through the deep, heavy drifts until he stopped between the wolf and the dogs, his fist raised, ready to strike.

"Snarling, the wolf flashed its teeth and leaped at Ujarak, its jaws about to close around his throat, when the animal yelped and twisted sideways in the air. Falling to the ground, the wolf struggled to stand but tumbled over again, the snow streaked with blood. Catching up to Ujarak, I saw the trimmed, white feathers of an arrow sticking out of the animal's shaggy fur. Behind me, my uncle lowered his bow. The commotion of the dogs had brought him outside just in time. Going to Ujarak, he kneeled beside the panting wolf.

"'It's time you learn how to use a bow,' he said to my brother. 'I will teach you.'

"I went and stood with them. The wolf lay dead, its narrow yellow eyes still open, as if it could see us. 'I didn't know what to do,' I told my uncle.

"'That's okay. I will teach Ujarak to shoot. Next time, he will be ready.'

"'I want to learn too,' I said.

"'Killing is not for you,' he told me.

"That night, I complained to my father that I wanted to learn to shoot like Ujarak. Uncle wasn't being fair.

"'You are going to be an *angakkuq* like me,' he said. 'You will learn about the unseen and you will know things. Our people will need your help as much as they will need Ujarak to hunt for them.'

"As the years passed and my brother and I were educated according to our natures, we became jealous of each other. I wanted to learn how to use the bow and arrow, and he wanted to learn the secrets of the *angakkuq*. But our father wouldn't allow it. He said if I learned to hunt as well as my brother, I wouldn't need Ujarak to feed the people, and he said if Ujarak became a powerful *angakkuq*, he wouldn't need me to find the caribou for him. Our uncle and father also worked together in this way. Our father told us the secrets of an *angakkuq* were dangerous in the hands of a hunter. For the same reason, an *angakkuq* should never take on the task of killing, for his advantage over the animals would be too great. But if my brother and I worked together, he said, the people would never go hungry.

"Instead of heeding our father, Ujarak urged me to demonstrate the things I was learning about how to be an *angakkuq*. In exchange, he promised he would teach me how to hunt. 'You need me more than I need you,' he argued. 'Who can an *angakkuq* feed?'

"'How are you going to feed anyone if you don't know where the caribou are?' I asked him. 'Without me, you'll be no better than a blind man searching for a hole in the ice.'

"But Ujarak was too stubborn for me to resist. And my desire to learn to hunt was too strong. Eventually, I surrendered to my brother's wishes, and by the time we reached our teens, I had become as skilled with the bow and arrow as Ujarak, if not as patient. And Ujarak had become as crafty with the *angakkuq*'s arts as me, if not as respectful of the unseen forces we were learning to use. If I could slow a fish by cooling its blood just long enough to grab it from the river, Ujarak could stay motionless for so long that he could cool the blood of a whole school of fish. But he was always showing off and ended up catching more fish than we could gut and clean before they spoiled. If my father had found out what we were doing, he would have stopped us. When you waste food, the spirits get angry and the animals go away."

With these words, the old man erupted in a fit of coughing that left him doubled over and gasping. Concerned, the teacher suggested to Rachel that they stop.

"Your grandfather can come back another day," she said.

"No!" the students chimed.

When Rachel told her grandfather what the teacher had said, he shook his head.

"How about some tea, then?" the teacher asked, cradling her stomach as she lowered herself from the desktop and went to plug in the kettle that always sat on the counter beneath the window.

"Okay," Rachel said.

Waiting for the water to boil, the teacher dropped a tea bag into a mug and gazed out at the barren expanse of trampled snow that covered the schoolyard. Maybe the baby would come if it had a name, she mused, thinking about how the old man's father had hastened his birth by naming him while his mother was in labor. At the teacher's last checkup, giving in to her curiosity, she had let the doctor tell her the baby's sex. To her relief, she was going to have a boy, a brother for her two young daughters. A third girl would have been one too many, thank you very much. Now, she just had to settle on a name.

As the kettle whistled, the teacher snapped out of her reverie, amused by her sudden turn to superstition. Smiling at her foolishness, she unplugged the kettle and poured out a mug of hot water. When the tea had steeped, she placed the dripping bag on a saucer to use again and brought the mug to Ataninnuaq, careful not to step on her students' fingers as she tiptoed between their knees and elbows to reach him. The old man took the mug in both hands and drank the tea in three scalding gulps as the teacher watched, startled by his gusto.

Seemingly reinvigorated, his eyes bright, Ataninnuaq returned the empty mug to the teacher, and she made her retreat, hoisting herself back up onto the desktop.

"The year I was twenty," the old man said, "I left my people and went to live in an igloo far from the winter camp. I ate very little and sat all day listening for the caribou. In the quiet, the wind whispered in my ears, mocking and taunting me as it filled my head with doubts. 'Go home. The caribou won't show themselves. You are too impatient. You'll never find them.' But I knew the wind was just the voice of my own fears, so I stayed put, waiting to hear the sound of hooves scuffling over the rock and ice.

"At last, one morning, as I lay on my bed of skins and watched the rays of the returning sun climb up the wall of my igloo, the snout of a caribou poked through the chimney hole above my head. I scrambled to my feet and went outside, squinting into the light, but I could see no caribou or tracks in the snow. Certain my visitor had been a spirit, I crawled back into my igloo to see if it would return. Shortly, a puff of icy air billowed in through the chimney hole, followed by the snout of the caribou again. This time, instead of going outside, I spoke to the animal. I knew if it was a spirit, it would talk to me. I asked it to tell me when the caribou would come. But the spirit huffed and said nothing. Then I remembered the bag of moss my father had given me. He'd picked the freshest, greenest, juiciest leaves just for this purpose. I quickly opened the bag and fed the moss to the caribou spirit by the handful until the animal had devoured it all.

"After that, the spirit spoke through the chimney hole. It told me when winter ended and I saw the hares with their babies and the first brambleberries were ripe and ready to eat, I should take my people back to the place where I was born. The herd would meet us at the water. 'But there is one more thing,' the spirit said. 'Your brother Ujarak cannot join the hunt.'

"'Ujarak is ready,' I protested. 'He may be young like me, but already he is one of our best hunters.'

"'He is greedy and proud,' the caribou snorted. "If he joins the hunt, we will not offer ourselves to you. Your arrows will miss the mark and you will go hungry.'

"What the caribou spirit said about Ujarak was true, and I blamed myself. I had taught him too many of the *angakkuq*'s secrets. It had made him ruthless in the hunt and reckless. One time, he had even threatened to turn our uncle to stone.

"That day, Ujarak was pestering me. 'Father has taught you nothing but tricks,' he said.

"'That isn't true,' I answered.

"'Then tell me. What would you do if a wolf attacked us now, like when we were kids?'

"Our uncle was coming toward us along the shore, and he looked angry.

"'I don't know,' I said.

"'I didn't think so,' Ujarak sneered.

"'I would turn it to stone,' I said under my breath.

"Our uncle had almost reached us.

"'What did you say?'

"'I would turn it to stone!'

"It was the first time I had told Ujarak about this power, and it surprised him.

"'You know how to do that?'

"'Not yet. But I could turn its heart to stone.'

"Ujarak's eyes shone. 'That's a good one,' he said.

"'Ujarak!' our uncle hollered as he strode to a stop in front of us. 'You left the sled with the dogs! They chewed up all the straps. It's in pieces!'

"'Ataninnuaq needed—'

"'He doesn't need anything from you,' our uncle bellowed. 'Useless!' He stomped past us through the snow. 'Come!' he shouted at Ujarak.

"We were quiet until he was gone. 'I'll turn Uncle to stone!' Ujarak blurted out. 'We'll see who's useless then.'

"When I returned home after meeting the caribou spirit and told Ujarak he couldn't join the hunt, he got angry. He had waited a long time to hunt the caribou with the other men. The next morning, without telling anyone, he packed up his things and walked off toward the sun. When our people set out to meet the caribou at the place where I was born, Ujarak still hadn't returned.

"On the day that the caribou arrived at the shore as promised, my father sent me to meet them. Watching from a hillside, I waited with the hunters as the leaders stepped into the water one after another and swam toward the island. The herd followed close behind, more caribou than the people had seen in years. When we had let the leaders pass, I motioned to the hunters. 'It's time!' I cried. And they clambered down the slope to the shore, their bows at the ready, as I looked on.

"But something was wrong. The leaders were trying to get back to shore. The caribou behind them had panicked, and some were swimming out to open water. Then I saw him. On the top of a bluff overlooking the coast sat Ujarak, his eyes on the caribou leaders. They were almost back to shore, but the harder they tried to reach the beach, the slower they swam. It was as if, oh no, as if they were being turned to stone. 'It's Ujarak!' I yelled.

"I ran along the shore toward my brother. 'Stop!' I shouted. 'Ujarak, stop!' But his power over the caribou leaders was too strong, and I couldn't reach him in time. One after another, Ujarak turned the leaders to stone. They froze where they stood, their antlers poking up out of the water."

The teacher stared at the old man in disbelief.

"Today, they call that place Tuktoyaktuk," Ataninnuaq said.

"That means Looks Like Caribou," Rachel explained.

"The caribou never came back there," the old man said, his eyes glistening with what the teacher thought might have been tears. "For years, I tried to find them, but I couldn't."

"I've heard of Tuktoyaktuk," the teacher said. "Is that really how it got its name?"

"Yes," Rachel said. "My grandfather saw it."

The teacher didn't know what to think. She peeked at her watch, the quiz she had prepared still in the back of her mind. It would have to wait until after recess, she decided. She shifted against the desktop, her bottom growing numb.

"And what happened to Ujarak after that?"

When Rachel told her grandfather what the teacher had asked, he grew solemn.

"My father banished him," he said. "Wherever he went, no one would let him stay. Even the animals wouldn't feed him. He went so far east looking for food that he reached the island the white men called

Victoria after their queen, who lived across the eastern ocean. People who saw him said he was starving and half mad.

"One time, I met a hunter who told me of a place called Marluk Amaroq," Ataninnuaq said.

"That means Two Wolves," Rachel added.

"The rocks there look like two wolves stuck together," her grandfather said. "Passing by when he saw the wolves eating a caribou, Ujarak had turned them to stone and taken the meat for himself. People said wherever Ujarak went, there were stones that used to be animals.

"Another time, a woman from far away told me she'd seen Ujarak change himself into a seal so he could catch a big fish. She said he pulled it up onto the ice with his teeth and gobbled it down in one bite. After that, he went back into the water and came out of the hole again in the form of a man.

"When the priests heard these things, they became angry. They told us not to believe what people said about Ujarak. Either the stories were lies, they told us, or he was a demon.

"Then a big priest from the south came to our camp with a policeman. People called the priest Father Sungaartoq because of his blond hair."

"*Sungaartoq* means yellow," Rachel said.

"That one, I know," the teacher said, smiling.

"I didn't like the priests. When they came to live with us, the people stopped listening to me. They broke the taboos and ate the caribou's lungs and heart, where the breath and soul reside. They dishonored the animals. But the priests said the people didn't need to worry about making the caribou angry because Jesus would protect them. Then the Hudson's Bay Company built stores to feed the people, and no one needed the caribou anymore.

"I didn't like the policemen either. The police said they had come to watch over the white people who lived with us because we had no laws of our own. But they were mistaken. We had a way to do things, we had things we needed to do, and we had things we should not do. When my people stopped listening to me, they forgot the way to do things. When they went to the store instead of feeding themselves, they forgot what they needed to do. And when they left the land and went to live in the villages, they forgot what they should not do."

When Rachel recounted her grandfather's criticisms of the priests and the police, the teacher found herself glancing toward the classroom door to make sure no one had stopped in the hallway to listen. In her opinion, it was best not to discuss religion and politics. Otherwise, you were asking for trouble. Still, she was eager to hear what happened next and gave no thought to interrupting.

"The yellow priest was looking for Ujarak," Ataninnuaq went on. "It was 1927 then, and I was almost forty. 'I have not seen my brother for many years,' I told him. The priest said Ujarak had stolen supplies from one of the whaling ships. The policeman had come to put my brother in handcuffs. He said I should tell him if Ujarak came to our winter camp. But I refused. That was not our way. Ujarak had been banished. There was no punishment worse than that.

"'You people need to see he's just a man,' the priest said, taking the policeman's rifle from him. 'And if we cannot catch him, we will shoot him. I don't care which.'

"'Ujarak is powerful,' I said. 'He might try to kill you.'

"'Without a gun?' The priest laughed. 'That sort of nonsense is the problem.'"

His eyes glinted, hard and gray, but through his bluster, I could see his fear. He handed the rifle back to the policeman.

"'Let's go,' he said. 'It's time we took care of this rascal.'

"The following morning," the old man said, "I found a dead ptarmigan outside my snow house. Someone had left it for me to eat. But the bird showed no wounds, and I couldn't tell how it had been killed. When I cut it open, I saw the bird's heart had been turned to stone. Ujarak had left it there.

"At that moment, I looked up to see my brother standing in front of me. Tied into his tangled hair were animal bones that rattled in the wind like angry spirits, and he had patched his cloak together from the hides of so many animals that I could not recognize them all. At his side hung a bag made from the face of a caribou with holes where the eyes used to be. He had grown thin, and whiskers grew on his cheeks.

"He said he had seen me talking to the yellow priest. He told me he would kill the man if he had to. 'If you kill him, more police will come with their laws, and our people will suffer,' I said.

"He told me I should have killed the priest myself. He warned me not to stop him.

"'Leave the priest to me,' he said as he started for the shore.

"I tried to follow, but the blowing snow stuck to his hair and cloak until he had turned as white as the sky and I could no longer see him. At the water, his footprints vanished. I thought it must be true that he was able to change into an animal or a bird. Maybe he had gone into the ocean or flown into the air above me.

"I could not let Ujarak kill the priest, and I could not let the priest kill Ujarak. I didn't know what to do, so I tracked the yellow priest on my dogsled until I caught up to him and the policeman. From the top of a slope, I could see them camped below me in the arm of a big river, their snowshoes poking up out of the snow next to the door of their tent house.

"As I descended toward their camp, a flock of gulls circled above it. They flew out over the bend in the frozen river and then back again. Drawing closer, I counted nine of them. Nine! Impossible. That kind of gull never traveled in odd numbers. Six, eight, ten, but never nine. One of the birds had to be Ujarak in the shape of a gull.

"The next time the birds flew above the river, the ice cracked open with a loud boom and water poured onto the land. The yellow priest came out of the tent as the torrent reached him. Soon he was up to his knees and the current was getting stronger. The ice cracked again, and more water rushed toward him. He tried to run away but fell and was dragged under until the policeman grabbed him by the arms and pulled him up onto a bank of snow.

"When the gulls circled back over the land, I saw bones tied into the head feathers of the lead bird. The priest saw the bones too.

"'It's the demon!' he shouted, pointing skyward at the passing gulls. 'He's trying to drown us. Shoot him! Shoot him, I say!'

"Lifting his rifle, the policeman pointed it at Ujarak just as my sled came to a stop at the edge of the rising water.

"They were going to kill him, so I put an arrow in my bow and aimed it at the policeman as I pulled back the string. But I had never shot a man before, and I hesitated. When the priest caught sight of me, he grabbed the rifle and swung it in my direction, pulling the trigger. As soon as I heard the bang, I saw the bullet coming toward me. I went into the unseen with my mind and stole the bullet's heat, making it sluggish and dense so it turned into stone and stopped in the air, falling to the ground in front of me. I tried to pull back the string of my bow, but I had used up all my strength. I slumped over by my sled as the priest cocked the hammer again. He fired a second bullet, but this time I couldn't stop it.

"In a blur, the gull who was Ujarak flew down, and the bullet hit him in the chest. As he plummeted into the water, his wings thickened into arms, and his talons shrank into toes. His beak softened into lips, and his feathers twisted themselves into strands of hair. When the breath had left him, the river retreated from the land, and his body went with it, pulled under the ice. The flood passed, and the priest was not drowned, but Ujarak was gone."

The old man sat quietly for a long while, as if he was trying to decide what to say next, the teacher thought.

"I should never have taught Ujarak my father's secrets," he said at last. "And he should never have taught me to hunt. But we were young, like you, and we didn't want to depend on each other. That is not the right way. The world of the hunter, what we can see, and the world of the *angakkuq*, what my father called the unseen, must be in balance. We lost our balance, and so did our people."

After the old man had struggled to his feet, departing without ceremony, and the teacher's students had returned from recess to puzzle through their end-of-term quiz, she pondered Ataninnuaq's story. His talk of spirits and an unseen world she had never heard of before, not in school and not in church, had left her confused. For him, the unseen and the seen could not be separated. One intruded on the other. She wanted to understand, but she didn't.

The next morning, when the teacher asked Rachel about the old man's cough, the girl said her grandfather was in bed with pneumonia. The teacher knew Rachel had taken a job at the gas station after school, where she was learning to use the cash register, and wouldn't get home until close to dark. Prodded, the girl disclosed that her mother, Sarah, the old man's daughter, wouldn't be home either, since she worked the late shift that week at the hospital, where the doctors and nurses kept her busy translating the complaints of her fellow Inuit. Seizing the chance to see the old man again, the teacher offered to stop in for a visit on her way home.

"I can stay with your grandfather until you get back," she said to Rachel.

"Why?" Rachel asked, clearly doubtful of the teacher's motives.

"Why not?" the teacher quipped, resorting to cheery enthusiasm. "I can bring him some soup, and maybe you can tell me the rest of his story."

Every day for the next week, the teacher trudged through the village to visit the old man, the snow-packed roads crunching underfoot as her swollen feet protested that her boots felt like they'd shrunk two sizes since morning. In a mittened hand, she clutched a brown paper bag with a thermos of chicken soup, the only medicine she knew.

Today, reaching the old man's squat clapboard house, built on stilts like all the others, the teacher spotted him in the front window waiting for her, his face shrouded by a thin strip of tattered curtain. Waving to him, her purse dangling from her shoulder, she hauled herself up the front staircase, its wooden steps so slick with ice that she had to grip the sagging handrail to keep from slipping.

Opening the door, the teacher put a hand to her nose as the dense, warm air of the room, sour with dishrags and sweat, hit her full in the face. Inside, she tugged off her boots with a moan and massaged her toes. Stuffing her mittens into her pockets, she unburdened herself of her coat and shoved it onto one of the hooks in the wall.

"What are you doing in the draft?" she asked Ataninnuaq, who was still seated at the window in the wheelchair that Sarah had brought home from the hospital. "Come away from there."

If the old man didn't understand the teacher's words, at least he could tell by her tone that she meant business.

"Come," she said, as she crossed the room and rolled his wheelchair to the dining table. "I have your soup."

She lifted the brown paper bag for Ataninnuaq to see and started toward the kitchen.

"*Ingippoq*," the old man said, pointing at the wooden chair next to him.

"I'll sit in a minute," the teacher said, hanging her purse on the back of the chair. "Just let me heat your soup."

"*Ingippoq*," the old man said again, his eyebrows arching.

Persuaded by his gravity, the teacher slowly lowered herself into the chair, wincing as she eased her aching back against the slats. Just then, a tremor of pain tore through her belly. Groaning, she gripped the edge of the table. Was it time? Was her stubborn little boy finally going to show himself? But the quake passed as quickly as it had come. The teacher looked at the old man. The rims of his eyes burned red and raw, and the whites had a yellow cast.

"You should be in bed," she said.

The old man pointed at her. "Atan," he said. He pointed again. "Atan."

He was trying to tell her something, but she didn't know what.

"Yes," the teacher said. "Atan-innu-aq. Did I say it right?"

Leaning forward in his wheelchair, the old man reached for her swollen belly.

"Atan," he said impatiently.

The teacher placed his outstretched hand in his lap.

"That's enough," she said, taking the tone that she used with her students.

When Rachel got home from work, she could explain what her grandfather wanted.

Thwarted, the old man slumped back in his chair, his breathing jagged and shallower than yesterday. The teacher leaned toward him and felt his forehead, her cold fingers warmed by his blazing skin.

"Not good," she said. "Let me fix your soup."

Heaving herself to her feet, the teacher went to the kitchen and plugged in the hot plate, its coiled element glowing as she emptied the thermos into a dented pot with a loose handle. The government built these houses like army barracks, she thought, each one elevated three feet above the frozen soil, its underside exposed to the elements. The rooms got so cold that a thin layer of ice formed on the floors when you mopped them. No wonder the old man was sick.

Steam rose from the pot, the broth about to boil. Unplugging the hot plate, the teacher ladled out a bowlful and brought it to the table. Ignoring his soup, the old man pointed at the teacher again.

"Atan," he said.

But she still didn't know what he wanted. He frowned and thumped his chair against the table, sending thin noodles slopping down the side of the bowl.

"Stop that," the teacher said.

She lifted a spoonful of soup to his mouth, but he pushed it away, sending bits of chicken and cubes of carrot splashing onto the white plastic tablecloth with its fading pattern of red and green poinsettias, in use since Christmas. The teacher sighed and went to get a cloth from the sink.

When she'd returned and sopped up the mess, the teacher sat down again, sliding her backside to the front of the seat and folding her hands on top of her stomach. Still refusing to eat, the old man scowled, his toothless bottom gum glistening in the light from the overhead bulb. The teacher thought he looked smaller in the wheelchair than he did in the bed. In the chair, he looked like a child, as if his life had carried him back to infancy. These outbursts of his were childish, too, even if he had good reason to be angry.

Not angry with her, of course. But as she had learned over the course of that week, seated there at the table with the old man and Rachel, home from the gas station and pressed into translating for her grandfather, his people had suffered indignities at the hands of the priests and the police in the years after Ujarak's death that had left wounds—things Ataninnuaq had not told her students.

"My wife died of tuberculosis in 1939 when Sarah was fifteen," Ataninnuaq had begun. "I was fifty then. It was the year that the government decided to lump the Inuit together with the Indians and treat us all the same. At last, we were under the authority of the white man's laws, as I had always warned would happen.

"In 1955, the year that Sarah gave birth to Rachel, the government was trying to move our people to villages far from the caribou, but I refused to leave. I had my bow and arrows and could still feed the family. We didn't need handouts. Then, when Rachel turned five, the police said she had to go to school. I used to take her with me on my dogsled to check our fox traps. I would tell her stories about the places where we hunted. That was our history. I wanted to keep her with me, but the police wouldn't allow it. They took Rachel away, so Sarah had to go with her. But I stayed behind.

"Only a few families with grown children remained in our winter camp on the shore of the northern ocean. The police wanted us to put an end to our seasonal hunting trips and leave the land too. But we wouldn't go. The officers thought we would have no choice but to comply if we faced starvation, so they shot the sled dogs that we used when hunting and left them for the bears to eat. Not long after that, the last of the families in the camp moved to the villages. But I wouldn't go.

"I had saved two dogs from the policemen's guns by hiding them in a woodshed, but the captain had broken up my sled with a hammer and burned the pieces. He was sure I would come to my senses and do what he wanted if I had no way to travel. Instead, I killed one of the dogs I had hidden, and I used its ribs to make runners for a small sled and its skin to make straps so I could tie the sled to the other dog. Then, defying the officers, I packed up the meat of the dog I'd killed, and I rode away into the night, never to be seen by them again."

When Rachel had finished translating her grandfather's words, the old man had smiled at the teacher with a wink, as if to say, "I may be exaggerating about that last bit." Or perhaps he'd meant, "I showed them, didn't I?" The teacher hadn't been able to tell.

"So, when did he come here to Frobisher Bay?" she'd asked Rachel.

"Four years ago. He came back when I was ten. Mom said he was lonely. Even the spirits couldn't keep him company anymore."

There, the old man's tale had ended, but as the teacher watched him today, his chicken soup growing cold, she was no closer to understanding the *angakkuq*'s mysteries than she had been after his visit to her classroom.

"If you don't eat, you won't get better," she said, stirring the soup so that the thin film congealing on its surface dissolved back into the broth.

The old man tapped his chest and said, "Atan! Atan!" Then he pointed at her stomach.

The teacher looked down at the arc of her belly.

"Atan?"

"*Ee*."

"You want me to name the baby Atan?" she stammered, unable to conceal her surprise. If her parents hadn't raised her so well, she might have laughed.

"*Ee*!"

The teacher frowned. It wasn't good to saddle a child with an odd name.

"Atan," he insisted, nodding resolutely.

The old man didn't have a son or grandson, the teacher reminded herself. It made sense that he wanted to give his name to a boy. She thought about his request. Would it be such a bad thing? A name, after all, was nothing more than a sound you either liked or didn't. It had associations that pleased you or not. Atan sounded a lot like Adam, a good Christian name. She didn't have to call the baby Ataninnuaq, except on his birth certificate.

Only later would she learn from Sarah that a name, as one of the Inuit's spirits, carried the residue of a person's character when passed along to a newborn. When explained to the teacher, this idea had confused her as much as it had vexed the first priests who lived with Ataninnuaq's people. Certain it referred to reincarnation, the priests had forbidden them to keep passing along the names of their elders, instructing them to use names from the Bible instead, like Rachel and Sarah, the wives of two great men written about in the Old Testament. But the priests, as the teacher would discover, had been mistaken. Naming had nothing to do with reincarnation at all—even if, in the case of a powerful *angakkuq* like the old man, a name could carry the weight of a spell cast from beyond the grave.

The teacher rubbed the curve of her stomach.

"It's not a bad name," she said, smiling at the old man. "I'll think about it."

"*Ee*?" Ataninnuaq asked, sitting up in his wheelchair.

"Yes," the teacher said.

Smiling, the old man pushed aside the spoon the teacher had placed within reach and lifted the bowl, slurping his soup straight from the rim. As he reached the bottom, broth dribbling down his chin, the front door opened, and Rachel bustled into the room wearing a shiny nylon parka with the gas station's logo on the back and big boots that made her look like a moonwalker.

She pulled off her boots and came to the table.

"I'm starving," she said. "Did Mom leave any food?"

"Check the fridge," the teacher said, rummaging for something in her purse. "But first, can you write down your grandfather's name for me?"

She placed a pen and a slip of paper on the tabletop.

"Why do you need it?" Rachel asked, sounding suspicious.

"I don't know how it's spelled," the teacher said.

Rachel wrote out her grandfather's name and handed the pen and paper back to the teacher.

"Why do you need to spell it?" she asked.

"Just in case," the teacher said.

"It means wise counselor," Rachel added.

"I remember."

The teacher smiled, no longer inclined to see boastfulness in the girl's admiration for her grandfather. After all, what his parents had said about him was true. He knew things. Perhaps what he knew belonged to another time, but in his way, the old man was surely wise.

Ataninnuaq coughed, frantically searching the room for the old coffee tin he used as a spittoon.

"Wait," Rachel said.

She rushed into the bedroom and returned with the can, holding it for her grandfather as he forced thick wads of green phlegm from his lungs and gulped for air. Looking on, the teacher felt helpless. What if the old man didn't get better? She pushed the thought out of her mind and waited for the coughing to pass.

Recovering his breath, Ataninnuaq fished a handkerchief from his pants pocket and wiped his brow. When he had finished, his hands in his lap, the teacher leaned over and took them in hers.

"See you tomorrow," she said, giving his fingers a squeeze.

The teacher thanked Rachel for helping her with Ataninnuaq's name, which she didn't want to spell wrong. Getting up, purse in hand, she went to the door and struggled into her boots and coat. Ready at last, she tugged on her mittens and trundled back outside, bracing herself for the walk home.

When the teacher left, Rachel went into the kitchen with her grandfather's empty soup bowl and found the teacher's thermos on the counter. Snatching it up, she started toward the front door.

"*Nuqqarit*," Ataninnuaq said, holding up his hand.

Rachel stopped. "But—"

"*Ingippoq*."

Rachel could tell her grandfather had something important to say. She sat down at the table next to him, the seat of the chair still warm from the teacher's bottom.

"She doesn't need it anymore," Ataninnuaq said in Inuktitut as Rachel set the thermos down on the tabletop. "She won't be back."

"Why?"

"Her baby will come tonight."

"Oh."

The old man's eyes grew wide.

"She will call him Ataninnuaq. My name-spirit is going to return in the body of a white man."

TWO

2042

Reaching Washington in darkness, the streetlights out because of the curfew, our taxi stops at a checkpoint. Soldiers in riot gear and gas masks crowd our windows as the car rolls to a stop. The soldiers carry shields and cattle prods, zip ties hanging from their belts in looped bundles. They have everything necessary to hobble and bind a person. Restrained like that, you can't lift food or water to your mouth. You can't open your pants to relieve yourself. As the soldiers stand over you, pretending you're not human, they can keep you on your knees in the sun, the cold, or the rain for hours. I escaped these things the last time I was here, but my friends didn't, and their running battles with the police never ended well.

A beefy fellow with a neatly trimmed mustache, who has a tablet clutched to his chest, pulls open the front and back doors of the car and orders us out—the taxi driver, then me, and finally the young man who came to fetch me from India. Sliding across the back seat, he follows me onto the curb, where we are hit by a gust of black smoke from a stack of burning tires. Standing next to the driver, I attempt to muffle a cough as the soldier with the tablet stops in front of us, his unblinking eyes scrutinizing me through the glass of his gas mask. I return the stare, timid enough to please but not so timid as to raise suspicion. The soldier is always performing for his brothers, whose ridicule he fears if he betrays any weakness. He uses fear to control others, but fear also controls him. I give no sign that anything troubles me. He will have no cause to get rough.

The soldier grabs me by the shoulder and yanks up my sleeve until he finds the chip that was implanted in my forearm before I left New Delhi. Without it, I couldn't have returned. My chip is fine work, I remind myself as he scans it with his tablet. The surgeon who did the work even lasered the scar to thicken its edges, creating the impression that the gelatinous chip, inserted under a layer of fat before it was sewn inside, has been there for a long time.

Releasing his grip on my arm as if tossing back a fish, the soldier scans my face with the tablet and checks for discrepancies between what he sees on the screen and the image my chip spits out. There are no differences, but he still won't be able to identify me. My chip is linked to an imaginary man with a false name and a fabricated history. Decades ago, my entanglement with a group of hackers called the Outliers forced me into a life on the run. But without their help, I could never have set foot in the United States again. With a cloned chip, they have erased the real me from the matrix of data that entraps us all.

Satisfied, the soldier clutches the tablet to his chest again and asks me a question, his words muffled behind his mask.

"Pardon?" I ask, playing the part of the half-deaf codger, a hand cupped behind my ear.

"Where are you going?" the soldier shouts, his breath fogging the glass between us.

As planned, I explain that we are headed to a retirement party for the young man's grandfather, a believable fiction since, at seventy-three, I am past retirement age myself.

After pondering my tale for a long moment, the soldier grunts and shoves me toward the taxi, turning his attention to my companion.

Shortly, the young man joins me in the back seat, his chip scanned, our story believed. Agitated, he keeps fidgeting with the strings of his hooded jacket.

"What's the matter?" I ask.

"Look at them." His eyes fall on the soldier with the tablet, who appears to be in a heated discussion with his superior. "He said they're watching out for old men like you."

"Who did?"

"The one who scanned us. He told me to be careful." The young man turns to look at me. "What if they know?"

"Maybe they're on our side." I steady his hand. "Is that possible?"

"It sounded like a threat, not a warning."

"I hope you're wrong," I tell him. "You'd better be wrong, or this general strike you're planning will never happen."

The driver jumps back into the taxi, slamming his door. "We have to hurry," he says as he starts the engine. "We must be off the road by nine o'clock, or there's no telling what they'll do—start shooting at us, probably."

Middle-aged with a slight frame and stooped shoulders, the man has an accent that suggests an earlier life somewhere in Eastern Europe. I want to ask him how he has ended up in the United States at a time when he would be better off anywhere else. He has likely come because of poverty or worse—the imperial reach of the billionaires knows no bounds—but it is wise not to pry, or he may have questions of his own that I don't want to answer.

As we drive across the Potomac River—named after an Algonquian village—the young man explains that he joined the underground because of me. His father was at the protests in Washington in 2022, he says, and the experience changed his life. "Turn your back," his father has told him more times than he can remember. "The state is the enemy. Turn your back on the whole damn thing." He looks at me as if waiting for a reaction. "Turn your back," he says again.

I know the words. I made them famous. They were emblazoned on ten-thousand T-shirts. Unsure what sort of response he expects, I meet his eyes with what must seem like a dumb stare.

"We tried," I say, shifting in the seat to gaze upon the fires blazing in oil barrels along the road. "We just didn't get very far." The taxi crosses over a cement culvert full of overturned shopping carts with rusted-out frames, their wheels in the air. "We never had a chance."

I'm sure the young man doesn't know what to make of me. He has heard only myths. I am the white man named after an old Inuk. I am Atan who performs miracles. I am the singer who vanished into India, where I lived like a tree rooted to one dusty spot. In the eyes of his generation, I am someone I don't recognize.

When we reach Independence Avenue, the illuminated Washington Monument towers before us as if waiting for someone to come along and pull it out of the ground, like Excalibur from its stone, so that the excesses of capitalism might at last be delivered a staggering blow and the crime bosses of the empire brought to their knees. It's a rousing thought, but it won't come to pass unless spirit stirs the effort. Are people ready for that? This is what I've come to find out.

THREE

1969

The teacher had barely reached the end of Ataninnuaq's street when the old man's prediction about the baby's imminent arrival proved true. There on the road, as she stepped between the ridges of ice formed by the snowmobiles, her water broke, sending hot liquid down her thighs, a cloud of frosty vapor rising from beneath her skirt. She wondered if she should turn back. Maybe Rachel could help her. But the hospital was almost as close. She just had to make it up the hill overlooking the bay. Worried more about frostbite than she was about the contractions that would follow, the teacher pushed on, her wet nylons stiffening as they froze.

Later that night, at home in bed, Ataninnuaq could feel the teacher's child emerging from the world of the unseen as surely as he was slipping back into it. As the hours passed, his chest wheezed and rattled under the blankets, each breath shallower than the last. His soul-spirit was ready to depart, but the baby wouldn't come. Unable to wait any longer, Ataninnuaq called out to his daughter, Sarah, as the morning's first light tinted the sky outside his bedroom window.

Shortly, Sarah appeared in Ataninnuaq's doorway, slumped against the frame, her thick black hair tumbling about her face, released now from the neat bun she wore at work.

"What's wrong?" she asked in Inuktitut.

"The child is stubborn," he said.

Sarah stepped into the room and stood at the bed.

"What do you mean?"

"He won't come," Ataninnuaq told her, lifting himself onto his elbows. "The teacher grows weak."

"I warned you, didn't I? You have no business interfering with that family."

"Ahh," Ataninnuaq grunted, gesturing as if to push Sarah away. "Go to her. It's time."

When Sarah left for the hospital, Ataninnuaq called Rachel to his room and asked her to fetch his drum. Still half asleep, one hand shielding her eyes from the rays of sunlight stretching across the planks of the floor, she shuffled to the closet in her slippers. Locating the drum and its mallet behind a Christmas tree stand, she came to the bed and set them down next to her grandfather.

"Help me up," Ataninnuaq said in Inuktitut.

Rachel wheeled her grandfather's chair closer to the bed, but he motioned for her to stop.

"Take my arm," he said, the mallet in one hand, the drum hoisted in the other, a tight grip on its short wooden handle as he inched toward the edge of the mattress.

When Rachel had pulled Ataninnuaq to his feet, he slipped his arm around her waist, and together they walked out to the front room.

Letting go of Rachel, Ataninnuaq circled to and fro, the large flat drum rising and falling, the mallet kissing wood again and again. With the last of his strength, he lurched from one foot to the other, beseeching the spirits of the land to draw the teacher's child safely into the world.

At the hospital, Sarah found the teacher's husband on a bench in the hall outside the delivery room, his elbows on his knees, his chin in his hands, great circles under his youthful eyes. The first time they met, she'd thought he seemed too young to be a school principal, even in the north, but this morning he looked his age and then some.

"How are they doing in there?" she asked, glancing at the closed door across the hall from them.

"I don't know," the principal said, checking his watch. "It's been nearly twelve hours."

Behind him, outside the window, wispy funnels of snow spun like drum dancers across the parking lot. Watching them approach, Sarah thought she heard the vibration of stretched hide, a mallet striking wood as it beat out a haunting rhythm. Where was it coming from?

"Do you hear that?" she asked, pulling her gaze away from the whirling snow.

"Hear what?" the principal asked.

Sarah thought it must be her father making mischief in the unseen. Either that, or there were spirits about.

Unbuttoning her coat, she sat down on the bench.

"You have to name the child," she told the principal. "If you don't name him, he won't come."

The principal sat up with a groan.

"I doubt that," he said. "Anyway, we haven't decided on a name yet." He stifled a yawn. "We only just found out it's a boy."

Sarah realized then that the principal had no idea the teacher had agreed to name the baby after Ataninnuaq. Oh, damn, she thought. There mustn't have been time for her to tell him. But it was too late to turn back, even if she doubted any good could come from her father's request. The child had to be named, and soon, or the teacher could be in danger.

The door to the delivery room swung open and a young nurse, recently arrived from the south, came into the hall.

"We're no closer than before," she told them, obviously crestfallen.

The principal exhaled in frustration and stood up.

"Call me when it's over," he said.

"You're leaving?" the nurse asked, shooting Sarah a shocked look.

"I've got two daughters waiting for breakfast and a babysitter who needs to go home," the principal said as he gathered up his parka, a scarf dangling from one of the armholes, his gloves protruding from the pockets.

Watching the principal withdraw toward the exit at the end of the corridor, Sarah shook her head. The poor man had no idea what was afoot.

"Come," she said, turning on her heel, the nurse close behind her.

Striding through the swinging door to the delivery room, Sarah saw the teacher propped up on an electric folding bed, her face hidden behind the sheet stretched between her raised knees.

"She needs an Inuit birth," Sarah declared.

Standing at the end of the bed, the doctor spun around to face her, his gloved hands extended in front of him like a quarterback waiting for the snap.

"Her?" he asked.

"Yes, her," Sarah answered. "You've done it before."

"But those were Inuit women."

"A woman is a woman," Sarah retorted, one hand on her plump hip. "You know it's safe."

"Why should it make any difference?"

"Because it works."

The doctor turned to the teacher and shrugged.

"If it's okay with you, it's okay with me."

"You will have to get down on your hands and knees," Sarah said.

Nearly delirious with exhaustion after a night of labor, the teacher laughed.

"On my knees?"

"It will only be for a moment," Sarah said. "It's the way I was born. Rachel too. It's the old way."

"Okay," the teacher said, pushing wisps of sweaty hair from her brow as Sarah helped her stand.

After the doctor and the nurse had lifted the mattress off the folding bed and onto the floor, the teacher stepped back onto it, getting down on her hands and knees as the doctor crouched behind her, the nurse hovering nervously. Reaching down, Sarah put her hand on the teacher's back just as another contraction hit.

"Ahee!" the teacher cried.

"It's time for you to name the baby," Sarah said, squatting beside her. "Will you call him Ataninnuaq?"

"I haven't spoken to my husband yet," the teacher gasped.

"There's no time now. You have to name him, or he won't come."

The teacher grimaced. "I think so—yes, okay."

"Yes?"

"Yes, yes! I'll name him Atan—Ataninnuaq."

Sarah pressed her palms into the teacher's lower back.

"Ataninnuaq, come out," she said in a firm voice.

At once, the baby's slick head emerged, and Atan slipped into the doctor's waiting hands.

"Good grief!" the doctor exclaimed. "How did you do that?"

At that moment, back at home in the front room of Sarah's house, Ataninnuaq lost his footing and tumbled to the floor, his drum crashing down beside him on the faded linoleum as the mallet rolled under the sofa, skittering to a halt amid pieces of hardened macaroni and dust bunnies tangled with silver tinsel.

"Grandfather?" Rachel called out in Inuktitut.

"It's done," Ataninnuaq said, breathing his last. "The boy is here."

As Sarah watched the baby squirm in the doctor's hands, the drum that had been resounding far off in her mind ceased to beat, and her stomach tightened. She could feel her father's soul-spirit departing, as if a color was draining out of the world, a shade never to be seen again. At the same time, she could feel the echo left behind in her father's name, a trace that even then vibrated in the teacher's newborn son.

The doctor handed the baby to the nurse while he took a scalpel and cut the umbilical cord. Beaming now, she wrapped little Atan in a blue blanket and placed him in the waiting arms of the teacher, who had gotten off her knees and collapsed onto her back, as bewildered as the doctor, Sarah could see, but no doubt grateful for her intervention.

With some spit on her thumb, the teacher cleared the mucus from her baby's eyes and looked into his face. What she saw surprised her. He looked old, like someone who'd lived and knew things.

"Atan," she said.

If only her mother could see her now, the teacher thought. Down on all fours, the old way, giving birth like an Inuit! Arriving in the north three years ago, in 1966, she never would have imagined such a thing. And she certainly wouldn't have agreed to give her child an Inuit name.

The teacher had been twenty-five when she and her husband came north with their two preschoolers, Eleanor and Libby, the second so called because Eleanor, sixteen months old when Libby was born, couldn't say Elizabeth. The teacher and her husband had just graduated from college and were drawn north by the high salary and subsidized housing. There was even isolation pay.

In August of that year, they left their home in Prince Albert, Saskatchewan, and traveled east by train to Montreal before flying to Fort Chimo on the coast of the Hudson Straight. The swarms of ferocious mosquitos that tormented them on the tarmac while they waited for the plane to be refueled made her anxious about what lay ahead for them in that new land, but they weren't in the north yet, she thought, at least judging from the pine trees and flowers lining the runway. Surely, there were no mosquitos where they were going. Flying on to Frobisher Bay, she was filled once more with high expectations, her stomach aflutter, so plentiful and majestic were the icebergs that rose from the sea far below.

"I was impressed with the town as the plane came in to land," the teacher wrote in a letter home to her parents that first week in the north. "The buildings are nestled amid rocky hills on the edge of the bay. After arriving on a lovely fall evening, if I can compare it to the south, we were met by a sweet little Eskimo lady from the school board who drove us to our new home."

There, the teacher's excitement had ended. When she walked through the front door of their assigned house, whatever hopes she harbored about their accommodations were swiftly dashed, and she had to choke back a sob. For one thing, the plastic liner of the no-flush toilet hadn't been replaced since mid-summer, "and you can surmise the rest," she wrote. The stench of feces was awful. For another thing, half the kitchen was taken up by a hulking oil stove that made the house smell like a garage, and the cupboards were coated inside and out with a film of grease that it would take her an entire morning to scrub off with an abrasive sponge.

Along the wall outside the kitchen stood a crude, gray dining table, a testament to the absence of the colonial-style furnishings they'd been promised. The living room, smaller than expected, had forest-green walls and matching upholstered furniture. "When it comes to the bedrooms," she wrote, tongue in cheek, "some of the more attractive features are the dark turquoise walls, the purple throw rugs, and the five strips of tape on the ceilings. I assume the roof leaks! I can hardly wait till spring thaw."

She went on to describe her struggles with the stove, which was constantly going out and flooding with oil. When it did work, it blazed so hot that she had to wear her bathing suit while cooking. She complained of the persistence of odd odors—"the smell of filth"—no matter how much she scoured and disinfected. She mentioned the Eskimo man who came once a week on behalf of the Privy Council to replace the toilet liner and carry away the family's waste. The liners leaked, and he always left a trail of poopy drops from the bathroom to the front door.

"My sanity sits in a bowl of artificial flowers that we brought with us, the only cheerful note in the place," she added in exasperation.

The world beyond her family's "smelly shoebox" was an entirely different matter. The window in the living room looked out on the bay, and although there were no trees in that place, she was captivated by the rugged beauty of the land and how the rocks changed color as the lichen in their cracks caught the sunlight. She promised herself that she would try to sketch the scene on a clear morning when the tide was high. She favored that view for the fullness of it—the pull she felt. It was as if the sea, like a field of wheat back home, wanted to draw her into itself. In these moments, she felt so small in the face of something so enormous that her frustrations and disappointments became insignificant. During those first days, she often found herself at the window in rubber gloves, a sponge in hand, staring out upon the shimmering water.

In her second letter home, the teacher narrated her adventures grocery shopping at the Hudson's Bay Company store on Friday evenings after the weekly supply plane arrived with new goods. The ship that came to Frobisher Bay each fall had brought them cases of canned bacon, canned butter, and many other things she'd never dreamed of eating out of a can. At the store, she got not-so-fresh fruit and the usual dry goods at an exorbitant markup. Twenty-five pounds of flour cost a staggering $3.40, and four bananas or a dozen eggs cost $1.25. "With the prices they charge," she wrote, "our food allowance of $200 for the year will be used up by Easter, never mind my best efforts to ration luxuries like oranges among the four of us."

The highlight of those shopping trips was getting to see the locals up close. "It's most amusing to observe the white man's influence on the Eskimos," the teacher wrote. "You can see something in nearly all of them that is a throwback to the days of integration. One stately gentleman outside the store was wearing a cowboy hat, complete with a child's plastic whistle hanging from the brim by a string, and he had a huge pair of sunglasses perched on his nose. It is not unusual to see adults sucking on lollypops, the sticks protruding from their mouths as they stroll home."

Nevertheless, the teacher couldn't help but note, there were many ways in which the white man hadn't influenced the Eskimos a whit, especially in matters of hygiene. Just as the pipes in her house drained directly onto the ground, the Eskimos had no compunction about flinging aside a finger of snot when outdoors. Worse, every morning as she passed through the school cloakroom where her students' sealskin parkas hung from a gauntlet of pegs along both walls, so pungent was the smell of the urine used by the Eskimos to soften and tan their hides that she had to keep from gagging.

Now, here she was, lying atop the mattress on the delivery room floor, Sarah cross-legged beside her, as the teacher watched her little boy trying to figure out how to suckle at her breast. Yes, she thought, if only her mother could see her today. She didn't even refer to the Inuit as Eskimos anymore.

"That's an Indian word," Rachel had told her one day, interrupting the class's math lesson. "It's not our word. We're called Inuit."

Suddenly, Sarah gasped, her gaze fixed on the window.

Turning to look, the teacher saw a fat crow on the sill, its head cocked, one beady black eye peeking at them through a crack in the blinds.

"What's wrong?" she asked.

Sarah frowned and shook her head.

"Nothing," she said. "I have to go home. I should check on my father."

Getting to her feet, she excused herself and went back out through the swinging door.

Only the next day, when Rachel came to visit the teacher at the hospital, did she find out why Sarah had been spooked by the crow.

"Do you remember the story about Ujarak?" Rachel asked, eating up the last of the teacher's green Jell-O, untouched since lunchtime.

"How could I forget?"

"Well, some people in town say when Ujarak was killed by the yellow priest, he cast his soul-spirit into a crow, never to depart the earth."

The teacher was skeptical.

"Even if such a thing was possible," she pointed out, "this crow would have to be ancient."

"Not true," Rachel said. "My grandfather told me Ujarak's soul has been jumping from crow to crow for years."

When word of the crow's appearance at the hospital spread throughout the town, everyone had an opinion about what it meant. Some people said the crow was nothing to fear—that Ujarak would look out for young Atan. The boy, after all, had been given a good name. Others said the teacher had been asking for trouble when she'd named her son after the old man. Ataninnuaq used to be a powerful *angakkuq*. He could be up to mischief. Besides, what did the boy's family know about Inuit ways?

A month later, when the baby got dangerously sick, the naysayers weren't surprised.

"Your grandfather never should have given that boy an Inuk name," Rachel's neighbor said in Inuktitut. "He's sick because his parents don't know how to please his spirit."

A bowl of brambleberries mixed with caribou fat sat between them on the old woman's kitchen table with two spoons sticking out.

"Eat," she said.

Rachel put a spoonful of the greasy concoction in her mouth.

"Mmm!" She hadn't tasted this treat for years.

"All the way from Resolute."

"So good!"

"When Ataninnuaq was a boy, he lived farther north than we do now," the old woman said. "The sun disappeared for many months. When it came back, the people took the wicks out of their stone lamps and put in new ones before lighting them again. It was bad luck to leave a lamp burning with an old wick. Taboo. That's how people started a new life when the sun came back. Your grandfather lived that way all his life. Now it's spring. The season has just changed. But the teacher hasn't put out her family's lamps. That's why the boy is sick."

"No one uses lamps anymore," Rachel said.

They ate up the last of the berries and put down their spoons. The days were still short, and it had become dark while they spoke. Standing up, the saggy skin on the underside of her arm jiggling as she reached above them, Rachel's neighbor pulled a chain, and the bare bulb that hung down above the table flickered to life, bathing them in yellow light.

"You have to change their light bulbs," she said. "Then the boy will get better."

The problem with little Atan was in his gut. His mother had found blood in his poop, and the doctors, upon taking a series of X-rays, had determined that his small intestine had collapsed into the large. He would have to be flown to a hospital in Montreal for surgery.

When Rachel found out the baby was going to be cut open, she got angry with Atan's mother.

"What do white doctors know?" she asked. "They never treat the cause of things, just what they can see."

"They know the cause," Atan's mother said. "That's why we're going to Montreal."

"They know the cause of the bleeding," Rachel said. "But what about the collapse? What made that happen?"

Atan's mother, who'd only stopped at Rachel's house to pick up the thermos she'd left behind the month before, didn't answer.

"Say a prayer for us," she suggested, descending the front steps, the mud squelching beneath her boots as she reached the street.

Rachel scowled. What good would praying do? Jesus didn't follow Inuit customs. No, she wouldn't pray. Her neighbor had given her a better idea, and she knew just how she was going to pull it off.

The next morning, while Atan's mother flew south with her son and the principal and his daughters were at the school, Rachel snuck into their house through a window above the back porch. After counting all the light bulbs she could find, even the one inside the night-light in the hall, she slipped out through the back door and went to the Hudson's Bay Company store. Upon returning to the house with new bulbs, she carefully unscrewed and replaced all the old ones, taking them with her in the plastic shopping bag when she left. That afternoon, she broke the old bulbs with a rock, one by one, and threw the pieces into the dumpster behind the school, discarding them as if they were old wicks.

Just then, as the plane to Montreal began its descent, little Atan stopped crying for the first time since taking off from Fort Chimo almost two and a half hours earlier. At the hospital, when the surgeon came to see Atan's mother in the waiting room, the man clutched a large envelope she'd brought with her from the doctors in Frobisher Bay.

"Are you certain these are your son's X-rays?" he asked.

"Of course."

"We aren't seeing the same thing." The doctor took a new X-ray out of a folder and showed it to Atan's mother. "Your baby is perfectly healthy."

"And the bleeding?"

"It seems to have stopped."

"I don't understand." Atan's mother was mystified. "So, he's okay?"

"He's okay."

"It's a miracle," she said.

The surgeon chuckled.

"I suspect that when the airplane was landing, the change in air pressure popped the small intestine back out again. Not a miracle really, but still a nifty trick."

When Atan's mother telephoned home from the hospital to give her husband the news, he said he concurred with the doctor.

"If science can explain it, then it wasn't a miracle," he told her, but she didn't see why that made any difference and thought it was a miracle all the same.

In any case, Atan's troubles weren't over. While under observation for almost a week, he was fed infant formula made from cow's milk, and during that time, his mother ceased lactating, only to discover when they got home that the formula gave her son gas and hurt his stomach, but there was nothing else to feed him. The pain made Atan cry for hours at a time, kicking and fussing in his crib. The noise kept everyone awake. At last, Atan's mother resorted to placing his bassinet on the porch outside the back door at night so the rest of the family could sleep.

"Are you crazy?" Rachel asked when she heard what Atan's mother was doing. "A dog will take him. Or a wolf!"

"The porch is six feet off the ground!" Atan's mother protested, bouncing the baby in her arms as they stood in the doorway.

"Have you ever seen a wolf jump?" Rachel asked, pushing her tuque back from her forehead.

"Nothing has happened. He's fine."

"Why don't you let one of the Inuit women feed him?" Rachel asked, about to head off for her shift at the gas station. "There are two new mothers in town who could do it."

That night, when Atan's mother told her husband about Rachel's idea, he flat out refused.

"We don't know anything about those women," he said.

Atan's mother sighed.

"And, no," her husband said, lying back down, "the light bulb in the lamp doesn't seem any brighter to me."

The following Friday, when Atan's mother bumped into Rachel at the Hudson's Bay Company store, both of them reaching for the same desiccated lemon, Rachel suggested feeding Atan reindeer milk.

"Where am I going to get reindeer milk?"

Atan's mother laughed, glancing around at the nearly bare shelves as Atan looked up at them from his stroller, his eyes dull, his skin pallid.

"I can get it," Rachel said.

But she couldn't. Frobisher Bay was too far from any reindeer herds. Instead, while Atan's parents waited for him to outgrow his allergy to cow milk, the boy suffered.

In the fall, Rachel asked if she could start taking care of Atan full time when his mother went back to her job. Rachel was too old for school, she complained. So Atan's mother made a deal. Rachel could babysit if she agreed to be tutored in reading on Saturday mornings.

"I expect you here on time and ready to work. No excuses."

"Yes, yes," Rachel agreed. It was the chance she'd been waiting for.

First off, to keep Atan safe, Rachel carved animals out of fish vertebrae and sewed them onto all his clothing. The size of buttons, they made a clicking sound when his sleeves brushed against the tray of his high chair. She told Atan's mother the amulets were for decoration, but the truth was she did it to protect him from the white man's ways.

Intent on teaching Atan to live and think like an Inuk, Rachel watched closely to see what interested him. It was important to know who he was so that when he got older she could direct his path. In school, all the students were taught the same things, no matter who they were. Rachel would find out what made Atan unique so he could take his proper place in the world. More than that, Rachel treated the boy as if he was her relative, thinking of herself as his granddaughter—his *irngutaq*.

"Tell *irn-gu-taq* what you want," Rachel said to him. "Tell *irn-gu-taq* what you see."

Determined that he should know the land and its spirits as old Ataninnuaq had known them, she made the whole world Atan's classroom.

When, at eleven months, the first word Atan said was *irngutaq*, Rachel was delighted, taking it as a sign her grandfather's name-spirit really was stirring inside him. Then, as Atan grew into a toddler, Rachel glimpsed traits of old Ataninnuaq in the boy, like the steadiness of his gaze when he was concentrating and his quick temper. On top of that, Atan could talk to animals, as if reading their thoughts, something only her grandfather could do.

The first time it happened, Atan was five and attending morning kindergarten. After school that day, seated at Rachel's dining table, he told her the story while Sarah made them lunch, listening from the kitchen. One of the boys in the class had peed his pants and made a mess on the floor, so Atan had volunteered to go fetch the janitor for his teacher, happy for any excuse to be outdoors. As he walked across the courtyard between his classroom and the school office, a famished husky stalked him silently through the snow, its white coat matted and thinning. Unfed for days because there were so few fish to spare in the middle of winter, the dog must have gotten loose and been on the hunt.

Atan didn't notice the husky until, slinking nearer, the animal snuffled at his coat pocket in search of a half-eaten peanut butter and jelly sandwich wrapped in brown paper. Turning around, Atan saw his teacher waving at him from the windows, her face contorted in fear. She'd warned the children about the huskies, known to tear one another to shreds for a bone or scrap of sealskin. There was no telling what a hungry dog would do to a defenseless child. Gathered around her, Atan's classmates banged their pudgy palms against the glass, trying to warn him. But it was too late. The dog was about to pounce, its teeth drawn, a low growl rising from its throat.

"Wait," Atan said as he slowly retrieved the snack and removed the paper. "What's your name? I'm Atan."

The husky whined and sniffed at the purple-stained sandwich in Atan's hand.

"Is it Desna?" he guessed. "Or Suka?" Atan stuck the ball of oily brown paper back in his pocket. "How about Qimutki?"

The husky shook its head.

"Oh, I know, it's Kilalurak!" Atan said.

At that, the husky whimpered and sat down, as if Atan had given the dog a command.

"Good boy," Atan said, dropping the soggy lump into the snow.

At once, the husky pounced on the morsel and devoured it whole as Atan, waving at his teacher, continued across the courtyard and walked safely into the office.

Rachel stared at Atan from across the table.

"Why did you pick those names for the dog?"

"I made them up."

"You don't know what they mean?"

"No."

"Desna means boss, like the dog that makes the other ones behave," Rachel explained. "Suka means fast. You know, like for the lead dog. And Qimutki means puller, for when a dog is really strong."

"What does Kilalurak mean?" Atan asked.

"White whale," Rachel said. "Was the dog at the school white?"

"All over."

Sarah brought three bowls and a handful of spoons to the table.

"Those were the names of your grandfather's dogs," she said.

"When?" Rachel asked, astonished.

"Before you were born," Sarah said. "Atan, do you like carrots?"

"Yes, please," Atan answered.

"Can you set the table?" Sarah asked Rachel before returning to the kitchen, where a pot of chili con carne bubbled atop her new stove, bought on installment.

"I told you," Rachel said, staring at Atan in amazement. "You've got my grandfather in you. How else would you have known those names?" She pushed the bowls and spoons into their places at the table. "It's proof. I really am your *irngutaq*."

Not long before Atan's seventh birthday, he was walking home from first grade with Rachel one afternoon when they got disoriented in a sudden blizzard. Although Atan's house was just around the corner, they lost their way in the blinding snow and ended up wandering out of town. As the storm subsided and the last of the icy squalls skittered around their feet, Atan realized they'd arrived at the edge of a bed of stones, a drift of snow curled over them like a shroud.

"Where are we?" he asked.

"This is Grandfather's grave."

"Why did you bring us here?"

"I didn't."

"Shouldn't he be buried in the cemetery?"

"He didn't want to be near the white man's church."

"What's wrong with our church?"

"He blamed the missionaries for a lot of stuff, that's all."

"Like what?"

"Man, you ask a lot of questions."

"Like what?" Atan insisted.

"Like how they shut God away in a little wooden building with a cross and cut our people off from the spirits."

"Oh." Atan looked around them at the bone-white tundra. "But why did you bury him way out here?"

"He didn't like the town. He said people have nothing to do there but take payouts from the government because we're too far from the caribou."

"You and your mom have jobs."

"He called what we do white work."

Standing there with Rachel, Atan suddenly felt gigantic, like he was astride the land. Rachel seemed far away. She was still talking, but English had become a foreign tongue to him, and he couldn't understand the words she spoke. As the wind gusted across a vast world of rock and snow, Atan could smell a herd of caribou passing nearby. Entranced by a vision, he imagined himself taking up a bow and going off in their direction. In the next instant, he found himself on the bank of a river where the caribou had stopped to drink.

The animals twitched and nodded as signals went up and down their flanks. A consensus was forming. They were about to stampede. Atan knew it when they did, but the lead bull had no idea. It was drinking alone. When the herd bolted, Atan ran toward the bull, his bow pulled back, an arrow ready. In a panic to overtake the other caribou, the beast started up the bank of the river and ran straight into Atan's shot. The flint entered the center of the bull's chest, and the animal tumbled over in the snow.

At once, Atan snapped out of his reverie. Looking down at old Ataninnuaq's grave, he felt sick and frightened. Somewhere, the caribou's scarlet blood seeped into the snow. Atan started to cry, feeling ashamed of his tears. He was too old to cry. But the tears kept coming.

"What's wrong?" Rachel asked.

One of Atan's mittens had fallen off, and his fingers had turned bright red. Rachel picked up the mitten and brushed away the pellets of ice that had become stuck to the yarn.

"Give me your hand," she said.

Atan's eyes had a faraway look.

"You had a vision, didn't you?" Rachel asked, as she slipped the mitten onto his hand. "What did you see?"

Atan wiped his nose with his sleeve, unable to answer.

"Come on, let's go" she said, dabbing at his tears with the end of her scarf.

When they arrived at Atan's house, his mother was outside on the front steps watching for them, the sky already getting dark.

"Where have you been?" she asked Rachel as they approached. "Dinner is already on the table."

"It was the blizzard," Rachel said.

"I was expecting you half an hour ago," Atan's mother scolded. "I didn't know what had happened. You had me worried sick."

"We got blown off course," Rachel retorted, getting testy.

"How far off course?"

"We ended up at Grandfather's grave."

"Just like that?"

Atan climbed the steps, his mother crouching in front of him as he reached the top.

"It wasn't on purpose," he said.

"Wasn't it?" she asked, removing his scarf and mittens. "And what's wrong with you? You look like you've seen a ghost?"

"It was Grandfather," Rachel said. "I think he gave Atan a vision."

"Oh, nonsense." Atan's mother stood up, looking down the steps at Rachel. "It was you who took him to the grave and scared him half to death."

"It was Grandfather—"

"Not another word. Your grandfather has no influence on my son."

Atan's mother took him by the shoulders and pushed him toward the door.

"Go wash your hands," she said.

"It wasn't her fault," Atan told his mother, lingering in the doorway.

"Don't go putting silly ideas in his head," she said to Rachel. "Nothing that happened was your grandfather's doing. At most, it was an accident."

"Then be prepared for many accidents," Rachel said, pushing off the bottom step with the heel of her boot as she turned to go.

"Foolish woman," Atan heard her mutter.

"Pardon me? Did you say something?" his mother asked.

"No," Rachel lied.

"You know what? I've been thinking. Atan can start walking home with Eleanor and Libby."

"What—why?"

"There's no need for you to do it."

With that, Atan's mother retreated, the door banging shut behind her.

The next week, as Atan walked home from school with his sisters, Rachel zoomed by on the back of a snowmobile, her arms wrapped around the waist of her boyfriend. Atan waved to her, but she didn't wave back. Laughing, her head flopping from side to side, she nearly fell off as the snowmobile rounded the next corner, sliding sideways as it fishtailed. Atan thought she looked drunk.

Missing his *irngutaq*, Atan passed his time with the dogs in town. He often stopped at their houses with pieces of leftover baloney sandwich or slices of Kraft singles snuck from the refrigerator in his kitchen. There wasn't a husky he couldn't talk to.

Then, late in the spring, when the ice on the bay melted and people went back to using their boats for hunting instead of sleds, all the dogs in town were loaded onto a skiff and taken to a nearby island, where they were fed on fish scraps and could run free until the wintertime, lest they grow fat and sluggish over the summer. In their absence, Atan became despondent. It felt like his friends had left without him. What was he supposed to do all summer? What if *he* got fat and lazy? Didn't he need to run around like them, instead of always clutching one of his sister's hands or sneaking away to wander on his own when his mother's back was turned?

When the moon was full, the sound of the dogs howling carried across the water and kept Atan awake. By the end of June, he missed them so much he could no longer bear it. One night, kicking aside his tangled sheets, he slipped quietly out of bed and got dressed. His toes squishing through the purple throw rug, he ventured into the hall and snuck past the closed door to the bedroom his sisters shared. He tiptoed past his parents' room, its door ajar, his father curved around his mother in the dark like he was a pod and she was a row of peas. Going into the kitchen, Atan took a hunk of raw fish wrapped in cellophane from the bottom shelf of the refrigerator. He went into the front hall, pulled on his jacket and sneakers, and eased open the front door, pausing to listen. Behind him in the house, no one stirred.

It was long before sunrise when Atan reached the docks, the moon bright as he deftly made his way between the boulders that lined the shore. As if he had done it a hundred times, he untied one of the boats and scrambled aboard, tossing the rope to the floor of the vessel. Pushing off with an oar, he felt the boat drifting as the current surged beneath him. His heart pounded. He could hardly keep the oars in place, let alone row them, but the huskies urged him on, their cries louder that night than usual. They wanted him to come.

At last, Atan had traversed the short distance to the island, the water lapping at the stern of the boat as it lurched to a stop on a gravel beach. Coming ashore, he grabbed up the rope that lay coiled on the floor of the boat and wrapped the untethered end around a big rock. Next, he headed inland, striding toward the clearing where the men emptied their pails of fish scraps for the huskies.

Atan had decided he wanted to live with the dogs until it was time to go back to school. Upon finding a spot in the clearing where the huskies had been sleeping, he flopped onto the ground and rolled around in their hair so he would smell like them. From his pocket, he took the piece of raw fish he'd snuck from the refrigerator and bit off a big chunk. After chewing it until his jaw was sore, he gulped the fish down. Now he would give off the same scent as the dogs.

Looking around, Atan realized the huskies had stopped howling. He pricked up his ears, listening for their chorus as the moon crept across the sky. Where had they gone?

Setting out to find his friends, Atan had gone no more than a hundred feet when he came upon the body of Kilalurak, the all-white husky he'd met in the courtyard at school, her tongue protruding stiffly from her mouth, her throat torn open.

On the path in front of Atan, something moved. Peering into the shadows, he saw a wolf as black as the sky, its yellow eyes glowing like stars. Now he knew why the dogs had run away. He clenched his fists, the pit of his stomach gnarled with anger.

"Bad wolf," he said.

The animal bounded toward him.

In that instant, an image of the wolf's heart, sinewy and glistening as it beat faster and faster, flashed before Atan's eyes. Letting his mind slip into the unseen, he squeezed the wolf's heart with all his might to stop it. With the animal at a sprint and only feet away, Atan closed his eyes and squeezed even harder, the wolf's heart thudding more slowly with each passing second. Just as the beast was about to leap upon Atan, it whined in pain and stumbled to its knees. It struggled to stand but toppled over. Exhausted, tears streaking his cheeks, Atan fell to the ground, returning to the world of the senses as quickly as he'd left it. Before him in the clearing, the wolf lay dead.

Shocked at what he had done, Atan fled to the boat and untied the rope from the rock, yanking it so hard that he fell backward into the water when it came free. On his feet again, he pushed off and climbed aboard, rowing back to the docks as quickly as he could. Just as the lights were coming on in the windows of the houses above the bay, he left the boat where he'd found it and slipped away. Before anyone knew he'd left, Atan was back at home and safe in bed, his wet clothes out of sight in the bottom of his laundry hamper.

Two days later, Rachel's neighbor told her about the dead wolf. The fishermen had found it when they went to the island to feed the huskies.

"They had no idea what killed it," she said in Inuktitut. "There was a dead dog there, too, its throat bitten into, but the wolf showed no signs of a fight."

The old woman stirred her tea, an open tin of biscuits at her elbow.

"Help yourself," she said, pointing at the tin, the golden biscuits stacked inside crisp-white paper inserts, all neatly crimped.

Rachel lifted a flower-shaped biscuit from the tin and popped it into her mouth, its buttery goodness making her smile.

"So, what killed it?" she asked.

"Well, they took a knife and sliced the animal from the belly to the chin so they could look at the organs. The liver wasn't swollen. The kidneys were the right color. But the heart—I'm told they stood back in amazement. The heart had turned to stone."

"Are you sure?"

"Yes, they've been showing it around. Some people think Ujarak must be back. They say no other *angakkuq* can do that kind of sorcery."

Rachel wasn't convinced. If Ujarak's soul-spirit still lived, it was in the body of a mere crow. It lacked the strength and power of a man. No, Rachel suspected Atan. Her grandfather had been capable of such a feat. Surely Atan was too.

The following Monday, when Atan left school, Rachel was waiting for him outside.

"You hear about that wolf they found?" she asked.

"Yeah."

"Was it you? Were you on that island?"

Atan turned to look at his sisters lingering on the sidewalk.

"Come on already, man!" Libby called to him.

"I'm coming."

"Well?" Rachel asked.

Ashamed, Atan didn't want to tell her what he'd done. He worried people would be afraid of him. He didn't want to be different. He wasn't an *angakkuq*. He wasn't an Inuit like Rachel. His parents were white.

"Leave me alone," he said. "I didn't even know your stupid grandfather. You're not my *irngutaq*. I'm a white boy. I'm not like you!"

FOUR

1977

When Atan was eight, right before the end of the school year, his father accepted a teaching job at a high school far to the south in Ontario.

"I won't be a principal anymore, but it's a start," he told Atan and his sisters, all seated in a row at the long, gray dining table outside the kitchen, Cheerios floating in the bottom of their bowls.

"But, Dad—," Libby protested, scraping up a spoonful of sugary milk.

"We can't live here forever," he said. "There's no future for us in the north. What will you do when you finish school? Where will you work?"

The Inuit had been asking themselves the same questions for years. Life in Frobisher Bay had been a dead end for many of them. But now, with their communal way of life abolished and no one able to survive on the tundra in the style of the white man—every household for itself—they could no longer go back to the land.

In the summer of 1977, fortunate to have a way out, Atan's family took it. Leaving behind their smelly shoebox on stilts, they moved to a city called Kitchener. Located on the edge of an old subdivision, their semi-detached house backed onto an expanse of thick weeds and towering grasses. A cornfield marked its east side, and a road lay to the west.

In the distance, rows of newer houses stretched for blocks, almost to the Grand River, built atop farmland that had once been the territory of the Five Nations.

"Herbert Kitchener was a British war hero like Martin Frobisher," Atan's sister Eleanor announced from her spot on the family room sofa next to Atan's father, his face buried in the evening newspaper. Fifteen now, Eleanor considered herself an expert on everything.

"The city was originally named Berlin by the German Mennonite farmers from Pennsylvania who came here in the 1800s. Then, in 1916, after Lord Kitchener and more than 700 people died when their ship struck a German mine near the Orkney Islands in Scotland during the First World War, the city changed its name to honor him and snub the Germans."

"Does that mean we can snub the Germans too?" Libby asked, cross-legged on the floor, her math homework spread out before her on the coffee table.

Seated in the armchair next to a floor lamp in the corner, Atan's mother looked up from patching the knees of Atan's jeans.

"No, you can't," she said, snapping a length of thread with her teeth.

"Who do you think makes the Schneiders hot dogs you like so much?" Atan's father asked, looking up from his paper.

"Who?" Libby asked.

"Germans," Eleanor said. "The factory's right downtown."

On the floor at the end of the sofa, sitting next to the glass doors to the backyard, Atan thumbed through a box of slides of his family's photographs from the north. His mother had shown the slides to Libby's ninth-grade class that afternoon because they were learning about the Inuit, and when she got home, Atan had asked her not to put them away. Holding one of the slides up to the light of the end-table lamp, he saw a dogsled traveling along the coast of Frobisher Bay, with a driver at the reins and three men in snowshoes running behind it. Atan put the slide down and looked out at the darkened yard, a patch of grass bordered by a straggly line of cedar hedges, the sky drained of color as dusk approached. Who cares what this place is called, he thought, when there aren't any spirits here?

In the north, in the spots where the men used to hunt, you could hear the spirits of the caribou. Atan had heard them himself when he was very young, the air stirring with the scuffle of hooves as he and Rachel walked along the bluffs at the edge of town.

"You see?" she had asked him. "There are spirits everywhere."

In the south, the rocks under Atan's feet didn't whisper. Everything lay hollow and silent.

Atan looked at his family reflected in the glass doors. Eleanor sat braiding her hair as Libby twisted her pencil in a sharpener, shavings drifting to the floor. His mother's hair glowed in the light of the floor lamp, his father in the shadows. In the south, Atan thought, it was as if all the birds had stopped singing, and no one noticed but him.

Worse, as he would learn the next morning, a Saturday, the dogs in that place wouldn't talk to him, at least not the one that had recently moved into the triplex next door, a big, hairy beast the color of ash. Woken by the dog's barking, Atan pushed aside his bedroom curtains to see a man with a fat belly below in the triplex's driveway, one hand clutching a thick rope tied to the dog's collar. Anxious to meet this marvelous animal, glimpsed only once while helping his mother carry in the groceries, Atan left his pajamas in a pile on the floor and pulled on his jeans and a T-shirt, still flailing to find the armholes as he dashed down the stairs.

Emerging onto the driveway through the side door, Atan froze as the dog, still barking, leaped toward him, only to be jerked back mid-stride by the rope at his collar.

"Hi," Atan said as he kneeled to lace up his sneakers.

"Hi, kid," the man answered.

"What kind of dog is that?" Atan asked.

"Don't know," the man said, his coffee slopping onto the asphalt as the animal strained at the rope. "He might have some shepherd in him, maybe some wolfhound. The thing's a mutt."

"Can I walk him?" Atan asked, his shoes tied.

The man sized Atan up.

"You won't be able to hold him."

"I can do it," Atan said, confident he was stronger than his thin frame and knobby elbows let on. "I've known huskies almost as big. I won't even need the rope I bet."

The man laughed.

"You think so, eh?"

"Yeah."

"Okay," the man said with a chuckle.

He had a thick mustache that hung over his lip and got wet when he drank from his mug.

"Babe, come watch this," he said, as a woman in tight denim pants and a fluffy white jacket appeared at the entrance to the triplex. "This little guy says he can walk Anvil."

"Is he crazy?" the woman asked. "Don't let him do that."

The man handed the rope to Atan and took out a cigarette.

"Just in the field," he said, as the dog sniffed at Atan, his slobbery jowls quivering.

Atan kneeled in front of the dog and searched its gold-flecked eyes.

"So, you're Anvil? I'm Atan," he said. "I just moved here from the north. Where are you from?"

Anvil twisted his head sideways, a dumb expression on his face. Atan waited for an answer, but it was no use. Unlike the huskies in Frobisher Bay, the animal wouldn't tell him what it was thinking.

When Atan stood up again, Anvil strained against the rope with such force that Atan fell forward and almost got yanked off his feet.

"Wait," Atan cried as he shortened the rope and tried to catch up.

Paying him no mind, the dog pulled Atan to the end of the driveway and lunged into the field.

"Stop," Atan shouted. "Stop!"

But Anvil was at a full run now, Atan trailing behind, his feet tripping through the tangles of undergrowth as he let out the last of the rope. On they sped, Atan going as fast as he could, until at last, heedless of his cries, Anvil pulled Atan off balance, and he tumbled to the ground.

Instead of letting go of the rope, Atan hung on, dragged by the dog, his hands burning, his knees cut, his elbows scuffed and bruised. As Anvil reached the backyards of the subdivision on the far side of the field, Atan lost his grip and slid to a stop on his belly.

Sitting up, Atan saw the dog circle back toward home as the man came into the field and got hold of the rope.

"You okay?" he hollered to Atan, laughing so hard that his cigarette almost fell out of his mouth.

Atan didn't answer.

The man pulled Anvil tight against his leg as he reached Atan.

"Why didn't you let go of the rope?" he asked.

"I thought he would run away," Atan said, dirt ground into his wounds and grass in his hair.

"Crazy kid," the man chuckled as he helped Atan to his feet, brushing him off before they started back across the field.

Humiliated, Atan trailed behind so the man wouldn't see his tears. Watching Anvil's backside sway back and forth through the grass, Atan couldn't understand why the dog hadn't talked to him. Was this place to blame, or had he changed somehow? Atan couldn't decide.

When he moped around the house that summer, complaining he had nothing to do, Atan's mother put her foot down.

"Out," she said, holding open the side door as she handed him his jacket. "It's a beautiful day."

"But, Mom—."

"Go on. And don't come back for at least an hour."

Making it as far as the concrete step in the driveway, Atan sat down.

"Go make some friends," his mother scolded through the screen.

"Like who?"

"I don't know. There are lots of kids around."

Atan was trying to come up with an excuse to go back inside when a boy his age from the townhouses across the street cruised to a stop on his bike at the end of the driveway.

"Wanna go see a cool house?" he called out.

"What's cool about it?" Atan asked.

"It's big," the boy said. "Like a mansion."

Atan got up from the step and went down the driveway to the sidewalk.

"Is it far?"

"No," the boy said, dirt in the corners of his mouth. "It's where the rich kids live."

Rolling his bike between them, the boy led Atan across the street, and they continued along the sidewalk until they reached a T-intersection.

"This way," the boy said, turning right, the sounds of the children in the playground behind the townhouses fading as they marched on.

Soon, growing in size, the homes became stately palaces with double garages and thick, wide lawns in front, not a dandelion in sight. Bigger than any house Atan had ever seen except on television, none of them were joined together like his.

Finally, the boys stopped in front of a three-story house with a deep veranda across the front and a brick path along one side that brought them to a steel gate. In the backyard, where half a dozen children were running about, Atan saw a play fort with climbing bars and slides, their metal chutes glinting in the afternoon sun.

"I don't know those kids," Atan said.

"That's okay," the boy from the townhouses reassured him.

Unlatching the gate, he led Atan into the yard as a ten-year-old boy with spiky hair started toward them.

"Who's this?" the older boy asked, striding to a stop in front of them.

Before Atan could say anything, the boy slugged him in the stomach, and Atan doubled over, unable to breathe as all the air rushed out of him.

"Get lost!" the boy shouted.

Atan had never been hit before. At his school in the north, he'd been the one who broke up shoving matches between his classmates at recess, not the one who got punched. The pain of being hit was a shock, but worse, it hurt him to the core, his heart constricting. The sun seemed to grow dim, the world darker. Mystified by the actions of the boy with the spiky hair, Atan retreated through the gate and retraced his steps home as a new thought took hold—rich people were mean.

After that, when Atan's mother forced him outside, the weather growing hotter, the afternoons stretching on forever, he ignored the neighborhood kids leaping through sprinklers in the front yards or scooting up and down the sidewalk on bikes, beach towels tied at their necks to flutter behind them like superhero capes. He preferred to play in the field behind his house, where the chirping crickets made a beautiful racket and the grasshoppers springing between the stalks of grass provided endless amusement. Taking refuge in the shade of the oak trees at the edge of the cornfield, Atan passed the time watching birds dart in and out of the grass, the flossy seeds of the milkweed pods set adrift in the sunshine by the rustle of their wings, the breeze sweet with the scent of fallen apples and manure. Walking back home, he was careful to avoid the nest of a mother killdeer near his trail through the field, lest he got too close and she darted out from the brush, trilling at him sharply, a wing dragging behind her on the ground like it was broken, all in the hope of drawing him away from her eggs. When they'd first met, Atan had gotten out of her way, promising not to come so close next time. Such a clever bird.

Early one morning at the beginning of August, Atan was in the kitchen making cookies with his mother, the last of the baking trays about to go into the oven, the bowl nearly ready for licking, when they heard the rumble of an engine and the cracking, mulching, scraping sounds of heavy, churning machinery. Running downstairs to the family room, Atan went to the sliding glass doors and looked out upon the field to see clouds of dust billowing into the air above a mower with long rows of rotating blades, their steel edges sparking against the biggest rocks, a shiny green tractor towing the contraption along. Sliding open the screen door, Atan ran into the backyard and out across the field. Soon, he was a stone's throw from the roaring monster.

"Stop!" he yelled as the tractor passed, leaving a swath of destruction in its wake. "Stop!"

The driver, wearing a pair of oversized earmuffs to dampen the noise, didn't seem to hear Atan, and through all the dust, the man clearly couldn't see him either.

"There are nests here!" Atan cried, frantically waving his arms as the tractor rolled on, the birds scattering into the air, their eggs and hatchlings left in its path.

When the tractor reached the west side of the field and turned around to cut another row, Atan went to meet it, an anger throbbing in his chest that he hadn't felt since the night he was on the island and killed the wolf.

"I could turn your heart to stone," he fumed, looking up at the driver inside the glass cab.

Atan didn't want to harm the man. He just wanted to stop the machine. Staring at the tractor as hard as he could, he tried to expand the air in its tires to burst them, but nothing happened. Attempting to overheat the engine, he imagined the water in its radiator boiling, but the tractor rumbled on. Desperate, he tried to heat the gas in its tank to ignite a fire, but it was no use. Atan was powerless.

It was his fault, he told himself. Instead of lying to Rachel, he should've told her the truth about the wolf. But he'd denied everything, and now he was just a white boy, not an Inuk, not an *angakkuq*, stuck here in a land without spirits where big, noisy, mad machines roamed the land.

The tractor continued to circle until the blades had mowed down every last weed and stalk of grass and all the birds had fled. As Atan took in the desolation of the shorn field, his eyes brimming with tears, a crow swooped down and landed beside him.

"Shoo!" he cried. "Leave me alone."

He kicked at the crow with a bare foot, sending the big black bird skittering out of the way.

"Caw, caw," the crow said as if to tell him, "Come, come."

Curious now, Atan watched as the bird hopped toward a cluster of woody stalks cut off half a foot above the ground.

"Caw, caw," the crow said again as if to say, "Look here."

As Atan followed, the crow fluttered up from the ground and landed atop the stalks. Nodding its head, the bird pointed with its beak.

Looking down, Atan saw a nest with two green-speckled eggs.

"Coo-ik, coo-ik," called a mother nightjar circling overhead.

"See?" the crow asked. "The tractor's blades didn't harm the nests. The birds will come back, and the grass will grow tall again."

With a squawk, the crow leaped into the air and sailed across the desolate field. As it flew higher, Atan thought he saw animal bones tied into its tail feathers, but it might have been a trick of the sun.

"Hey, wait, you talked to me!" Atan shouted, only then realizing he'd understood what the crow was thinking. "Come back!" he called, but the bird was too high to hear him.

Turning around, Atan saw his mother watching from the edge of his yard, her apron speckled with icing. She must have seen him shouting at the driver of the tractor, he thought. Had she seen him kicking at the crow too? Since leaving the north, Atan had grown so forlorn that his mother had bought him one of those yellow T-shirts with a happy face on the front that were all the rage with the teens.

"I'm worried about you," she'd said, holding the shirt up to his chest to see if it was the right size. "Rachel once told me you carry her grandfather's grudges. Was she right?"

Unable to explain himself, Atan hadn't answered. Now, reaching his yard, dandelion fluff in his hair, bits of grass coating his sweaty legs and arms, he wondered what his mother was going to say. Bracing himself, he stopped in front of her. At a loss, his mother shook her head.

"Go get cleaned up," she said, starting back inside.

After his encounter with the crow, Atan looked for it every morning, scanning the sky through the glass doors in the family room as dust devils whirled in the now-barren field and fat flies buzzed against the screen. After a week with no sign of the peculiar bird, Atan went to look for it in the cornfield. Making his way between the gigantic stalks, their leaves swaying in the breeze like underwater creatures, their cobs fat and ripe, Atan heard the squeaky chatter of swallows passing overhead. Wondering if their eggs had hatched, he turned and followed them, his sneakers scuffling over the troughs in the coarse earth as the birds flew on toward an abandoned barn next to the cornfield where Atan had seen their mud nests in the rafters.

As he emerged from between the rows of corn, Atan was surprised to find a station wagon parked in the dirt driveway outside the barn's open doors, its faux wood paneling dented, the roof rack showing rust. Most of the time, there was no one around in the morning, and it wasn't even noon yet, but that summer a lot of hippies had been hanging out at the barn. Sometimes, there were so many of them that they had to park underneath the chestnut trees lining the property. When they stayed overnight, you could hear them making music long after sunset. One time, Atan's father had needed to go over to the barn at one o'clock in the morning to ask them to quiet down.

"They looked like good enough kids," he'd said at breakfast. "And I didn't see any bikers."

Bikers were the ones who wore black leather vests with scary patches. They had lots of tattoos and never smiled.

Looking out upon the gravel lane that ended at his street, Atan didn't see any bikers, at least not on that side of the barn, which was built next to a rise in the land, its sloped driveway descending to the doors of the basement garage around the front. There, a decaying tractor with cracked headlights had once stared out at Atan from the dark. Then someone had towed it away and locked the doors tight. That's where the bikers usually parked. If they were at the barn, he wasn't allowed to go.

Approaching the doorway, Atan saw a girl in her twenties crouched next to a camp stove, a pot of water perched above its flickering blue flame. Inside, eating eggs and potatoes out of mugs with spoons, sat two guys on a bench fashioned from cinder blocks and a wooden plank. Behind them, at the back of the barn, two more girls were hanging laundry to dry on a rope strung between beams under the loft.

"Hi," Atan said, gazing down at the girl in the doorway.

"Hi there," she said, smiling warmly.

"What are you doing?"

"Making coffee. Want some?"

"No," Atan laughed. "I'm not old enough to drink coffee."

"What's your name?" the girl asked as the water in the pot came to a boil. "I'm Deloris."

"I'm Atan."

"Atan, huh? What kind of name is that?"

"Inuit," Atan said.

Deloris looked confused.

"Eskimo," he added.

"Oh yeah? Cool. I've heard of them. They live in igloos, right?"

"Not anymore."

"You don't look like an Eskimo. I mean, you're a blondie. And those blue eyes!"

"I'm not. I was born in the north. That's all."

"Cool."

Turning off the stove, Deloris swiveled around to face her friends.

"Hey guys, this is Atan from the north. He's practically an Eskimo."

"Welcome, little man," the guy closest to Atan called out as he set his empty mug on the hay-strewn floor between his feet and picked up a guitar.

"That's Ransom and his cousin Spyder," Deloris said. "And those two fine women you see back there are my best sisters in the world, Corinth and Ruby."

"Are you living here?" Atan asked.

"Maybe," Deloris said with a carefree smile. "Hey, can you bring me their mugs?" she asked, glancing at the boys.

Atan went and picked up Ransom's mug, waiting while Spyder scooped the last of his potatoes into his mouth.

"Why are you called Ransom?" Atan asked.

"He was kidnapped as a baby," Spyder said, licking his spoon clean.

"Really?" Atan asked.

"No, he's just joking around. My name's Randy, but Ransom sounds cooler. We call him Spyder cuz the bike he had when we were kids was called the Spyder 500. It was black and had long front forks and long handlebars that looked like spider legs. Really groovy."

After washing the mugs in a tub of water outside, Atan brought them to Deloris, who filled them with coffee made right in the pot.

"You just gotta pour it through a strainer," Deloris said, tipping out a long stream of brown liquid. "Cowboy-style."

As Atan carried the mugs to Ransom and Spyder, Ruby sat down across from them on an apple crate and picked up a guitar, too, strumming a minor chord as Corinth and Deloris sat together on the floor with mugs of their own, their knees pulled up under flowing skirts that

Atan thought made them look like fairies. Sitting down beside the girls, he noticed the leather necklace Corinth was wearing—a big black stone hanging in the center of her chest.

"It's called obsidian," she said when she saw Atan looking at the pendant. "That's a fancy word for volcanic glass. It protects me."

"From what?" Atan asked.

"From myself. Obsidian is like a mirror of your inner shadow. It shows you your bad stuff, like your hatred and fear. Just like the earth has night and day, your soul has light and dark. You gotta clear out the dark vibes in your psyche if you want to live in the light. I mean if you really want to love, you know?"

"Corinth is a spiritual warrior," Deloris said. "She loves everybody."

Atan thought about that.

"Jesus says we should love everybody, but I don't think I do. Sometimes I don't like people very much."

Ruby stopped strumming her guitar.

"From the mouths of babes," she said.

"There are a lot of people I don't like very much either," Deloris said. "But we still gotta love them. They just don't know what they're doing."

"There's too much ignorance in the world," Ruby said. "That's all."

"It's cuz of ignorance we ran away," Spyder said, looking at Ransom.

"From home?" Atan asked.

"The United States," Ransom said.

"We're what they call draft dodgers," Spyder told Atan. "We snuck into Canada like four years ago, so we wouldn't have to go kill people in Vietnam. You know where that is?"

Atan shook his head.

"Anyway, ever since then, we've been traveling around, working on farms, or picking grapes in Niagara. Stuff like that."

"You don't have a house?" Atan asked.

Deloris sighed. "Who needs a house, man? People weren't made to sit in one place. It's better to move around."

"Like the Eskimos used to," Atan said.

"Yeah, little man, exactly like that," Ransom said. "We're Eskimos like you."

Atan felt a surge of pride that made him grin.

Strumming her guitar, Ruby smiled at Ransom, and he smiled back, flipping his hair out of his eyes as they played a song, the notes rising to the rafters while swallows darted in and out of the barn, their wings glinting in the sunlight that streamed through the cracks in the walls. After a moment, Corinth joined in, singing about some bad people somewhere who had paved over paradise just to make a parking lot. Atan thought she sounded like an angel. He felt the way his mom always said church was supposed to make you feel, even though it never did, like the music was inside him and he was inside the music.

Deloris began singing, too, her low, raspy voice full of devil-may-care gusto, and the song became a chant. Using an empty, overturned bucket as a drum, Spyder lay down a beat with the palms of his hands, matching the speed of Ransom's strumming. As the music got faster, Atan jumped up, rocking from side to side. Closing his eyes, he danced in a circle, around and around on the same spot in time with the rhythm, each tap of the drum and strum of the guitars taking on form and color in his mind.

Soon, Atan was in a trance. The bucket sounded like a skin drum, and Corinth and Ruby sounded like they were throat singing the way Inuit women did, trying to see who could go the longest on a single breath. Atan swung his arm as if banging a stick against the rim of an Inuit drum, imagining he was a drum dancer as his spirit soared to heights he'd never known.

When the song ended and Atan opened his eyes, he saw the others looking at him with admiration.

"The boy's got rhythm," Spyder said.

"He sure can move," Ruby agreed.

"Wow," Atan said when he'd caught his breath. "That was cool."

"Very cool," Ransom told him.

"I have to go home for lunch," Atan said. "Will you be here tomorrow?"

"Yeah, for sure," Deloris said. "Come visit."

"Okay."

Going out through the barn doors, Atan dashed off along the driveway.

"See you!" he hollered.

The next day, for the first time in the south, Atan awoke happy. He ate his cornflakes, gulped down his orange juice, and hurried outside, going straight to the barn. About to depart for the shopping plaza three blocks away, the girls invited him to come along.

"The grocery store throws out tons of good stuff," Corinth said. "Like bread and sometimes cheese with hardly any mold on it."

"Last time, we found two packs of those little white powdered donuts," Deloris said. "They were stale, but I toasted them in the frying pan and, I swear, they melted in your mouth. Who knows what we'll find?"

As Atan traipsed up the street with the girls, he spotted his mother cutting chives with a pair of scissors in the front garden of his house. Coming to the sidewalk, she stopped him in his tracks.

"Where do you think you're going?"

"The plaza," Atan said.

"Why?"

"I'm going with my friends from the barn."

"You don't have any money."

"I'm just walking with them."

Atan's mother glanced at the girls.

"It's almost time for lunch," she told Atan.

"No, it's not."

"It will be."

"But, Mom—."

"Stay close. Do you hear me? I mean it."

With that, having spoiled all the fun, Atan's mother went back into the house, still brandishing the scissors.

With exaggerated frowns, the girls left Atan behind, promising to bring him a treat if they found anything good in the dumpster.

Inside, Atan found his mother in the kitchen putting eggs into a pot of boiling water.

"Why didn't you let me go with them?" he demanded.

"They look like trouble," she said.

"They aren't."

"They have more dirt on their necks than the sand eaters across the street," she said, sounding harsher than Atan was used to.

Maybe she had a headache. But he also noticed something in his mother's sternness that he would have called "prejudice" if he'd known the word. Since arriving in Kitchener, she'd made a point of distinguishing her children from the ones who lived across the street in the townhouses with the sand-filled playground.

"You can always tell the kids from the other side of the street by the ring of dirt around their mouth," he'd heard her say. That was why she called them sand eaters.

Later, after eating his egg salad sandwich, Atan went back to the barn to see if the girls were there, but everyone was gone. He was about to leave when he heard the rumble of a motorcycle and saw a biker riding toward him, followed by a black van that kicked up dust as it sped along the gravel lane.

Before the biker could spot him, Atan ran into the barn and hid in one of the old cow stalls, listening as the motorcycle stopped, its engine cutting off. The van skidded to a halt, and he heard footsteps in the gravel, followed by the creak of old hinges as the men outside swung open the doors to the barn's basement garage, flooding the cracks in the floor at his feet with daylight.

Lying flat on his belly, Atan looked through the biggest gap. What he saw down there made his mind reel—shelves of stuffed animals wrapped in plastic, rows of new bicycles, and boxes of stereos piled to the ceiling alongside racks of fur coats. In the middle of the garage, a punching bag swung from the rafters.

Hearing someone come into the barn, Atan peeked out to see Ransom in the doorway. Behind him stood the biker, an ugly scar under his eye, a snarl twisting up his face.

"You shouldn't be here," the biker said to Ransom as he pulled a long-handled knife from a sheath on his belt.

Turning around, Ransom put his hands out in front of him.

"Hey, man," he said. "I can leave. I dig it."

Wondering what to do, Atan looked on as Ransom scanned the makeshift home he'd created with his friends.

"Just let me gather up this stuff," he said. "When my buddy returns, I'll load up the car, and that's it. It'll be like we were never here."

"No, you weren't," the biker said, and he swung the knife, cutting Ransom's forearm.

Scrambling backward, Ransom slipped in the hay and fell to the floor.

"Man, what the fuck?"

The biker strode forward and kicked Ransom in the jaw with the heel of his boot.

"You didn't see me, either. Understand?"

"Yeah," Ransom moaned, spitting blood. "I wasn't here, man."

"Good," the biker said, sliding the knife into its sheath as he went back outside.

Atan inched out of the cow stalls and went to the doorway to make sure the biker wasn't going to come back. At the bottom of the sloping driveway, two other men, their jackets bearing the same patches in the shape of a skull with wings, were unloading microwave ovens from the van. Atan listened as they went in and out of the basement, relieved when he heard the doors swing shut with a bang, followed by the clatter of a chain pulled through the handles and the thudding clank of a padlock. Coming back into view, the men closed up the van and hopped inside, the tires spitting out gravel as they tore down the lane. Back on his motorcycle, the biker stomped on the kick-start with his bloodied boot, the engine roaring to life as he sped away, dust billowing in his wake.

As a cold silence fell upon the place, the girls stepped out from behind the chestnut trees across the driveway from Atan, each laden with shopping bags from their adventure at the plaza. They must have gotten back right when the bikers showed up, Atan thought, as Ruby ran past him into the barn.

"Are you okay?" Ruby asked, kneeling beside Ransom where he sat on the floor.

"Yeah," Ransom said, his jaw swollen.

Atan came and stood at Ruby's side, Deloris and Corinth following him.

"That's it. We're leaving," Deloris said, pulling clothes off the line under the loft.

"Where's Spyder?" Ruby demanded as she wrapped a T-shirt around Ransom's forearm, the cut still bleeding. "He should have fuckin' been here."

"He went to see about some work. It's not his fault."

"Hey," Corinth said, crouching in front of Atan. "You alright?"

"Huh?" he asked, feeling sick to his stomach.

Corinth hugged him tightly, her obsidian pendant pressed between them.

"You should go. We'll take care of Ransom."

"Are you guys gonna leave?"

"No. Deloris is just upset. We'll see you tomorrow, okay?"

"Okay."

As Atan walked home through the field, swatting the clouds of tiny insects that circled his head, the sickness in his gut turned to anger at what the biker had done to Ransom. Why did those men have to come to the barn? Now, everything with his friends was spoiled. And why was the basement full of all that new stuff? What would happen if anyone found out what he'd seen?

That evening, claiming not to be hungry, Atan refused dinner and shut himself away in his room, brooding in his beanbag chair, his anger and fear all twisted up together. A little after eight o'clock, long before the sun set, he went to bed without kissing his parents good night and slept fitfully.

Just after three o'clock in the morning, Atan awoke with a start, the clouds above his house streaked with furnace orange and molten yellow, an eerie light dancing upon the walls of his room. Going to the window at the end of the hall, he looked out at the shorn field to see his neighbors streaming across the dark expanse in housecoats and slippers, their flashlight beams bouncing along in front of them.

Running to his parents' room, Atan bumped into his father, who came into the hallway as Eleanor and Libby appeared in the doorway of the bedroom they shared.

"What's going on?" Libby asked.

"I'm going to find out," Atan's father said.

"I'm coming too," Eleanor insisted.

"And me," Libby said.

"No!" Atan's father barked. "Stay here until I get back."

But Atan was already halfway down the stairs. Crossing through the living room, he ran out through the front door and sped off along the sidewalk, dressed in his pajamas. Reaching the end of the gravel lane that led to the barn, he saw a row of three fire trucks under the chestnut trees, their corrugated leaves painted red by the flashing lights. Behind the trucks, an ambulance and two police cars had come to a haphazard stop.

Running up the lane, Atan saw smoke pouring out of the barn's open doors and tongues of fire licking at the cracks in the walls all the way to the roof, where long tentacles of flame reached high into the night sky. The barn was ablaze.

"My friends!" Atan cried, racing on until he came to a length of yellow tape stretched across the lane, each end tied to a fence post, a policeman standing in his way.

"Where do you think you're going?" the officer asked.

"My friends are in there. I need to find them."

"There's no one in there now, son. I can assure you of that."

Atan looked past the officer to see Ransom and Spyder in handcuffs, shoved along by two more officers as they approached the police car nearest him.

"We didn't do anything, man," Spyder protested. "It was those bikers."

"I don't see any bikers," the officer behind him said.

"Me neither," the other one smirked.

"Bullshit!" Ransom shouted. "I saw you talking to the motherfuckers when you got here."

"Shut it!" the officer with Ransom said.

"Let them go!" Deloris cried, trailing behind. "This is fuckin' harassment!"

The officer with Spyder turned around and pointed a gloved finger at her.

"You'll stay back, Miss, if you know what's good for you."

"Hey, little man," Ransom called out to Atan. "I'm being kidnapped after all."

He tried to smile, but his swollen jaw made him wince.

"These pigs work for the bikers," Spyder said. "They're crooked. That place was full of stolen shit. Never trust the cops, kid!"

As the officers forced Ransom and Spyder into the back seat of the police car, Ruby and Corinth caught up to Deloris.

"They're going to get deported," Ruby said.

"They'll be okay," Corinth assured her.

"Ransom's going to end up in jail for desertion," Ruby cried. "Don't you get it?"

The officer standing across from Atan lifted the yellow tape, stretching it above the roof of the police car as it backed up and passed underneath. Swiveling its rear end into the grass under the trees, the car turned around and sped down the lane, the heads of Ransom and Spyder silhouetted in the back window.

When the police car was gone, Deloris came and stood with Atan as they watched the barn burn.

"It wasn't us," she said. "Those bikers came back with a bunch of guys and a big truck, and they moved a ton of stuff out of the basement. After the truck left, one of them started the fire."

"I know it wasn't you," Atan said.

"Those cops are bullshit," Deloris said.

The next evening, after the cinders had cooled, Atan went to the barn with his father, its blackened concrete foundation still standing next to a stubby, soot-streaked silo. Atan hadn't known concrete didn't burn. The steel roof beam, lying in the debris, hadn't melted either. But everything else had turned to ash—the cow stalls, the loft, the rope on which the neighborhood children had swung before dropping into the hay. Good things always got taken away, Atan told himself. First the field, now the barn. And why did his friends have to go to jail when they didn't do anything wrong? Nothing seemed fair.

FIVE

2042

I awake to the glare of a searchlight in my eyes, the staccato of propeller blades rattling my windowpanes as a helicopter flies over the house. Sitting up, I squint into the gloom to see my laundered socks dangling from a bootlace stretched between two chairs, each weighted down with a stack of old magazines pilfered from under the steps in the hall. In the shadows cast by the streetlights, the contraption looks like a bombed-out city overgrown with vegetation, as if my socks were hanging vines. At the end of the room, the refrigerator shudders and goes quiet. Still startled by the helicopter, I lie back down, my heart jumping in my chest like a grasshopper caught in a jar.

The helicopters have heat sensors. The soldiers can see I'm here. Intended to terrorize, the searchlights tell them nothing they don't already know. The state's preferred weapon, the potent ingredient of its dark arts, has always, after all, been fear. So why am I so unnerved? No one knows who I am, I remind myself.

Unable to sleep, I lie awake, waiting for daylight.

As the first rays of sun trickle through my thin curtains, the drunk in the room next door gets up and starts throwing things. He's searching for something, maybe his pants, amid what I imagine is terrible squalor. His door creaks open, and I hear him go out onto the side porch, now used as the front entrance, his lighter clicking as he sparks up a cigarette. Smoking isn't allowed inside the house, which has been carved up into apartments, two upstairs and four down, a shared bathroom on each floor.

The woman living in one of the apartments across from me, who is often distraught and likely mentally ill, comes into the hall and stomps to the front door. "I can smell the smoke!" she shouts.

"No, you can't," the drunk says.

"You're trying to kill me. Don't hide it already."

"Kill you?"

"Sidewalk! Go to the sidewalk!"

"Get out of my way," the drunk says, coming back inside, his cigarette crushed out and tossed, I suspect.

Both retreating, the clash over, their apartment doors bang shut behind them. The drunk and the schizophrenic. It feels like the lead-in to a bad joke.

I should get out of bed, brush my teeth, wash my face, comb my beard. I should make some eggs and boil water for coffee. Instead, I stay put. The room is so bleak, the human hour so late. But here I am, stowed away in this safe house, waiting for a general strike. It all seems too preposterous.

"Damn it," the drunk mutters behind the wall separating our rooms.

I imagine him standing before his mirror in his postal uniform, his hair slicked flat in the apocalyptic style. Having nicked himself shaving, he is trying to stanch the bleeding, a bit of toilet paper stuck to his face.

A television drones away in the schizophrenic's room.

"Turn it down!" the drunk hollers.

The university student who lives above me clomps down the stairs and goes out the front door. No doubt she has her backpack with her. I wonder what books it holds. Anything banned? Does she know what life was like before the chips? She was born after the changes began. Maybe she goes about her days believing that everything is as it must be.

Or perhaps she just pretends to. At least she has her small acts of joy. Sex in the middle of the night, her lover beside her when she wakes. These moments are still hers. But if they are taken away, will she wish she'd fought for them now?

Something is scratching at my door. Sitting up, I see a kitten's paw in the gap at the bottom. I push back my blanket and get out of bed, the kitten meowing plaintively. When I open the door, I find a scrap of paper at my feet. The kitten gives it a swat and scampers inside as I pick up the paper and glance into the hall. No one is there. Closing the door, I go in search of my intruder, who has gone under the bed, I think.

The postman comes back into the hall, a ring of keys jangling on his belt. "I said, turn it down!" he shouts at the schizophrenic's door as he leaves.

"Animal!" the schizophrenic screams back in a voice so shrill that it shakes me every time I hear her carrying on. It is the cry of a mind at odds with itself. How many people feel like she does in these times but never show it?

Turning on the light above the stove, I realize the paper is a cash register receipt from the days when money was still something we carried in our pockets. The date is illegible and the numbers have faded, but there are words written on it. In a shaky hand, it says, "I know who you are."

Startled, I go to the window and pull open the curtains to glimpse the postman as he strides down the hill in front of the house. He didn't hesitate outside my door or wait for a reaction from me. And the student from upstairs never so much as glances at this room as she passes my window. What about the actress who lives in the other apartment across the hall? Did she write the note? The kitten is hers, I think. Is she about to come knocking?

Emerging from beneath the bed, the kitten leaps for the bootlace that I tied between the chairs, pulling one of my socks to the floor. I should lace my boots, I think. If I have to run, I don't want to be the old fool stumbling along in boots without laces. Scooping up the kitten, I put it back in the hall and lock the door.

Whoever left the note may have reported me. If someone knows who I am, then it is no secret my arrest would be big news. I'm sure I would be branded a terrorist all over again just for being here. That would be nonsense, of course, but at least there would be a trial this time. At last, I could explain myself. Still, if that was the writer's intention, why warn me?

Shutting the curtains, I sit down in the armchair by the window and wait for something to happen, but nothing does.

SIX

1979

When Atan was ten and had just started the fifth grade, his sisters got into an argument with their father one Sunday morning about having to go to church.

"It's so boring," Libby complained.

"We're not children anymore," Eleanor said. "You can't force us to believe if we don't."

"I'm not raising a bunch of pagans!" their father shouted. "Now get in the car."

"What's a pagan?" Atan asked his mother.

"Not a Christian," she said, fussing with his tie.

"My children are going to know God the way I always did—through Jesus," his father said as he followed the girls outside, his best suit jacket draped over one arm. "And for that, you need to go to church."

The screen door banged shut behind him.

Atan had heard the word "pagan" before. The Catholic priest in Frobisher Bay had called old Ataninnuaq a pagan because his church was in nature.

"The priest didn't like that," Rachel had said. "He feared the spirits in the land. He said they were demons."

Atan loosened his tie.

"So, I'm not a pagan?" he asked his mother.

"Most definitely not," she said.

At that time of year, Atan liked to wander in the forest at the end of his street for long spells, the trees stretching their bare limbs into the blue sky, the path hidden by fallen leaves as orange as pumpkins. With the forest floor crunching under his boots, Atan felt like he was in the north again, where the land breathed and the wind told secrets anyone could hear if they listened.

"What if I want to be a pagan?" he asked.

"Why would you want that?" his mother asked as she hurried him toward the door.

Later that week, Atan's mother made an announcement. Worried her children were drifting away from God, she'd been looking for an alternative to the United Church the family had attended since coming to Kitchener. Now she'd found it. A woman in the church choir had told her about a Christian retreat on the edge of a stream surrounded by woodland. It would be perfect for a weekend outing, Atan's mother explained. And with a passionate young minister adored by the teenagers, it sounded like an answer to prayer.

The following Saturday, the grass in the front yard white with frost, Atan's parents herded him and his sisters into the family's orange Volkswagen bus and headed to the Bezak Center. Inconsolable the whole way there, Eleanor and Libby complained they would rather have been at the mall with their friends. But when they arrived and saw other teens milling about near the front doors, they cheered up. Like at a regular church, the minister stood by the entrance to greet them, but instead of a black gown, he wore bell-bottom jeans and a loose yellow shirt with a V-neck and flowing sleeves. Judging him to be in his early thirties, Atan thought his oversized sideburns and bushy hair made him look like a musician.

"I'm Archie Spencer," the minister said with a boyish smile. "Call me Archie. Welcome to the Bezak Center."

Atan liked him right away. But more than Archie's charm, what captivated him was the way Archie talked about Jesus during that day's sermon. The stories Atan had heard at church made Jesus seem otherworldly like he was more god than man, but Archie made Jesus seem as if he could walk through the door at any minute, with dust on his sandals, maybe even a glint of anger in his eyes, like when he kicked over the moneylenders' tables in the temple.

"One time," Archie said, "when a pompous Roman king rode into Jerusalem on a white horse, trailed by slaves taken in war, a red carpet rolled out to meet him, Jesus traveled the same road into the city on a humble donkey the very next week while the people scattered lowly palm leaves on the ground in front of him and hailed him as the Lord of Peace."

Archie's Jesus was a fiery rabble-rouser who went out of his way to anger the Romans with a brazen act of street theater. He was a radical who stood up for others. Atan liked the sound of that.

Driving home, Atan's parents said they liked Archie too. Jesus was a living force for him. He wanted people to show love, not just talk about it. Atan's family decided to return the next week, even though his father said there were maybe a few too many "flakes" in the crowd for his liking.

"Flakes?" Atan asked.

"Holy rollers," Eleanor said, picking at her chipped nail polish. "You know? Jesus freaks. For them, Jesus is like a drug they can't get enough of, and they want everyone to love Jesus as much as they do."

One of the holy rollers was Greta, who had recently arrived in Ontario on a cross-country bus from the East Coast after a messy breakup. Atan's family met her at the Bezak Center's fall potluck a month after their first visit. Stationed at the dessert table under the clock in the center's main hall, Greta was serving up red Jell-O salad with chunks of pineapple and mini marshmallows, and Atan kept going back for more.

"Are you sure it's okay?" his mother asked. "He's had more than his share."

"He's welcome to it," Greta said. "There's plenty."

When Minister Archie introduced Greta to the congregation that evening at a special evening service to celebrate the autumn harvest, explaining she needed a place to stay while she looked for a job and got on her feet, Atan's mother quickly volunteered the family's spare room in the basement.

"Are you sure we want to do that?" Atan's father asked her.

"Why not? We've got space."

"Okay," his father said, although Atan could tell he was reluctant.

"Her?" Libby asked as she turned in her seat to look at their father.

"I can show love too," he said, nudging Libby in the ribs.

"Why not her?" Atan asked.

"She seems kinda weird," Eleanor said.

Within days of coming to stay at Atan's house, Greta announced she was a psychic. To show how grateful she was for their help, she wanted to do free readings for everyone in the family. She said she could tell them their futures. Declining, Atan's parents told the kids they didn't believe in that sort of thing and didn't want them exposed to her foolishness. That was fine with Eleanor and Libby, who weren't interested either. But Atan was curious.

Finding Greta alone in the basement on a Tuesday after school, Atan asked her if she could really see the future.

"It depends on the person," she said.

She wore big loopy earrings that swung back and forth as she spoke, her bright red lipstick glistening in the sunlight that fell through the high, narrow windows.

"Bring me something that belongs to you," she said. "It has to be something you care about."

Atan went upstairs to his bedroom and came back with his favorite Matchbox car, a purple Volkswagen bug with fat tires and a souped-up engine rising out of the hood. It had a rear spoiler, two big silver exhaust pipes, and a number eight on the door. Greta held it in her hand.

"How long have you had this?" she asked.

"Since last Christmas," Atan said.

"Hmm, do you have anything older?"

"Maybe," Atan said.

He went back to his bedroom and rummaged through his Lego blocks and game boards. After flipping through his hockey cards, he dumped out his container of colored markers but found nothing he could use. Then, in a wooden bowl on his bookshelf, Atan found one of the bone amulets Rachel had sewn onto his clothes when he was a toddler. Shaped like an owl the Inuit called an ukpik, it was just what he needed.

Holding the ukpik amulet in her palm, Greta closed her eyes.

"You died already but are still here," she muttered. "You are old, so old."

Atan wondered what she meant.

Greta gasped, her lids twitching. What was she seeing? Why wouldn't she tell him? Suddenly, her eyes flew open.

"They will shoot you again!" she cried. "You can't escape it."

She stared at Atan, her face scrunched up in bewilderment.

"Who will shoot me?"

"It was you, but it was the old man's fate," Greta said. "You are living his story, not your own."

Atan knew she was talking about old Ataninnuaq.

"No, I'm not," he said. "I'm just named after him."

That evening, over dinner with Atan's family, Greta asked about his namesake.

"So, the old man was an Eskimo?"

"An Inuit," Libby said. "He was a shaman."

"Really? A shaman?" Greta asked. "That's powerful sorcerer stuff!"

"He wasn't a sorcerer," Atan's mother scoffed. "He claimed to have done some strange things, but I don't know if I believed everything he said. And I certainly don't think there's any such thing as what the Inuit call a name-spirit. Atan is just a name."

"It's more than a name," Greta said. "You have to drive the old man out of your son."

"Drive him out?" Atan's mother asked. "What does that even mean?"

"He's practically possessed! I'm telling you for his own good."

"He's not possessed," Atan's father protested, cutting into his meatloaf.

"He's possessed!" Greta cried. "If you guys are good Christians like you say, you'll give him a new name too. For his own safety. He's in danger. I won't tell you what I saw, but trust me, his name is gonna get him killed one day."

"Bullshit," Atan's father declared, pushing his chair back from the table with so much force that Atan's cup toppled over, spilling milk in his lap. "I won't hear another word of this," his father said to Greta, getting to his feet. "It's time for you to take your things and go."

"Go where?" Greta asked, turning to Atan's mother.

"I don't care!" Atan's father shouted.

He got to his feet and came around to Greta's side of the table as she stood to meet him. Grabbing her by the shoulders, Atan's father marched Greta to the top of the basement steps.

"Get down there and gather up your stuff."

Greta descended in a fury, banging about the makeshift room as she crammed her belongings into a duffle bag.

Intimidated by their father's anger, Eleanor and Libby sat at the table, transfixed, while their mother sopped up the milk with a cloth.

"Go change your pants," she said to Atan, whose thighs were sopping wet. "Put on your cords."

Before Atan could do as he was told, Greta came up from the basement and headed toward the side door.

"Jesus will cast out the demon," she hollered. "Pray to Jesus if you know what's good for you!"

"That's enough!" Atan's father shouted, kicking the screen door open as he ushered Greta out onto the driveway.

"Fuck you!" she hissed, storming down the sidewalk as Atan came and watched from the doorway.

Atan's father went back inside, and Atan followed him into the kitchen.

"How's that for love?" he asked.

No one answered.

For the rest of the day, Atan couldn't stop thinking about what Greta had said about the old man.

"Is it true? Does he have power over my life?" he asked his mother when she came to his bedroom to say goodnight. "Is someone going to shoot me?"

"That's just crazy talk," his mother assured him. "Superstition."

She smoothed out her son's *Star Wars* bedspread and sat down beside him, an X-wing starfighter circling her back. "We don't go in for sorcery or magic. Do you understand?"

"What about Jesus?" Atan asked. "Isn't it superstitious to say he turned water into wine and walked on water?"

"That's different," Atan's mother said. "Those were miracles, not everyday things. That's what made them holy."

Trying to fall asleep, Atan recalled a story Rachel had told him once about how she'd healed him when he was a month old and needed to be flown to Montreal for surgery. She'd claimed to have done it by changing all the light bulbs in his house because of an ancient taboo, and he'd never doubted her. Now, he wasn't sure. If miracles were separate from everyday life—if normal people couldn't make wondrous things happen—then Rachel had lied to him. Her story sounded like something only a pagan would believe.

And so it was that Atan, his childhood superstitions firmly in the past, didn't recognize the crow watching from the rooftop almost three years later on the day his family moved out of the semi-detached house they'd been renting. The idea that he had once talked to that very crow in the field behind his backyard would have struck Atan as foolish. And when their van came to a halt in the driveway of their new house on the other side of the city and Libby slid the side door open, Atan had no inkling the crow he saw hopping about on the lawn was the same one.

For a week, the crow followed Atan to and from his new school, perching on the light posts as the boy trudged along, awkward in the body of a thirteen-year-old, his feet and hands too big, his gangly arms making him clumsy. Immersed in sullen misgivings that seemed to arise out of nowhere, Atan dismissed the recurrence of the crow as mere chance. If he hadn't, he might have known he wasn't alone after all, even at a new school, where strange faces filled the halls, the girls shooting him sideways glances, the boys aloof and menacing.

When Atan's family had settled into their new home, a place of their own at last without a townhouse in sight, his mother renewed her quest to find a church that could close the gulf she felt growing between her family and God, which had only widened since the incident with Greta. After that, they'd abruptly ended their visits to the Bezak Center and resumed attending lukewarm services at the United Church.

As luck would have it, a few weeks into her word-of-mouth search, Atan's mother learned of a downtown congregation whose retiring minister had recently been replaced with an evangelical preacher from the Christian talk show *100 Huntley Street.* Elated by the thought of a ministry with passion, Atan's mother insisted the family give the man a try.

"Just because he's on television?" Libby asked, nineteen now and no longer obligated to go to church with her parents. "Count me out."

With Eleanor away at university, that left Atan, who was curious to see what this minister, the Reverend Dale Holdsworth, was all about.

At first sight, Reverend Dale was almost the model of conservatism, his smiling wife at his elbow, the couple flanked by their three children as they greeted congregants inside the church's vestibule. Next to his wife stood their sixteen-year-old daughter, wearing a short dress and a tight sweater that made Atan self-conscious when they shook hands, and next to the reverend stood their fourteen-year-old sons, identical twins. As Atan would learn, one was a shy would-be scholar and the other an affable would-be dropout who longed to start a rock band. The only thing out of the ordinary during that morning service was Reverend Dale's call for people to stay behind at the end if they felt the pull of Jesus and wanted to accept him as their savior.

Reverend Dale's belief that you had to be saved by Jesus to escape damnation was well known. It wasn't enough just to be a Christian. But he kept the fire and brimstone stuff out of his sermons, and Atan, for his part, didn't see anything all that remarkable about the man. In time, however, the number of people answering the call to salvation became so numerous that the television preacher had to add an evening service just for this purpose, and the twins soon invited Atan to come along with them so he could see the goings-on for himself.

Nothing like church services, these gatherings resembled old-style revivals, with people coming to the altar in tears to be born again in Jesus while Reverend Dale—cradling an open Bible, a hand upon the parishioner's head—summoned the Holy Spirit, which seemed to pass from the preacher into the saved, some of whom even fell to the floor and writhed about, kicking and thrashing until, exhausted, they lay still.

Watching the raucous proceedings, Atan suddenly rose from his seat to answer the preacher's summons—not because he was afraid of going to hell or because he wanted to be like the twins, both saved, but because he now sensed a power at work in the imposing man, a former professional football player with shiny black hair and big meaty hands.

Kneeling at Reverend Dale's feet, Atan bowed his head.

"Jesus, I am a sinner," he began, repeating what others before him had said. "I ask for your forgiveness. I dedicate my life to you and ask for your salvation."

"Do you acknowledge Jesus died for your sins?" Reverend Dale asked, placing a fat, sweaty palm atop Atan's head.

"I do," Atan answered.

"Do you accept Jesus as your personal and everlasting savior?"

"I do," Atan repeated, catching the scent of shaving cream on the preacher's cuff.

"Do you want to be born again in the spirit of Christ?" Reverend Dale boomed.

"I do," Atan declared, feeling dizzy.

"Holy Spirit, I beseech you, enter the heart of this young man," Reverend Dale cried as he snapped the Bible shut, his breath hot in Atan's ear.

With these words, Atan fell to the carpeted floor, overwhelmed by a rush of energy that emanated from his core, connecting him to everyone and everything as he entered the unseen world, now illuminated by a light that shone in every direction, penetrating the infinite at once and forever—its source, Atan himself. Filled with peace, his heart surging with love, he stared up at the ceiling, amazed to realize the energy stirring his soul hadn't been passed to him by the minister but instead had erupted from within.

Returning home that night, Atan felt elated, like God needed him for something. He'd always longed to right the wrongs he saw in the world. Now, he believed God was going to show him how. Finding his mother at the piano in the dining room, her choir music open in front of her, he told her what had happened.

"I think I want to be a minister," he declared.

"That's a new one," she said.

Atan had talked about being an actor, even though he hadn't auditioned for the school musical that year because, according to him, the songs weren't about anything. Then he'd set his sights on journalism, only to discover he wouldn't be able to say what he wanted.

"The newspapers just print what the Man tells them to print," Eleanor had said, home from university for the Thanksgiving break, her hair cut short. "It's called propaganda."

Being a minister made sense, Atan's mother told him. If actors were extroverts and writers were introverts, ministers had to be a bit of both, which he certainly was. After only a month at his new school, despite his initial misgivings about being there, Atan had been elected class president on the strength of his promise to get pop machines in the foyer and his plan to organize a winter carnival when the snow arrived. But, preferring to pass his time after class in the wood shop or the art room instead of kibitzing with the other students while they waited for the bus home, he was also the sort who tended to avoid people.

The way Atan saw it, he was a mix of his parents. Like him, his mother had once longed to act, even winning a summer scholarship when she was eighteen that enabled her to travel from Prince Albert to Stratford, Ontario, where she landed the part of Shakespeare's Juliet in a production that got her picture in the paper. At the same time, like his father, Atan could be remote, only stepping to the fore when leadership demanded it. Atan just had to find a way to combine his mother's idealism with his father's pragmatism. Maybe as a minister, he could do that.

What Atan didn't see was that he had always straddled two worlds—a material plane, where the ego took its lumps and tasted its triumphs, his personality born of expedience, and the vast and timeless inner plane that old Ataninnuaq had known how to access, going deeper than most. Now, having rediscovered that unseen place lying on the church floor, Atan wanted to hold onto that transcendent feeling more than anything.

But the elation that followed Atan's salvation by Jesus drained away. At first, he told himself the letdown had to be normal, like when you got excited about Christmas only to be left deflated after it was over—the cheery wreaths, lights, and ornaments put away, the gray of wintry days returning. But if the Holy Spirit was inside him, Atan wondered, then why couldn't he feel it anymore? Was the Holy Spirit at Reverend Dale's command?

Now fast friends with the twins—Karl a kindred rebel who played a mean electric guitar and Fred a kindred thinker inclined to ponder the world in puzzlement—Atan often stayed over Saturday night at their three-story brick house next to the church before meeting up with his parents the next day for the morning service. A month after his born-again experience, Atan awoke one Sunday in the twins' den to the clickety-clack of Reverend Dale's typewriter as he sat in his study upstairs working on that week's sermon. Getting up from the foldout couch, Atan went to talk to him.

"Why can't I feel the Holy Spirit anymore?" Atan demanded.

"You should be happy you felt it at all. Some people don't," Reverend Dale said, balling up a sheet of paper torn from the yellow notepad at his elbow.

"Can I be saved again?" Atan asked.

Laughing, the preacher tossed the paper into a trashcan in the corner.

"It doesn't work that way."

"Then how does it work?"

"All that matters is you're saved," Reverend Dale said, ignoring the question. "Now, let me finish this."

The next Sunday, at the end of the evening service, as newcomers headed to the altar to receive Reverend Dale's promise of salvation in Christ, Atan slipped out of his chair on the edge of the aisle and followed them, his head bowed. One by one, the eagerly faithful recited their prayers of redemption and promptly tumbled over at the preacher's feet, seemingly entranced by a wily magician, as volunteers from the congregation hovered with water and pillows at the ready. Finally, it was Atan's turn.

Seeing the boy kneel before him, Reverend Dale frowned, his exultance turning to scorn.

"What are you doing?" he barked under his breath, his gaze darting to the next person in line as he grabbed Atan by the shoulder with his free hand, the other cradling his Bible, and thrust him to the side. "Go help the others!" the preacher said, motioning at a volunteer who was attempting to heave one of the fallen congregants up from the scarlet carpeting.

Speechless and humiliated, Atan scrambled to his feet and did as he was told.

Having taken to hinting during morning services that congregants who hadn't been saved by Jesus weren't quite as close to God as those who'd answered the call, Reverend Dale eventually found himself in hot water with the church's board members, who demanded he terminate the evening services and put an end to theatrics like people falling over and making undignified displays of themselves. All claims of miraculous doings, healings, and so forth within church walls were to be retracted. A return to the orderly services of old was expected, with a focus on instructing churchgoers in the ways of self-sacrifice and good neighborliness. Reverend Dale refused.

"God's work cannot be curtailed," he told the congregation.

The board had no choice but to fire the preacher and evict his family from their house, which belonged to the church.

Unthwarted, Reverend Dale's supporters raised funds to buy his family a home of their own and rented a school gymnasium where he could continue to preach every Sunday morning and evening. By the start of the new year, the mornings had taken on the high emotions and strange doings of the evenings, the two services becoming indistinguishable. Now, after every service, congregants were slain in the spirit, as Reverend Dale called it, and people spoke in tongues, an ancient, holy language he claimed no one understood but him. While the stricken person uttered an unearthly stream of words for the preacher to translate—florid recitations full of "almighties" and "all powerfuls" and "all redeemings"—Atan looked on in amazement, wondering if he could learn to speak in tongues too.

When Atan asked Reverend Dale what a person needed to do if he wanted to speak in tongues, the preacher rebuffed him again. On this occasion, in light of Atan's antics when he'd wanted to be saved a second time, the rebuff was less kind.

"Don't be a nincompoop," Reverend Dale said, approaching his car as Atan followed him across the school parking lot. "Have some respect for the mysterious."

Incensed, Atan doubted Reverend Dale, wondering if the Holy Spirit wasn't nonsense, just like Rachel's paganism. Try as he might, whether with prayer or by dint of sheer will, Atan couldn't recover the sensations of the night he was saved. Despite his efforts, no force stirred in him. No illumination flashed through his mind.

A few weeks later, a middle-aged woman, seated two rows in front of him at the morning service, began to speak in tongues, her tightly permed hair bouncing above the collar of her red turtleneck sweater as she launched into a purportedly spirit-inspired missive about seven angels of mercy, said to be in attendance that day. At once, another congregant, a scruffy, unshaven man in a shabby suit, leaped out of his seat, speaking in tongues too. Reverend Dale, trying to translate the woman's impassioned words, one hand on his temple, the other pointing in her direction, became flustered, for he couldn't translate both messages at once.

"Quiet, you!" he said to the man, gesturing for him to sit down.

But the man's incomprehensible ramble only grew louder, drowning out the woman's voice. At last, unable to keep translating, the preacher went along the aisle to the man's row and shoved him down into his chair.

"That's enough out of you," he said sternly.

Angered, the man sprang back up to face Reverend Dale, strange words continuing to gush from his throat, as the woman in the red turtleneck fell silent. Still, Reverend Dale refused to translate what the man was saying.

Across the aisle, Atan looked on in astonishment. "What's going on?" he asked Karl.

"That guy's just mad. He's had like three divorces, and my dad told him he shouldn't keep doing that. You know, because marriage is supposed to be for life." Dubious, Karl smirked. "He wants my dad to tell him it's okay."

"But he—your dad," Atan stuttered, "—he can't tell the Holy Spirit to be quiet, can he?"

"I don't know," Karl said, seeming not to care.

"Shh," Fred told them, nudging Karl in the arm. "Get up."

They all stood, along with the rest of the congregation, as Reverend Dale, having returned to the front of the room, sang the first lines of a hymn called "Nearer, My God, to Thee." Obediently, everyone joined in, backed by the pianist and the choir in a half-circle behind her, including Atan's mother, a soprano who sometimes sang the solo part. She was smiling, too, if a little nervously.

"You don't know me," the man hollered over the singing voices. "You don't make the rules!"

He found an opening between the rows and headed toward the gymnasium's side exit.

"You don't know me!" he shouted. "You're bullshit!"

The doors swung open with a bang as he went out, his voice echoing through the school's hallways until he reached the exit and was finally out of earshot. Still, the singing went on.

Atan wondered what was wrong with everyone. Didn't they see what just happened? Who was Reverend Dale to say who the Holy Spirit could inspire? Why not two people at once? Maybe the divorced man was the one really talking in tongues, and the woman with the bouncy perm was faking, putting on a show in cahoots with Reverend Dale. Atan had seen enough. The preacher was a fraud, and all the smiling congregants were his fools, weak-willed people who never dared question him.

That week, looking for an excuse to avoid church, Atan went in search of a job. Fourteen now and old enough, there was nothing to stop him, and he soon found work clearing tables and washing dishes at a restaurant called Mother's Pizza. Popular for screening films from the silent era in its dining rooms, the restaurant had been a hit with his family when they first came to Kitchener. Atan fondly recalled the jugs of root beer that crowded their table, a checkered kerchief tucked under his collar when he ordered spaghetti. He was sure his parents would have no grounds to object. On Saturday nights, he was told, his shift wouldn't end until two o'clock in the morning, and by the time the managers had cashed out and someone was free to drive him home, it would be the middle of the night. That would be far too late for him to get up for the morning service, Atan reasoned.

"What time will you finish?" Atan's mother asked when the restaurant telephoned on Friday during dinner to tell him he was hired.

"Not late," he lied, ladling creamed corn onto his mashed potatoes. "I won't have to stay until closing unless it's super busy."

"And you'll wake up for church?" his father asked, a pork chop hoisted on the end of his fork as he refilled his plate.

"Yeah, probably."

"As if," Libby quipped.

"You promise?" his mother asked.

"I think so," Atan said.

On Sunday morning, waking to the sound of his parents in the kitchen, Atan stayed in bed and waited until they had left for church. When they came home mid-morning, he was lying in front of the television, blurry-eyed and disheveled, the remote in his hand as he flipped through the channels.

"I know what you're up to," his mother said. "Well, you can just go to the evening service. I've asked the twins to pick you up."

"I can't. I have to work."

"Not on a school night, you don't."

"I'm not closing. It's just till nine."

"Every week?"

"Yeah, every week."

"What about church?"

"What about it?"

Atan's mother snatched the remote from his hand, turning off the television with a click.

"When are you going to go?"

"I'm not."

"But you never miss. What's going on?"

Atan wouldn't say, and true to his word, he didn't go back to church. Just as he'd once lost his connection to the spirits of the north and his pagan bearing, he now denounced his Christian beliefs and, along with them, God, Jesus, and the Holy Spirit in one fell swoop. Gone was any sense of connection to something larger than himself. With no recourse to the unseen world, Atan had only himself to fall back on—only his ego. Forswearing the vastness of what he didn't know, he imagined he knew more than he did. Indeed, if he had recognized his ignorance and vulnerability, he would have been terrified, so bereft was he of any means to overcome them. Instead, he became an ass, annoying his teachers with his cockiness and his parents with his distance. At school, Atan was the mover and shaker who chaired student council meetings, organized charity drives, landed roles in the spring musicals, his voice as good as his mother's now, but he always came home late, eating a plate of food left for him in the oven before he disappeared into his bedroom. For the rest of high school, it went on like that.

In the middle of Atan's graduation year, staggering home from a party late one January night, drunker than he'd ever been, he stopped to rest at an unfinished house on the edge of a new subdivision, its walls not yet erected, no roof overhead. Descending to the basement on a wooden ladder, he lay down on the floor and quickly passed out.

A while later, hearing a girl's voice calling his name, Atan opened his eyes to see stars spinning madly in the clear sky. Shivering, he lifted his head and looked around. Where was he? In the light of a quarter moon, he could make out concrete walls and a floor littered with construction debris. He was going to freeze, he thought, laying his head back down.

The stars kept spinning, and he closed his eyes to make them stop. Soon, he'd passed out again.

"Atan?" the girl's voice called out, louder this time.

Atan groaned and clutched his head. He could hear his teeth chattering. It was okay if he died there, he told himself, trying to deny the devastation welling up inside his chest. He was ready to die. He'd lasted eighteen years. That was pretty good.

It had started to snow, the moon eclipsed by a rogue cloud as tiny flakes drifted down out of the blackness and melted on Atan's face, his jacket and jeans turning white. He'd never felt so tired.

"Atan?" the voice called out again, close now.

It sounded like Vanessa, Atan thought, his lab partner in chemistry class, a brunette with sweet brown eyes as bright as a doe's. He tried to get up but felt sick to his stomach and lay back down. Above him, a large crow landed on top of the wall, squawking loudly as it used the tips of its wings to brush bits of dirt and snow over the edge.

"Stop it," Atan cried as the dirt spilled onto his face. "Shoo!"

The bird took to the sky, and Vanessa's face appeared in its place.

"Atan?" she called down to him. "Is that you?"

"Vanessa?" he slurred.

"What are you doing in there?"

When he didn't answer, Vanessa went down the ladder to the basement. Sitting him up, she pulled Atan to his feet. Then she helped him climb back out, holding his legs steady on the ladder's rungs as he wobbled above her.

Reaching the sidewalk, Vanessa brushed the snow off the curb, and they sat down under a streetlight. She had watched Atan leave the party blind drunk and in a gloomy mood, she explained, and she'd been trying to catch up, only to lose sight of him.

"Are you okay?" she asked.

"No."

"What's going on with you?"

Atan shrugged and tried to smile. "I wish I knew."

SEVEN

2042

I am asleep when I hear tapping inside the fireplace. Reluctant to open my eyes, I cling to a sweet calm that has taken hold of me—free of troubles, beyond doubt and regret, adrift in a dream about caribou that slips away as my mind is forced back to this room. The tapping grows insistent, and I awake, slowly unfolding my legs, stiff these days, now that I'm cooped up and no longer walking mountain trails every morning, as I was in India. At last, I lift myself off the bed and manage to stand.

I go to the fireplace, covered by a cast-iron plate embossed with a winter scene of pine trees and tobogganers. The plate once hid a bricked-up flue, but the bricks were removed before I arrived, and a tunnel was dug that leads to a safe house on another block. It's my escape hatch. It's also my lifeline since I can't go out. Old men like me are being targeted and detained, even if they're not suspected of anything. The young man who brought me here was right about the soldier at the checkpoint. The military has somehow found out that I've come back to Washington. They're onto us.

I remove the cast-iron plate to see a "mule" crouching in the tunnel's opening with two cloth bags full of groceries. This is what the runners call themselves—mules. "It's the mules," the young man said, "who will win the fight." If the fight can be won, I agree with him, for the mules are surely stubborn in their resolve, refusing to be chipped and living off the radar, which must require all kinds of sacrifices others are unwilling to make.

The cupboards were well stocked when I arrived, so this is my first delivery. I'm curious to see what my visitor is like. How does one end up a mule? What inspires a person to embark on such a dangerous path? Is it anger or love—or both?

"Come up," I say, sitting down on the edge of the bed as a figure in a hooded coat climbs into the room.

The curtains are closed, and in the light from above the stove, I can't tell if it's a boy or a girl.

The mule puts the groceries on the counter. I see a full-length skirt, so it could be a girl. Then again, through my front window, I've seen boys dressed in long skirts too. It has become a sign of manliness to be brazenly unmanly. Beneath the skirt are chunky boots, so it could be a boy. The mule pulls the hood down and turns to look at me. It's a girl after all, no more than twenty, perhaps younger. Her hair cropped, she wears no makeup, her full lips framed by high cheekbones. She looks familiar, but I don't know why.

She notices my handwashing—socks again and a shirt—hanging between the chairs I've piled with magazines. "Are those what I think they are?" she asks, pointing at the small towers of *Good Housekeeping* and *National Geographic*.

"Shh," I say, indicating the wall. "The neighbors will hear us."

She takes a magazine from one of the stacks. "Wow, real paper!" she barely whispers. "Brisk."

"What?"

"That's brisk. You know, *cool.* I love old stuff." Putting the magazine back, she steadies her gaze on me, searching my face, like she has something to say. Or maybe a question to ask. Seeming to lose her nerve, she returns to the counter. "I'll put these away for you," she says.

"What have you brought me?"

"Everything." She pokes around in the bags. "Lentils, beans, rice. Onions, garlic, and peppers." She pulls out three ruby-red apples, holding them up for me to see.

"Curry?" I ask, trying not to sound too eager.

"No. Sorry. Whatever we can't grow ourselves, we have to get on the black market. Couldn't find any."

"You have your own gardens?"

"Roof-toppers."

"And what do you use for money when you have to buy things?"

"We barter. No chip, no money, you know?"

"You barter for everything?"

"Mostly, but sometimes we get chipped people to buy stuff for us. The scalpers. Then we pay them in work usually."

Putting the apples down next to the toaster, she fishes a packet of oatmeal from one of the bags, then a burlap pouch of coffee. Efficient and poised, she doesn't rush as she places the items in the cupboard. She has a remarkable presence about her.

"Is there any news?" I ask.

"No. But there will be." She turns to face me, smiling. "Any day."

"You seem sure."

"I am." She peers at me through the dimness. "Aren't you?"

"Well, I'm not allowed to go out, am I? The military doesn't seem to be on our side."

"They are. They're just following orders so no one gets suspicious."

"Why a general strike now?"

"You have to ask?"

"I do. I've come a long way. I'd like to know what our chances are."

"It's because of this martial law stuff. We know it's based on lies. China isn't going to attack us. The government's using that as an excuse. We're fed up. We've suffered enough."

"Have you?"

"Of course. Take a look around."

"I'm not so sure. People can convince themselves things aren't bad even when they are. Unless the facades of all the buildings turn black with mold and little girls stop wearing colored ribbons in their hair and all the politicians grow sinister mustaches, they imagine nothing's wrong. For them, the curfew is no more than an inconvenience. Life goes on."

"What about the debtors' camps? The debt slaves? People are being dragged away in broad daylight. No one is safe anymore."

"I've heard what's going on. But when it's their neighbors and not them who are the ones suffering, people swallow the madness along with their eggs and toast. They wash it all down with orange juice that wouldn't make it to their tables if not for the labor of migrants working for dollars a day. No amount of suffering has ever been enough to make people act."

"Maybe not in your day."

Upset with me, she finishes putting away the groceries and closes the cupboard door, swiftly stuffing the empty bags into the front pockets of her coat.

"I just want to know what's different this time."

She shakes her head, like she's mystified I would even ask. "You. That's what."

"Me?"

"We've been waiting for you."

"I don't understand."

"You can inspire people. If they hadn't tried to kill you, things might have changed a long time ago."

I want to tell her I doubt it, but I hold my tongue.

"When the president is gone, we can elect a new government, free of the cabal."

"The deep state?"

"Yes."

"I hope you're right."

"I am. You'll see."

Defiant, she pulls up her hood and descends into the fireplace.

"Wait," I call after her.

She stops and turns back.

"What's your name?"

She looks at me, hesitant to answer.

"I'm not supposed to say. It's safer that way."

"Okay. Well, thank you for coming."

"Sure."

She ducks out of sight, and I listen as she retreats along the tunnel before getting up from the bed to put the cast-iron plate back in place. I don't know whether to envy or pity her for harboring such certainty. Was I ever that young?

EIGHT

1988

"Why haven't you applied for university?" Atan's guidance counselor asked, opening a folder on his desk. "You should have done it before Christmas."

"I don't know," Atan said, seated across from him.

With only three months before graduation, Atan had no idea what he wanted to study or where.

"If you don't apply now, you'll miss a year," the counselor told him. "At this late date, you've probably already lost your chance at a scholarship." He leveled his gaze on Atan, his glasses sitting low on his nose. "And that's a shame because your marks are top-notch."

On the wall behind the counselor's desk was a map of Canada, its ten provinces arrayed from sea to sea. Above them stretched the northern territories, whose mysteries Atan rarely thought about anymore, their islands scattered far into the Arctic Ocean. He cast his eyes east from Kitchener's spot on the map amid the Great Lakes in a marigold Ontario, across a rose Quebec by way of the Saint Lawrence River, and all the way to the peach maritime provinces, where there were many good schools. Too close, he thought.

He looked west out of Ontario across a pea-green Manitoba, a taffy Saskatchewan, and a robin's egg Alberta. That was pretty far away, but his mother had a brother in Calgary, so his family would likely visit if he lived there. He loved them. That wasn't the problem. He just needed to be himself, on his own terms, and he couldn't do that with his parents—or God—looking over his shoulder. Next was a mauve British Columbia with an island off its southern coast near the United States border. Atan couldn't get any farther away from home without leaving the country, he thought, unless he went north. He glanced up at the vast expanse covered by a teal Yukon and a gray Northwest Territories. Nothing there, he told himself, at least nothing you would call a school.

Atan pointed at the island off the coast of British Columbia.

"Are there any universities there?" he asked.

The counselor swiveled his chair to look at the map.

"Vancouver Island?"

"Yeah."

Scratching the bald patch on the crown of his head, the counselor swung back around.

"Just one," he said. "The University of Victoria. You interested?"

"Yeah."

"Let's see if it's still accepting applications," the counselor said, picking up a sheet of paper in the folder. "Not many are."

Atan pulled his chair a little closer to the counselor's desk.

"You're in luck."

"Yeah?"

"But the deadline is soon." The counselor looked at the calendar on his watch. "You have ten days."

"Shit."

"Pardon?"

"Sorry. What courses do they have?"

"No idea."

The counselor went in search of a course calendar. But Atan had already made up his mind. That was where he would apply.

As for what Atan would study, he couldn't decide. He was no scientist or mathematician, that much was clear. He had good grades in economics, but that was only because of his paper on the collapse of the German economy in 1923, the result of a money-printing spree that left the country's currency worth nothing. In any case, still scornful of the lenders confronted by Jesus in the temple, Atan had no interest in getting rich. Business courses weren't an option. Neither politics nor law appealed to him since both demanded moral compromises, he figured, as if the truth could be relative. He loved art but didn't draw that well. He could sing, but in his first year of high school, he'd wound up in a class of troublemakers whose antics had lost them the privilege of using the school's instruments. Music was out. That didn't leave much, Atan thought, only literature, writing, and history, where his strong grades made up for his weaker showing in the disciplines with sharper edges and little room for rebellion. In the end, he applied to the Faculty of Humanities and was accepted late that summer. He even landed an entrance scholarship of almost $12,000, enough to set him free.

That fall, perched on the rim of the Pacific Ocean, over 2,500 miles from home, Atan found new life at the University of Victoria, its rolling green campus dotted with low buildings tucked beside rises and knolls lined by old trees. Between classes, he liked to sit beneath the Garry oaks outside the library with his notebook, a trunk at his back, writing thoughts that verged on poems or, lately, something closer to song lyrics. Other times, he holed up at the Student Union Building, the hub of campus life. Boasting a cafeteria on the first floor and a bar downstairs, it even had an art house cinema, where Atan, upon seeing European films for the first time, had quickly become obsessed with the Swedish director Ingmar Bergman's bleak meditations on human torment and spiritual doubt.

One afternoon mid-semester, Atan's philosophy professor, a petite, slightly hunched woman in her fifties with a vaguely Eastern European accent, gave a lecture on Immanuel Kant, whose name she pronounced exactly like the foulest word for the female genitalia that one could ever utter in public. Every time she said it, the students squirmed, some of the young women sighing with annoyance, some of the male students cringing in embarrassment. The burly guy seated next to Atan in the last row of tiny desks couldn't stop snickering.

Oblivious, the professor proceeded to discuss "Kunt's" *(squirm)* take on God and how seeing no place for the divine in matters of moral truth, he had argued against the existence of spirit, or innate ideas. For him, all human knowledge came from experience alone. Picking up where "Kunt" *(cringe)* had left off, the professor explained, Friedrich Nietzsche had gone even further in denying the divine, claiming that the idea of a moral good sanctioned by God was a fiction created to force human meaning upon an inhospitable reality.

"What does that mean?" a young woman in the front row interrupted, pushing a floppy knit hat out of her eyes as she looked up from her frantic note-taking.

"What does what mean?" the professor asked.

"Inhospitable reality," the woman said, reading what she'd scrawled.

"It means life is shit," the burly guy chimed in.

"That's right," the professor said. "Nietzsche declared God dead. Then he said a life without God is inhospitable because life doesn't love or care about us."

That was true, Atan thought. Life wasn't fair. People suffered all the time for no good reason.

"So that's why bad things happen to good people?" Atan asked.

"It depends on your frame of explanation," the professor said. "For instance, if you believe in animism, or paganism, as the Natives traditionally did here in British Columbia, you will perceive the world as inspirited and thus responsive to your wishes and actions. You will take responsibility for your own reality, recognizing you play a part in bringing it about. Long before Kunt *(sigh)*, Baruch Spinoza imagined something similar to animism, arguing that God was in fact consciousness itself, resplendent in nature and cloaked in human form."

"I don't know about you guys, but I definitely feel like I'm God," the burly guy quipped.

"Then you misunderstand," the professor said. "The mountaintop god, the one Søren Kierkegaard said required a leap of faith to believe in, the one Nietzsche declared dead, is the one you mean. But that was not the god Spinoza meant. He was talking about god in every atom, god as energy and spirit. That is a different idea of God."

She glanced at her watch. Next week, she told the class, they would look at readings by Jean-Paul Sartre and Albert Camus, who had articulated the existential anxiety that came with Nietzsche's view of life. But first, she wanted to know if there were any more questions about "Kunt" *(groan)*. There weren't.

After the philosophy lecture, Atan had a Shakespeare class taught by a tall, wiry man in his fifties, who had a British accent and tended to stuff his hands into the front pockets of his trousers when he spoke, frequently using them to emphasize his point with an outward tug, as if he had once been told his hands were flailing about and it was best he try to keep them still like a good thespian.

Sitting in the middle row of the classroom, Atan noticed the Shakespeare professor's fly was undone. Every time he tugged at his pockets, the front of his pants opened wide, closing only when he unclenched his hands again. Atan felt bad for the man but didn't dare point out the obvious and risk embarrassing him. Instead, he tried to keep his eyes on the page of his text, *Macbeth* this time, the third play the class had read in nearly as many weeks.

"Fair is foul and foul is fair," the professor read from the book on his podium. "Where have we heard those words before?" He approached the first row of desks and peered into the students' faces. "Anyone?" he asked, his fly opening.

Atan put up his hand. "Macbeth's first line," he said.

"Yes!" the professor said. "Act one, scene thirty, line forty. Everyone have it?" He looked at Atan, his fly closing. "What does Macbeth say?"

"So foul and fair a day I have not yet seen," Atan read.

"Pardon? Did anyone hear that?"

The room was silent.

"I barely heard that," he chided Atan. "Macbeth has just come from triumph in battle. He's tired and bloody, but elated. Let's hear it again."

Atan considered the mind behind Macbeth's words, his recognition of the foulness of death in war even as he welcomed the fair fortunes of victory. As the rows of students in front of him turned around in their desks to watch, Atan mustered all the actorly bearing he could and repeated the line, reveling in the mad delirium of victory while also showing hints of the torturous self-doubt that would grow in Macbeth as the murderous consequences of his ambition became clear.

"Bravo," the professor said with a wide grin. "Much better."

Lately, showing an interest in Atan, he had taken to challenging him in this way.

Atan didn't mind. When looking at the university's course calendar, he'd been happy to see the school boasted a theater department with a brand-new building that housed three stages—one in the round, one a proscenium, and one a black box. During the first weekend of the school year, he'd auditioned for the fall season's main-stage productions, landing a part in a dark comedy by Christopher Durang called *The Marriage of Bette and Boo.* His role as a Catholic priest had required impressions of bacon frying and coffee percolating for the attendees of a couples' seminar. The newspaper reviews had been full of praise for his performance, and Atan had been a minor celebrity for a few brief weeks, long enough for his Shakespeare professor to take notice and start steering him toward more serious work.

"Fair is foul and foul is fair," the professor repeated, his fly opening. "What else do the witches say that suggests a world where things are not one thing but two?"

A young man two seats in front of Atan stuck his pen into the mass of red curls atop his head and put up a freckled hand.

"When the battle's lost and won," he read.

"Yes," the professor said, his fly closing. "Fair is foul and foul is fair. Lost is won and won is lost. Nothing in *Macbeth* is as it seems. But he does not understand this truth. He does not perceive reality clearly. This is the tragedy of the play. What do we call such a reality?"

"Inhospitable," Atan said.

"Yes," the professor said, his fly opening. "Macbeth's world is inhospitable to him. It ultimately does not want him to be king. It thwarts his ambitions. But that is only because he has contravened the cosmology of the play by taking the throne from the divinely appointed king. Shakespeare's world is constructed according to a hierarchy, atop which sits God. Beneath him, as God's deputy, sits the king. No disobedience is permitted in such a world. You can bemoan the acts of an unjust ruler, you can pray to God for intervention, or you can flee the kingdom. But you cannot kill the king and take his throne."

The professor paused, his fly closing.

"When Macbeth does that, the sky turns dark at midday and the horses eat each other. Nature is in chaos. Order is restored only when Macbeth is killed and the crown falls to the king's rightful heir. There is fairness in the foul end Macbeth meets. Fair is foul and foul is fair."

In the hallway after the Macbeth lecture, Atan stopped his Shakespeare professor with a tap on the shoulder.

"Sorry, sir, but just so you know, your fly's undone."

"Oh!" the professor said, quickly zipping up. "Was it terribly noticeable?"

"No, not at all," Atan lied.

"I've been doing that quite a lot lately. Good thing you caught me before my next class."

His cheeks crimson, the poor man hurried off.

Walking home, Atan reflected on what his professor had said about the cosmology of *Macbeth*. Was there really an ordering force that could stand against the chaos of life? In his philosophy course, Atan had scoffed at Kierkegaard's claim that nothing more than a leap of faith was needed to know God. Instead, he'd sided with Nietzsche, taking solace from the idea that God was dead. Convinced life was unfair and inhospitable, Atan had taken to thinking of himself as an existentialist. But sometimes, like today—one professor riling the class with her pronunciation of Kant, the other diminished by his open fly—Atan sensed a mischievous spirit, a trickster full of mirth and humor, lurking beneath the surface, and he wondered if he wasn't wrong about things after all.

That first semester, an even greater influence on Atan's thinking than the existentialists was his roommate, the simultaneously brash and insecure Brad Wheeler, who'd turned up at the door of Atan's basement apartment in a downpour late on a Tuesday night three weeks into September, soaked to the bone, an overstuffed backpack at his feet, a ten-speed bicycle at his side.

"I'm your new roommate," he chuckled. "I guess the landlady told you?"

Eight years older than Atan, Wheeler sported a droopy mustache that shook when he laughed.

"Yeah, she told me," Atan said. "Come in."

Wheeler rolled his bike inside and leaned it against the wall, letting water pool on the cement floor beneath the tires.

"Didn't think I'd make it. It's been raining for two days."

"You've been cycling for two days?"

Wheeler laughed again. "More like three months."

"Where from?"

"Toronto."

Atan didn't know whether to believe him. Judging by Wheeler's gut, which protruded into view as he pulled off his windbreaker, he wasn't in good enough shape to cycle around the block. And even though the sleeves of his Pink Floyd sweatshirt were cut off at the shoulders like he was some kind of muscleman, with an obscene amount of armpit hair sticking out from the edges, his arms weren't big and solid but flabby. He looked like a bum.

"Shit!" Wheeler exclaimed. Going back outside, he soon returned with a padded guitar case. "Can't be forgetting this," he chuckled. "Not after lugging it so many miles."

"You're serious?" Atan asked. "You biked here from Toronto?"

"Yeah. A couple of truckers helped me over the Rockies, but I made it to Alberta and through the foothills on my own." Slipping off his wet running shoes, Wheeler picked up his backpack. "Which room is mine?" he asked.

"This way," Atan said, leading him through the kitchen.

"The worst part was the thunderstorms on the Prairies," Wheeler said. "There was nothing taller than me for miles in every direction, lightning crashing into the fields on both sides of the road." He bellowed with laughter. "Man, it was terrifying. But beautiful too."

The guy was telling the truth, Atan thought. Wheeler had ridden his bike across the country. Either that or he was a damned good liar.

"This one's yours," Atan said, opening the door to Wheeler's bedroom. "Don't worry, mine isn't any bigger."

"This will do," Wheeler laughed.

As it turned out, Wheeler told the truth. One morning at the beginning of July, six days into an addiction rehab program, he'd jumped up in the middle of Group and berated the other residents.

"All we do is sit around and whine!" he shouted. "Fuckin' poor me." He pointed at the guy at his elbow. "Fuckin' poor him." He pointed across the circle at the woman whose story he'd interrupted. "Fuckin' poor her." Knocking over his chair, he clambered toward the door. "Get me the fuck outta here!"

From there, Wheeler had gone straight to his younger brother's place to see about borrowing some camping gear.

"Where're you going?" his brother wanted to know.

"West," Wheeler told him.

"Where west?"

Wheeler sighed. "I don't know."

With no idea where the road would take him, Wheeler had packed what he could carry, oiled up his old ten-speed bike, and started pedaling. If a few months with no one but himself for company couldn't sober him up and put an end to his self-destruction, he told Atan, then nothing could. Arriving in the Rocky Mountains at the end of August, the temperatures already turning cold, he'd pushed on to Vancouver, which he'd hated on sight, he said, because it was too clean and too orderly.

"A city that young is socially engineered," he said. "It's totalitarian. Walk here, use this ramp, descend on these stairs, stay to the right, do not pass fuckin' go. Fuck you!" he chortled.

In any case, the rents were too high in Vancouver, so Wheeler had checked the listings for places in Victoria and found a room in Atan's basement apartment on Beach Drive, one block from the ocean, beneath the long slopes of a gabled roof that gave the house the air of a cottage.

The night Wheeler arrived, he introduced Atan to avocados. The meals in Atan's house growing up had always been a variation of meat and potatoes, vegetables on the side, maybe peas or corn. Never had anything as exotic as an avocado crossed his plate.

"What's that?" Atan asked.

Sitting half-lotus on the carpeted floor of the TV room, as the landlady called it, his belly on top of his thighs, Wheeler ate spoonfuls of the strange food directly out of its dark-green skin. In front of him on the coffee table, a stick of incense burned in a wooden holder shaped like a half moon, its wisps of fragrant smoke drifting up to the low ceiling.

"Ambrosia," he said.

"What?"

"Food of the gods."

Atan was confused.

"It's called ambrosia?"

Wheeler laughed. "No, it's an avocado. You've never tasted avocado?"

"No."

"Try it."

Atan ate his first spoonful of avocado and smiled. Wheeler wasn't exaggerating. It tasted divine—earthy and nutty, so creamy, almost buttery. Maybe Atan was wrong about him. Sure, he looked like someone Atan's mother would've called a sand eater, a guy from the wrong side of the street, but that was no reason not to take him seriously. Although years ago Wheeler had dropped out of university after only a couple of months—disgusted, he said, with everyone's self-importance—he'd read way more books than Atan, a lot of them about esoteric things.

One was called the *Tao Te Ching*, an ancient book by the Chinese philosopher Lau Tzu, who wrote it against his better judgment, Wheeler explained, when asked to leave behind some wisdom before retreating from the world to live out his old age in solitude. For Lau Tzu, the truth of things could not be expressed in words. A person who spoke did not know, and a person who knew did not speak. His answer to this conundrum was eighty-one cryptic verses, which Atan did not fully grasp but soon took to quoting whenever it felt appropriate.

Watching a fellow student destroy Hamlet's "to be or not to be" monologue with overacting, Atan said, "Fill your bowl to the brim and it will overflow. Sharpen your knife too much and it will blunt."

When Wheeler heard Atan parrot Lau Tzu that way, he told him, "It's not a set of rules, man. It's nothing like that. Just think of the Tao as a current. It's invisible but moves through everything. Once you're aligned with it, you can forget what you've read. You'll just be in the flow."

"Okay," Atan said, not really understanding.

"With the Tao, you can replace the dictator God of Christianity with one that makes life possible," Wheeler told him.

"I don't believe in God."

"Yes, you do."

"No, I don't."

"Yeah, you do. You just need to redefine what God is."

"Change my frame of explanation?"

"Exactly."

Atan didn't like what he was hearing.

"I'll kill myself before I believe in God again," he promised.

"You just might," Wheeler said. "Nothing and no one exists outside the Tao."

Apart from introducing Atan to the Tao—another name for the unseen, even if Atan didn't recognize it—Wheeler's deep hostility toward so many things in the world around him had a noticeable effect on Atan, spurring the anger that had festered in old Ataninnuaq.

One time, seeing the latest Benetton ad on the side of a passing bus, Wheeler turned livid at the gratuitous image of a white firefighter with a rescued Black baby cradled in his arms, denouncing as vehemently as any race scholar the idea that Black children needed heroic white interveners. Looking on, impressed by Wheeler's passion, Atan had to pull his friend back from the curb as the bus hurled by, splashing them both with rainwater.

Another time, when Atan insisted that Canada, with health care for everyone, was more socialist and less capitalist than the United States, Wheeler gave him a history lesson he would never forget.

"Canada was founded on theft and murder!" Wheeler retorted. "We started as the glorious Hudson's Bay Company—a corporation!"

"That's true," Atan said, thinking about it. "But—"

"The company pushed all the Natives into war with each other over furs. Why? So it could sell beaver hats to rich pricks in Europe. There's your socialism!"

Back in Ontario, visiting his family for Christmas, Atan told his father what he thought of Canada's criminal history.

"Hogwash," his father said. "The Indians would still be rubbing two sticks together to light a fire if left to their own devices."

"What's wrong with that?" Atan protested. "At least they knew enough to take care of the planet. That's more than you can say about us."

"The Eskimos in Frobisher Bay were the worst polluters I've ever seen. Homes half taken apart, doors and drywall strewn about on the ground, yards full of garbage."

"Inuit," Atan corrected him.

"Yes, yes, Inuit."

"And it's called Iqaluit now, not Frobisher Bay. That means Place of Fish."

Atan's father took off his glasses and closed the Tom Clancy novel he'd been reading.

"Did you know some of the mothers in town used to feed their kids baby formula spiked with dish soap so they would get diarrhea?"

"Why would they do that?"

"So they could leave the kids at the hospital for the weekend while they went drinking. I never told you this, and you were too young when it happened for you to remember, but one night a drunk couple got into a fight and set their house on fire with a candle. I was one of the first from the volunteer brigade to get there. The husband was slumped over in the snow, couldn't even stand up, and his wife was blubbering hysterically. I couldn't understand anything she said. It turned out her son was asleep in the bedroom. The fire was too hot for us to use the front door, so we had to go in through the back wall with axes. When we got into the room, it was too late. The boy was curled up on the bedsprings, just a pile of cooked meat."

Atan didn't know what to say.

"Those people were given everything they needed, yet they became drunks," his father said.

"Not until they started living in that town."

"Stop romanticizing them. They are no better and no wiser than us."

Yes, they were, Atan thought. He couldn't explain what he sensed. He just knew his father was wrong.

That winter, Wheeler also introduced Atan to the marvels of the guitar. It wouldn't have been his first choice of instrument. He didn't like things he couldn't master quickly, and when Wheeler showed him the chords, the guy's fingers seemed to contort in impossible ways. But then one rainy night near the end of March, Atan went to see Wheeler play at an open-mic coffeehouse downtown, and that changed his mind.

Wheeler was third on the list of people who signed up to perform. When the master of ceremonies called out his name, he was in the washroom and almost got passed over.

"I'm still here," he laughed as he squeezed between the tables of spectators, grabbing his guitar from the chair next to Atan.

Watching Wheeler plug in, Atan thought his friend might be headed for disaster. Not that Wheeler couldn't play well. The guy's fingers moved like lightning. But he had no self-esteem, which Atan blamed on Wheeler's father, an overweight character actor Atan had seen in bit parts as a hard-assed judge or a boss. When Wheeler was very young, the story went, his father had told him and his brother they had no talent.

"Show me your hands," he'd said to them one day while they were heading downtown on the bus. "You see?" he'd asked, holding up his own hands for comparison. "Neither of you has the hands of an artist. The shape of your palm and the length of your fingers are all wrong."

Wheeler had believed him. In a way, he still did.

After tuning his guitar, Wheeler pulled the mic stand an inch closer, his head cocked to one side as he ripped into a wild cover of "Psycho Killer," a song by the Talking Heads that Atan had never heard.

"I can't seem to face up to the facts," Wheeler sang. "I'm tense and nervous and I can't relax. I can't sleep 'cause my bed's on fire. Don't touch me. I'm a real live wire."

Atan marveled at the speed of Wheeler's strumming as the song kicked into the chorus.

"Psycho killer, qu'est-ce que ç'est?" Wheeler belted out, eyeballing the people at the tables closest to the stage as if he was a little crazy himself. "Fa-fa-fa-fa, fa-fa-fa-fa-fa, far better. Run, run, run, run, run, run, run away oh oh."

With his hair hanging in his eyes, he leaned his face close to the strings and drove home the rhythm with each downward thrust of his bare fingers. Picks weren't Wheeler's thing, he'd told Atan. He needed to "feel the steel."

By the time Wheeler got to the second verse, droplets of sweat were flying from his hair and spattering against his guitar.

"You start a conversation," he wailed. "You can't even finish it. You're talking a lot, but you're not saying anything. When I have nothing to say, my lips are sealed. Say something once, why say it again?" He flashed the audience another crazy grin and sailed back into the chorus with a new reserve of fury. "Psycho killer, qu'est-ce que ç'est?" he asked.

Right then, the forefinger of his strumming hand split at the tip, sending a stream of blood onto the stage floor. Instead of stopping, Wheeler finished the chorus and strode into the final verse.

"We are vain and we are blind," he intoned. "I hate people when they're not polite." The blood kept spurting, and he kept singing. "Psycho killer, qu'est-ce que ç'est? Fa-fa-fa-fa, fa-fa-fa-fa-fa, far better. Run, run, run, run, run, run, run away oh oh oh. Yeah yeah yeah yeah oh!"

Wheeler was in his glory, riding the song's final forty-five seconds of spectacular licks and riffs like he was on the back of a wild mustang he'd tamed. When the song was over and his guitar went silent, no one made a sound for the briefest second before the whole place erupted in astonished applause. Wheeler shoved back his hair and gave the audience a sheepish smile.

From that moment, Atan was hooked. The actor in him wanted to be up on the stage where Wheeler was, all eyes on him. And the writer in Atan was just as mesmerized by the words of the song Wheeler had sung. It was about something. That song had attics and cellars in it that Wheeler's voice had flung wide open for all to peer into. Atan wanted to write and perform stuff like that.

"Teach me to play," Atan said to Wheeler as they walked home from the coffeehouse in a drizzle, having missed the last bus, both of them too broke to afford a taxi.

"It won't be any fun. It'll be fuckin' boring. And until you grow callouses, your fingertips will hurt like hell."

"I know."

Atan looked at Wheeler's bandaged finger and eyed the blood on the leg of his jeans.

"Can I use a pick at least?"

"Sure," Wheeler laughed.

"So, you'll teach me?"

"Yeah, but be warned. Most people quit after a couple of weeks."

Atan pulled the collar of his jacket up around his ears to keep out the rain and dug in for the rest of the walk.

"I won't," he said.

NINE

1991

"What's wrong with my story?" Atan asked his writing professor, a kind-natured, grandfatherly sort who had published a few novels Atan thought were pretty good, even if a little dated.

"Fiction is about small truths," the professor said. "Big truths are for the signs you kids wave around at protest rallies."

"So, just because my story is actually about something, I get a C?"

Atan hadn't seen a C since the third grade when the teacher at his first school in Kitchener had given him a C in everything, a fate so troubling that his mother had needed to reassure her eight-year-old that C meant satisfactory, which was just fine.

"It's not a story," the professor said with a warm smile. "The characters are types, not people. I don't know how they feel. Show me that, and you'll have a story."

"So, I get a C?" Atan asked again.

"You get a C," the professor said. "But you can always rewrite it."

No matter what Atan tried, he couldn't get the story to work. The fact was that he didn't like the characters, a villainous crew of loggers whose tale he'd cobbled together from news articles about the clear-cutting in Clayoquot Sound on the west coast of Vancouver Island. He hadn't located their humanity, so he couldn't make them breathe. Instead of soldiering on, he gave up.

That same week, he got stuck on a paper he was writing about the symbolism of the trees in Anton Chekhov's *The Cherry Orchard* for an English class. Like the trees in Clayoquot Sound, the trees in Chekhov's play were being cut down for profit. Atan wanted to argue that in any production of the play, the trees could never be shown but had to stay offstage lest they lose all significance as nature's last stand against the onset of the industrial age and become mere stage props. However, to his frustration, Atan's insight about Chekhov's trees was hardly enough to fill a whole paper. Try as he might, he couldn't reach the required word count.

Atan soon ran aground with the papers for his other courses too. Unable to get his ideas to line up, he kept trying to say a hundred things at once, as if he could fit every caveat and qualification into the opening paragraph. He was holding on too tight, trying too hard. He knew it, but he couldn't stop himself. With the first semester of his final year barely underway, he'd already missed a deadline in almost every course. He was quickly falling behind.

A paper about Albert Camus and suicide that he needed to write for his philosophy class finally brought Atan's discouragement to a head. Camus said a person had to decide whether life was worth living despite the absurdity of meaninglessness. Atan wanted to argue life was meaningless only if it wasn't lived the right way—that the modern world's capitalist cruelties and disconnection from nature broke a person's heart precisely because they betrayed life's meaning and spirit. But he couldn't put his finger on what this meaning was and kept coming back to the impression that life was absurd no matter how you lived it, his words tumbling over in a heap. After spending the better part of a Saturday morning on the first page, Atan cracked.

He was at home when it happened, typing away on his new computer, a Macintosh Classic purchased with money his parents had given him on his twenty-second birthday. In front of his desk stretched the bay window of the studio apartment he'd rented above an all-night diner midway between the university and downtown Victoria. After sharing digs with Brad Wheeler for three years, Atan had moved into his own place, a landmark popular with the nurses at the mental health center two blocks away and a hub for the city's taxi drivers, their cars lining the curb at all hours.

Deleting everything he'd written that morning, Atan thrust himself out of his chair and picked up the nearest heavy object—an old-style ten-gallon milk can the last tenant had left behind, now used as a garbage pail. Holding the can by the neck and hoisting it above his head, he glanced at the small rectangular screen of his new computer. Frenzied, he looked up at the pane of shop-sized glass in the window above his desk. To his right, propped against the wall by his bookshelf, sat a two-inch slab of wood on which Atan mounted watercolor paper to keep it from buckling when it dried. Catching sight of the slab, he turned and swung the can with all his strength, its bottom edge ripping a crescent-shaped gouge in the wood.

"Fuck it!" Atan hollered as he struck the wood again, the chips skittering across the floor. "Fuck it, fuck it, fuck it!"

Dent, dent, dent. At last, he collapsed to his knees, the milk can destroyed, his desperation dissolving into a finely honed misery. It was time to give up, he told himself.

On Monday, Atan went to the registration office at the university and dropped all his courses. It was just two days before the cutoff date, after which he would've been assigned failing grades and lost his tuition payment. Now, he wouldn't be able to get the student loan he was expecting and would have to live off his tuition money for as long as he could.

Pretending to be doing okay, Atan told himself he'd quit school because what he wanted to do was write. As the world went by in the street below his window, the day full of people shuffling in and out of the diner downstairs, he would write a great play or even an epic novel. He didn't know what it would be about, only that he had something to say.

But as the hours and days passed, with the blank screen of Atan's computer glowing in front of him on his desk, the cursor silently blinking, no words came. Glancing up at his face reflected in the bay window, night coming on, another afternoon wasted, Atan was met with a crushing thought. He wasn't ready to be a writer. He wasn't ready to be anything.

When Atan was young and living in the north, Rachel had told him the most important thing was to find his "right place" in the world. That was how she put it.

"How will I know what it is?" Atan had asked, tossing a stone into the water at the edge of the shore as a tern swooped low, searching for fish.

"Life will show you," Rachel had said. "Life will test you. Then it will show you who you are. But you have to listen, or you won't hear what it's saying."

Thinking of Rachel's advice, Atan looked at his computer screen, mocked by the cursor's incessant blinking. Life was testing him, he thought, but it wasn't showing him much. Had he forgotten how to listen? He needed Rachel just then. For the first time in years, he missed her. But it was too late to do anything about it. Rachel was dead.

The previous January, after getting into a fight with her boyfriend, her lips swollen and bleeding, Rachel had been on her way to a friend's house in the middle of the night, stumbling along drunk in the dark, when she'd fallen down and passed out in a snowbank. There, at the end of her street, she'd frozen to death. Sarah had told Atan's mother about it in a letter. Then, in a phone call with his parents that February, he'd gotten the news that Rachel—his *irngutaq*—was gone.

"She'd had a drinking problem for years," Atan's mother had said. "She was starting to get like that even before we left."

"How old was she?"

"Only thirty-six. Too young."

Atan watched a bus pass as it shuttled students to the university. Everything that had allowed him to make sense of himself had been stripped away now that he'd left school—his acting, his studies, his reputation with his professors as someone to turn to when they asked a question and none of the other students had the answer. If he wasn't a writer, he was nobody.

Not only that, but Atan was broke. Having just paid November's rent, he barely had enough money left for dinner—a can of soup and a potato, if he played it right. How was he going to survive? He thought of asking his parents for help but knew his father would end up telling Atan the same old thing: "You would make a good teacher if you just stopped messing around with acting and writing and that damn guitar we gave you, which I always said was a foolish gift. No one ever learned to play the guitar in their twenties and got any good at it. If you had any talent, we would have seen it long ago. Teaching is in your blood, after all."

Atan didn't want to hear it, and anyway, what choice did he have? He needed to find a job. In the meantime, maybe he could score an advance if he got hired somewhere. Or maybe he could hit Wheeler up for a hundred bucks.

The next morning, passing through the lobby of his building on his way out to look for work, his novel abandoned, Atan noticed something in his mailbox. Just what he needed, a bill, he grumbled. But instead of a bill, what he found was an envelope redirected from his prior address on Beach Drive. Tearing it open, he pulled out a check from the children's recreation center where he'd worked the previous summer as an acting teacher. The center's union had been renegotiating its employees' contracts, and by the time the new terms had been finalized, the camp was over and Atan was back at school. A deal for higher wages had been struck, and he was owed retroactive pay. In his hands, he held a check for $200.40.

Atan had to admit he was amazed at this small miracle of timing, not that his sudden rescue from the indignities of poverty was enough to restore his faith in life or himself. Stuffing the check into his pocket, still sore that he had to look for a job at all, he stepped out into the sunshine, the fall air turning crisp.

In the window of a coffee shop at the corner of Fort Street and Foul Bay Road, not five blocks from Atan's apartment, he saw a sign that read, "Baker Needed." In his teens, working at Mother's Pizza, he'd moved up from dishwasher to dough chef. That was kind of like a baker, he thought. Figuring it was worth a shot, he went in to apply. The place sold muffins, carrot cake, and brownies, nothing too complicated. The owners, a middle-aged couple from Prince Albert, the same town on the Prairies where his parents had grown up, were happy to give Atan a try. The only catch was he would have to work the night shift, which started when the shop closed at eleven o'clock and ended when it opened again at seven.

At first, Atan was relieved to be free of the stress of being broke. Each morning at the end of his shift, he liked to see the results of his work, all the muffins in their baskets on the shelves behind the front counter, their golden edges bathed in light from the display bulbs, the chocolate ones with a swirl of frosting on top. After icing the carrot cake and brownies, which he always did last because they had to cool first, he mopped up and took the garbage out back, lingering in the twilight while he waited for the floor to dry. There was nothing more peaceful than the ripe stillness at that hour, the black of night slowly bleeding to blue, the whole day about to burst forth from the skin of the sky.

Yet these moments of respite weren't enough to sustain Atan. As the weeks at his night job stretched into months, he withdrew from the world, growing ever more despondent. The only people he spoke to were the girl who locked up each night after he got to work and the girl who came in each morning to put on the first pot of coffee as he was leaving. Thanks to the light that seeped in through the blinds in his front window and the noise of the traffic, never mind that the door to the diner downstairs shut with a bang every time anyone went in or out, he barely got enough sleep. Even covering the window with a bedsheet nailed to the corners of the wall and resorting to earplugs didn't help. He could never stay in bed for more than a few hours, and even then, he slept fitfully.

Every day, up before noon, Atan went downstairs for breakfast, the regulars seated at the counter nodding to him as he came in, the diner's staff the closest thing he had to friends. Alone in a booth, he leafed through the *Globe & Mail*, ignoring the news in favor of the arts coverage. Despite his sense of the world's troubles, he'd grown complacent about the global scene. It was 1992, and now that the Soviet Union had broken up and a liberalizing China had been released from trade sanctions, the victors in the war against communism were free to move about the world, indebting poor nations with their schemes. It was open season for the greedy, but in the face of what was obviously colonialism by other means, Atan showed no signs of the revolutionary fervor old Ataninnuaq had expected of him.

After breakfast, Atan dragged himself through the downtown streets and along the harbor during the many hours he had to fill before going back to work each night. There were only so many bookstores to browse, only so many magazines to read, only so many cups of joe he could drink, lurking in the coffee shops of all the neighborhoods his wanderings discovered. Peering out from behind his table tucked away in a corner, he could see that everyone came and went with purpose, spent sugar packets and creamers kicked aside by their passing feet. He was the only one with nowhere to be and nothing to do. For them, there were never enough hours in a day. For him, time itself had become a torment, something to be filled and endured, a prison against which his mind now rebelled. How could he escape time?

On his way back home late one day as Atan passed a corner store, an old woman in the doorway, a broom in her hand, looked up at him.

"Smile," she said. "You never smile."

Atan threw her a hostile glance and scurried away like a cockroach caught in the glare of a bulb turned on in the middle of the night. Damn, it was true, wasn't it? He was that unhappy guy creeping around at the edges of the frame with no part to play, no role, just miserable. Now, he felt spiteful too. He wanted to tell that nice old woman to mind her own business. What did she care if he smiled? Screw her. Screw everybody!

Not long afterward, Atan was alone in his darkened apartment one evening, a Leonard Cohen cassette playing on his boom box, the singer's unmistakable baritone laden with defeat, when he heard Wheeler hollering to him from the street.

"Hey, Atan! You up there?"

After moving out of their place on Beach Drive, Wheeler had rented a room by the marina, not far from a little dive where he tended bar—a working-class joint with wooden rafters and peanut shells strewn about the floor. During his first months in Victoria, when he'd managed to survive by way of odd jobs, he'd always ended up quarreling with the wealthy people who hired him. The tensions typically arose over minor affronts like being required to enter a client's home through the back door, not the front. He said these things were symbolic of the class warfare he perceived in the opulence of the homes where he worked and in the ostentatious displays of money he bemoaned when yachts as big as palaces docked in the harbor across from the Empress Hotel. Eventually, word had gotten around that he was a pain in the ass, and the work had dried up.

To get by, Wheeler had turned his hand to busking on the waterfront, charming tourists with renditions of Janis Joplin's "Me and Bobby McGee," The Guess Who's "American Woman," and Johnny Cash's "Folsom Prison Blues," along with a slew of other countercultural tunes that he'd made his own—all the while secretly hoping someone would be impressed enough to offer him a gig at a club. But that hadn't happened. His unkempt hair and armpit scruff, like a ring of dirt around his mouth, marked him as an outsider in an upwardly mobile culture. And since Wheeler flaunted this whiff of poverty like an ironic badge, a big "fuck you" to the rich, he'd never gotten a break. In the end, not missing the irony that he was a recovered alcoholic and drug addict, he'd caved in and taken a job pouring drinks.

"Atan!" Wheeler hollered again.

Slumped on the floor between the bookshelf and the bed, his back against the wall, Atan listened as Wheeler heaved his ten-speed bike up the stairs, his feet appearing in the light beneath Atan's door as he reached the top.

"Atan?" Wheeler called out, knocking loudly. "You in there?"

Atan didn't want to see anyone. He wished Wheeler would go away.

"I can hear the music, man. You alright?"

"It's unlocked," Atan said at last.

Wheeler left his bike in the hall and came into the apartment, the door open behind him. He found the light switch and gave it a flick—but nothing happened.

"You've got no lights?"

"The bulb's burned out."

"So, buy a new one."

Cohen's song "Dress Rehearsal Rag" was playing. "That's right, it's come to this. Yes it's come to this," he sang. "And wasn't it a long way down? Ah wasn't it a strange way down?"

"What are you doing?" Wheeler laughed, seemingly amused by the pathos of the scene.

"What do you want?" Atan asked.

"Let's go out," Wheeler said.

"Where?"

"What's it matter where? Downstairs, at least. Come on. You can't stay here in the dark."

"I'm good. Anyway, I've gotta work later."

Wheeler sat down on the edge of the bed, a stream of light from the hall falling at his feet.

"You been practicing?" he asked, looking around for Atan's guitar.

Buoyed by Wheeler's enthusiasm, Atan had put in countless hours of practice on the guitar when they'd lived together. As promised, the fingertips on his left hand had calloused over, his stubborn digits eventually able to move between the chords as swiftly as if he were tying his shoes. Then, instead of learning cover songs, Atan had tried to come up with his own tunes and write his own lyrics. A couple of the songs weren't bad, but most of them weren't very good, and his inspiration had waned.

Wheeler located the guitar in the space between Atan's desk and the wall, its strings dusty, a cobweb in the sound hole.

"I guess not," he quipped.

"I'm thinking of selling it."

"Why would you want to do that? Hell, it's a nice guitar. Nicer than mine."

"I might need the money."

"Why? You not getting paid enough?"

"I wanna quit."

"What's the matter?"

"I can't take it. I'm having a nervous breakdown or something."

"No, man. No, you're not. Your nerves are fine."

"I don't know what I'm doing anymore."

"That's alright. You'll figure it out."

Atan shrugged.

Outside, the wind had picked up, the branches of the tree across the street casting long, thin shadows that dipped and swayed on the wall above Atan's head.

"You'll be okay," Wheeler said. "You should start playing again. It'll be good for you." He put the guitar beside him on the bed and stood up. "I gotta go. It's gonna rain. Come see me at the bar when you've got a night off."

"Alright," Atan said, watching from the floor as Wheeler let himself out and closed the door, the hall echoing with the thump of his tires on the stairs as he sloughed his bike back outside.

Atan still had two hours to kill before it would be time to go to work. He crawled onto his bed and stared at the ceiling. "Now Santa Claus comes forward," Cohen sang. "That's a razor in his mit. And he puts on his dark glasses. And he shows you where to hit." Wallowing in his melancholy, Atan listened to the song end, the cassette player shutting off with a thwack as raindrops splattered against the awning outside the window.

The next Saturday, while walking between bookstores downtown, Atan ran into a girl from the theater department at the university. It'd been seven months since he'd quit school, and he hadn't seen her in all that time. Her name was Euphemia, and he'd had a crush on her since they'd met. He would have asked her out, except she'd been with the same boyfriend as long as he'd known her.

"Atan!" she cried, giving him a big hug, her wool poncho tickling his nose. "I haven't seen you in ages. What have you been doing? Any acting?"

"No. Just a little writing. I mean, when I have time."

"What are you writing? A play?"

"A novel," Atan lied.

"Yeah? Impressive."

"What about you?"

"I'm in a show. We open tonight, actually. You should come."

"What play?"

"Long Day's Journey into Night."

"Eugene O'Neill."

"Yeah. There's a part in it you would've got for sure. You would've been better than the guy they cast."

"Oh yeah?" Atan managed a rare smile. "Which part?"

"Edmund. He longs to be a great writer, but he's dying of tuberculosis."

The similarity between Atan's circumstances and Edmund's wasn't lost on him. Not that Atan was dying—it just felt like he was.

"I don't know," he said.

"Why not?" Euphemia asked, pretending to be insulted. "You should come."

"Maybe. Are there any tickets left?"

"I think so. There are always a few seats empty. I'll leave you a ticket at the box office, alright?"

"Okay."

"And we're all going out after, so don't disappear."

"Sure."

As Euphemia departed along the path next to the waterfront, the tall grasses brushing her bare knees, her skirt swishing just so, Atan regretted having said yes. For one thing, her boyfriend would be there. Worse, Atan would be forced to answer everyone's questions about why he wasn't in school anymore and what he was doing instead. Would he lie to them, too, and say he was writing a novel, or would he tell the truth—that he'd quit university to be a baker? He just wouldn't show up, he decided.

But that night, when 7:30 came around, there was Atan in the fifth row, way over on the left, having come early to avoid running into anyone he knew as he passed through the lobby. Three hours later, after hunkering down in his seat during two fifteen-minute intermissions, he was still there, standing to applaud, a dry ache in his throat as the lights came up and his former classmates took their bows. He'd missed out on a great role.

Afterward, Atan got on a bus with Euphemia and her boyfriend, accompanied by most of the cast, all in heavy eyeliner, traces of rouge brightening their cheeks, and they headed to a restaurant downtown, where everyone drank too much, including Atan, off work until Monday.

Shortly after midnight, as Atan sat with the play's director at a table overlooking the street, a fight poured out of a nightclub in the building's basement. A long-haired, overweight fellow in a lumberman jacket was swinging wildly at a slick-haired, skinny guy in a white button-down shirt. The overweight fellow tripped and fell as he stepped backward off the curb, and the skinny guy started kicking him in the head. Looking on, his field of vision suddenly shrinking, Atan saw nothing but a bloodied face and a sneakered foot.

"You can't do that," he heard himself say, and before he knew it, with no sense of his own actions, he was on his feet and running.

Threading his way between the tables, he lunged down the stairs and burst out into the street.

Strangely calm, Atan stood between the men and held up his hand.

"Stop," he said. "It's over. It's done."

The skinny guy looked bewildered. Rage swam behind his eyes as he searched Atan's face, unsure what to do. Unable to get up, the bigger fellow lay on the pavement, curled into a ball.

"Fuckin' right, it's over," the skinny guy hollered, thrusting a finger at the fellow on the ground. "Loser."

Then he ran from the scene, joined by three male friends who greeted him on the sidewalk with jubilant hoots and high-fives.

"Fuckin' hillbilly," one of them hollered.

"Kicked his ass!" another shouted.

In a daze, Atan could barely remember how he'd gotten there. One moment he was watching from above, the next he was in the street. The director of the play came and stood beside him.

"What are you doing?" he asked. "That was crazy."

Atan didn't respond. He just turned and walked away. In his despondency, the fight seemed like a stand-in for all that was violent in men—everything that was wrong in a world men had created.

As he continued along the street, Atan passed a fifties-style eatery where the hookers hung out and all the waitresses had beehive hairdos. The students went there after the bars closed to ward off hangovers with plates of greasy eggs, home fries, and sausages. Tonight, the girls standing out front in miniskirts and gaudy makeup seemed awfully young. Atan let his gaze linger on their bare arms and legs, feeling a pang of desire that filled him with loneliness and self-disgust all at once.

Farther along, outside a convenience store, a boy sat on the pavement with his hand out, no more than thirteen. Seeing him crouched there with dirt on his face and holes in his jeans, Atan took a five-dollar bill from his pocket, the only cash he had left, and shoved it into the boy's hand as the flickering neon lights overhead painted the kid's face blue, then yellow, turning him into a ghoul one second, a saint the next.

Trudging up Fort Street toward his apartment, Atan saw a man and woman arguing on the stoop of a house.

"Bitch," the man said, spitting the word in the woman's face as he leaned closer. "What did I tell you?"

Thinking of Rachel's fight with her boyfriend the night she froze to death, Atan felt like crying. He wanted to say something, maybe see if the woman needed help. Instead, he crossed to the other side of the road and kept going. The longer he walked, the fewer cars there were, until at last the seething misery of downtown was behind him, the air humming with the song of crickets. In the stillness, a strange and awful peace fell over him, a numbness unlike any he had ever known.

Entering his building, Atan went up the stairs to his apartment. He let himself in and closed the door, deliberately leaving his key in the lock outside. From the ceiling of his room hung a chandelier someone had painted white. Flecks of gold peeked out where the paint had chipped away. Standing on his desk chair, Atan tied one end of his bedsheet to the bottom of the chandelier and the other end around his neck. Through a crack in the window blinds, he watched the traffic light on the corner turn red.

"Stop," it said.

But Atan didn't believe in signs. Ignoring the light, he pulled the knot tight and stepped into the air.

TEN

2042

I'm out on the tundra hunting caribou. For days, I follow them, living like they do, eating what they eat until my own scent disappears and I smell like them. Wedged between their flanks for warmth, I sleep with them at night. Clumps of their hair stick to my coat. No longer hunting them, I take off my boots and run with the herd all day. My feet freeze, the pain growing into a perverse kind of bliss so hard-won and rare that I'm sure it will transform me.

People say I've gone crazy. But I would rather live like the caribou than remain in the white man's village. At last, I change into a caribou and become their leader. Taking the herd to the river to drink, I suddenly realize I've been here before. The first time, I was a child, and a winter storm had blown me off course, bringing me to the grave of my namesake, an old shaman called Ataninnuaq. In a vision, I saw this moment. I know what is going to happen. At once, the herd bolts, and in a panic to overtake the others, I run up the bank of the river and straight into an arrow. The flint enters the center of my chest and I fall over in the snow.

I awake, shivering, my feet like blocks of ice. Agitated, I pull them under the blanket, unable to decipher the dream. What was it trying to tell me? Swinging my stiff legs off the bed, I go to the kitchen counter and turn on the light above the stove as a cockroach scurries down the drain of the sink. That's a wise move, I think. Only idiots and stubborn old men remain in the fray until it's too late.

The pipes thud inside the wall as the student who lives above me opens the taps to fill the tub in the upstairs bathroom. Her boyfriend has spent the night and is walking about, likely gathering up his clothes. Soon, he descends the stairs in a few heroic leaps and dashes out of the house. At the curb, the engine of his restored Volkswagen bus rumbles to life, powered by the methane of animal waste, or so says his bumper sticker: "Fueled by shit!" As he drives off, the racket fades, the street growing quiet again.

Did he write the note I found under my door? Was it left there to see if I would panic? Maybe he was sent to keep an eye on me. His Volkswagen seems a little obvious. It could be an attempt to show his countercultural moxie so I won't suspect him. And isn't it true the student didn't move in until a week after I got here? Then again, it was the start of the school year. No doubt, lots of students had just arrived, taking up residence in cheap rooms all over the city.

The words of the note strike me as ironic now. "I know who you are." I've spent most of my life trying to figure out who I am, and now that I'm back in Washington, I'm no longer sure I do.

I fill a pot of water and put it on the stove to boil. As the flame ignites, I remember the face of the hunter who shot the arrow. It was me. I was both the hunter and the hunted. In a flash, I see what the dream was telling me. Leaders don't lead. They merely try to stay ahead of the herd. If they fall out of step, they defeat themselves. To topple a leader, one has to detect the will of the herd and sense when the leader is out of step. Until that moment, the leader mirrors our unspoken consensus. We get the leader we agree to—and maybe even deserve.

I don't think I ever really understood how a revolution works but instead imagined we could turn our back on the government, never recognizing that the president was able to take the pulse of the voters better than I could. I tried to lead people where they weren't ready to go without seeing we had already consented to so much that was destructive.

The hippie ethos of love into which I was born at the end of the 1960s, the strength of unionized workers, the movements for Black and Red Power—these things were all stomped out by imperial globalization during my teens in the 1980s as we conceded to the destruction of the planet by colonizing bankers to feed a demand for stuff we were told to want but didn't need. Like the Inuit cut off from the spirit world and forced into churches, we were cut off from our better natures and ushered into the temples of commerce, reduced to watching the hands of the clock and the tallies of our bank accounts for signs of success. Yet we agreed to it all.

I put two heaping spoonfuls of coffee into the pot of boiling water, along with a dash of cinnamon. When the grounds have settled, I turn off the gas and fill my mug, careful to leave as much of the sediment behind as I can. A young woman I once knew called it cowboy coffee. Having no machine, this is the best I can do, but after living wild for almost two decades, it's also what I'm used to, and there is some comfort in this low-tech ritual, as if I'm not really here after all but half a world away and still free.

I take my coffee to the window, the outlines of the rooftops across the street glowing as the sun returns, the sky tinted blue. My dream has left me wondering if I'm perhaps mistaken about the young woman who brought my groceries. Maybe she can read the herd better than I could. She might be right that most people—from the janitors to the generals—are at last ready to rebel. The truth is that I've been away too long to know. That's the problem I faced the last time I came to Washington, finding myself caught up in a protest that, the same as now, had plunged the country into chaos. Like a foolish caribou bull, I could be running right into another bullet.

ELEVEN

1992

As Atan's windpipe constricted and his face turned crimson, the veins at his temples swelling with blood, he heard the shuffle of a dancer beating on an Inuit drum and a man chanting.

The drumming stopped, and Ataninnuaq appeared before Atan in the unseen.

"This is the medicine," he said, his English oddly perfect, as he handed the drum and mallet to Atan. "Play."

Atan beat the wooden rim, delighted by the twang that reverberated through the stretched skin with each thwack.

"You have the medicine," Ataninnuaq said. "So play."

Atan had barely registered these words when the drum in his hands melted into air and old Ataninnuaq vanished, the bedsheet tightening around Atan's throat as he came back to his room above the diner.

Astounded, Atan put his feet back on the chair almost as soon as they'd left it, the blood draining out of his cheeks. Desperate for air, he untied the bedsheet from around his neck and slumped down on the seat. Trembling, he cried for the first time in years, terrified by what he'd almost done, awed by his encounter with old Ataninnuaq. Had he imagined it?

As the tears flowed, Atan saw his future with a clarity he'd never known. He would write songs, and he would sing. There wasn't anything else he wanted to do. In the gap between his desk and the wall stood his guitar, untouched since Wheeler's visit the week before. Pushing himself to his feet, Atan pulled out the guitar and sat down with it on the bed. Still drunk, his fingers clumsy, he strummed a few chords as the words of a new song came into his head.

"My mother said I was too radical to be a scholar," he began. "My father said I was too cynical to be a saint." He looked around the room, thinking about where his life had carried him. "I knew I was too honest to be a politician and too gentle to be a warrior," he went on, strumming the final chord lightly as his voice wavered over the note. Then he kicked up the tempo as he found his way into the chorus. "So I scramble on. I carry only words. I run with the poets now, the gypsies, and the birds. I scramble on. I will until I die. I run with the poets now, the ones who kiss the sky."

The words came from an unknown place. He had to write them down. But the next verse followed, his fingers working their way up and down the frets as if of their own accord. Atan felt entranced.

"My mother thought I'd have myself a wife and a child or two," he sang. "My father thought I'd learn myself a trade and work every day. But I was just too restless to live that sort of life and too far gone to ever settle down."

As Atan repeated the chorus, the presence of old Ataninnuaq swelled within him, bringing forth a timeless spirit, the source of the *angakkuq*'s power, which some people called the Holy Spirit. It had been there inside Atan all along.

Feeling light-headed, Atan sang the final verse with all the conviction of a storyteller.

"My mama said I could go mighty far if I wanted to. My papa said if I was only brave, I could master fear. Yeah, I knew I could've been some kind of sweet contender. But I refused to follow all the rules."

Thrilled by the rebel's credo in the last line, he played the chorus once more, the notes coming out of the guitar as if he'd strummed them all that way before.

"So I scramble on. I carry only words. I run with the poets now, the gypsies, and the birds. I scramble on. I will until I die. I run with the poets now, the ones who kiss the sky."

Letting the guitar slip from his fingers, Atan lay down, the song still bursting in his mind like a flower in the desert. He thought again about writing down the words but quickly fell into a heavy sleep, a bruise beginning to show across his throat.

In the morning, waking to the sound of a car's horn, his head throbbing, his mouth as dry as chalk, Atan was puzzled to see his bedsheet tied to the chandelier and dangling in the air. Images from the night before unreeled in his mind like a nightmare. Sitting up, he almost knocked his guitar off the bed. He checked the pockets of his jeans, wondering where his keys were. In the hall, he found them swinging from the lock but had no memory of having left them there. Returning, he picked up his guitar and fingered the neck as he tried to find the chords of a song he vaguely recalled playing, but he couldn't summon them. The words were gone too.

The next Sunday, during Atan's weekly telephone call with his parents, he told them he'd decided not to go back to school. What would he do with his degree anyway if he didn't want to be a teacher? And he wasn't going to stick around Victoria, he said. No, he wanted to be a musician, and for that, he needed to go to New York. That's where people got their start, wasn't it? His parents balked at the idea. Even if he didn't go back to school right away, they said, he still needed to support himself, and what was he going to do in New York with no way to work there as a Canadian?

"A lot of musicians get gigs under the table," Atan said.

"You're not even a musician," his father grumbled.

That week, when Atan told the couple who owned the coffee shop that he was planning to quit his job, they sided with his parents, but he wouldn't listen.

It was finally Wheeler who dissuaded Atan from going to New York. They were at the bar where Wheeler worked, and Atan had come by to tell him he was leaving Victoria.

"Giving up school for music is a gutsy plan." Wheeler laughed. "You might even succeed. But not in New York."

"Why not?" Atan asked as he cracked open a peanut shell and popped the nuts into his mouth. "I can play almost as good as you, and if I start practicing again—"

"It's not that. You've got a good voice too. The problem is New York." Wheeler stopped wiping down the bar and looked at Atan. "That city eats nice people alive. It will break you and kick you into the gutter."

"I'm not that nice."

"Yeah, you are. But that's not the point. You don't know how things work."

"How do they work?"

"My dad did off-Broadway shows all the time. New York is a crooked scene. You have no idea how bad people can be."

"Then come with me."

Wheeler let out a hearty laugh that made his jowls ripple. He'd gained weight, Atan thought, looking at the apron stretched over his friend's bulging belly.

"I can't write songs," Wheeler said. "I'm a hack, not an artist. You, on the other hand, could get somewhere."

"You like my songs?"

"Some of them. When you don't try too hard."

Atan watched as Wheeler filled two mugs of beer from a tap on the bar and placed them on a tray for the waitress.

"How long are you going to keep working here?"

"I don't know. There're worse things."

"What's your boss like?"

"He's a pompous blowhard. But what else am I going to do?"

Atan drank his beer, the place beginning to empty out.

"So I shouldn't go to New York?"

"Not yet. You should start somewhere smaller, like Toronto."

"Forget that. I'm not going there."

Atan had visited Toronto countless times growing up. Everyone at school who wanted to do anything big with his life had left Kitchener on Highway 401 bound for Toronto, or T.O., as they called it, which wasn't even an hour away. No, Atan wasn't going to be one of those guys. He would carve out his career behind people's backs and surface at the top of the scene to everyone's surprise. He couldn't do that in Toronto.

"What about Montreal?" Wheeler asked. "You'd be in Leonard Cohen's old stomping grounds."

Montreal suddenly seemed like the obvious choice.

"That's a good idea. They've got a good music scene there."

"Lots of blues too. The blues suit you."

That decided it. Atan would move to Montreal.

Setting a tumbler on the bar, Wheeler opened a bottle of Jack Daniels and poured himself a double.

"Here's to Montreal," he said.

Atan raised his glass of beer.

"You're drinking?"

Wheeler chuckled. "Occupational hazard."

"To Montreal," Atan said, their glasses clinking.

Gulping his drink, Wheeler looked out at the street, a mist rolling in from the harbor, the windows streaked with drizzle.

"If you ever return, I'll be here groveling for a paycheck, the Man's boot on the back of my neck."

"I doubt that," Atan said. "Anyway, we'll see each other again, yeah?"

"Yeah, you know, go with the flow," Wheeler said. "Could be." He tossed back his whiskey and set the glass down. "Who knows?"

Wheeler sounded bummed, Atan thought, feeling guilty he hadn't seen much of him since they'd moved out of the place on Beach Drive.

"I love you, man," Atan told him. "Thanks for everything."

Wheeler dried his mustache with his fingers.

"I love you too, Atan," he said. "Now get out of here so I can close up."

Laughing, Atan finished his beer and went to the door, peanut shells crunching under his boots. Stepping into the street, where the wet pavement glistened beneath the streetlights and the fog encircled the lampposts like ghostly fish in an invisible river, he had a gut feeling their paths would cross again.

Atan arrived in Montreal on a Saturday in January after almost ten hours on the bus from Kitchener, where he'd gone to visit his parents for Christmas, their attempts to persuade him not to throw away his life only stoking his determination to play his music, as old Ataninnuaq had urged. As the bus traveled along Saint Urbain Street at dusk, Atan noticed the cross atop Mont Royal, a sculpture made of steel beams outlined in glowing light bulbs. It reminded him of the cross above the entrance of the Anglican church in Frobisher Bay, which extended to the peak of the roof, the town prostrate below the church's hillside perch. He was back in the land of the yellow priests, he thought, their traces everywhere.

Atan also noticed a crust of English conquest layered over the city's French veneer. It was there in the street names he saw from the bus window, like Milton Street, probably named for the British poet John Milton, whose *Paradise Lost,* Atan knew, had appeared shortly before the Hudson's Bay Company landed its monopoly over one-third of what would become Canada. And beneath these strata, unmarked by street names, lay the lands of Indigenous peoples, their paradise lost forever.

With no apartment lined up and nowhere to sleep that night—except the YMCA, if it came to that—Atan checked his map book. Milton Street, it turned out, was on the edge of the McGill Ghetto, where a lot of students lived. That sounded perfect. McGill University had a good music school. Maybe he could find some other musicians to jam with. When the bus reached its destination, he hopped off with purpose in his stride, traveling light with nothing but his guitar and a duffel bag. Trudging along sidewalks deep with snow, the bitter cold a shock, he retraced the bus's route until he was back at Milton Street. It might be tough to find a rental in the middle of the school year, he told himself, but maybe he'd luck out and find a place left vacant after the first semester.

Continuing west for two blocks, his fingers numb inside his gloves, his earlobes red and stinging beneath the rim of his tuque, Atan saw nothing but three apartment buildings, each one uglier and more depressing than the last, their steel balconies rusted and decrepit, their front lobbies awash in fluorescent light, coupons and takeout menus strewn over the cracked tiles. Then, after crossing Sainte Famille Street—named for the holy family of Jesus, Mary, and Joseph—Atan spotted an "*À Louer*" sign in the second-story window of a triplex, a tiny dry cleaner's on the ground floor.

Slowing down, he saw students milling about at the entrance to a pizza parlor on the opposite side of the street as they waited for a table, stamping their feet to stay warm. Two doors away, he stopped outside the window of a packed greasy spoon with three small tables along one wall and a line of stools at a counter facing the grill. Deciding right then that he liked the neighborhood, Atan went into the greasy spoon to see if anyone knew where he could find the owner of the triplex. The cook, wielding a spatula as he flipped a row of fat burgers sizzling on the grill, said the man lived just around the corner on Sainte Famille.

When Atan came back outside, a big crow strutted toward him along the windowsill of the dry cleaner's as it let out a cheerful squawk.

Unlike in the past, Atan didn't ignore the crow but instead acknowledged that it might be there to greet him. Ever since old Ataninnuaq had appeared to Atan in Victoria, he'd started to trust in the irrational, taking tentative steps into the unseen.

"Yes, this is the place," he said to the crow.

Atan was right. It turned out he could afford the apartment—a cozy two-room setup with a little gas furnace out in the main room and a kitchen along the far wall. He signed the lease and paid the rent that very evening.

Throughout the winter, Atan busked inside the entrance to the Place-des-Arts Metro station, just a few blocks away, polishing his new songs as the icy wind whistled in through the doors with the passersby, his guitar case open to catch their coins. Unable to bring in enough money that way, he also found a job, convincing the chef at Sir Winston Churchill Pub in the heart of the English tourist district that his time baking muffins qualified him to serve up pasta dishes four evenings a week from five o'clock until eleven. It was thankless work, the wait staff barking demands, the surly sous chef forever scolding Atan for letting the pasta grow a skin under the heat lamps before the steaks were ready.

"Put it back in the pan!" the sous chef hollered, the veins bulging in his sweaty neck.

But working in a place like that motivated Atan to play his guitar even more and to write songs when they didn't come easily. He hadn't turned his back on school to punch a clock.

At the same time, Atan started taking gigs anywhere he could get them. Most nights, when his shift ended, he showered in the staff changing room and put on a crisp shirt and sharp jacket. Grabbing his guitar from his locker, he would head to the Upstairs Bar two blocks west on Mackay Street, where there was sometimes an open mic. Or he went east to the House of Jazz on Aylmer Street, where some of the old cats from back in the city's heyday still played the blues. Now and then, they would let him join in.

Pretty soon, people recognized Atan at the different clubs. He was the serious guy who sang his own songs, his voice a cauldron of emotion, his fingers tripping across the neck of his guitar with the lightness and speed of a blind man reading brail. He was the guy with the odd name that no one could pronounce.

"Hi, I'm Ataninnuaq," he would say. "I know. It's okay. Just call me Atan."

In the spring, he busked in Cabot Square before work, surprised to find a lot of Inuit there, more than he'd seen since leaving Frobisher Bay. Many were secretaries from the offices of the nearby Makivik Corporation who came to the square on their coffee break to soak up the afternoon sun. As one of the secretaries told Atan, Makivik oversaw millions of dollars paid to the Inuit of northern Quebec in compensation for their land. Originally stolen by the Hudson's Bay Company, later ceded to Canada, and finally transferred to Quebec before the First World War, this land had never been returned to the province's Inuit, who now lived in fourteen villages spread along the coasts of Hudson Bay and Hudson Strait.

At the center of the square stood a statue of the explorer John Cabot, who'd voyaged to North America in 1497 to claim land for England, or so said the plaque on the pedestal beneath his feet. The offense of his northward gaze, one hand raised to shield his eyes, must be obvious to the secretaries, Atan thought. Nor could the insult have been lost on the other Inuit who passed through the square, many in town to seek medical care for their children down the street at the Montreal Children's Hospital, as Atan's mother had done for him when he was a month old.

The square also attracted lots of Inuit from the derelict apartment buildings around the corner on Tupper Street, men and women who'd come south to Montreal hoping to escape alcoholism or poverty, only to fall into worse trouble in the big city. There to panhandle, they were ghostly reminders to Atan of a devastating project of cultural genocide in which his parents, as teachers in the north, had unwittingly participated.

Before leaving the square, he always made sure to give them some of the coins people had tossed into his guitar case.

Among this lot was Isaac, in his mid-fifties, who often bummed for beer money on the corner of De Maisonneuve Boulevard and Peel Street. They'd first met on a brutally cold day in February when Atan, rushing by on his way to work, his legs freezing inside his jeans, dropped a dollar coin in Isaac's cup.

"*Nakurmiik*," Isaac called out, hunched on the pavement in torn snow pants and what looked like a thrift shop winter coat.

"*Ilaali*," Atan said, glancing behind him as he passed.

"Ohh, my friend." Isaac smiled. "How do you know my language?"

Atan stopped and came back.

"I used to live in Iqaluit," he said, hopping from foot to foot to stay warm.

"Baffin Island."

"That's the place. Where're you from?"

"Akulivik. Top of Hudson Bay. Way up there."

"Nice to meet you. I'm Ataninnuaq."

"Oh, that means wise man." Isaac puffed on the cigarette butt he was smoking, his bare hand red with cold. "My name is Isaac."

"Like in the Bible."

"Yeah, the Bible." Isaac doubled over, coughing as he spit out a great wad of phlegm that froze when it hit the icy pavement and skittered into a ball. "Excuse me," he said.

"Do you have anywhere to stay tonight?" Atan asked.

"Yeah. But I need a beer."

"Where do you live?"

Isaac tossed the butt aside and pulled a glove from his coat pocket.

"I'm going to my friend's place."

"That's good. Don't stay out here too long."

"I need a beer right now."

"Okay," Atan said, thinking Isaac was already plenty drunk.

When Atan got off work that night, instead of heading to the Upstairs Bar for open mic, he went back to make sure Isaac had gotten out of the cold. Nagged by thoughts of how Rachel had died, he reached the corner of Peel Street to find Isaac passed out on the sidewalk under the front window of a florist's shop, the display of lilies behind the glass mocking him with the glow of spring. At his feet sat a half-empty beer bottle, the jumbo size sold in Quebec.

"Isaac?" Atan said, squatting beside him. "Isaac, wake up."

At the lingerie store next door, a blonde mannequin, still dressed for Valentine's Day in a red silk bra and panties, smiled down at them with absurd indifference.

Isaac rolled over with a grunt. "Ahh? Who is it?"

"It's Ataninnuaq."

"Oh, Ataninnuaq. Do you have a cigarette, my friend?"

Atan laughed at Isaac's dedicated quest for small comforts despite the danger he was in.

"No, I don't smoke."

"That's okay."

"It's late. Are you going to your friend's place?"

"No. He came and took my beer, but he left me."

"There's one here."

"Oh!" Isaac propped himself up just enough to spy the bottle near his feet.

"Do you want to stay at my place?"

"Is it far? My knees are bad. I can walk, but I'm weak."

"We can take the metro. I'll help you. It's right here."

Atan got Isaac to his feet and helped him gather up his belongings—a brown paper bag with an uneaten sandwich wrapped in cellophane that someone had given him and a piece of soapstone the size of a fist that had fallen out of his pocket.

"Oh, yes, I need that," Isaac said when he saw the stone. "It's for carving. You know, carving? To make things."

"Uh-huh." Atan handed Isaac the stone. "Are you an artist?"

"Yeah, an artist."

Clutching the beer bottle to his chest, Isaac slung an arm across Atan's shoulder for balance, and together they shuffled across the street. They went into the metro through its swinging doors and descended on the escalator to the train that would carry them beneath what Atan called the "cathedrals to commerce"—the Eaton Centre, Promenades Cathédrale, and the Hudson's Bay Company—the second actually built under the Anglican Christ Church Cathedral. He liked to imagine Jesus kicking over the tables in that place. Finally, they reached Atan's apartment, where the gas furnace would radiate heat all night, keeping them both warm.

After that, when Isaac came to Atan's part of town to pick up his welfare check, which barely covered his food, never mind giving him enough money to rent a place, he stopped in to visit. On very cold nights, he ended up sleeping on the futon in the front room, a jumbo-sized bottle of beer at his feet, lest he wake up sober and get the shakes. One Sunday, he arrived with a white plastic bag full of meat he'd brought from an Inuit feast hosted by a church in the suburbs. Along with Arctic char and seal—the first oily and pink, the other black and stringy—the bag held slabs of caribou, all flown in from Pangnirtung, almost two hundred miles farther north than Iqaluit.

"Can I boil this on your stove?" Isaac asked, pulling out a glistening red hunk of caribou.

The smell of the meat as it cooked made Atan nostalgic for the rare times at Rachel's house when her mother had prepared caribou and let him eat with them.

Eventually, Atan learned Isaac's story. After failing out of school in his village, he'd gotten into trouble when he'd started drinking as a teenager. Once, he stole a snowmobile. Another time, he set a toolshed on fire. Angry and idle, he was always getting into fistfights. With his barrel chest, thick arms, and wide jaw, Isaac looked like the sort who would have thrived on the land. Indeed, as a child, he'd traveled with his father by dogsled to check their traps for foxes, the pelts fetching twenty-five dollars apiece at the Hudson's Bay Company store. That was before his father's huskies got distemper, brought north by a German shepherd owned by the man who ran the airport. Twitching with seizures, their eyes caked with pus, the huskies were shot one by one. Without enough money to replace them, Isaac's family lost their way of life.

At twenty, after Isaac slashed his girlfriend's face with a broken beer bottle during a drunken argument, he was banished from the village and went in search of another community that would take him in. Wherever he landed, his problems with alcohol continued until, finally, he ended up in Inukjuak, where an officer of the Royal Canadian Mounted Police showed up at his house one day, flown in to arrest Isaac for public intoxication. When he resisted, stabbing the officer in the leg with a fork, he ended up in prison for ten months. Over the next nineteen years, he was repeatedly put back in jail for drinking, a violation of his parole. At last, ducking further run-ins with the law, he had slipped off the radar of the prison-parole system and had avoided jail ever since.

Isaac had a way of looking at things that Atan admired. Recounting the death of his father's dogs, caused by a careless intruder from the south, Isaac showed no anger.

"That guy made a mistake," he said. "We all make mistakes."

Describing how the police had beaten him up after driving him to their depot when he was first arrested, Isaac was philosophical.

"I think they felt much better," he said.

When it came to begging for change, Isaac had the secret figured out.

"Smile, be happy for everyone!"

In these words, Atan heard a generosity of spirit that went beyond Isaac's need to charm beer money out of passersby.

"Do you know what your name means?" Atan asked Isaac one day as they passed a joint between them in Atan's front room, winter over, the windows open again at last to the fresh air of spring and the chatter of birds.

"Nope."

"I looked it up. It means, 'He will laugh.'"

"He will laugh," Isaac repeated as he melted into mirth, smoke coiling above his head.

His glee infectious, Atan laughed too.

"It suits you."

In the fall of 1995, after more than two years on Milton Street, Atan got a letter in the mail from the Government of Quebec summoning him to appear at an office downtown to prove he'd been a resident of the province for at least twelve months. If he didn't comply, he would be forbidden to vote in a referendum that October to decide if the province should separate from Canada—another episode in a long history of clashes between the French and the English in the country.

The French woman in the apartment above him didn't get this letter, but her English boyfriend did, even though they'd both lived there for over a decade. To Atan, it looked like the government was demanding proof of residency only from anglophones, who mostly opposed separation and were going to vote no. He figured a lot of them wouldn't bother to go to the downtown office as instructed, and even if they did want to go, many wouldn't be able to take the time off work. By keeping anglophones off the voter list, the government was trying to rig a victory for the yes side.

Intending to vote no to separation and piqued that the government—supposedly the face of the people—would resort to subterfuge to serve its ends, Atan answered the letter's summons. For more than three hours on a Monday morning, he stood in a long line on the tenth floor of a building on Sherbrooke Street—named after a nineteenth-century governor-general of British North America—determined to do his small part to thwart the government's anti-democratic plan. There, as he inched along the hallway, his gaze retracing the maze-like pattern in the carpet for the hundredth time, Atan was approached by a reporter for the English television network CTV—an old hand known for his silver hair and fatherly demeanor.

"Are you planning to vote yes or no in the referendum?" the reporter asked as the cameraman hovered behind him and a young woman held a microphone above Atan's head.

"I'm voting no," Atan said.

"Can you tell us why?"

"It's not because I'm English or don't think the French have been mistreated. But we're part of a bigger story. After centuries of warfare so notorious Shakespeare wrote epic dramas about their battles, what happened? The English chased the French across the Atlantic, only to stop fighting with them and forge a new nation. Instead of imagining that great differences divide us and trying to break up the country, we should be proud of this history. And don't forget we built this nation on the backs of Indigenous peoples, who have real grievances we need to answer. That's the part of our story we have to put right."

When Atan got to Sir Winston Churchill Pub that afternoon for work, the interview had already aired on the midday news, and his face had been splashed across the widescreen television mounted above the bar. As he headed to the staff changing room, the waitresses teased him about being a celebrity. He appeared again at six o'clock and once more at eleven. The next day, when a French radio station replayed the piece for its call-in audience, Atan was pilloried for his rosy picture of French-English relations and his love of Eskimos and Indians over the French. When the referendum was decided in favor of the no side, leaving Canada intact, his interview surfaced again, bringing more ridicule.

But Atan didn't care. In the end, he figured, all anyone had to lean on were stories. A nation, like a person, lived or died by its stories, and Canada's story of French-English strife was killing it.

In his own life, too, Atan had begun to adopt a frame of explanation—as his professor had called it—that allowed for a grander, optimistic, even providential story, and he'd resolved to live by this story no matter what it took, bringing what old Ataninnuaq had told him was the medicine of song to anyone who wanted it.

The following spring, now twenty-seven, Atan played his first solo gig, a sold-out show at Café Campus on Prince Arthur Street. At the end of the night, when the audience called for an encore, he realized he'd run out of original material, but not wanting to admit it, he stalled for time.

"I might have one more," he said, unsure what he would sing.

Buoyed by the energy of the crowd and propelled by something like faith, he suddenly heard himself say, "This one's called 'I Scramble On.'"

Strumming the guitar, he found the chords, and out came all the words of the song he'd conjured on the night of his near hanging, the final lines a transcendent hymn to Atan's right place in the world: "I scramble on. I carry only words. I run with the poets now, the gypsies, and the birds. I scramble on. I will until I die. I run with the poets now, the ones who kiss the sky."

After Atan's triumph at Café Campus, the old bluesmen on the circuit said Montreal was too small for a cat like him. It was time he grew a pair and hauled his ass south of the border.

"It would help with your songwriting," Brooklyn Willy said, taking apart his saxophone after a show one night at the House of Jazz.

"What's wrong with my songwriting?" Atan asked.

"There's nothin' wrong with it, son. I don't mean that. But you ain't seen hardship. You don't know how bad people can be." Putting the mouthpiece of his instrument to his lips, Brooklyn Willy blew a stream of spit onto the dressing room floor. "You gotta get your hands dirty in this world if you want to write the blues."

Hadn't Brad Wheeler told Atan the same thing the last time they spoke—"You have no idea how bad people can be"? History was full of horrors inflicted by tyrants and maniacs, he reasoned. What else was there to know? But Brooklyn Willy was right, and Atan knew it. His life had been sheltered.

It wasn't long before he packed up his belongings and took the red-eye bus down across the Canada-US border, rolling into Midtown Manhattan as the sun rose, its rays glinting orange in a thousand windows as pedestrians massed at the intersections and fleets of taxis moved along the wide streets like schools of fish amid the hulking garbage trucks. He got himself a bunk at a hostel around the corner from the Chelsea Hotel, made famous by Leonard Cohen's song about Janis Joplin.

"I remember you well in the Chelsea Hotel," the ladies' man sang. "You were famous, your heart was a legend."

Soon Atan found a basement apartment in Greenwich Village, home to venues like Groove and Terra Blues, and best of all, Café Wha?—where singers and poets the stature of Bob Dylan and Allen Ginsberg had once hung out. After cutting his teeth in Montreal for three years, Atan was in New York City.

TWELVE

2042

Like a cat, I watch the street through a gap in the curtains. Curved in the shape of an elbow, the street connects two roads, one at the bottom of the hill and another up around the bend. Every morning, the elderly couple who live upstairs descend the hill empty-handed, she with a bonnet tied in place to keep her hair set and he stooped and doddering. When they return, always an hour later with a full shopping bag, I'm glad to see he hasn't been hauled away by soldiers out looking for me. Today, as they pass, I wonder what it would be like to grow old with someone. Then I catch myself. I'm already old. A long time ago, I was thrust onto a solitary path, and I have followed it to its only end.

In the front yard stands the gnarled trunk of an ancient cedar, all its branches cut off. What remains resembles a raised fist. I have chosen to take this tree as a sign of steadfastness in the fight. I sense it knows I'm here. I even sense it was put here long ago and took this very form just because I was going to be here now. It's here for me. You may call that crazy. How could the past have bent itself to the present? I don't pretend to know the answer. Wiser men have explained it better than I ever could. But experience has shown me it happens all the time. Every minute is an intersection of what was, what is, and what will be. All of life unfolds within a web of spirit that is not bound by time. Words cannot convey the symmetry I perceive as I look upon that tree.

You may say I am grasping at straws, and perhaps I am. But I was woken early by the cries of the schizophrenic woman across the hall, and the tree has calmed my frayed nerves.

"No transmissions! No transmissions! No more!" she hollered again and again, spewing her disquieting torment.

I've heard her telling the postman next door that a captain taunts her, demanding she do his bidding. This captain, I guess, is supposed to be hovering somewhere in a spaceship and beaming thoughts into her wretched head. But she insists he's dead—a ghost—so I may be wrong.

Even stranger, she claims he communicates to her in a rudimentary code that her mind must convert into words no matter how hard she resists. It may even be Morse code, for her ranting often dissolves into what could be taken for incoming dots and dashes. "Dah, dit, dit-dah-dit-dit, dit-dah-dit-dit, dit-dit-dit-dit, dit-dit, dah-dah!"

More than unnerved, I'm also terribly hungry. It's been more than two weeks since the young woman came with groceries, and I'm almost out of food. For the past three days, I've consumed nothing but coffee and oatmeal. Soon that will run out too. I've been meditating to distract myself, but I need to keep my strength up. If no mule comes today, I will have to take my chances and try to get out of here. That may seem foolhardy, but then my foolishness is legendary. When you believe that even the trees are on your side, you tend to throw yourself into things.

A sedan pulls up to the curb and I withdraw from the window a little. One by one, the doors of the car open and slam shut at identical intervals, followed by the cold click of military boots on the cement path that leads to the side porch. Through the crack in the curtains, I see four men pass. They are dressed in matching forest-green sweaters and black ball caps. Each has a pistol on his hip. With machine-like swiftness, they mount the porch steps and pass into the hallway outside my room. It all happens so fast that I barely have time to think of getting into the tunnel beneath the fireplace. So much for my great escape.

But the men are not here for me. Instead, they pound on the schizophrenic's door.

"Open up!" one of them calls out.

"Go away," she screeches.

"Incoming transmission," another says. "It's the captain. Ready to beam up?"

His taunt is met with laughter from the others, and I find myself at the peephole in the door spying on these goons who have come to harass a sick woman.

"Fuck you!" she screams amid what sound like jagged sobs.

"Open up!"

The pounding resumes, each blow shaking the ceiling. The woman has gone silent. She must be cowering in a corner. Who are these maniacs?

"So? Do we kick it in?"

As the men take turns throwing themselves against the door, the lens in the peephole stretches and contorts their bodies, each one a player in a grotesque charade. All my life, I have seen people tormented by men like this lot, sociopaths with power. I want to confront them. I want to unlock the door and go out into the hall. My hand is on the knob. I'll do it, I think. Can't they feel my eyes on them? Don't they know I could turn their miserable hearts to stone?

The noise in the hall is suddenly very far away. It grows fainter, and I realize I'm falling. I drop to my knees and tumble over on the floor. I can hear heavy breathing—my own. I stare up at the ceiling as darkness engulfs me.

THIRTEEN

2001

Atan's first gig in Greenwich Village was a one-off at Terra Blues. Brooklyn Willy was a legend there and got him in the door. But gigs were hard to come by, and after five years in New York, Atan still made most of his money busking at Washington Square Park. He usually started his mornings at the Waverly Diner on the corner of 6th Avenue, fueling up on eggs and coffee before sessions in the park that could stretch to five or six hours. Today, the sky cloudless, the air kissed by the last warmth of summer, Atan was hoping to find lots of people strolling about. He had just paid his rent and was low on cash, so he needed a good day.

When he arrived at the diner just before nine o'clock, Atan found the tables empty and all the customers and waitresses pressed together at the back counter. They were peering into the kitchen at a small television on a shelf above the butcher's block. On the screen, Atan could see the World Trade Center towers in Lower Manhattan, not thirty blocks away. One of them spewed black smoke from a gash in its side, high above the skyline.

"What's going on?" Atan asked the waitress at his shoulder, an elderly Hispanic woman, as she dabbed her moist eyes with the corner of her apron.

"They're jumping," she moaned, choking back tears.

"It was a small plane, they think," said the man in front of Atan, his eyebrows arching above thick-rimmed glasses as he loosened his tie, a briefcase at his feet. "I was on my way there."

At that moment, a passenger airliner appeared on the television, its belly in shadow as it banked toward the sun and flew straight toward the World Trade Center. No, Atan thought, his disbelief scarcely taking form before the plane, defying the unthinkable, slammed into the upper floors of the other tower and erupted in a ball of orange fire.

"*Dios mío*! *Dios mío*!" the waitress whispered.

"Christ! What the hell is going on?" the cook gasped, his voice rising above the cries of shock from the patrons as they pulled themselves away from the scene unfolding on the television.

"Now it's both towers," the cook said, turning to look at Atan.

"*Mi familia*," the waitress moaned as she untied her apron and hurried outside.

Fleeing the diner, the patrons scattered along the sidewalk, apparently determined to get as far away from there as they could, or maybe as near as possible to the people they loved.

The man with the thick-rimmed glasses sat down at the counter, his face pale.

"I guess we're as safe here as anywhere," he muttered.

Atan joined him, his plans for the morning forgotten, the world contracting until nothing remained but a dark knot of terror.

"Who would do this?" he asked.

The answer came from the CBS news anchor Dan Rather and a parade of pundits.

"Bin Laden," they said in unison. "Al-Qaeda," they repeated.

As if reciting a mantra, they lay the blame at the feet of the Muslim terrorist Osama bin Laden and his al-Qaeda network, the fires in the towers still burning.

Atan stared at the television and listened to every word. When a thirty-something waitress with a southern accent asked him if he wanted to order his usual, he shook his head. He didn't feel like eating.

"How about some coffee?" she suggested, her fake eyelashes brimming with tears.

Atan nodded.

As the steam rose from his cup, he counted out a handful of nickels and dimes he'd collected while busking the day before and slid them across the counter.

"Sorry," he said.

"That's okay, honey," the waitress said, glancing at Atan's guitar case on the stool next to him. "I'm sure these coins were hard won."

Atan didn't know her well, other than to exchange words about the weather, but in that moment, her kindness was a balm. He felt a deep comradery with the few people still gathered in the diner as the television replayed the sickening image of the airplane striking the tower yet again.

Within the hour, once more defying the unthinkable, that same tower let out a roar and exploded, all 110 stories disintegrating floor by floor. People trapped by the flames were dying in front of Atan's eyes, along with all the police and firefighters who had gone inside. It seemed unreal, and he couldn't fathom what he was seeing. Lasting no more than ten seconds, the collapse left nothing behind but great billows of dust. The tower was gone.

Watching the replays, no one spoke, not Atan, not the man at his elbow with the thick-rimmed glasses, not the waitress with the southern accent, her mascara dissolving into rivulets of black tears that ran to her chin. Then, half an hour later, it happened again. The other tower roared its last, and in barely more time than it takes a baseball to sail out of the park, nothing remained but monstrous clouds of dust looming above Lower Manhattan like volcanic plumes.

Dan Rather was as startled by the events of the day as anyone else.

"First, one of the World Trade Center towers collapsed," he said as replays of the falling towers unspooled on the television screen above the butcher's block. "Yes, collapsed! It just—it looks like one of those scenes of an old building being, you know, purposely dynamited and blown up. First one tower and then the other collapsed, completely collapsed."

Atan wondered how that could be. How were the towers rigged for demolition without anyone knowing? It didn't make sense. Surely, the answer would emerge, he thought, if he just stayed there long enough and watched the story unfold. Instead, retreating from their first impressions, the news anchors dropped the question of demolition as quickly as the towers had vanished until the consensus was reached that fire alone had caused the collapses—nothing but fire.

By noon, the investigation was all but over, a formality to be undertaken in the days ahead. The jury, it seemed, had already ruled. Bin Laden, operating from a base in Afghanistan, had ordered jihadists to fly airplanes into the towers because Americans didn't love the right God. As for the destruction of the towers, that was merely a happenstance that had worked wildly in bin Laden's favor, multiplying the dead manyfold and leaving the witnesses to dread what might come next. It was terrorism on an unprecedented scale, an audacious success for a gang of foreign purveyors of evil.

Atan wasn't convinced. In the coming weeks, a memory nagged at him. As a child, he'd seen the effects of a fire after the barn near his house burned down. He knew concrete didn't burn. Neither did steel. The barn's silo had survived, along with its basement walls, and there had been a long steel roof beam lying in the ashes that the heat had not melted or warped, even though the firefighters had given up in their attempt to save the barn, letting the flames rage through the night, far longer than the towers had burned.

Nearly four years after the attacks, on an August night in 2005, Atan surprised the crowd at Café Wha?—where he now had a regular gig—with the anti-war bent of his new songs. By that time, the story about a clash between Christian and Muslim nations had killed hundreds of thousands of brown-skinned people in Afghanistan and Iraq, and Atan couldn't be quiet about it any longer.

In one, he sang, "How can I smile when people are dying and the president grins like he can't hear them crying? How can I sing when so much is unspoken and liars spin news like our brains were all broken?"

"I have to weep cuz it's all true," he lamented in the chorus. "I have to weep just to get through. I have to weep, it's what I do. I'm the prophet sent to ask you."

In the next verses, he continued the litany of his bewilderment.

"How can I dance when my heart's always aching and bankers fund wars like all life is for taking? How can I love when it won't change anything and God's always used like the Devil's own plaything?"

Singing this last line, Atan embodied all the sorrow of one who had loved God and lost him, only to come to God's defense in the face of the tragically self-righteous slogan God Bless America.

By the time Atan segued into his next tune, the two guys in the nearest booth were openly scowling, apparently offended by his lack of enthusiasm for the ever-sprawling War on Terror. Noting their hostility, with both men into their fourth pint of beer, their empty glasses cluttering the table, Atan looked directly at them.

"I pay my taxes like I should," he sang. "They say it's for the common good. But I know what the money's for. They rob us blind to pay for war." He stepped closer. "Forgive us for the dollar bill. Forgive us for the blood we spill. Forgive me for this face I wear. It isn't that I just don't care."

Striding toward the other end of the narrow stage, Atan sang the chorus with the pathos of someone bludgeoned by the enormity of the wrongs in his midst.

"My pain is deep. It's a mile wide. This mask you see keeps it all inside."

Thumping his glass down on the table, the bigger of the two men rose from his seat.

"No one gives a shit about your pain!" he hollered at Atan.

"Shh!" a buxom woman in the next booth hissed at him as her girlfriends looked on.

Rising to the bait, Atan spun around and strummed his way back to the two men.

"I think of Orwell's '84, thought-police knockin' at the door," he sang. "This is the Nine-Eleven age, liars struttin' across the stage. They lie to me, they lie to you, so what's a decent guy to do?"

Atan stopped playing his guitar, and silence rushed into the room.

After a beat, singing a capella, he answered, "I smile so they'll never see the rage that's boiling up in me."

He went back to the center of the stage, shimmering in the purple glow of the overhead lights, and struck the first notes of the chorus again, letting them tremble in the air as he sang.

"My pain is deep. It's a mile wide."

"Nine-Eleven was a tragedy," the bigger guy yelled.

Atan reached down with the little finger of his right hand and swiveled the volume knob on his guitar up to eight.

"This mask you see keeps it all inside," he bemoaned, letting the notes stretch out and screech and finally crash down around him as the audience hooted applause.

"Fuckin' hippie, give us some blues," the smaller guy shouted.

It was true. Atan's music had veered away from the blues, some of it sounding more like rock and some of it more like folk. Mostly, it sounded like him. He'd found his voice.

Seated on a stool at the microphone, Atan tuned his guitar for the next song while the waitresses moved along the row of booths, gathering up empty glasses.

"Nobody lied about Nine-Eleven," the bigger guy said.

"We're living different pasts," Atan said. He strummed his guitar. "We're living different truths." Strum. "You saw the towers fall and you believe what you heard." Strum, strum. "I saw the towers fall and I don't believe a word." Strum, strum, strum.

"Fuck you!" the man shouted.

"Boo!" a few people called out.

Atan shrugged. "Just sayin'."

"People died," a middle-aged woman yelled at him.

Her encouragement must have been all the bigger guy needed. He got to his feet and came at Atan with both fists swinging. But Atan was too agile for him. He slid down off the stool, pivoted on one knee, and dodged the punches. Before the man could launch another volley, a bouncer pulled him off the stage and marched him along the red velvet carpet to the exit. Up the stairs they went, past a gauntlet of photos of legends who'd played gigs at Café Wha? over the years, the smaller guy close behind, threatening to sue, until at last both men were shoved out onto the sidewalk.

At the end of the night, after last call came and went and everyone made their way outside, Atan was coiling up his amp cable, his guitar case open beside him where he kneeled on the stage, when he heard a sweet voice at his ear.

"That was either gutsy or stupid."

Looking up, he saw a woman in her mid-twenties, maybe older, her long dark hair swinging across her face as she tilted her head. Under her denim jacket, she wore a summer dress with tasseled beads that twinkled in the footlights.

"What was?" Atan asked.

"Mouthing off like that."

Her eyes, green with a rim of gold around the edge of the iris, were twinkling too.

"I was just telling it like I see it. That guy can think what he wants."

"I agree with you. But most people don't want to hear that stuff."

Atan tucked the amp cable into his guitar case and closed the lid.

"I'm Sam," she said, extending her hand.

He took her slender fingers in his palm, and she let them rest there for a moment.

"You doing anything now?" she asked.

She was a pretty girl, Atan thought, and her company would do him good. He'd been feeling restless lately. Walking back to his apartment after his gigs had become a letdown. Nothing was worse than the loneliness that followed the high of a show when everybody had been grooving on the vibe he was laying down, connected to him and each other by the spell of the music. He would drink up the crowd's energy like a thirsty castaway come ashore until he felt so alive that he wanted to cry and laugh all at once.

Sam twirled the end of her hair around a finger as she waited for an answer. Atan had been here before, too many times to count. Some girls just had a thing for musicians. They'd slink backstage after the show or linger in the shadows when the place emptied out. Atan could have hooked up with lots of them, but that wasn't what he wanted. Random sex left him cold. He'd only ever made love once, he figured, and that was back in high school when he'd been too miserable to be anyone's boyfriend but had still found bliss with Vanessa, the girl who'd saved him from freezing to death the night he'd passed out drunk in the unbuilt house.

Sam was too young, he thought. He was midway through his thirties. He didn't need someone hanging off his arm who was a decade younger and still trying to figure out her shit. Then he laughed at himself. She probably wasn't even looking for a boyfriend, just a shag, he thought.

"Where're you from?" he asked her.

"Why?"

"Your accent."

"Good ear. Most people don't notice. All the accents are mashed up here anyway, right? You got Puerto Ricans talking like Jamaicans, and Hondurans talking like homies."

She was lively, Atan thought.

"So, are you going to tell me?"

"The Western Sahara."

"Really?"

"Yeah. My parents were missionaries there until I was fifteen. They named me after the city where I was born, Samara. I read somewhere that your name means wise man. Is that right?"

"Yeah, someone who gives wise counsel."

"Do you?"

Atan laughed. "Those guys tonight didn't think so." He picked up his guitar case and stepped down off the stage.

"So? You want to hang out?" Sam asked.

"Sure. Walk with me?"

"Alright."

Happy to be outside in the fresh night air of late summer, they strolled up Minetta Lane until they arrived at a playground with looping steel bars for climbing. Without hesitating, Sam dashed across the grass to the sand and leaped into the air, wrapping her arms and legs around one of the coils as she leaned her head all the way back, her face upside down.

"Come on," she called to him.

"I'm good here," he said, watching from the sidewalk.

"Where do you live?" she asked.

"On Christopher."

"Is it far?"

"Five blocks."

Sam unwrapped her legs and released her grip, falling gracefully to the ground.

"Show me?" she asked coyly.

Damn, she had a nice smile, Atan thought, trying to decide what he would do when they reached his place. Would he ask her to stay?

The truth was that Sam had nowhere else to go. She'd only ended up at Café Wha? that night, she told him, because she was on the run from the immigration authorities and afraid to go home. She was Canadian, not American. After leaving Africa, her parents had lived in New York doing inner-city work, but when Sam was twenty, they'd gone back to Toronto, where the Christian foundation that signed their checks was headquartered. Not wanting to give up her life in New York, Sam had stayed behind, working under the table and rooming with American friends who could sign the lease for her.

Since the attack on the Twin Towers, the government had cracked down on illegals, and now they were onto her. That afternoon, returning from her job at a bookstore on West 84th Street, she'd found two Homeland Security thugs waiting on her stoop. Seeing the men before they saw her, she'd kept walking and ducked into the nearest subway station. She'd gone as far south as the Washington Square stop and was wandering along MacDougal Street, not sure what to do with herself, when she'd reached the café, happy to read on the marquee that Atan was playing.

"I'd been wanting to see you live for a while," she said. "It was fate."

By the time they arrived at Barrow Street, the ambivalence that Atan had been feeling about Sam was gone. Attracted by her outlaw status, he wanted nothing more than to help her. As they ran across the street, a speeding taxi barreling toward them, they took each other's hand and didn't let go until they'd reached the steps that led down to his single basement room.

"So you're stranded?" he asked her.

"Well, I could crash with a friend, but that's where they'll look for me next, and I don't want to cause anyone trouble."

"Stay here."

Sam blushed.

"Are you sure?"

"Yeah, but I don't have a couch. We'll have to share the bed."

"Okay, if we have to," Sam joked.

Atan let them in and went to shower. When he came out of the washroom, he found Sam sitting cross-legged on the bed. The candle on the bedside table was burning, and she'd lit a stick of incense she'd found protruding from the soil of a potted cactus on the bookshelf. Atan climbed onto the bed and sat facing her, cross-legged, too, as he searched her eyes, looking for the person beneath the skin. There she was, he thought, vulnerable amid the sass. And her? Did she see a gentleness behind the cockiness that had almost gotten him punched out that night? At last, they held each other, their hearts pressed together, as they stepped into the unknown. Soon their breathing took on the same rhythm. To Atan, they felt like one entity pulsing in the flickering candlelight. They stayed like that until, the incense burning out, they lay down in a beautiful heap and fell asleep.

Two days after rolling out his new songs at Café Wha? Atan got a phone call from an arts reporter for the *New York Post*. The guy was writing a review of the show and wanted to know the rest of the lyrics to Atan's song about Nine-Eleven, the one he'd been about to sing when he was attacked by one of the patrons.

"What song about Nine-Eleven?" Atan asked, hunched over a bowl of granola at the table next to his front window.

"I saw the towers fall and I don't believe a word," the reporter quoted him as saying.

"Oh, that," Atan laughed. "I was improvising."

"So, what exactly are your views on Nine-Eleven?"

"Are you asking me to speculate about what happened?"

"Yes. If you don't believe a word, what do you believe?"

"I'm not playing that game," Atan said. "I don't know what happened. But I can spot a lie when I hear one."

"Who's lying?" the reporter asked. "What's the lie?"

He needed a quote to nail down his story.

"Ask Dan Rather."

"The news anchor?"

"He can spot a lie too."

"What did he say?"

"He said it looked like the towers fell as if rigged for demolition. And he wasn't the only one. At least three dozen reporters on the ground said the same thing. You can watch all the footage from that morning on a new website called YouTube."

"And you agree?"

"Don't you?"

"As far as I know, the investigators didn't find any evidence of explosives."

"They didn't look."

"Of course they did."

"No, they didn't. Explosives weren't a likely scenario, they said, so they didn't look for any. It's like they were standing over a body full of holes, but they refused to look for bullets. Why not? Why cover up what happened unless you're the criminal?"

"So you're suggesting the government—what? Killed its own people?" the reporter stammered. "You believe that?"

Atan did believe it. In the deepest part of his being, he thought it was true. But why? In a flash, the reason came to him, and he spoke the words as they entered his head.

"That's how bad people can be," he said. "When there's money to be had, the innocent will be killed. It has been that way on this continent since the first Europeans arrived. Most history in the Americas is a story of organized crime."

"Now you're confusing the issues."

"Am I?"

Atan looked out the window at the pedestrians passing on the sidewalk, all in their own worlds, as unaware of his concerns as he was of theirs.

"Anyway, people shouldn't care what I think," he said. "They can decide for themselves, no?"

When the *New York Post* review came out, it gave a blow-by-blow account of Atan's fracas with the two men, suggesting his views on Nine-Eleven were suspect, but without any statement from Atan about what he thought had really happened and apparently unwilling to acknowledge Dan Rather's speculations about controlled demolitions, the reporter mostly let him off the hook. Instead, he called Atan a "devil-may-care rabble-rouser reminiscent of a bygone era with a light touch on the frets and a mournful voice."

Among a jaded generation born into the aftermath of the 1960s, with its parade of assassinated heroes, Atan's songs were soon selling fast enough at a website called MySpace that he didn't need to busk anymore, and before long, an agent from Nonesuch Records showed up at one of his gigs to offer him a recording deal.

"I'm doing fine on my own," Atan said, seated across from the agent in a booth at Café Wha? between sets. "What do I need a million dollars for?"

"No one said anything about a million dollars," the agent laughed. "You're a niche artist, after all."

"I'm not interested," Atan said, getting to his feet. "But thanks."

When Atan told Samara about the record deal, she said he was crazy for turning it down. She'd been living with him for almost three months by then, and it was the first time they'd fought about anything.

"Are we going to stay in this little room forever?" she asked. "Look around. We're on top of each other."

Atan looked at the dirty clothes, hers, piled on the floor next to the bed. He took in the empty beer bottles, hers, on the window ledge; the dishes, hers, stacked on the chair next to the door; the hula hoop, hers, that leaned against the stove in the kitchen nook.

"We would be fine if the place was tidier," he said.

"It would be tidier if it was bigger," Sam snapped.

"I doubt it."

"So I'm messy now?"

"A little."

"There's nowhere to put anything!"

"Okay, okay, I get it. We won't be here forever."

"Really?"

"Yeah. I'll release my album. Just not with these guys. They pretend to be independent, but they're owned by Warner Brothers. They'll make me into a commodity. They'll cut off my balls. Is that what you want?"

Sam smiled.

"Well, is it? Do you want me without balls?"

"No."

"I'll find another label, alright? I don't need to be famous to make a living. And with the Internet, that's possible. It's not like the old days. Okay?"

"Alright."

"Remember, we live like this because we're outlaws. If Brooklyn Willy hadn't signed the lease, we wouldn't even have this place."

"I know. You're right."

And that was it. They were in the same groove again. With Sam, for the first time in his life, Atan felt like he had an accomplice. More than anything else, that was why he loved her.

It also helped that, growing up, both had suffered from their entanglements with Christianity. If Atan's quest for the Holy Spirit had left him disillusioned in his teens, the evangelism of Sam's parents had left her jaded when it came to religion.

"Samara is in the Moroccan part of Western Sahara," she told Atan one morning as they walked along Christopher Street. "The people are Muslim. They already have a religion! They didn't need my parents' help."

"So, why were they there?" Atan asked.

"To feed the poor, they said, but their ulterior motive was always to convert people to Christianity."

"It's an old story," Atan said as they neared the Hudson River, which always made him think of the Hudson's Bay Company, also named for the explorer Henry Hudson. The company's agents, he knew, had also brought along the priests when they'd gone to trade for furs with the Indigenous peoples of the Northwest.

With spring upon them, the snowdrifts along the sidewalk had melted into puddles in the muddy grass. At the end of the street, finding the crosswalk flooded, the sewer covers blocked with clumps of dead leaves, Atan scooped Sam up in his arms and carried her to the other side of West Street. He could feel the moisture seeping through the lace holes of his boots, but he didn't mind. Sam was smiling at him, the sunlight in her eyes. He would have swum across the river with her on his back if she'd asked him to.

They walked along Pier 45, the water lapping at the concrete abutments beneath them, the breeze almost warm.

"But you know I believe in God," Sam said. "Not God as a male on some throne, like a dictator king. And not God as just energy. It's more than that. It has personality."

"I don't really think of God that way."

They stopped at a railing and looked down into the water, seagulls squawking overhead.

"There was an old woman on my street who I used to talk to when I was a kid," Sam said. "Like really old! A bush woman, tribal. She didn't answer the call to prayer with her neighbors or cover her head with a hijab. Religion didn't mean anything to her. But she showed me things, serious stuff I'll never forget."

"Like what?"

Sam smiled at Atan. "God," she said.

"Oh yeah?"

"Yeah. Come sit down. I'll show you."

They sat on a bench under a swath of canvas awning stretched like a sail above the end of the pier.

"Close your eyes."

"Okay. They're closed."

"Now listen to the air, just the air."

A long moment passed.

"Imagine the air gathering water droplets from the surface of the river, climbing the face of the pier, stirring in the trees."

Atan could hear the thin, bare branches clicking together as the breeze moved through them.

"Listen to the air as it enters you and leaves you."

Atan did as he was told, letting the air fill him like a bellows and escape again. Soon his breathing made no sound, and the more he focused on the air passing in and out of his lungs, the less he heard.

"Listen to the silence behind everything—the air, your thoughts—everything."

Suddenly, Atan didn't know where he was. He heard the hooves of caribou and a drum dancer singing in Inuktitut. Somewhere far off, a wolf howled. He felt a hand on his forehead and smelled shaving cream. A rush of energy flashed through his core, about to obliterate all thought, when his eyes sprang open.

"What the hell? What did you do to me?"

"Why? What's wrong?"

Atan didn't know what to say.

"Did you feel it?" she asked.

"Yeah, but it was more like a place than a person."

"I know, right? Like somewhere timeless. Everywhere and nowhere."

"I've been there before—when I was young. But it was too much too fast, I think."

"And now?"

Atan shrugged. He sensed there was a holy dimension to life. It moved him when he wrote songs and filled him when he played live. It was the common ground at which he and Sam arrived in moments of carnal bliss he'd never known was possible. Even the bravado of his youth had given way to the fearlessness that comes with trust in the unseen. But he had only ever accessed what Sam called God in an ecstatic state, the experience fleeting. He didn't know how to ground into it.

"It still felt like too much," he said.

"I know just the book for you," Sam told him, pulling him up from the bench as they started back along the pier.

"What is it?" Atan asked.

"You'll see."

The next afternoon, Sam came home from her shift at the bookstore with a copy of *The Miracle of Mindfulness* by the Buddhist monk Thich Nhat Hanh.

"If you want to learn how to meditate, this will help," she said, setting the book beside him on the bed, where he sat with his guitar, a new song in the works.

The book was a quick read, and soon Atan was trying out the exercises, like washing the dishes *to wash the dishes*, which meant that instead of thinking about what he would do when he was finished, he observed the weight of each dish and felt the water trickling over his hands. Trying out walking meditations, he counted in time with his steps until breathing was his only focus.

Next, he replaced the counting with a mantra: "Breathing in, I am. Breathing out, I am." At last, he dropped the mantra and gave his attention to the silence behind everything—where the spirits stir, Rachel would've said. Only then did he feel ready to sit down and try to meditate in the way Sam had shown him, merging his consciousness with the unseen—with God.

But when Atan reached this stage, something unexpected happened. His ego behaved like a child. Using the silence to demand attention, it replayed his arguments with Sam about their living situation, filling his head with conversations they would never have—maddening, pointless, angry thoughts that circled around and around, getting him nowhere. Their fights had become so frequent that he found himself longing for the peace that would surely come if ever he could silence his ego long enough to truly quiet his mind.

"It's easy for you to act like poverty is some kind of badge," Sam said to him one night when he got home from a gig, almost a year to the day since they'd met. "You idealize being poor because you grew up with all the privileges of middle-class life. Well, I didn't. My parents had nothing. I didn't leave home to end up living in a place with about as much space as we had in our little hut."

"Then get your own place," Atan said, feeling trapped. "Or go live with your friends."

"Fine."

Sam stuffed some clothes and her toothbrush into a backpack.

"Don't forget your hula hoop."

"It's not mine. Heather left it here."

Heather was Sam's co-worker and best friend, the sister she'd never had.

"So? Take it with you."

"Okay, I will!"

Sam grabbed the hula hoop from under the bed and shoved past Atan. Stomping out the door, she headed off along Christopher Street.

As soon as Sam was gone, Atan regretted telling her to go. Lighting a candle, he went outside and placed it next to the potted fern on the table beside the door. That way, if she came back, she would know he was waiting for her—that he was sorry.

Lying in the dark, wondering where she'd gone, he found the words to a new song.

"I'll light a candle for you, Sam. I'll leave it on the table. I'll light a candle for you, Sam, whenever I am able."

He'd rolled off the bed and picked up his guitar, searching for the chords to the chorus.

"So tether the hawk and bring out the dove," he sang as he strummed. "Tether your heart to that thing called love. Tether your soul to no kind of pain. Tether me, dear one, with your sweet name."

The tune had a country twang, which Atan kind of liked.

"I'll light the fire in your eyes, Sam. I'll light it with my own," he sang, looking out the window. "I'll light the fire in your eyes, Sam, to see where we are going."

Uncertain of the next verse, he went outside to see if Sam was anywhere in sight, but the sidewalk was empty, the city asleep except for the taxis zipping by. Above him, a few stars defied the urban glow.

"I'll light the heavens with your stars, Sam," Atan whispered. "I'll take them from your smile. I'll light the heavens with your stars, Sam, and we'll walk a crazy mile."

Back inside, Atan slumped down on the edge of the bed, the guitar across his knees.

"I'll light the world with your words, Sam," he sang, finding the final verse. "I'll speak them where I go. I'll light the world with your words, Sam, and watch the wisdom grow." It was the first love song he'd written, and it felt like a prayer. "So tether the hawk and bring out the dove. Tether your heart to that thing called love. Tether your soul to no kind of pain. Tether me, dear one, with your sweet name."

When Sam came back three hours later, dragging the hula hoop and smelling of tequila, Atan sang the song for her while she sat on the floor by the stove. Holding the candle he'd lit, she wept.

"No one's ever written a song for me," she said. "It's like I'm the only girl you've ever loved."

"You are," Atan said, another argument behind them.

But he couldn't deny the difficulties of their living arrangement, and it didn't help that Atan's career had stalled. He still had no record deal, and he'd released only a handful of new singles on MySpace in the past year. Even though he was writing all the time and had lots of material, he couldn't figure out how his songs fit together. He didn't know what he wanted the album to say.

On top of that, in the years since Nine-Eleven, a truth war had been brewing that Atan couldn't escape. When the *New York Post* interviewed him in 2005, YouTube had just gone online, offering a pulpit for every point of view. A true cacophony of consciousness, it laid bare the doubt and fear roiling beneath the surface of American life. At the center of it all was Nine-Eleven, with the collapses of the Twin Towers viewable for all in uploaded videos. Now anyone could see what Dan Rather had seen. The towers looked like they'd been rigged to explode. The emperor had no clothes.

But the mainstream media still insisted they couldn't see Uncle Sam's pimply ass, even when scientists found traces of explosives in the debris of both towers. For Atan, this evidence was the smoking gun. Nevertheless, people clung to the story about how the fire had brought down the Twin Towers, unable to broach the unfathomable. He couldn't understand why. It didn't matter, he told himself. It wasn't his fight.

Unfortunately for Atan, the media didn't see it that way, and as the truth war raged on, his statements to the *New York Post* were dragged into the debate. The Nine-Eleven skeptics co-opted him for their cause, and the press dismissed him as a dupe, a lunatic, and a fuckin' Canuck. Some of the club owners, claiming loyalty to the New Yorkers who'd died in the towers, blacklisted Atan. Worst of all, in 2007, when Atan was finally about to sign a two-album deal with the indie label Jagjaguwar, he was dropped at the last minute. It just wasn't the right time, the agent told him. Maybe the label could sign him in six months or a year—after things had quieted down.

Seated at the table next to his front window, the sun faint in a gray December sky, Atan hung up the phone. Bewildered, he turned and looked at Sam as she cracked an egg into a pan on the stove.

"Well?" she asked.

Atan shook his head.

"Now what are we going to do?"

She threw the eggshell into the sink.

"Fuck!" she cried.

Atan had lost the deal because of his politics. Despite himself, he was in the middle of the fight against the covetous and murderous ways of the white man, as old Ataninnuaq had always intended. But that wasn't what Atan wanted, and he wasn't prepared.

FOURTEEN

2011

After five and a half years with Atan, two of those as manager of the bookstore where she worked, Samara felt stuck in her life. The owner of the store, who never came in anymore, would have sold her the business and been done with it, but Sam didn't have the money. Cooking school was an option, but that took money too. She'd asked Atan if he would consider moving to Canada, where she could get a student loan, but he had no interest in going back.

"That would be like giving up," he'd told her.

One Friday near the end of February, Sam had to work late. The store was hosting a reading by a novelist from Toronto named Tyler Blake. Traveling by taxi at the bookstore's expense, she met his flight at LaGuardia Airport in East Elmhurst and took him out to eat at a Thai restaurant on West 46th Street before the launch. The place was his choice and cheap enough that the bookstore owner wouldn't balk at paying the bill. Thai food was his favorite, Tyler Blake told Sam, not that he'd ever been to Thailand, but he was learning to cook it himself.

"You like to cook?" she asked, chopsticks poised above a bowl of pumpkin fried rice.

"Yeah. If I wasn't a writer, I'd be a cook," he said.

"Really? I'm thinking of going to cooking school. I like books, but I can't write."

"Why don't you open a cookbook store with a restaurant in it? You could use recipes from the books in the store so people could taste the food first."

"Wow. That's a cool idea."

Sam smiled at him like she hadn't smiled in a long time.

Tyler Blake was a writer on the rise. At thirty-five, with two violent tragicomic novels under his belt, he was about to go mainstream with his latest. Although published by a small press, his new book was going to be made into a film. He had just sold the rights and was in New York to finalize the deal.

The reading attracted about thirty people, from ardent fans to the curious, most with tuques on their heads and scarves hanging from their necks, some still standing in their coats, sweating as the slush from their boots melted on the floor. Tyler Blake's new book was set in a dystopian future where the fate of humankind was in the hands of two robot boys, one named R-Naught and the other named R-Two. The reading was lively, verging on the theatrical, as Tyler Blake took on the robotic voice of R-Naught and the growly inflection of his nemesis, Doctor Evangeline, who'd unleashed an outrageous parade of woes upon harnessing the subatomic matrix of the universe to alter the past.

When the reading was over, Tyler Blake signed books while Sam refilled people's wine glasses. As the store cleared out, she filled her glass, too, along with his, until they were both more than a little tipsy. After Sam had locked up the shop, they left together and wandered the streets of Hell's Kitchen. Along the way, she pointed out restaurants he should try while he was in town, like Lily's on Ninth Avenue, where she liked the roasted cauliflower au gratin best, and Amy's Bread, across the street, where they stood at the window, drooling over the golden loaves that lined the shelves. It was almost eleven o'clock when they went into O'Neill's Irish Bar, where Tyler Blake picked up the tab for three rounds of Guinness that left them both stone drunk.

At two o'clock—just about when Atan would have been finishing his show at Café Wha?—Sam was falling over in her chair.

"I'm so tired," she said when Tyler Blake tried to sit her up. "Just let me sleep."

He helped Sam to her feet and out the door. They took a cab to the Walker Hotel in Greenwich Village, where the film company had booked him a room for five days. There, they lay down together on his bed and promptly passed out on top of the duvet.

The next morning, when Sam came home to find Atan brooding at the table as he scribbled ideas for lyrics in his notebook, she had to assure him that nothing had happened between her and Tyler Blake.

"We were fully clothed," she said.

"That's not the point. You were six blocks from here," Atan hounded her. "Why didn't you just come home?"

"I said I'm sorry. I didn't even know where I was until this morning."

"I kept waking up to check my email. I hardly slept."

"It would be easier if you had a cellphone like a normal person," she pointed out. "Now that we don't have a landline anymore."

"Sam, I didn't know where you were!"

"I got drunk. It happens. But I wasn't in any danger, okay?"

"And you slept together on this guy's bed?"

"Yes, slept! I just wanted to fuckin' sleep. And that's what I did!"

"Do you like him?"

"No—yes, he's smart. He's interesting. So what? I meet smart people all the time."

"Yeah, but you don't spend the night with them."

"I was tired! I just wanted to sleep!"

The day after Tyler Blake's reading, Atan had another show at Café Wha?—part of a rare two-night bill to kick off his album, which he'd finally decided to self-release. The attitude at Café Wha? had always been "Fuck the Man!" so Atan's troubles with the media had endeared him to the management all the more. They were rooting for him, and he didn't fail to deliver, bringing down the house at the end of the night with the album's title track, "Love Is Not Democracy."

Sitting on a stool in a single spotlight, Atan bent over his guitar and peered into the dark.

"They say I was born tired, with a heavy stride, and the memories of an old man's life blazing in my eyes," he sang. "They say I was born weary of this mortal frame, with an upturned lip and a sour mind, like God was to blame." The crowd was quiet, as if gathered to hear a story. "They say I was born ready to turn 'round and go, but the years have passed and now I've learned what the prophets know."

The last note hovered in the air, almost disappearing into the silence as the audience waited to hear what the prophets knew.

"Love is not democracy, a bank trust, or a factory," Atan sang, bursting into the chorus.

The audience hooted and whistled.

"Love is not shiny pearls, the War on Terror, or a girl."

This mention of the ongoing Nine-Eleven wars brought cheers.

"Love is not a tragedy, a butcher's feast, or a fallen tree," Atan wailed. "Love is not! Love is not!"

He stopped playing and waited as the room grew silent again.

"Love is what will set us free."

Reaching the end of the last verse, Atan sang, "They say that God is waiting on the other side to send me back here for another chance to rise up and cry."

Again, he let the note quiver into near silence, but this time, before he could begin the chorus, the audience joined in with a rousing "Love is not democracy!"

"No, it's not," Atan said as he strummed the chord again. "Love is not democracy," he sang, "a bank trust or a factory. Love is not shiny pearls, the War on Terror, or a girl."

Just then, Atan caught Sam's eye. She was sitting alone at a high round table in the back with a bottle of beer. She'd been hung over all day, and he knew she hadn't felt like coming. She raised her bottle and nodded at him, but she didn't look happy.

"Love is not a tragedy, a butcher's feast, or a fallen tree. Love is not! Love is not!"

Atan watched Sam slug back the last of her beer and slip down from her chair.

"Love is what will set us free," he sang softly, glancing at the frets of his guitar as he strummed the final chord, the audience erupting in applause. When he looked up, Sam was gone.

Atan got home from the show to discover Sam wasn't there, and she hadn't emailed. Lately, on her days off, she would leave as soon as Atan rolled out of bed around noon. They were hardly at home together anymore except when they were sleeping. The only time they connected was when they were naked together, vulnerable in their lovemaking. In these moments, it felt like they left their egos behind, united by something untainted and timeless, each blissfully unable to tell where the other began or ended. It was this feeling that kept him holding on.

Atan lit a candle and left it on the table outside the door before going to bed. Sleeping fitfully, he awoke at a little after three o'clock to see Sam still hadn't come home. He checked his email again. This time, he found a message. She was at Heather's place—Heather of the hula hoop. "I'm drunk," she'd written. "I'll crash here. I know you don't like it when I drink this much. Too tired to fight."

"Why did you leave the show?" Atan wrote back.

When he got up in the morning, Sam hadn't answered.

Waking up on Heather's couch wrapped in an orange afghan, Sam turned on her phone and scrolled through her messages. She read the one from Atan and sighed, thinking of last night. "Love is not shiny pearls, the War on Terror, or a girl," he'd sung, looking right at her. If love wasn't a girl—if loving her made Atan feel trapped instead of free—she asked herself, then what was the point? She scrolled on, cheered to see Tyler Blake had emailed, too, inviting her for brunch at Olio e Più if she was free. He'd heard their salmon benedict was to die for, he wrote.

"Count me in," she answered. "Meet you there?"

After a feast that stretched into the afternoon, Sam and Tyler Blake went to the Rubin Museum of Art on West 17th Street and got lost together in six floors of Himalayan artifacts. Transported to a world awash in carpets woven with threads of peacock blue, turmeric yellow, and ruby red, they became enchanted by a surfeit of deities carved of wood and ivory or cast in gold, losing all track of time.

Sam received another message from Atan mid-afternoon.

"Come home," it said. "We need to talk."

But Sam didn't want to talk.

At six o'clock, when Sam and Tyler Blake were at Amy's Bread in Chelsea, bigger than the one in Hell's Kitchen, its display cases overflowing with pastries, tarts, and cakes glazed in chocolate, Atan wrote again.

"Come home tonight, or don't bother."

Was it an ultimatum? Was Atan breaking up with her? To Sam, it sounded that way, but right now, she didn't care. She was having fun for a change. Turning off her phone, she sipped her hot chocolate while Tyler Blake expounded on the merits of his espresso, which he thought quite good.

That night, Sam didn't return to the basement apartment on Christopher Street, and Atan lay awake tormenting himself about where she was. Had she been at Heather's all day, or had she gone to the

Walker Hotel to see Tyler Blake? Atan thought Sam had crossed a line when she'd spent the night passed out on the novelist's bed. He feared she wasn't going to cross back. Was she fucking him right now? He got out of bed and checked his email. She hadn't written. He lay down again and tried to sleep, squirming like a cockroach on its back, legs kicking, desperate to right itself but unable.

Sam didn't return the next night either, or the one after that. On the third morning, she wrote to say she was coming to get her stuff in the afternoon. She showed up in a taxi with four big lettuce boxes scavenged from the fruit market down the street. Watching her through the window, Atan felt his stomach tighten as she pulled the boxes from the back seat and dragged them down the icy stairs to the front door.

"Is this really what you want?" Atan asked after he let her in.

"You told me not to come back."

"I was angry."

Sam took a box and headed to the kitchen nook.

"At least tell me where you've been staying," Atan said.

"It doesn't matter now."

"What do you mean, it doesn't matter?"

"You broke up with me."

"I did not. I just—I didn't!"

Sam grabbed whatever utensils were hers and tossed them into the box—a grater, a peeler, the oven mitts, and an apron.

"Were you with that writer?"

"I didn't cheat on you if that's what you're asking."

"No?"

"No! You broke up with me, remember?"

"Stop saying that."

Sam filled the other boxes with books and clothes, tossing in hairbrushes, shampoo bottles, all the makeup that cluttered the bathroom counter, everything jumbled together.

"Atan, we argue so much about the future, it's unbearable," she said, looking around the room. "This place is unbearable."

Sitting on the edge of the bed, Atan watched as she stacked the last of the boxes next to the door.

"So what's your plan?"

"I'm going to Toronto."

She looked up at her bike, suspended from the ceiling by two large hooks.

"Sell my bike and send me the money, okay?"

"Is that where he's from?"

"Who?"

"You know who."

"Yes, that's where he's from. But I've been talking about going to Toronto for a long time."

Sam opened the door and went up the stairs, lugging the boxes one by one, the taxi driver there to load them into the trunk.

Hoisting the last box, Atan followed her, shivering, his arms bare in a T-shirt.

"I'm sorry," she said as she got into the taxi beside the driver. "You're a beautiful man. I didn't mean to hurt you."

The sun glinted off her cheeks, and Atan saw tears in her eyes. She pulled her door shut as the taxi sped away from the curb, its wheels spinning in the slushy snow. She was gone.

Before meeting Samara, Atan had grown used to his solitude, made bearable by his brief exchanges with the staff who worked at the coffee shops and diners he frequented. The only other thing that kept him going was the intensity of his connection to his audiences in the fever of performance. In the days after Sam departed, he felt bereft in a way he'd never known. He ached to love but was alone.

Time passed, but it did him no good. He thought about Sam constantly, flinching at the thought of her naked with Tyler Blake, the song of the goddess in her throat, each sigh giving language to the pleasure of love. How had it come to this? How could she do this? Didn't she know it would destroy him? Had she ever really seen him?

"Son, you better stop thinking like that," Brooklyn Willy said. "You got yourself tangled up in the world's oldest story. Boy meets girl, loves girl, loses girl."

They were at East Village Pizza on First Avenue, a block from Tompkins Square Park, where they were scheduled to share the stage at the Charlie Parker Jazz Festival in mid-August.

"I should have seen it coming," Atan said. "The night we met, she told me she was on the run from immigration, but later she said the guys she saw on her doorstep could have been friends of her ex-boyfriend, who'd been stalking her. She went from a life with that guy right into a life with me, and now she's doing it again."

"Listen," Brooklyn Willy said, "you can't take it personal. The way things were going, you two had to break up sooner or later. The girl knew it and got scared. That's all. Scared people do bad things."

He bit into his slice of pepperoni and double cheese with the same gusto he showed when playing the saxophone, grease running down his fingers and chin.

"Go on—eat."

Atan wasn't hungry.

Brooklyn Willy put down his slice of pizza and wiped his mouth with a napkin.

"I said eat with me. Show some respect now."

Atan shook some chili flakes onto his slice of mushroom and feta and took a bite.

"That's right," Brooklyn Willy smiled. "They don't let a woman kill you, not in the Tower of Song."

Atan looked up. "That's Cohen," he said, surprised.

"What? You think I don't know white music? I know good music. Period. And Mr. Cohen was right. Losing this girl ain't gonna kill you."

That was true, and Atan knew it. But part of him had to die—the self that suffered the nights, the self curled up in the pit of his stomach like a wounded animal, the self that felt Sam's absence like a missing tooth whose gap he kept poking his tongue into. He knew this self. He had come face to face with it in his attempts at meditation. It was his ego. His time with Sam had been built on the needs of his ego, he told himself. His whole career as a musician had been spent pursuing the goals of his ego. He couldn't do it anymore. He wanted to kill his ego and end its accumulation of sorrows.

Atan stopped writing songs and canceled his weekly gig at Café Wha? All that spring and summer, he didn't pick up his guitar. By the time the Charlie Parker Jazz Festival rolled around, he'd started to draw on his savings and would have skipped it if not for the money. As it was, the organizers would refuse to cut him a check after he showed up without his guitar and spent the first ten minutes playing a djembe he'd bought from a guy in Washington Square Park, where Atan had been passing his days smoking weed and learning to drum. At last, taking the microphone from its stand, he began to sing a cappella, making up the words as he went.

"This one's called the death of a man," he sang. Drum, drum. "This one's called the death of a beautiful man." Drum, drum. "This one's called the death, the death of a man." Drum, drum. "This one's called the death of a beautiful man." He looked up to the sky, where the moon cut the clouds like a scythe. "I'm returning the madness that you left with me. I'm taking back my serenity. Endless hours, endless bed, don't you see? No more kneeling down to pray. No more tears at break of day." As his voice trailed off, he struck the drum. "This one's called the death of a man," he sang once more. Drum, drum. "This one's called the death of a beautiful man." Drum, drum. "This one's called the death, the death of a man." Drum, drum. "This one's called the death of a beautiful man."

Atan slung the drum from his shoulder by its strap and walked toward the footlights.

"Will you love me when I'm broken?" he sang. "Will you love me when I fall? Will you love me when I'm sorry, or not love me at all? He paced across the front of the stage. "Will you love me in the morning when the rooster crows? Will you love me at sundown when the darkness grows? Will you love me, mmm-hmm? Will you love me, ohh? Will you love me when I'm broken or not love me at all?"

Atan stopped singing and peered out at the audience, the many-headed beast whose approval he'd courted night after night for so many years.

"I didn't think so," he said.

Chased by a rising chorus of murmurs and boos, he set the microphone at his feet and exited backstage.

The next afternoon, Brooklyn Willy went to Atan's apartment and found it empty. Out front, his belongings were piled on the sidewalk—stacks of books and compact discs, pans and dishes, a potted cactus, an unused notebook still in its cellophane, and even his guitar. Taped to the stair railing was a paper sign in black marker.

"Free," it said.

Yes, indeed, that boy was free now, Brooklyn Willy thought. Atan had up and burned all his bridges. But where the hell had he gone? Brooklyn picked up the guitar and the cactus, about the size and shape of a swollen thumb, and took them with him as he shuffled home in the August heat.

At that moment, Atan had just crossed the United States border at Laredo, Texas, on his way down to the Mexican state of Nuevo León, where the cactuses that flashed by were as big as a man. Having flown into San Antonio mid-morning, he'd gone straight to a car dealership he'd found online and bought himself a 1984 Volkswagen van the color of cream, with a gas fridge and stove, a water tank installed for the kitchen sink, and a roof that popped up into a tent. It had cost him most of his savings, but with no rent to pay, he wasn't worried about money.

Before long, the sun dipped low, streaking the desert sky with blood reds, tangerine yellows, and lipstick mauves, the cactuses turning to silhouettes against the horizon. The first stars appeared, along with the planet Venus, the brightest light for miles. Atan turned on the van's high beams and continued into the darkness. He was crossing the dry bed of an ancient ocean, the crushed shells of a hundred thousand years of sea life crusting the hubcaps as if he were traveling back in time.

Close to midnight, Atan reached the state of San Luis Potosi, with no more than an hour to go before he would be at his destination, the town of Real de Catorce, located 9,000 feet above a desert plateau on the side of a mountain in the Sierra de Catorce range. He'd heard about the place from the guy in Washington Square Park who'd sold him the djembe. Once the site of a silver mine and now a sleepy town of about a thousand people, Real de Catorce—or Royal Fourteen—had been so named to commemorate fourteen Spanish soldiers killed there in the 1500s by Chichimeca warriors determined to thwart the invasion of their silver-laden lands.

"The spirits are alive in that place," the guy had told Atan.

It was the company of spirits, not people, Atan sought as he let his headlights draw him farther into the desert, the barren plateau taking on the look of windswept snow like he was back on the flat, haunted tundra of his youth.

At the turnoff for Real de Catorce, Atan came to a stop when he saw the steep incline he needed to travel if he was to reach the town. The van was running hot, and he'd already stopped twice to refill the cooling pump with water. Not wanting to risk the engine overheating halfway up the mountain, he drove on in search of a place to pull over for the night and ended up on a dirt track that wound through a desolate outpost of shacks before arriving at an arroyo. Ahead on the left bank, Atan saw a stand of trees, their gnarled limbs shining in the headlights. Swinging the van into the circle formed by their trunks, he came to a halt at last, exhausted and ready to sleep.

At sunrise, waking to what sounded like wind chimes, Atan pulled aside the curtain in the van's back window to see strings of tiny tinkling bells and translucent glass beads hanging in the trees. Sliding open the side door, he was greeted by a riot of colored ribbons and shells tied into the branches, their crooks adorned with makeshift shrines bearing feathers, seed pods, and stones—obsidian wrought by volcanoes, amber formed of tree resin, opals born of water. As a dry wind moved through the sparse canopy, causing the ribbons to flutter and the shells to clatter, the effect of the whole impressed upon Atan's senses something like wonder.

He thought he must be in a temple, a destination for pilgrims in search of peyote cactus and the wisdom of the desert. He stepped outside to see a firepit with blackened logs amid the ashes. Clusters of stubby brush, thick with thorns, dotted the plateau in every direction. For the first time since leaving the north, Atan felt connected to the pulse of something wildly alive and primal. Right then, he decided he would stay there rather than travel up the mountain to Real de Catorce. He wouldn't leave this place, he told himself, until he'd buried his ego.

That night, a deer came to Atan in a dream and showed him where to find peyote. He didn't put much stock in dreams. He rarely remembered them anyway. But this one was too vivid to ignore. In the morning, with the sun peaking over the top of the Sierra de Catorce range and the air still cool, he went to look for the four peyote buttons the deer had shown him, one larger than the others. But he was unable to tell one stand of desert scrub from the next and could see no traces of peyote. For an hour, he searched, until the sun was too hot and he had to give up.

Atan went back to the van and sat by the firepit, trying to remember the dream more clearly. Behind him, something moved, and he turned around, startled to see an old man on a donkey emerging from beneath the trees, a blanket with geometric designs in shades of adobe and chocolate draped over his shoulder and a large cowboy hat on his head. Atan couldn't figure out where the guy had come from. It wasn't like a person could sneak up on this place. The old man steered the donkey into the clearing and started toward the mountain, gesturing for Atan to follow him.

After no more than a hundred feet, the donkey stopped, and Atan soon caught up. Looking down, he saw a dime-sized patch of grayish green peeking up at him from beneath a thorny bush. The old man made a sweeping motion with his hand, and Atan got on his knees, gentling clearing away the sand to find a family of four peyote buttons, one of them larger than the others, like in his dream.

Holding up two fingers, the old man nodded at the cluster, and Atan sliced away two buttons with a knife he had brought for that purpose. The man made a sweeping motion and handed Atan a canteen. He covered the exposed roots of the cut cactus with sand and sprinkled them with water, presumably to help them grow back.

Retrieving his canteen, the old man turned in the direction he had come, and the donkey whinnied to Atan as it started forward, leaving him to trail behind, the freshly cut peyote buttons clutched in his hand.

"Hup, Cierva," the old man said, and the donkey took to a trot, carrying him back to the clearing under the trees.

When Atan got there, the man was gone, the plateau empty as far as the eye could see. Atan wondered if he'd imagined him. Suddenly, he remembered what *cierva* meant. At the Waverly Diner in New York, he'd seen the word printed on one of the flash cards used by the Hispanic waitress to teach her granddaughter Spanish. Above the bold black letters, he recalled a cartoon drawing of a deer.

Humbled that his dream had come true, right down to the donkey named Cierva, Atan sat down by the firepit, his literal-minded ego surrendering to the inexplicable. Peeling one of the peyote buttons to reveal the wet fruit beneath the thick skin, he sliced it into quarters and popped one in his mouth. To avoid the bitterness, he swallowed it nearly whole, followed by another. As he waited to see what would happen, his stomach rebelled. Jumping to his feet, he ran out behind the trees and threw up. Back at the firepit, he tried again, this time chewing the pieces slowly and swallowing the juice as he went. This is the way to do it, he realized.

As the hours passed, Atan entered a more vibrant world, his senses alive to the desert in new ways. Colors grew brighter and sounds sharper. Wandering away from his encampment, he noticed things he'd overlooked—chamomile bushes with swaying yellow flowers, aloe plants with towering stalks a deeper yellow still, spiky round cactuses festooned with pink and orange flowers. Hummingbirds darted and drank. Chattering birds fluttered out of prickly bushes, full of song and light. Lizards, roadrunners, and mice were his companions.

When the sun reached the horizon and the night insects began to whir and chirp, Atan gathered kindling from beneath the trees to build a fire, stoking it with logs he'd bought by the bagful at a gas station in San Antonio. A blanket wrapped around his shoulders, the heat of the day seeping from the land, he peeled the second peyote button and cut it into pieces, eating them one by one. As he stared into the flames, the plant's medicine surged within him, and he felt time stop, the present and past merging.

Gazing across the desert, Atan saw people with torches approaching from the foot of the mountain. A dog yelped, and he heard children laughing. An ancient man dressed only in a loincloth stepped into the firelight, his face tattooed, his upper arms sporting straps of leather. Behind him, two younger men carried a boar on a spit ready for roasting. The first man piled stones into pillars on opposite sides of the fire for the young men, who set the boar to cook above the embers as husbands and wives arrived with their children to sit by the fire, passing gourds of drink among them. Some had drums and began to thump out a steady, hypnotic rhythm. Finding nothing odd about their sudden apparition, as if he'd been expecting them all along, Atan got his djembe from the van and joined in.

Dancing and drumming, the people feasted until the middle of the night before unrolling their mats and falling asleep beneath the trees. Atan didn't go to bed but stayed up to tend to the fire. When the sun rose, seeing a river flowing in what had been the arroyo just hours ago, he took a pot from under the sink in the van and went to fetch water for coffee. On the opposite bank stood two ancient men fishing, and nearby crouched three women washing clothes at the water's edge. In place of the shacks that had lined the dirt track, a tamarind grove had sprung up overnight, its boughs rustling with fruit pods.

Returning to the clearing with a pot of water, Atan saw the trees next to the firepit were younger now and full of foliage. One bore avocados, the other mangoes. He gathered fruit for breakfast and shared it with the people there. In exchange, they gave him beans and corn. In this way, like a skilled *angakkuq*, Atan contrived to bring forth from the past everything he needed to subsist in the present.

Over the next weeks, the ancient people of the plateau came and went, fading in and out of Atan's experience like ghosts as he fell deeper into a trance dream where the silence in his mind was the desert, desolate but alive, empty but pulsing with spirit. Growing thinner, bearded, unrecognizable, he came to see he wasn't meant to kill his ego after all, only to bring it into balance with this inner stillness he had long neglected—the part of himself Sam had said was God.

FIFTEEN

2042

I open my eyes to the glare of the light above the sink. Someone is kneeling beside me with a cup of water.

"Drink," whispers a familiar voice, and I realize the young woman who brings me groceries has come.

She helps me to sit up, and I empty the cup slowly as I get my bearings.

"What happened?" I ask.

"You must have fainted."

"That's no surprise, I guess. I'm almost out of food."

"Sorry about that. I've been trying to get here for days, but there was another roundup of debt slaves, with soldiers all over the place. In New York, they even went into the towers on Wall Street and dragged people out. Word is they got trucked straight to the camps."

"Do you know what happened to my neighbor—the woman across the hall? There were men here pounding on her door."

"I know. They took her away. When I got here, I heard them leaving, and you didn't open the fireplace. I was sure they'd found you. I had to kick it in."

I see the cast-iron plate behind her on the floor. She's worked up, and I try to reassure her.

"Well, they didn't. I'm still in the game."

She smiles.

"Here, get me up," I say.

Taking back the cup, she helps me to stand and gets me to the bed, my head throbs, and I realize just how weak I am.

"More water?"

I shake my head.

"I need to eat," I tell her. "What did you bring me?"

"Lots of stuff. Spinach and sweet potatoes, even beets. I can make you something if you want."

"I do," I say. "But just soup, please. Nothing heavy."

She puts a pot of water on the stove and sets about chopping vegetables.

"The irony is the debt slavers have started trading shares on the stock market," she says. "So those guys are going to end up being traded like cattle by their colleagues."

I can hardly get my mind around it.

"Human cattle," I mutter.

"We'll all be cattle if they have their way," she says.

"So, how do you fight that?"

"We don't fight it, not directly. We turn our backs, like you taught us. We refuse to consent. We consciously outgrow it so it has no purpose anymore and crashes on its own."

"Is that happening? Where is the evidence a coup won't bring more of the same? All I've seen since I got back is madness."

She tosses a handful of grated beet root into the steaming water and turns around. As her eyes meet mine, her gaze goes straight into me, and I feel exposed, like she can see all my contradictions.

"I'm the evidence," she says. "My generation."

She washes a sweet potato in the sink, scrubbing away the caked-on mud before peeling and dicing it.

She possesses what the acting professors at university called presence. An undeniable force drives her. She could be an angel. I want her to be.

"Have you figured out how to infect everyone else with your wisdom?" I ask as she shoves the cubes of sweet potato off the cutting board and into the pot. "Unless you can do that, your sacrifices, the secret meetings, your movements between safe houses—all of it will be for nothing."

"You taught us that too. Well, my mom, at least. She called it dehypnosis."

"Dehypnosis? And she heard about that from me?"

She looks at me, an eyebrow cocked. "I'm starting to wonder."

She cuts up a red onion and adds it to the boiling water, along with salt and pepper and some freshly chopped rosemary, its sweetly pungent scent filling the room.

I don't want to discourage her, but I need to know I haven't risked my freedom for no good reason.

"What about the men who took away my neighbor?"

"They belong to the past."

"Do they know that?"

She turns down the flame on the stove and comes to the edge of the bed, staring at me now as if taking my measure.

"If they don't know it yet, they will soon."

I'm reminded of a song.

"Come senators, congressmen, please heed the call," I half sing.

"Huh?"

"Bob Dylan."

She sits on the edge of the bed. "What song is that?"

"'The Times They Are A-Changin.' He wrote it before I was born."

She frowns. "That's a long time ago."

"Don't stand in the doorway, don't block up the hall," I sing softly. "For he that gets hurt will be he who has stalled. There's a battle outside and it's raging. It'll soon shake your windows and rattle your walls, for the times they are a-changin'."

"Oh, abrupt!" she laughs. "My mom had a bootleg of you singing that song in Lafayette Square. I used to listen to it all the time."

"You did? I don't even remember singing it."

"Do you still play guitar?"

"Not for years. Look at my hands." I show her my gnarled knuckles. "Arthritis."

She takes my fingers in hers. "I'll bring you something for that. Works great. You'll see."

She returns to the counter and tears the spinach into small pieces before adding it to the pot, removing the stems as she goes.

"I'm making a big batch, so you'll have some left over."

After washing the knife, grater, and cutting board, everything put neatly away in the cupboard, she ladles out a bowl of soup and brings it to the bedside table with a big spoon. Piping hot, it smells wonderful.

"I have to go before those Borg come back," she says. "I heard them tell your neighbor they were taking her for some kind of injection, and the hospital isn't far from here."

"Borg?" I ask.

"Yeah, one mind, no soul."

"If the shoe fits."

She nods. "Will you be alright?"

"Yes. Thanks to you."

She hesitates as if there is more she wants to say, but then seems to change her mind. Pulling up her hood, she steps down into the tunnel, lifting the cast-iron plate back across the opening before she goes.

SIXTEEN

2022

As the 2010s unfolded, with the criminal cabal that pulled the strings of government moving on from Afghanistan and Iraq to train its guns on Libya, Syria, Yemen, and Iran, Atan was nowhere to be seen. Peyote tourists passing through Real de Catorce told of seeing a man who could have been Atan living in a van near an arroyo on a plateau west of the Sierra de Catorce range. They couldn't be sure, they said, on account of the man's thin face and long beard, but when he spoke, the voice was Atan's, recognizable because it was everywhere, his self-released album, *Love Is Not Democracy*, now an underground hit getting radio play at a time when the words of his songs matched the sentiments of so many. But if the man in the desert was Atan, they said, he had clearly gone crazy, for when he spoke, he seemed to be talking to people who weren't there.

Speculation about Atan's whereabouts surfaced again in the late spring of 2022 when a middle-aged couple from Montreal, who had attended his sold-out Café Campus show back in 1996, found his van on their way to Real de Catorce and posted pictures of it online. He wasn't there, they said, just the van, the color of stained teeth, the pop-up tent bleached by the sun and torn by the wind, the wheels half buried in blown sand. From the mirror on the passenger side hung a dirt-streaked blanket with a hole burned through it. Nesting mice had chewed up the wiring in the engine. Under a tree lay a djembe, its skin ripped and sagging—the same one Atan had played at Tompkins Square Park, people said, proving the bearded man seen there years before really had been him. But no one knew where he'd gone.

Forty-two when he went into the desert, Atan had never intended to stay away so long, but living as if in dream time, he had no idea how many years had passed. If not for the desire to see his family again, he would have given no thought to going back. After all, he was happy. The ancient people of the plateau had healed his heart with their generosity and freed him from the woes of his ego, yoking it to the needs and rhythms of the tribe. One foot in the world of the unseen, he had found an Eden more beautiful than anything he'd ever dared hope for.

Away with the men of the tribe hunting deer when the couple from Montreal passed through, Atan returned to find their tire tracks next to the firepit. On one of the altars in the crook of a tree, he spied a tiny piece of meteorite, or maybe it was an ancient bullet shard. Whatever its origin, it felt like a bad omen, but he left it alone and helped the other men skin the deer. That night, festive after the hunt, they feasted on venison, washed down with pulque, and drummed until after dark.

The next morning, following a night of fitful dreams, Atan woke to a blood-curdling cry. Sitting up on the foldout bed in the rear of the van, he looked out the front window to see men on horseback wielding swords and muskets, their steel helmets flashing in the sunlight as they chased down the people of the tribe. Sliding open the van's side door, he saw conquistadors raping two of the women beneath the trees, their hands tied behind their backs while they kicked and screamed. He watched horsemen set upon several of the elders, cutting them down with bullets as they fled into the tamarind grove. On the riverbank, a marauder grabbed a baby from the arms of his dead mother and plunged the wailing boy under the water, holding him there until the current carried away the tiny corpse. Turning around, Atan saw a conquistador stride into the clearing with four young men captured in the fighting. Forcing them to kneel in front of him, he went along the line with his sword, their severed hands thudding into the dirt like wet fish as he passed.

Upon seeing what the conquistador had done, Atan lunged at him, intent on getting hold of his sword and striking him down—the rapists about to feel his wrath, too, if he got his way—but he merely stumbled through the man, who was more ghost than not. Realizing he was unable to intervene, Atan closed his eyes to the nightmare, willing himself to return to the present, but after so many years, he couldn't pull free. Returning to the van, he passed a wretched day as the rest of the tribe fought on, their spears and arrows no match for the breastplates worn by the Spanish, whose bullets tore into their flesh, leaving the plateau strewn with bodies.

Within a month, those who survived to bury the dead were overcome by an illness they had never seen, their skin erupting in boils until, weakened by fever and vomiting, they were dying too. Unable to escape the carnage, Atan witnessed it all—the first days of genocide in a conquest for wealth by the already rich, a global scouring that had continued throughout old Ataninnuaq's life and up to the present.

Not long afterward, as Atan sat alone by the fire one night, he heard a sound foreign to that place but familiar to him—the rhythm of the large flat drum played by the Inuit. Roused from an abject sorrow, he was startled to see old Ataninnuaq step into the light with his drum. Leveling his gaze at Atan, the old man, to Atan's surprise, spoke to him in Elizabethan English.

"This visitation," Ataninnuaq said gravely, "is but to whet thy almost blunted purpose."

Atan knew the words. They were Shakespeare's, spoken by the ghost of Hamlet's murdered father, come to coax the prince to exact revenge for the fallen king's death.

But it wasn't revenge the old *angakkuq* wanted from Atan. It was resistance.

"Have you seen enough?" Ataninnuaq asked, turning to look at the sick people lying on mats beneath the trees, disbelief in their eyes.

"Yes," Atan said.

More than Nine-Eleven or the hundreds of thousands left dead in Afghanistan and Iraq, Atan's last days in the desert had brought him face to face, after more than half a lifetime, with just how bad people could be. Yes, he had seen enough. He wanted to resist. But what chance did he have when Ataninnuaq himself had not been able to stand up to the colonialists? Why did he expect Atan to succeed when he, a powerful *angakkuq*, had failed?

"Why me?" he asked.

"Because you're white," Ataninnuaq said.

It was true. Thanks to the color of his skin, Atan had power that old Ataninnuaq had never possessed. There was nothing he could say to refute it.

"What should I do? Where should I go?"

"The wolf has three heads," Ataninnuaq said, sitting down next to him, the fire almost out. "Choose one."

"I don't understand."

"Vatican City sent us the priests, didn't it? The City of London sent the bankers, and Washington, DC, sent the soldiers."

"Three heads."

"One brought deception, one brought debt, and one brought death. But Washington is closest. That would be best, don't you think?"

Atan thought about it. "My passport's no good."

"I know. But I've made arrangements. A fisherman named Oscar will take you over the border."

"Where?"

"Follow Highway 2 to the coast and walk north to a beach called Costa Azul. He's waiting for you."

With that, Ataninnuaq stood up and thumped his drum, chanting in Inuktitut as he stepped under the trees to perform the last rites for the dying. Dancing from foot to foot, he swept low over their bodies, his guttural cries rising and falling with the rhythm, each syllable echoing into the darkness. As Atan watched him, the branches of the trees withered, barren of avocados and mangoes once more. He looked about to see the water in the river cease to flow, no longer lapping the shore, as the arroyo returned. Ataninnuaq's voice grew dim, like he was a long way off, and he vanished, too, taking the last of the people with him.

The next morning, after trimming his beard and cutting his hair, Atan swapped the loincloth he'd been wearing for a clean T-shirt and jeans. Touching his forehead to the hood of the van, he thanked his desert home for its shelter and said farewell. His canteen still full from the river, he stuffed the last of the harvested mangoes into his duffel bag, along with his worn blanket, and walked the dirt track—no longer a tamarind grove—out to the road. On the first highway going east, he pushed on through the state of San Luis Potosi and walked across the state of Tamaulipas, reaching the Gulf of Mexico five days later.

When Atan arrived at the beach called Costa Azul, a bare-chested fisherman rose from a hammock outside his hut.

"*Hola*," the man hollered as he strolled across the sand to meet the traveler he'd been told was coming, extending a calloused hand.

"You must be Atan."

"That's me," Atan said, meeting his grip.

"*Bienvenido*. I'm Oscar."

"I guess you've been expecting me."

"Yes, come inside. My wife is making tortillas."

Over a dinner of red snapper, rice, and beans, with a generous stack of handmade tortillas, Atan learned that Ataninnuaq had appeared to

Oscar in a dream. A descendant of the Atakapa people, whose civilization had thrived there years before, Oscar was old enough to remember the ways of his grandparents. He'd been taught never to ignore a dream, he told Atan, so he was going to do what Ataninnuaq had asked of him.

After dark, when Oscar went out in his boat to fish, he took Atan with him, the stars a current they followed north, the moon not yet out. Before long, crouched at the bow, Atan saw a light bobbing toward them across the water. Waving his flashlight in response, Oscar cut the motor, and another boat came alongside them.

"This is my brother, Jorge," he said. "He's going to take you from here."

Atan tossed his duffle bag into Jorge's boat.

"Thanks for everything," he said, stepping across the gunwales.

"Don't let the old man down," Oscar said.

Atan smiled, trying to hide his uncertainty about what lay ahead. "I'll try not to."

Jorge handed Atan a blanket, telling him to get down and cover himself up. Seated on a bench in the stern, his bony knees drawn up to his chin, he turned the boat around while Atan tried to find a comfortable place to lie down amid the nets and buckets in the bow. Then Jorge revved the motor, and they were off.

Jorge lived in Port Isabel, a town in Texas, Oscar had told Atan. As long as he stayed hidden, the agents along the border would suspect nothing and let old Jorge go about his business.

Before sunrise, just as planned, Atan scrambled out of Jorge's boat under the cover of dark.

"I'd tell you to avoid the highway," Jorge said, "but no one's going to figure on a white guy sneaking into the United States. If anyone asks, say you got here from Brownsville, to the west."

"Brownsville," Atan repeated. "Got it."

On the road leaving Port Isabel, Atan hitched a ride with a man and his young daughter, the girl sitting between them on the front seat of a late-model pickup truck as they cruised north toward San Antonio.

"Seems everyone's going to Washington," the man said when Atan told him where he was headed.

"Why's that?" Atan asked.

The man tilted his baseball cap back off his forehead.

"The uprisings. Don't tell me you haven't heard what's going on."

"I've been away a while."

Hunched between Atan and her father, the little girl, freckled and shy, had become immersed in a video game she was playing on a cellphone—at least, it seemed to be a phone—the likes of which Atan had never seen.

"What year is it?" Atan asked.

"Seriously?" the man chuckled.

"Yeah."

"Twenty twenty-two."

"What?" Atan sat bolt upright. "Oh, you're kidding, right?" he asked, starting to smile.

"Nope. Even the kid knows that."

His stomach sinking, Atan thought about his parents and sisters—how much his long absence must have worried them. He looked out the window at the passing landscape, more green than he'd seen in years. What had he missed while he was gone? What world was he returning to?

As the asphalt rolled away beneath them, the young girl asleep with her head against Atan's arm, the man explained that uprisings had been rocking the capital off and on for more than two years. Massed in Lafayette Square across from the White House, people had first gathered in 2020 under the banner of a protest called Black Lives Matter in response to the serial murders of unarmed, handcuffed Black people shot dead in the streets or in their homes by racist police.

Racist police—the age-old arm of the state's power over those deemed wild, uncivilized, less than human, Atan thought. The Black Lives Matter Movement sounded like pre-emptive self-defense.

But the protests, the man went on, had morphed into something else, becoming a stand against racist wars in the wake of Iraq, Libya, and Afghanistan, each decimated and abandoned by the marauders of the day.

"What we've done to those countries is ugly," he said.

Atan felt sick, recalling what he had watched the Spanish do to the people of the desert.

"I can imagine."

"Now, the surveillance state the feds created for the War on Terror is watching us," the man explained. "All dissidents are criminals, not just the usual scapegoats, but everyone else too. They're all there protesting—Blacks, whites, Indians, immigrants. You name it, they're there."

"What are their demands?" Atan asked.

"They want a new system, one where we don't have to choose between millionaires backed by other millionaires, both sides suckin' the dicks—"

Catching himself, the man glanced down at his sleeping daughter.

"I mean, *sucking up* to the deep-state bankers and billionaires."

As they drove past Corpus Christi, the young girl awoke just long enough to rub her nose and tell Atan he smelled like fish.

"Sorry about that," he said.

"That's okay. I like fish," she said with a yawn.

"They want to kick over the moneylenders' tables," Atan said.

"Yup. They want all the crooks out. But it ain't gonna happen. You can't change a system. You gotta change people. And people like money. That's just how it is."

In San Antonio, the man insisted on dropping Atan at the bus station. His ex-wife's place was close by, he said, so it wasn't a problem. Anyway, he was happy for a few more minutes with his little girl. As

Atan got out of the truck, the man told him to stay clear of the uprisings.

"You'll just get your skull cracked open," he said. "And who will that help?"

"Not me," Atan said.

Aboard the next bus to Washington, Atan fell fast asleep, feeling like an apparition, back in the world but not fully. The changing parade of passengers to which he awoke when the bus stopped in Houston seemed carnivalesque, so exaggerated were people's personalities, as if everyone had taken up one stance or another, all trying to shout over the rest with the volume of their clothes and hair, their sexual convictions, their blunt politics. Some people were stances unto themselves, declarations that ended with an exclamation mark! Had people always been that way? Atan couldn't recall.

Two days later, arriving in Washington, he was thrust into the world of the living and all the cares it entailed. With his cash almost used up and his bank card expired, he would have to see about getting his hands on some money if he was going to rent a place. Locating a branch not far from the bus station, he explained his predicament to the teller, who was happy to help.

"Looks like you haven't used this account in a while," the woman said, gazing at her computer monitor, the tips of her fake fingernails clicking against the keys as she typed. "But that shouldn't be a problem."

"Can you tell me the balance?" Atan asked.

"Sure, just one sec—."

The woman stopped typing and looked at Atan. Picking up a pen, she wrote an amount on a slip of paper and passed it across the counter.

The number floated before Atan's eyes, so many digits. Was that thousands or was it—no, wait—millions? It was millions.

"Is this my account?" he asked.

"Uhm, yes—yes," the woman assured him. "Do you want to make a withdrawal?"

Outside the bank, his wallet full of hundreds, enough for rent and then some, no YMCA for him that night, Atan sat down on a bench, bewildered, uncertain whether to laugh or cry. Surely, what Atan thought of as spirit, or God, must have been grinning. Despite himself, his album had given him what he'd always forsworn—wealth. He felt elated but dirty, blessed but tarnished. As soon as he could, he would find a way to make his songs downloadable for free, he decided. In the meantime, all he could do was make good use of his windfall.

First off, that meant buying a guitar. His encounter with old Ataninnuaq in the desert had made him want to play music again. Coming into town, he'd even pulled out his notebook and jotted down some new lyrics, his pen bouncing up and down on the page as the bus navigated potholes.

After renting an apartment on the top floor of a townhouse on Twenty-Third Street, about twenty minutes on foot from the uprisings at Lafayette Square, Atan went out and got himself a new Gibson J-45, its rose-hued body fading to burnished honey under the sound hole and around the bridge. Compared to playing his old guitar, it felt like he was putting on a stiff pair of new boots every time he picked this one up. But he practiced till his fingers bled, his skills slowly returning as he sat by his open front window, the din of the traffic on Washington Circle carried on the warm spring air.

Two weeks later, his days given over to meditation, music, and long looping walks along Rock Creek Trail that brought him back to Twenty-Third Street, Atan was starting to feel like his old self, only better. He'd even managed to fatten up on falafels and pizza at the Aroma Cafe around the corner on Pennsylvania Avenue. However, he hadn't yet ventured east to Lafayette Square. He would go when he was ready, he told himself. He wasn't going to rush in.

Then, on a Friday night in mid-May, Atan woke to blaring sirens, an endless cacophony that stretched on nearly till morning as if living itself had become a crime to which every police car was racing, an emergency calling forth every fire truck and wailing ambulance. Atan could no longer ignore the maelstrom gripping the city. It was time for him to do as Ataninnuaq had asked.

In the morning, he made his way along H Street, startled at the sight of so many police cars and military vehicles. Ducking under a barricade on the north side of Lafayette Square, he stepped into a world of chaos where torn tents and scattered belongings littered the ground at the feet of a seething throng of people, many wounded and bandaged, the air crackling with the energy of alarm. Walking deeper into the crowd, Atan came upon a skinny white college-aged kid sitting under a tree with his phone.

"What are you watching?" Atan asked him.

"Last night's riots," the kid said, handing Atan his phone. "Some cop lost his gun."

On the screen, Atan saw a curbside reporter clutching a microphone as she tried to keep her hair from blowing in her eyes.

"So, there you have it," she pronounced. "The chief of police says a firearm is unaccounted for after last night's standoff with protesters. She could not tell me how the officer was separated from his gun or where it is now, but clearly, the situation in the capital has deteriorated over the past twenty-four hours. Back to you, Joy."

"Thanks, Gloria," said a studio anchor seated behind an orange desk in the station's newsroom.

"So, what happened?" Atan asked the kid, returning his phone.

"We got attacked. The police were itching to do it for a while now, ever since that new order from the president saying we had to take our tents down."

Atan sat next to him cross-legged in the grass.

"There were a lot of tents here?"

"Hell yeah, hundreds. A whole city. They came in on horseback in the middle of the night swinging poles with hooks on the end, and they were just galloping by and pulling down tents. People got trampled and shit. Then a wave of cops on foot came through, beating everyone with clubs, binding their wrists with zip ties. All along H Street, they had these paddy wagons lined up just waiting to haul us out of here. I think almost four hundred people got arrested in less than an hour."

"Where were you?" Atan asked.

"I climbed a tree," the kid laughed. "Now, everyone's pointing fingers at each other. The Black Lives Matter folk, who outnumber the rest of us, they blame Antifa—"

"Who's that?" Atan interrupted.

"Antifa?"

Atan nodded.

"Man, you just crawl out from under a rock or what?"

Feeling out of his depth, Atan shrugged.

"You could say that."

"You're not a journo, are you?"

"A reporter? No. Not even close."

"Okay. Well, the Antifa people are the so-called anti-fascists. They're all about direct action, which is like code for violent action. They don't want to change the government—they want to overthrow it. If you ask me, they're government agents. You know, provocateurs. They almost always wear bandanas over their faces, and they're the ones looting and setting stuff on fire—storefronts, cop cars, shit like that. Anyway, the Black Lives Matter folk blame Antifa for last night, but Antifa blames them because a bunch of Black guys got into a battle with the cops at the barricades yesterday."

"What do you think?" Atan asked.

"I'd like to know who dropped off the pallet of bricks that mysteriously appeared at the entrance to the park yesterday morning. If there weren't any bricks, no one would've ended up throwing them at the cops. No bricks, no violence. Know what I'm saying?"

"Makes sense," Atan said.

The kid went back to staring at his phone, head bowed, his spine curved against the tree trunk. Watching him, Atan mulled over the young man's words, certain the opposed factions had been easy to divide—their energy bled off into squabbles with each other—because at the root they were afraid. The Black protesters had been terrorized across the years into fearing for their lives. The others, not used to overt oppression, feared losing their freedom to the state under full-spectrum surveillance. And all of them feared a president who daily used the military to assault peaceful demonstrators, filling the air with drones and swooping helicopters, the streets a theater for armored vehicles and roving snipers. It was fear the protesters had in common, and this fear had put them into a collective hypnosis that had blinded them to the real power they had. After all, united in their stand against the deep crimes of an elite few, they were a formidable force and should have been unstoppable.

Atan wondered what would happen if the protesters could tap into this trance that had taken hold of them, using it as a bridge to the unseen self, to the inspirited and inspirational, to the timeless well of the mind. What if spirit could be brought to bear on the struggles that were culminating there in Lafayette Square, uniting the opposed factions like a tribe?

"How long have you been here?" Atan asked the kid.

"Since last fall. Left school and never went back. Don't plan to either, not until we see this through."

"Where's home?"

"Nashville."

"Oh, yeah? I've always wanted to go to Nashville. For the music, you know."

"Yup. That's the place for it."

"So, do you know any of the leaders here?"

"There're really no leaders. It kinda depends on what's happening. But yeah, sure, I know a few. There's one guy who has been here as long as anyone. When he says shit, people listen."

"Can I meet him?"

"Uh-huh. He should be around here somewhere—unless he got arrested."

Getting to their feet, Atan and the kid pushed through the crowd until they reached the center of the square, where a handful of protesters lounged beneath a statue of President Andrew Jackson, a cruel slave owner reviled for his hand in the Indian Removal Act of 1830, Atan knew, which had forced Native Americans of the south to surrender their ancestral lands and relocate. Treating the people like cattle, government militias had herded tens of thousands to a territory west of the Mississippi River in migrations that saw countless thousands die. The statue, with four cannons at its base ready to fire in all directions, each draped in vines of purple flowers, showed Jackson poised for battle atop a rearing horse, a fluttering peace flag tied around his neck like a cape—the man now a paragon of racist evil and genocide that no one in the square was ever going to celebrate again.

"Anyone seen Wheels?" the kid from Nashville hollered.

Behind the low, spiked fence that encircled Jackson's statue sat a young woman with bare feet, a pair of combat boots beside her in the grass.

"Over there," she said, pointing past the statue. "He's holding court."

"Any news?" the kid asked.

"They trucked in more bricks this morning."

"You serious?"

"Yeah. There're pallets of 'em piled up by the intersection."

"Fuckers!"

Stepping over the fence, Atan and the kid went around to the other side of the statue, where the one they called Wheels, sitting half-lotus in the grass, regaled his listeners with tales of the night before. Sporting a big belly that made him look like a Buddha, he had a boisterous laugh that started as a nervous chuckle before erupting into mirth. Atan recognized the man at once. Staring up at him, his face eroded by time, his mustache as unfashionable now as it had been on the day they'd met, was Brad Wheeler, a bandage across the brow of his badly swollen left eye.

"Fuck me!" Wheeler shouted. "I'm seeing a ghost!"

Leaping to his feet, he wrapped Atan in a bear hug and wouldn't let go.

"What the fuck?" he kept saying.

At last, he thrust Atan away from him with both arms so he could get a good look at his old friend.

"Do you guys know who this is?" Wheeler asked the others sitting there.

There were blank faces all around.

"This is Atan!"

"The singer?" the kid from Nashville asked.

"Yes!" Wheeler boomed.

"I heard you were dead," the kid said.

Atan laughed. "Not nearly."

"I knew you weren't dead," Wheeler said, all smiles.

Struck by an idea, Atan was smiling too. Here was the ally he needed. Together, he and Wheeler might be able to change what was going on in Lafayette Square.

"What are you guys doing tonight?" Atan asked him.

"Same as every night," Wheeler said. "Trying to stay one step ahead of the cops."

He touched the bandage above his eye.

"Last night, I got thirteen stitches for my trouble."

"Let's try something different," Atan said.

"Like what?"

"I want to do a show."

"Where—here?"

"Yeah. Tonight."

"How're you gonna do that? We got no stage, no sound."

"We could bring all those bricks and pallets in from the street and use them to build a stage right here in front of the statue," Atan said. "And we can get the people I saw making speeches at the barricades to let us use the portable speakers they've got over there. Instead of facing off with the police tonight, you guys can turn your backs on them and face the stage. We can turn our backs on the White House, the cops, all their shit. If we ignore them long enough, they might just wither up, no? Why give them your energy? Why bleed for them?"

Just then, a big black crow landed on top of the head of Andrew Jackson's statue and let out a squawk, as if to affirm the idea. It was Atan's crow, the one that had reappeared across his life. He hadn't encountered the bird since the day he'd moved to Montreal, but a vision of animal bones tied into its tail feathers flashed before his eyes, and he knew it was the same one.

"So?" Atan asked, grateful for the omen. "What do you say?"

"Won't work," Wheeler said. "The police will come in here to clear the park, just like always."

"Not if there're too many people," Atan said. "Not if everyone's packed in shoulder to shoulder so the police can't get near the stage. Not if the television cameras are rolling and the crowd is peaceful and the vibe is high."

Atan was electrified but calm. He knew exactly what needed to be done.

"Alright," Wheeler said. "When word gets out on social media that you're doing your first live gig in over a decade right here tonight, people will come by the busload."

Wheeler swung around to look at the protesters he'd been talking to when Atan and the kid got there.

"Well, you heard him," Wheeler said. "Go get those bricks and as many pallets as you can find."

A gaggle of twenty-somethings roused themselves in the afternoon heat.

"You got it," said a young man with a goatee and horn-rimmed glasses, his gaze hard and serious as he looked at Wheeler.

"That's Terrence," Wheeler said.

Beside Terrence sat a round-faced boy of the same age, his pudgy hands folded in his lap.

"And that's his cousin Marcus."

"Hi," Atan said, nodding to the boys as they pulled themselves up from the grass. "Thanks for the help."

"They grew up in Harlem and graduated from MIT together. They're smart *and* street-smart. If you need to know what's what on the ground, ask them."

"We'll get us a crew," Marcus said, and off they went.

"You seen Kara?" Wheeler asked the kid.

"Combat Kara?"

"Yeah."

"She's over there," the kid said, pointing back the way he and Atan had come.

"You guys get online and tell people what's going on. Start with the activist forums and then the music blogs and the gossip sites." Wheeler grinned. "Tell everyone Atan's alive, and the son of a bitch is performing here at nine o'clock—just in time for the new curfew that came down this morning. Got it?"

"Done." The kid's phone was already out as he went off to tell Kara.

"You've got some pull," Atan said to Wheeler.

"Nah. They just like having someone to look up to."

"I'll be back later. Bring your guitar."

"You just got here," Wheeler protested.

"I've got a new song to rehearse."

Hopping back over the spiked fence, Atan navigated through the mass of people as he made his way out of Lafayette Square, intimidated, he had to admit, by so many Black people in one place. There it was—the racism, he thought. Where did that fear come from? It had to be the white man's lies. The same old bullshit stories.

Heading home, Atan stopped at the Aroma Cafe, where he used the pay phone to call up Terra Blues in New York and get a number for Brooklyn Willy. It turned out he was still living in the house he'd always shared with his sister in New York. But Brooklyn was away.

"You know how he is, always roaming," his sister said. "But he's got his phone with him. Let me get you the number."

After jotting down the digits on a napkin with the waitress's pen, Atan plugged more quarters into the phone and made the call.

"Brooklyn?" he asked, hearing a voice on the line that was familiar but gruffer than he remembered.

"Yeah, this is Brooklyn. Who's this?"

"It's Atan."

"What!"

"It is. It's me."

"Good God, boy, you trying to give me a heart attack?"

"Where are you?"

"Son, I'm in Washington, DC. Where the hell else would I be? Question is—where are you? More than ten years you don't call me."

"I'm sorry about that. But listen, you got your sax?"

"You know I do. Why?"

"I'm here too. I'm doing a show tonight in Lafayette Square and I need you to play."

"Lafayette Square? Boy, are you crazy? The po-po gonna crack your head if you're in there after dark."

"Not tonight."

"Why not?"

"Trust me."

"Why should I trust you?"

"I need a band too."

"A band? You want me to get a band together just like that?"

"Brooklyn, there's not a city in this country where you don't know at least a half-dozen top-notch players. Am I wrong?"

There was a long pause.

"What time?"

"Nine o'clock."

"Okay. I'll make some calls. But son, you better be right. I'm too old to be running from the police."

At nine o'clock, when Atan climbed up onto the makeshift stage erected between two of the cannons at the base of Andrew Jackson's statue, the crowd in Lafayette Square stretched out in front of him all the way to Pennsylvania Avenue, its flanks hemmed in by Madison Place to the east and Jackson Place to the west. Behind him, more people pressed in from H Street. As Wheeler came on stage and picked up a microphone, buses continued to roll in with people from out of town.

"Shit, this is big," Atan said, glancing at Brooklyn Willy, who was seated stage left in a Black Lives Matter T-shirt, looking dignified in his gravity.

He'd brought along a bass player and a drummer, two young cats hot from the clubs. Everyone was plugged in and ready to go.

"See these guys in the front here with their phones trained on us?" Wheeler asked Atan, pointing. "They're going to be live streaming the show for the people farther back, so don't worry about the volume. I've got you covered, man."

Atan was impressed. "Okay."

Wheeler looked out at the crowd.

"Welcome!" he bellowed into the microphone. "This is the Turn Your Back concert."

The crowd whistled and roared.

"For you guys way out there, you can find us at #TurnYourBack and watch us on your phone. Tonight, we turn our backs on the White House and the cops. We turn our backs on the whole damned shit show!"

The crowd erupted again, hoots of approval rippling toward the stage.

Atan took his microphone from its stand and looked out at the crowd as the people grew quiet again.

"It's been a long time since I said anything political," he began.

"It's a long time since you said anything," Wheeler quipped.

"That's true," Atan laughed. "The last time I did, it was about Nine-Eleven, and it got me in hot water. I know, I know, we're not supposed to talk about Nine-Eleven. But, hell, we can call a lie a lie in this country, can't we?"

The crowd whooped and hollered its agreement.

"There's another lie we've been told," Atan said. "It's the lie about race. There are no races. Racism is real, and it's ugly. But we don't look at the Joneses and say, 'Man, those Joneses all got similar-looking ears. They must be a different race.' No, family members look alike because they share genes. What we call race is not race, but family resemblance. And across families, we share more genes than not, don't we? These genes make us a single race, the human race."

A few "amens" and "hallelujahs" rose above the cheers of the crowd.

"I'd like to ask a question," Atan said. "When the white nations get together and launch illegal wars that kill hundreds of thousands of brown-skinned people, why doesn't anyone cry racism? What makes our white leaders any different from cops who murder Blacks in America? There is no difference, and until we stop consenting to these wars, along with the genocide of Indigenous peoples on reserves and reservations, we're all implicated in racism."

A few "uh-ohs" drifted toward the stage, but there were some more "amens," too, for Atan had struck a chord of truth that people acknowledged. Nationalism was at its root racist.

"And more than our genes," Atan said, "what binds us together is spirit, the animator of us all."

Atan put his mic back in its stand, and he had just picked up his guitar, ready to start the show, when three cordons of black-helmeted police officers with shields and batons entered Lafayette Square from Pennsylvania Avenue, pushing their way far into the audience. As the officers advanced, one hundred strong, the panic of the crowd swept toward the stage like a portentous wind. A glint of fear in his eyes, Brooklyn Willy got to his feet and took Wheeler's microphone out of his hand.

"Shame!" Brooklyn Willy shouted into the mic, pointing at the marching lines of police, robotic in their movement, anonymous behind their face guards. "Shame!" he shouted again, his finger wagging. "Shame! Shame! Shame!"

Like a flock of sparrows swooping as one, the front of the crowd swung around in the same instant and, spying the advancing officers, joined in with Brooklyn Willy, fingers wagging.

"Shame!" the people shouted. "Shame! Shame! Shame!"

The cry was taken up across the square, everyone pressing in upon the police, whose cordons soon melted together into a jostled mass, the crowd closing in behind them to block their way out. At last, the advance stopped, the officers shoved so closely together that they could not even lift their arms to raise their batons, never mind strike anyone.

"Shame! Shame! Shame!" the crowd hollered, fingers pointing.

From the video drone flying overhead and streaming live to Facebook, the police looked like a black poison injected into a single brightly colored cell that was determined to force it out again. For over ten minutes, the blot of poison swayed a little this way and a little that way, the chanters never letting up—"Shame! Shame! Shame!"—until the officers, exhausted, turned around and pushed their way back toward Pennsylvania Avenue, the crowd parting just enough to let them out.

Arrayed behind the barricades, their tails between their legs, the police could do no more than look on as Atan stepped up to his mic and strummed a long, mournful note that drew the attention of the audience back to the stage, stillness descending once more as the sound of crickets in the trees rose on the night air.

"This is a new song," Atan said. "It's about these days we're living in. It's called 'Biblical Times.'"

He nodded at the bassist, who came in with a low *"du-doh-du-doh,"* a smile creeping out from under his newsboy cap, pulled low over one eye.

"Bah-bah," Atan strummed.

"Du-doh-du-doh," the bassist replied.

"Bah-bah," Atan strummed again.

"Du-doh-du-doh," the bassist played again.

"Wah-wah," Brooklyn Willy added.

"Got blood on the wall," Atan sang. "Blood on the street. Blood in the water. Blood at your feet. Oh yeah, child, these are biblical times."

"Ta-ta, ta-ta, ta-ta," the drummer played underneath.

"Maybe I should run for cover," Atan sang. "Buy a gun. Get ready for slaughter. Hide my son. Hide my daughter. Oh yeah, child, these are biblical times."

Wheeler joined Atan for the bridge to the next verse, their guitars talking to each other like old women at prayer.

"They tell me that my enemy is my brother standing next to me," Atan crooned. "Got to close my heart and lose an eye. Oh yeah, child, these are biblical times."

"Amen," a woman near the stage called out.

"Got blood on the wall," Atan sang. "Blood on the street. Blood in the water. Blood at your feet. Oh yeah, child, these are biblical times."

"Wah-wah," Brooklyn Willy continued, taking the bridge this time. *"Wah-wah, wah-wah."*

"The battles of forgotten years grow rotten with the mold of old men's tears," Atan sang. "We fight their wars again for fun, and bodies fall one by one. Oh yeah, child, these are biblical times."

Throughout the crowd, heads nodded in solemn agreement, the soulful groove of the song working its way into people's hearts, Atan thought, the mood becoming evangelical.

"You ask me what it's all about," Atan sang. "It ain't no mystery. There's no doubt. The world's standing at hell's gate. Oh yeah, child, these are biblical times."

As the final bridge ended, the drummer and bassist fell silent, Brooklyn Willy's last note trembling underneath the strumming guitars until only Atan and Wheeler continued playing.

"Got blood on the wall," Atan sang. "Blood on the street. Blood in the water. Blood at your feet." Almost whispering now, the guitars growing silent, he brought the song to a close a cappella. "Oh yeah, child, these are biblical times."

After a brief hush, the crowd broke into an outpouring of what Atan could only think of as love, thunderous applause flowing over the stage like a river and touching all the musicians. Something big was happening, something important, and he could tell they all felt it.

The show carried on past midnight, the players buoyed by adrenaline and infectious energy as Brooklyn Willy led them in funkified covers of jazz and soul standards that had the audience dancing like they hadn't danced in a long while. Just when it looked like everyone was too tired to carry on, a van from New York rolled up, and almost a dozen musicians tumbled out, their instruments in tow. As the crowd parted and they neared the stage, Atan turned to Brooklyn Willy.

"What's this?"

Brooklyn grinned. "I told you I'd make some calls."

He pointed at the approaching musicians.

"And see there. They've brought you something that will kick the daylights out of that slick-ass Gibson J-007 or whatever it is you got now."

Looking closer, Atan saw that the first musician over the spiked fence was carrying his old guitar.

"How—?"

"Found it on your stoop," Brooklyn said. "Thought you might need it one day."

With a crop of fresh players, the show continued all night, stopping the next afternoon only long enough for a crew to set up a proper sound system and erect a circular stage around Andrew Jackson's statue that left him sticking up out of the middle, his cannons immersed beneath the floorboards.

The show stretched on for days and then weeks, with musicians arriving from all over the country and as far away as London and Cape Town to join in. To make it all work, the restaurants in the neighborhood fed the audience, posting signs in their windows that read #TurnYourBack so people would know where to go for food. Homeowners posted signs, too, so people would have a place to sleep and shower. Wheeler was on the phone with the mayor's office every day to coordinate garbage collection and maintenance of the portable toilets lined up along Sixteenth Street, which the mayor had renamed Black Lives Matter Plaza when the uprisings began back in 2020.

The protesters had created their own tribal utopia within feet of the White House, but as the days passed, it all started to feel too good to be true. Atan knew the government hadn't lost the battle, just the upper hand, and he worried it couldn't last forever. He needed to figure out their next move.

SEVENTEEN

2042

It's almost midnight, and I can't sleep, a book open on my chest, a pair of drugstore reading glasses perched on my nose. The young woman who brings my groceries gave me the book the last time she was here, along with a jar of arnica ointment for my arthritic hands, made from plants she grows herself. The book is a Western by Zane Grey called *The Fugitive Trail*. Printed in 1963, its pages are yellowed and falling out. It's not something I would have chosen to read. I've never cared much for genre fiction. But she said the book is one of her favorites, so I agreed to give it a try.

The book's cover describes the hero as a man "doomed to lie, kill, and forever ride the fugitive trail," and even though I've never killed anyone, there are unsettling parallels between his fate and mine. Like him, I've lived for years in danger of discovery without ever knowing which quarter it might come from. And like him, I'm growing paranoid. I still don't know who wrote the taunting note I found under my door, and I am preoccupied with speculation about who left it.

As if on cue, there is a knock at the door, and I jump. Who can it be at this hour? I hear the postman snoring in the room next to mine, so it isn't him. And the student upstairs left with her boyfriend not fifteen minutes ago, the sputtering engine of his Volkswagen bus making me nostalgic for a van I owned years ago, the last time I felt truly free. It could be my schizophrenic neighbor, but she has been silent since returning from the hospital, and in any case, she seems too fearful of people to go knocking on the door of someone she hasn't met. In fact, come to think of it, that makes her exactly the sort of person to leave a note.

"Hello?" a plaintive voice calls out.

I'm immediately relieved, certain it's the actress from across the hall. I've never seen her, but I've heard her rehearsing for auditions. She has the gravelly vocal chords of a longtime smoker and favors monologues by the likes of Lady Macbeth and Blanche DuBois. She must be at least middle-aged, maybe the high-strung type.

"Yes?" I ask.

"Hello?" she whispers. "Sorry to trouble you."

Getting out of bed, I open the door to see a woman who looks nothing like I imagined—a tall blonde, not a short brunette—her eyes darkened by stage makeup.

"Hi, I'm your neighbor, Margaret," she says, turning to point at her door. "Or just Margie is fine."

"Everything okay?"

"Is my cat in there by any chance?"

"No," I say, and right then, her cat emerges from under my bed, rubbing against my ankles, bigger now than when I last saw it. "Oh, I guess it is."

"There you are, Mr. Naughty Pants." The actress bends down and scoops up the cat. "He got out when I left this afternoon."

"I didn't know he was here. He must have slipped in when I went to the bathroom."

"Oh, it's terrible how there's only one per floor, isn't it?" She glances through the open bathroom door at the claw-foot tub, a rubber hose attached to the faucet because there's no showerhead. When I bathe, I have to crouch down and hold the hose over my head to rinse off.

"Sorry to be knocking so late, but I've just come from a show—a play."

I recall my own days on the stage—how I hated the letdown of going home to an empty apartment at the end of the night.

"How did it go?" I ask her.

"Fine," she says. "But I have a small part. That's what happens when we age, doesn't it? We get smaller and smaller parts to play." She looks at me with a conspiratorial glint in her eye, seeming to imply that, as an old man, I must know what she means. "Especially when you're a woman," she laughs ruefully.

"I suppose that makes for a lot of waiting around in the green room."

"Where?"

"The green room. Do they still call it that?"

"Oh, yes. Yes, it does. A lot of waiting." The cat paws at her hair. "Well, I should get him some dinner." She peers past my shoulder into my dimly lit room. "Good night. Sorry if I woke you."

"Good night." I close the door and lock it.

Now, I'm troubled. An actor would know the name of the room where you listen to the performance so you don't miss your cues. Perhaps she's an agent. Then again, maybe "green room" isn't a common term anymore. How would I know? But what was all that about having a smaller part to play? Did she mean to suggest I'm deluded to think I might have any role in the events now unfolding, even if I can do nothing more than inspire. All this conjecture is going to drive me mad.

I get into bed and try to quiet my mind, but I toss and turn for the longest time. The more I think about it, the more convinced I am the note was written by that poor woman with schizophrenia. But how on earth would she know who I am?

Falling asleep, I dream of a frozen shoreline littered with slabs of broken ice that jut skyward, piled there by a turbulent sea. The voice of my schizophrenic neighbor drifts toward me. "Over here! Over here," she cries. In the distance, across a wasteland of snow and rock, I see her waving her arms. Behind her, tucked into a bay near a ring of cliffs, sits a whaling ship that would have been used early in the 1900s, its sails furled, rows of gulls perched along the rigging. Dwarfed by the ship, my neighbor keeps waving. "Over here!" she cries again. "I found the captain."

The captain, I think. So it's not a spaceship she's been going on about but a whaling ship. The captain appears on the deck and calls down to her, pointing at me, but I can't hear what he's saying. My neighbor becomes frantic, waving her arms again. "Come!" she shouts at me. "Come!" But I stay where I am. "Commme!" she screams, her voice jolting me wide awake. The house is silent. A shimmer of daylight has formed around the edges of the curtains. It's almost morning, and I've been asleep for hours.

Dreams, I learned long ago, belong to the world of the unseen. They are as real as the ground we stand upon. Last night I was in that world with my distraught schizophrenic neighbor and a whaling ship captain. I don't know what the dream meant, but I'm sure the woman has something to tell me.

EIGHTEEN

2022

Onstage in Lafayette Square four months after the first night of the Turn Your Back concert, Atan strutted across the screen of the television mounted above the gas fireplace of Bacchus Altwied in his penthouse suite on the eighty-fifth floor of 432 Park Avenue in New York, one of the highest residential buildings in the Western Hemisphere and a jewel of Billionaires' Row.

Still spry at eighty-three, Bacchus thrust himself out of his high-backed, brass-studded leather armchair and stood scowling at "this hooligan," as he'd taken to calling Atan. For Bacchus, a retired president of the World Bank Group, an adviser to every American president since the days of Richard Nixon, and the oldest descendant of nineteenth-century sugar baron Lloyd Altwied II, there were only two kinds of people: winners and losers. The Altwieds had been winners. Bacchus was a winner. And it was the duty of the winners to direct the lives of the losers, who were ignorant of what was best for them but deluded enough to believe they weren't. In Atan, Bacchus saw the worst kind of loser—an idealist who didn't know his place. Most troubling, Atan had ended the violence in Washington after Bacchus had gone to so much trouble to keep the intersections stocked with pallets of bricks.

"Didn't we learn anything from the sixties?" he grumbled to himself, an embroidered gold peacock fluttering the length of his silk sleeve as he muted the volume on the television and took his phone out of the pocket of his royal blue housecoat.

"Why is this singer still making so much noise in Washington?" Bacchus asked when his assistant answered. "Find out who signed him. Tell them to cancel his record deals if he doesn't shut up. Track him down on Facebook, Twitter, and all the rest. Look at all the pissers and moaners who follow him. Find something! I want him ruined by dinnertime."

Slipping the phone back into his pocket, Bacchus sat down in his chair and unmuted the volume on the television. On the screen, Atan stormed to the end of a virtuoso performance of "Love Is Not Democracy," the crowd singing the chorus with him as the image cut to footage of the sprawling thousands in attendance, the stage a tiny oasis in their midst. "Love is what will set us free!" Bacchus heard Atan promise as the song came to a close. This was a powerful idea, a dangerous idea, Bacchus thought. Surely no one believed it. But as he watched Atan bantering with the audience, Bacchus could see this hooligan was planting buoyant, radical thoughts in people's minds that shouldn't have been able to take root in a time of fear. In these matters, Bacchus was well versed, for not only could he entrance and manipulate the unwashed masses, he also fancied himself a practitioner of the esoteric arts who could access the astral plane for his own ends.

At the age of twelve, browsing the shelves of his father's library in the east wing of the family home in Upstate New York, Bacchus had come across a book on occult wizardry from which he had gleaned a few tricks for focusing the mind and casting spells. It was true that in matters of outright indoctrination and enforcement of his will, he had relied on the teachings of Edward Bernays and Niccolò Machiavelli. From Bernays, the godfather of propaganda and a nephew of Sigmund Freud, he had learned the art of manipulation. And from Machiavelli, for whom politics was a game not subject to the common morality of life's losers, he had learned the arts of treachery, crime, and murder.

However, in a few instances, Bacchus had found it necessary to resort to direct intervention in the astral realm to get his way.

This hooligan Atan was just such a case, Bacchus decided. Along with whatever dirt his assistant might find, a little bad luck was sure to trip Atan up like so many pretenders before him. Shutting off the television, Bacchus got to his feet and drew the curtains. He dimmed the lights and crossed the room to an alcove in the wall, where a black candle stood in the center of a pentagram. After lighting the candle, he took a kernel-like, blood-red pomegranate seed out of a golden bowl and placed it in his mouth. Swallowing it, he fell into a trance that made him feel invincible.

"As above, so below," he uttered three times, summoning the astral plane to bear upon the earthly world. "Bring this hooligan to submission, rid him of all ambition, render him my fool," Bacchus intoned. "By the power of the ancients bent to my will, I make it so!"

Bacchus was about to blow out the candle to seal the spell when a loud bang spun him about. In a flurry of royal blue silk, he ran to the window and pulled aside the curtains to find a nickel-sized hole in the outer pane of glass. There, on the sill, perched a large black crow with a chipped beak and menacing yellow eyes. Opening its beak, the crow screamed into Bacchus's face. Terrified, he let go of the curtains and fell to the floor. In all his life, he'd never seen any proof his incantations actually sent ripples into the astral realm. Humbled and emboldened all at once, he scrambled across the carpet on his knees, pulled himself to his feet, and blew out the candle with great gusto, certain now this hooligan Atan was truly someone with whom he needed to reckon.

As Atan left the stage in Lafayette Square in Washington, he heard the bang, too, far off across the desert of his mind like a memory surfacing, but more urgent. Before he had time to wonder what it was, a Fox

News reporter named Larry Smiles thrust a microphone in Atan's face and dragged him into his third interview of the day. He should write a manifesto, he thought, so he wouldn't have to repeat himself all the time. But the fact was that he didn't know what he would write. Atan was making things up on the spot, as if improvising a song.

"How long can this concert keep going?" Larry Smiles asked.

"As long as it needs to."

Atan knew the reporter had been scolded by the network for his feel-good coverage of the Turn Your Back movement, which had spawned concerts and utopic enclaves across the world. Now, it seemed, Larry Smiles had decided to adopt a more critical stance. His boss had likely told him to.

"Who's going to decide how long that is—you?" Larry Smiles asked.

"No. We'll all decide, including you. This concert is a conversation."

"What's the end game, a world of lazy freeloaders looking for a handout? I'm seeing a lot of that around here."

There it was, Atan thought—no one could deny the crimes decried by the protesters, so it was time to attack the messengers.

"The end game may be a general strike," Atan said. "If that happens, the economy will suffer, and the tax base might even dry up, leaving governments unable to fund themselves. But only then will better ways be possible. It's not like we don't have enough for everyone. We have more than enough. And no one can say we don't deserve to be free of control. We were born with that freedom. The problem is a system run by criminals. It can't stand."

"You want socialism?" Larry Smiles asked. "Or maybe communism?"

"No, I want—" Atan thought about it. "I want a world where materialism is not the grounds for all action and art."

"We live in a material world. How could it be otherwise?"

"No, our world is inspirited. We are inspirited. We ignore spirit at our peril."

Larry Smiles looked dumbfounded.

"So, you want a system based on spirituality?"

"No. Why do you need a word? Call it spiritism."

"I don't understand."

"Spirit can't be understood, Larry. You have to feel it. Stick around, and you'll see what I mean."

With that, the interview ended, and Atan was back on stage.

That night, at the kitchen table in Atan's apartment on Twenty-Third Street, Wheeler watched Atan's exchange with Larry Smiles on his phone.

"Spiritism?" Wheeler asked. "I always said you'd make your peace with God. But what the fuck?"

Atan had been jousting with Larry Smiles and talking off the cuff. But he couldn't deny what Wheeler said. Atan had come to see God and consciousness as inseparable—the stuff of spirit. The ego was just a mask worn by spirit so it could know itself in relation to itself. Yoked to the material world, the ego was lifted by joy and buffeted by pain, but spirit, what Wheeler used to call the Tao, was the timeless and unperturbable well of the mind, the source of truth and love. While in the desert, Atan had learned to listen to the promptings of this spirit-self like an *angakkuq*.

As for Wheeler, he'd changed too. His pent-up anger at the Man had become focused, he'd told Atan, when his now ex-wife took him to live in Seattle and introduced him to the Outliers, a tight crew of computer anarchists known for punishing immoral corporations with crippling downtime. Money was the only thing capitalists understood, they argued. The bastards had no hearts, so you had to hit them in their wallets. Wheeler hadn't learned to hack, but he'd come up with some of the group's more audacious escapades, like when they'd hacked the locks on the Saint Lawrence River to shut down shipping, which Terrence and Marcus had spent almost a year figuring out how to do. In fact, Atan realized, Wheeler was being modest when he said he had some pull around Lafayette Square only because the younger folk needed someone to look up to. Many of them were hackers, too, and for them, Wheeler was a legend.

When he'd arrived in Washington, Wheeler had stayed in the suburban basement of Combat Kara, a hacker with the Outliers. Since the Turn Your Back concert began, he'd been crashing on Atan's couch, the two hashing out plans to redirect the revolution. If they weren't on stage at Lafayette Square, they were holed up at Atan's apartment debating strategy.

For his part, Atan was growing weary of the speeches threaded throughout the music each day. The rhetoric of the various activists who took the stage was as old as slavery and as outworn as capitalism. Yes, police brutality needed to end and communities needed to be safe for everyone. No, of course, no one should be silent in the face of injustice and inequality. But people had been saying these things forever. The protesters lacked a frame of explanation to support the aspiration for change. Their unity had no foundation beyond the old adage to love your neighbor as yourself, which was rooted in self-interest, not in mutual recognition of each other as spirit. People had to know the unifying force of spirit before there could be change, Atan insisted.

But Wheeler wasn't interested in Atan's preoccupation with the unseen. Having tasted the thrill of direct action with the Outliers, Wheeler wanted more of the same. He was willing to go along with the Turn Your Back strategy for a while, but what he really wanted to do, he said, was bring the whole system down and start over. In this way, he had more in common with the Antifa faction among the protesters than he did with Atan.

"The deep state is like the Mafia," Wheeler told Atan again and again. "You've got to wake up to that. These people don't play by everyone else's rules. History shows it. The Kennedys? Malcolm X? King? Assassinated! Same thing with Nine-Eleven. Outright murder! Snuff TV. How do you fight that? Fire with fire."

"That's all you can come up with?" Atan asked, seated at the table opposite Wheeler.

"These are biblical times. You said so yourself."

Atan looked out the kitchen window.

"Listen to that."

Beneath the sounds of traffic in the street, the patter and boom of distant drums rose on the night air. In recent days, the show at Lafayette Square had turned into a jam, with audience members joining in on djembes Atan had bought by the dozens and distributed to the crowd. For blocks in every direction, day or night, you could hear what people were calling the peace drums.

"Listen to what?" Wheeler asked.

"The drums. We did that. We can turn that into something."

"Then we'd better do it soon. When the summer ends and it gets cold, everyone except the diehards will pack up and go home. This is all gonna be a sweet memory, and we'll be back where we started."

"We could launch a pledge, something everyone could agree to do even after this is over."

"That's just more words. More talk. We've got to hurt the fuckers."

"What about decentralization? We could pledge to turn the whole system on its head. Instead of money trickling down from the feds, people could pay their taxes to the states and the cities, where they actually live, and starve the feds."

"A pledge to defund the federal government?"

"Yeah, defund the feds and you defund the military."

"It won't work."

"Why not?"

"Because people are cowards. They're terrified of the IRS kicking in their door. Or the FBI. You haven't seen what goes on now. They won't do it."

"Then we have to make them fearless."

"How do you do that?"

"You wake them up to spirit."

The conversation had come full circle, neither Atan nor Wheeler giving or gaining any ground. They agreed that everything had to be decentralized, from taxes to food and energy, so households and cities could become self-sufficient enough to free themselves from the deep-state pirates, but they couldn't agree on how to do it.

"'Turn Your Back'?" Bacchus snarled at the morning's headline in the *New York Times*. "Not on my bloody watch!"

Picking up a serrated spoon, he carved a perfect triangle of pink flesh from the half grapefruit on his plate and slipped the morsel into his mouth. In the headlines of the other newspapers spread out before him, even in the *Washington Post*, he found the same endless dribble about these so-called back-turners. If anything, instead of breaking into competing factions and stumbling under its own weight, the Turn Your Back movement was gaining momentum as if animated by a spirit that could not be resisted.

Three weeks after casting his little spell, Bacchus had failed in all his efforts to bring Atan low. Learning he did not have a record deal after all, Bacchus had called up the CEO of Warner Brothers to put in motion an offer from Nonesuch Records in the hopes of bringing Atan to heel, unaware he'd already declined an offer from the company more than a decade ago. Bacchus hadn't known what to make of it. Didn't this guy crave money like everyone else? Prepared to play hardball, Bacchus had scrambled to find some dirt on Atan but could get no leverage. Off the radar for more than a decade, he had no Facebook page, no Twitter account, not even a phone. Except for a page on MySpace that hadn't been updated in years, he was a ghost.

Done with his grapefruit, Bacchus wiped the juice from his chin with a linen napkin and dialed his assistant.

"Who the hell sells his music?" he asked.

"Well, he was using iTunes and Google Play but—"

"Then have him yanked!"

"That's the thing. He stopped. You can get his songs for free now."

"Son of a bitch. The mockery!"

Bacchus picked up a crystal carafe and tippled some vodka into his coffee.

"Has he been paying his taxes?"

"I couldn't find out. He's Canadian."

"Canadian? Then get him deported for Christ's sake! What are you waiting for?"

"I can't. He renewed his passport at the Canadian embassy last spring, and thanks to the mayor of Washington, he currently has a work visa as a performing artist."

"Goddamned Washington!" Bacchus bellowed, shoving the newspapers into a heap at his elbow.

There was nothing left to do, he decided. Atan would have to go. He took a deep gulp of his coffee. The more he thought about it, the more he liked the idea. A public shooting would be best. It would terrify the onlookers, putting them once more under fear's spell, and it would get the conspiracy mill churning so the revolutionary energy that was so distressing him could be bled off into squabbles between the protesters about the trajectory of the bullets, the angle of the sunlight, and whatever other obfuscating nonsense Bacchus could come up with. Oh, after all these years, he still got a kick out of leading fools around by the nose.

Bacchus planned the assassination to a tee, particularly pleased with his idea to use a new drone gun in case the shooter missed the mark. Light and stealthy, able to fire fourteen rounds, it would get the job done. Most important, the gun had been tested exclusively by Israel against Palestinians in the West Bank, so witnesses to the shooting, having never seen the gun before, wouldn't be able to imagine it. There would be no end to the speculation he could create, Bacchus reasoned, to say nothing of the outright denial it made possible for those on the inside. As for the shooter—a meth addict in debt to a bookie Bacchus knew—he had been easy enough to find. The chump could either do what he was told and go to jail or refuse and go to his grave.

On the first day of October, during an afternoon break in the music at Lafayette Square, Atan went on stage for a press conference to announce what the protesters called the People's Pledge. In its pages, they vowed allegiance to leaders who would decentralize the banks and put an end to usury so money could never again be used to amass more money. They vowed to seek the decentralization of capitalism by turning corporations into co-ops so the excess fruits of people's labor could never again accumulate in the hands of a few. And they vowed to turn taxes on their head so communities could thrive while the military went begging.

As Atan picked up the microphone, he saw the spark of a gun barrel an instant before he heard the shot—the lightning before the thunder. Shocked into a trance, he could sense the bullet in the desert of his mind as it sped toward him through the still air, its atoms vibrating so fast and hot he could smell the steel. With an intensity of focus he hadn't managed since the day he'd killed the wolf in Frobisher Bay, he willed the atoms to grow sluggish. As the bullet slowed, it became colder and denser until, just inches from Atan's face, it turned to stone and fell straight down at his feet, making a dull thwack as it hit the floorboard.

At that moment, a second bullet zipped toward the stage from above—so high above that even in a clear blue sky, whatever had fired it was invisible to the naked eye. But this shot didn't hit Atan either, for as soon as the first bullet fell at his feet, Atan's crow, watching from its usual perch atop Andrew Jackson's head, soared into the air and screeched past Atan's head, the bullet passing through its chest as the bird slammed into the stage in a mess of gore and strewn feathers.

As Atan lunged to the inner edge of the floorboards and jumped beneath them, hidden with Jackson's cannons, a third bullet tore through the air. Peeking out, he watched it slice into the neck of Brooklyn Willy, who slumped over on the stage, crushing his saxophone with his hip. Crawling on their bellies, the drummer and the bass player reached the side of the circular stage and scrambled down into the crowd of panicked spectators now rushing toward H Street. Motionless amid the chaos, eyes wide as a stone bullet rolled toward his feet, stood Wheeler.

Atan came out from under the stage and crawled to Brooklyn Willy, whose blood had pooled beneath his head. Frantic, Atan glanced around the park for anyone who could help, but there was no point, and he knew it. Brooklyn was dead.

"Look there," Wheeler said, pointing.

Atan got up and walked toward him. In the grass not ten feet away lay a white man—the shooter?—bloodied and unconscious, with two angry Black men looming over him, ready to kick the man again if he needed it.

Wheeler pointed at a gun on the ground where the man had fallen. "Recognize that gun?"

"No," Atan said.

"That's a police gun—a motherfuckin' police gun, Atan!"

As a cordon of police rushed into the park from Pennsylvania Avenue, the two Black men picked up the shooter and dragged him along the paved path to meet them. By the time the men dropped the shooter at the feet of the officers, the park was empty, litter tumbling across the grass as a swift breeze, strangely icy for mid-fall, swept down from the trees and whistled around Atan's ankles.

"It was them," Wheeler said, his eyes flashing as he pointed at the police officers who had come to retrieve the gun from the grass, a pair of paramedics rushing behind them with a stretcher for Brooklyn. "It was fuckin' them."

In the distance, the shooter, cuffed and conscious again, was being hauled out of the park by two more officers, one pulling him by the hair.

"What do you mean?" Atan cried. "I don't understand what you're saying."

Wheeler shook his head, disgust clouding his face. "I know you don't."

With the news cameras on hand in Lafayette Square for the press conference to announce the People's Pledge, Bacchus had watched the shooting live on television, unable to believe his eyes. Seeing Atan duck beneath the stage and Brooklyn Willy fall over dead, Bacchus was as mystified as he was enraged. The shooter's bullet had gone astray—that much was clear—but how had the drone missed Atan?

"Goddamn it to bloody hell," he shouted into his phone as he pressed his assistant for a sensible account the poor man couldn't give.

Soon, a contact at the Washington Police Department called to say the detectives at the scene had located two bullets.

"Only two?" Bacchus asked. "There should be three."

"No sir, just two," came the reply. "The one that killed the saxophonist passed right through his neck before it got stuck in the stage floor, and the other was lodged in the spine of a crow we found spattered on the floorboards."

"A crow?" Bacchus sputtered, recalling the one that had cracked his penthouse window.

"Yes, sir."

"Well, never mind that. Officially, there was only one bullet, understand? One shot, one bullet!"

With Atan alive, the plan foiled, there was nothing for Bacchus to do but get out in front of the story and spin it to his advantage. First, he had his assistant parade a crop of crisis actors in front of the news cameras to testify they'd heard the shooter shout a racial slur before he pulled the trigger. In the interest of verisimilitude, the actors gave slightly different accounts, two of them saying it was "Die, nigger!" and the others insisting it was "Die now, nigger!" By dinnertime, this motive for Brooklyn's murder had been set in stone, along with the shooter's status as a lone gunman, a view unchallenged by the slew of videos of the shooting streaming online, all of which recorded a single gunshot, the drone inaudible and unseen. Adding to the credibility of the lone gunman story was the claim that the weapon used was the same one a Washington police officer had lost in a scuffle with a protester earlier in the summer—a brilliant touch, Bacchus thought, regardless of what had happened, as it nicely wove in a pre-existing detail no one could deny.

Next, Bacchus asked the president to declare the whole of Lafayette Square a crime scene, and work crews quickly erected an eight-foot fence around the park, pushing the protesters onto Sixteenth Street. As tear gas billowed beneath the streetlamps along Jackson Place, the city growing dark, Bacchus sat back in his brass-studded armchair and watched a return to the looting, burning, and running battles with the police that had marred the protests and delighted him so much before Atan showed up, the peace drums silent now, the people in wild revolt against yet another racist murder, their piddling pledge forgotten.

"Bullshit!" Wheeler bellowed at the news anchor on the television in Atan's living room when he heard the shooter's gun was supposedly the one lost that summer. "That wasn't the same gun. The police gave it to him!"

Thrusting himself to the front of the sofa chair, he picked up the half-empty bottle of Jack Daniels on the floor between his feet and took a long gulp.

"The higher-ups tried to kill you, man!" he said to Atan, wiping his mustache with the back of his hand.

"We don't know that," Atan said, sunk into the couch, a bag of weed in front of him on the coffee table as he rolled up yet another joint, his nerves shot.

"You still don't get it," Wheeler said. "Well wait—just wait. When Kara gets here, you'll see."

Close to midnight, acting sheepish, Kara arrived with a package for Wheeler, a brown paper bag she pulled out of her steel-buckled, red velour purse and placed on the coffee table in front of Atan.

"Open it," Wheeler said, slugging back the last of the whiskey.

Atan reached into the bag and pulled out a gun identical to the one he'd seen in the grass—the same gun the media had been broadcasting pictures of all evening. A police gun!

"That's the gun the cop lost," Wheeler said. "That's the gun right there."

"Where did you get this?" Atan asked Kara.

"I've been hiding it for Wheels."

"Why? Where did it come from?"

"I'm the one who took it off the cop," Wheeler said. "Remember that little tussle I told you about?" He touched the scar above his left eye.

"You beat up a cop and took his gun?" Atan asked.

"No—well, yeah. But it wasn't like that. I was running from those cops on horses when I ducked into the alley by the YMCA and slammed into the guy. He was about to crack my head open with his baton."

"Why did you take his gun?"

"He wasn't going to chase me without his gun."

"Nope," Kara said, taking a hit of Atan's joint.

"He would've shot me."

"He would've, Atan," Kara said.

Atan stared at the gun where it lay next to the ashtray on the table.

"The shooter got his gun from the police," Wheeler said. "And there was more than one shot."

He struggled to his feet and fished around in the front pockets of his jeans, finally pulling out the bullet Atan had turned to stone.

"They can lie all they want, but they didn't count on this, did they?"

He placed the bullet on the coffee table in front of Atan.

"You picked it up?"

Wheeler nodded. Too drunk to stand, he sat back down, the cushion sagging under his weight.

"Want to explain how you did that?"

"I didn't—"

"Is this some of that desert shit you were telling me about?"

"I don't know how I did it."

"They're calling it a miracle," Kara said.

"Who are?" Atan asked.

"Everyone. It's all over the Web."

It was true. If Brooklyn's murder had succeeded in thrusting the protesters back into aimless violence, as Bacchus had intended, it had utterly failed to thwart Atan. Instead, when people looked at videos of the shooting frame by frame, they saw a bullet slowing to a halt mere inches from Atan's face and dropping out of the air. Some even claimed the crow seen crashing to the stage had saved Atan's life when it was hit by a second bullet, visible only as a blur. That was two miracles in one! The propaganda trolls unleashed online to bolster the cover story denied that anything out of the ordinary had happened, disparaging the stone bullet footage as fakery and the bird footage as a fantasy, but the damage was done. Within hours, among a generation hungry for more than the deadening materialism of their times, Atan had been elevated from a singer to a saint.

Kara snuffed out the joint in the ashtray and went to answer a knock at the door.

"Who is it?" Atan called after her, shoving the gun back into the paper bag.

"It's Terrence and Marcus," she answered from the hall. "And Nash." The cousins from Harlem shuffled into the room, followed by the kid from Nashville.

"Good. Everyone's here," Wheeler said.

"What's this?" Atan asked, moving over to make room for Terrence and Marcus on the couch.

"A meeting," Wheeler said as Nash and Kara sat down on the floor. "It's time we got serious."

"I'm not waiting for no cops to come shoot me in my bed," Terrence said.

"We're no Mark Clark and Fred Hampton right here," Marcus added.

"Why would they do that?" Atan asked.

Wheeler looked at Atan.

"They sent someone to gun you down, man. What's next?"

He cast his eyes upon each of his friends.

"How many years now have these fuckers been killing us? And all we do is sing songs about love and democracy. That's what they want. From now on, we're gonna play by their rules, okay? Their rules! I don't like it, but they made them, not me. We're done with street protests. They don't change fuck all."

"So, what are we gonna do?" Nash asked. "Tell me what to do, and I'll do it."

"We're gonna put the fear of almighty God into them, that's what," Wheeler said.

"Uh-huh," Marcus said. "I hear that."

Atan looked at the brown paper bag on the coffee table.

"We've got the gun. We can prove they lied. We'll go to the media—"

Wheeler laughed, frustration erupting from deep in his belly like he was a beast waking in its lair, surly and vicious.

"Yeah, just like we proved they lied about Kennedy and Nine-Eleven?" he asked, his words soaked in scorn. "No, we've tried truth. We've given them facts and evidence, but they don't care about all that. They've won. We'll play by their rules now."

"You're right," Kara said, lighting another joint.

"They want us to kill, we'll kill," Wheeler said.

"Word," Terrance said, pushing his horn-rimmed glasses up the bridge of his nose.

"Yeah, they win," Nash said.

The room was silent except for the sound of rain spattering the front balcony and the splash of tires in the street below as a storm front swept in, threatening snow.

"You're drunk," Atan said.

"Listen. Tell me this," Wheeler said, holding up a finger. "If there were a hundred people on an island and one of them was living off the backs of everyone else, sending them into wars for no reason, murdering anyone who disagreed, would we stand by and do nothing or cut the fucker's throat while he slept?"

"We're not on an island," Atan said. "So, unless you want to start killing innocent people, hacking traffic lights and subways and whatever else—I don't know, elevators—then shut up."

"He's right," Nash said. "We can't kill just anyone."

"Elevators," Marcus said, a grin creeping across his round face. "Elevators have cameras. It's easy to see who's in them and when. We can target people."

"What people?" Atan asked, angry now.

"The richest of the rich," Marcus said. "The deep-state gangsters."

"The penthouse dwellers," Terrence said. "The higher they are, the harder they'll fall."

"Oh, that's poetry," Wheeler chortled. "Icarus scorched by the sun."

"We should do it," Kara said.

"Oh, we're doing it," Marcus said.

"So, we're murderers now?" Atan asked.

"In war, there's no murder," Wheeler said.

"What about you, Nash?" Atan asked.

"I don't know anything about hacking."

Wheeler laughed. "Don't worry. We'll find something for you to do."

"Killing won't change anything," Atan said. "You guys know that. The world's problems are spiritual, not material. They can't be fixed in a material way. I've said this before. You've heard me say it. People need to see, at root, we're united by spirit. When people get that, things will be different. Evil comes from one illusion—the idea we're not inspirited, that we're divided. But we're connected by spirit, all of us, even our enemies. The people you want to kill are evil because they're ignorant of what we are."

"Not all of them," Wheeler said. "The worst of them know what they're doing. They play with the spiritual plane while telling us it doesn't exist. You've said so yourself."

"They deny it because they don't want us to use its power," Atan said. "If we give up on spirit, we surrender that power. And that power is your soul. What does it profit us to gain the whole world but forfeit our souls?"

Wheeler shook his head and chuckled. "You're quoting Jesus now?"

"The guy knew a thing or two," Atan said.

"Why should our souls be more important than this world?" Wheeler shouted. "If we keep doing things your way, there'll be nobody left to save and no planet. A few nukes, and it'll all be over. Time's up. When are you going to get it?"

Outside, the wind whistled down off the rooftop, the rain turning to sleet as Atan tried to find the words to explain a truth that seemed too obvious to need repeating but too illusive to express.

"We don't exist for our own sake but for—love. Call it love," he said. "If you become killers, you'll be giving up on love. Without it, the soul is lost, and there's no point to anything."

"Love gave up on the Black man a long time ago," Marcus said.

"A long, long time ago," Terrence said. "And now Brooklyn's dead, yeah?"

"Shot down," Wheeler said.

"And killing people is the way of the Tao?" Atan asked Wheeler.

"It's the way of the world," Wheeler slurred. He looked at the others. "That's where people like us live."

Atan had heard enough. "We're done talking about this," he said. He was met with blank stares. "I'm serious—the meeting's over. Get out."

"Yeah?" Marcus asked.

"Yeah. Out."

Marcus got up from the couch. "Okay. Our bad."

"Let's go," Kara said to Nash, pulling herself up off the floor.

Atan looked at Wheeler. "You too. Get your shit and go." He shoved the paper bag with the gun across the coffee table. "And take this with you."

The last one out was Wheeler, stumbling down the stairs with his guitar dangling from his shoulder by its strap, a backpack under one arm. Watching from the doorway, Atan knew a gulf had opened between them that hadn't been there before, leaving each man stranded. Too saddened to say anything that might close it, Atan let Wheeler go, looking on as he staggered outside and into the coming storm.

NINETEEN

2022

When Brooklyn Willy's sister, Maybel, came to Washington to get her brother's body, Atan met her at the morgue, and they flew back to New York together. He stayed in her spare room on Bergen Street in Crown Heights, where the townhouses with outdoor staircases reminded him of the ones in Montreal.

With her brother dead, Maybel had no one to help with the upkeep of the house.

"Winter's coming, and the front steps need mending," she said, sitting on the sofa in her front room, her feet up on a cushioned stool. "The fence is falling down, too, and the brickwork around the windows is crumbling. They tell me I can be forced to sell my home if I don't fix it up. That's right. My father took forty years to pay for this place and now they want me out. New bylaws or some such cockamamie diddle-daddle."

Maybel looked out the window at the darkening street, her eyes rheumy.

"The Italians and the Irish left Brooklyn along with the Dodgers in '57. That's when they turned Ebbets Field into housing for us Blacks coming in from all over—mostly the South, but Jamaica and the West Indies too. The strict Jews were the only ones who stayed. You've seen 'em. Got their long black coats and tall black hats. Now the white folk want it all back. Gonna kick us out and make condominiums."

Atan decided to stay put and help Maybel. It seemed like the least he could do since he was the one who'd gotten Brooklyn killed. After all, Atan had been warned, hadn't he? When he was a boy, Greta from the Bezak Center had said someone would try to shoot him. Atan's mother had told him the stories about Ataninnuaq and Ujarak, the hunter who'd been killed by the yellow priest's bullet. When the crow had first turned up in Lafayette Square, Atan should have seen what was coming. And what about the day he'd talked to Larry Smiles from Fox News? Hadn't Atan sensed someone meddling with his spirit just before he'd heard a bang far off in his mind? What was that all about?

Now Brooklyn was gone, his murder pinned on a patsy, and Atan could do nothing to set the story straight unless he told the press he really had turned a speeding bullet to stone. That would either make him into a miracle worker—and everyone knew how well that had turned out for Jesus—or else make him look like a crazy man, especially since he wasn't about to try to repeat the spectacle.

Worse, even if Atan had stopped the bullet, he felt like a fraud. He wasn't an *angakkuq*. If he'd inhabited the unseen while living in the desert, that was only because of the peyote and the years of ritual that had altered the energy of that place, making it a well for excursions into the spirit world.

Feeling lost and guilty, Atan retreated into himself. When Maybel's friends came to pay their respects, he stayed in his room, watching from the window as they added flowers to the pile blooming on the sidewalk at the bottom of the steps next to an album cover showing Brooklyn Willy in his youth, all smiles. Maybel knew that Atan didn't want to see anyone, but the women insisted on saying hello.

"Now, Maybellene, we won't trouble the boy long," one of them said, using Maybel's full name—the title of Chuck Berry's first hit song, recorded in 1955, the year she was born—just to remind her friend of how close they were.

"Okay, come on up," Maybel called to them.

As the women congregated in the kitchen, Atan came downstairs, saving Maybel the trouble of having to holler for him.

"Boy has the Holy Spirit in him," another of her friends said, putting sugar in her coffee at the kitchen table while Maybel served up slices of lemon loaf.

"Atan and Willard used to play the clubs in Montreal," Maybel said, setting a plate in front of him.

Atan wanted to tell the women that if he had the Holy Spirit in him, they did too. Just like government and money, God needed to be decentralized.

In the desert, Ataninnuaq had told him, "Go to Washington. Go to the City of London," naming the global seats of money and war. But he'd also said, "Go to Vatican City," the global seat of Christianity. Before money and government could ever be decentralized and power returned to people, God needed to be taken off his throne and recognized as the shared animating spirit of all. Atan still yearned to explain these things, but he'd lost the will. Eating his cake, he said nothing.

When a reporter from the *New York Times* finally cornered Atan at a diner on Franklin Avenue, he was tempted to tell her all about the spirit world, if only to throw her off her game. He thought of pouring out his whole life story. But he could tell she wasn't there for that. No, she was clearly hoping Atan would say something she could use against him, aligning him with the so-called conspiracists.

"Was there more than one shot?" she asked as a fly landed on a plucked eyebrow, settling amid the stubble to wash its legs. "How many shots did you hear?" she coaxed.

Atan waited for the reporter to swish the fly away, but she didn't.

"What do you think of this stone bullet story?" Here, the reporter giggled, and the fly zipped down to the tabletop. "What about the people who claim a crow took one for you? What do you say to them?"

"What should I say?"

"Is it true?"

"Could it be true? In your frame of explanation, what is possible?"

"Not magic. Not intelligent crows." The reporter laughed again, a stray hair stuck to her lipstick.

Atan wanted to unstick the hair. He wished she would stop standing over him and sit down. Tugging on his growing beard, he watched the fly alight on the chrome lid of the sugar dispenser.

"The FBI has started a file on you. Is that why you're hiding?" the reporter asked, taking a different tack.

"On me?"

"On all of the protest leaders."

"Well, I'm sure they know where to find me."

"So, why the silence? What have you been doing since you left Washington?"

"Not getting shot."

"But the shooter was caught. He was crazy. What are you afraid of?"

"The shooter was caught?"

The reporter smiled, apparently happy to be back on topic. "Wasn't he?"

Atan watched as the fly buzzed to a halt on the tip of the reporter's nose. This time she swatted it away with ninja precision, causing the dazed creature to crumple into the wall and tumble to the floor.

"Who put you on this story?" he asked.

"My editor."

"And him? I assume it's a him."

"It is."

"Who does he answer to? Whose lies does he peddle?"

"Lies about the shooting?"

Atan knew the reporter was fishing for some kind of grand and unprovable declaration about people scheming behind the scenes of power, but he wasn't about to give her what she wanted.

"Lies about the ego and the spirit," he said with a sigh. "Lies about Satan and God, about all of it, right down to consciousness and the human condition."

Atan watched the reporter's face droop, thinking she must be struggling to fit what he'd said into her desired narrative. She looked like a frustrated child unable to match shapes to their correct slots in a toy. Clearly, she had no idea what Atan was talking about, and he wasn't going to explain.

Walking back to Maybel's house, Atan turned the reporter's words over in his mind like he was counting worry beads, troubled by her revelation the FBI was watching him. Hadn't the FBI kept a file on John Lennon—and hadn't he been gunned down too? There was a spiritual war going on between the hunters and the healers. Everywhere Atan looked, the material had been purged of spirit and bent to commerce. And when someone came along who had the ability to remind people of spirit, showing them their better natures, the hunters gunned them down, covering their tracks with entrancing, hypnotic lies.

What was Atan supposed to do? Should he write more songs and get on with being a singer? How could he ever go on stage again without the risk of someone getting killed? Should he run away? But why do that? The deep state had failed to kill him. He'd stopped the bullet, turning it to stone. Whoever sent the shooter must be afraid of Atan—or at least convinced that he mattered. No, Atan wouldn't run. He would use that fear and attention to locate his enemy. He would be an *angakkuq* and confront his tormentor on the plane of the unseen. But he wouldn't harm anyone. An *angakkuq* wasn't a hunter.

For weeks, Atan holed up in his room at Maybel's house, like a monk in a cave, and meditated, trying to find his way back to the source of the bang he'd heard in his head the day Larry Smiles had interviewed him. For hours, he wandered in the unseen, listening for voices, waiting for apparitions, grasping in the dark. He heard Inuit drumming and caught sight of Ataninnuaq more than once, but the old man never spoke to him. Some days, Wheeler was there, seated half-lotus and floating in the air, a sly grin on his face as he drifted by in what looked to Atan like a beer-induced satori. The only thing he brought back with him from these excursions was a string of numbers that echoed in his mind like a countdown—four, three, two. But he had no idea what they meant.

When he wasn't in his room, Atan helped Maybel however he could. After she'd buried her brother beside their parents in the Cemetery of the Evergreens in East Brooklyn, Atan had cleared away the wilted flowers at the bottom of the stairs, setting aside the cards and notes, along with a teddy bear playing a saxophone and a Terra Blues keychain he'd found in the grass. Now, with the first snow expected any day, he raked up the leaves and mended the front steps, replacing the broken boards with new ones he'd carried home from the hardware store. After straightening the posts of the low picket fence that skirted the sidewalk, he gave it a fresh coat of paint. Most days, he ran errands and did the grocery shopping, avoiding the coffee shops and diners.

Reflecting on his life from the vantage of a middle-aged man who'd failed in love, lost his career, and almost been shot after stumbling into a protest, Atan had grown solemn. Here he was, living in a spare room in Crown Heights, his shipwreck hidden behind a veneer of charity as he tried to pretend he was only there for Maybel. At the same time, his connection with spirit left him alienated from the culture in which he was raised, adrift among others.

Preoccupied with these thoughts, Atan took up his old habit, formed in his university days, of walking the streets for hours at a time, pulled by emptiness and longing toward he knew not what. Hidden by sunglasses and a winter tuque, he took the subway under the East River to Lower Manhattan and went on to Central Park, getting off at the 5th Avenue Station. Here, he found himself at the feet of Trump Tower, right in the shadow of eight ultra-luxury skyscrapers boldly named Billionaires' Row.

It was a part of New York City that Atan had never visited, not once, in all the years he'd lived there, and he wondered why he felt drawn to it now. Day after day, he came back to walk among the people on Madison and Lexington Avenues, the snow-dusted sidewalks glaring in the sun beneath their clicking heels and wing-tipped loafers as they scooted in and out of Barneys and Bloomingdale's with their polished briefcases and brightly colored paper bags.

Was Atan there because he wanted to know the enemy? No, the people he passed in the street weren't bad, he thought. What did he care how much another spent on clothes or shoes? What difference did it make to him if this person or that lived in a swank condo? True, he didn't see the appeal of owning stuff that he figured would just end up owning him, but he had no quarrel with those who did. Live and let live. Like the pickup driver from Port Isabel had said, people liked money, and Atan could understand why. What troubled him was the lie at the heart of the system that made so much wealth possible—the lie that capitalism and democracy were compatible. In a world where individuals could accumulate more money than many small nations, enough to infiltrate and influence every strata of life, enough to direct coups and wars, there could be no real democracy. Instead, Atan figured, the ultimate outcome of capitalism, as waged across time, had always been organized theft and murder—piracy and war.

Seeing himself reflected in none of the blank faces flashing past him along West 55th Street, Atan imagined what it would be like to live among people who experienced reality as he did—as a material fact, yes, but also as an inspirited place where the material is kept in check and the ego along with it. Were there such people, and how would he find them? This question had just formed in his mind when he looked up to see a big red sculpture on the corner of 6th Avenue made of an L and a tilted O atop a V and an E.

Yes, that was what Atan wanted, he thought. Where could he find people who lived for love? A block later, he turned left onto 7th Avenue and stopped in front of Central Park Travel, where a poster in the window for destinations in India declared, “Come feel the love!” Atan had to smile. First the sculpture and now the poster. In his reality, where there were no accidents, nothing was just a coincidence. Everything was a clue. The unseen must be trying to tell him something, Atan reasoned. Maybe he should go to India and seek out its sages, who knew that God itself was the ultimate unseen ground of reality, which they called Brahman. This account of the world could have originated only with the shamans of old, Atan thought. And didn’t the greeting “namaste” say something about the divine in me bowing to the divine in you? Surely, love had to reside among a people who saw the world this way. Atan went into Central Park Travel and grabbed a brochure about India from a display next to the door.

In the street again and heading east, this time on West 54th Street as he looped back toward the subway, Atan flipped through the brochure, reading about the seasons and the monsoons in India. He would need a travel visa and vaccines, he learned. Preparing for a trip like that would take time. And then there was Maybel to think of. He couldn’t leave her in the middle of winter. No, early spring would be good—before it got too hot in India and the rains started. That still gave him a couple of months.

Absorbed by his plans, Atan walked two blocks past 5th Avenue without noticing, but instead of turning back, he made his way toward the subway along Park Avenue, where he soon found himself at an intersection in front of a skyscraper on Billionaires’ Row. To his surprise, exiting the building’s glassed-in lobby in bicycle gloves and a helmet, an orange messenger bag slung across his back, was Nash, his cycling shoes slipping on the snow-slick front steps as he hurried down to the sidewalk and mounted his bike.

Atan ran toward him, calling out Nash’s name, but his voice was muffled by the honking taxis and sighing buses as Nash sped off along East 57th Street. Giving up, Atan came to a stop at the foot of the steps.

Above the front doors of the skyscraper, as tall as a man, gleamed the street number 432. It was the countdown Atan had heard while searching in the unseen for the person who wanted him dead. Had his efforts borne fruit, first leading him to seek his quarry in the haunts around 5th Avenue and at last bringing him to this address? Atan didn't know, and he couldn't fathom what Nash had been doing there at the very same moment. It had to mean something.

One Sunday afternoon near the beginning of January, the tree branches white with snow, Atan and Maybel sat together on her screened-in porch at the back of the house and shared a spliff. The smoke was popping out of her mouth in perfect little rings that drifted through the vines of the potted ivies suspended from the ceiling. The herb helped with her eyes, she'd told him.

"I'm going to be sixty-seven this year," she said. "I'm getting tired, and come spring, all the yard work is gonna need doing."

"Sixty-seven's not that old," Atan said, thinking of his parents, both in their eighties now.

But then Maybel, he could see, had endured a much harder life than them.

"Now that you've got things fixed up, it's probably time for me to sell."

"Not to the developers."

"Heavens, no. I know better. No one's putting a condominium on this land. And no white folk are going to get their hands on this house either. They don't need it. They got their fancy jobs in Manhattan but don't want to live there. Too bad for them. They're not living in this house."

She took a long haul on the spliff.

"My mom used to say white folk were just like white rice and white flour—white cuz the beautiful brown husk with all the goodness had got stripped away, making them dull and mean. I know that's poppycock. I know a good person when I see one. You're a good person for sure. But that don't make any matter. I'm not going to sell this house to white folk. I'm going to sell it to a Black family who don't want to be renting no more, people who need something to hold onto."

"Where will you go?" Atan asked, taking the spliff.

"Oh, I've been looking at one of those communities for us seniors where you get your own apartment, and you can cook your own food, the whole deal. But there're people around to help out when you need it. If Willard were alive, I wouldn't think of it."

Soon Maybel found a buyer for the house, a couple with two children who attended the same church as she did. They were an upstanding family, Maybel told Atan, and the father had a good job at an auto glass shop over on Flushing Avenue, the same job he'd been at for nearly thirteen years. The catch was that they didn't have the down payment for a mortgage. Atan offered to give them the money himself. He had more than enough just sitting in the bank. But Maybel insisted on calling it a loan, to be repaid by the family as they went along.

When the deal was settled, Atan told Maybel about his plan to go to India in the spring. That week, he applied for a travel visa and submitted to a round of hepatitis vaccines before buying a ticket for the first day of March. Flying out of LaGuardia Airport in Queens, he would stop to visit his parents on the Toronto Islands in Lake Ontario, where they had moved after his father retired. Anxious to be gone, Atan counted down the days, longing to be free of his dark sunglasses and tuque, which only made him feel doubly removed from a world that didn't seem to understand him. Soon he would lose himself among India's billion and a half people, ideally in some rural outpost that civilization hadn't reached yet, where the fabric of life was spirit itself.

On February 22, at 8:07 a.m., Bacchus Altwied left his penthouse suite at 432 Park Avenue and boarded the elevator for a long descent to the restaurant on the twelfth floor. Two minutes later than usual because he'd misplaced his heart pills, only to discover they were in his breast pocket all along, he was looking forward to his usual salmon benedict breaded with braised pistachios, to be downed with a mimosa or two, the orange juice freshly squeezed. As soon as the elevator moved, Bacchus knew something was wrong. He was gaining speed. Too much damn speed! Harried, he pushed the emergency stop, but nothing happened. The illuminated buttons had gone dark. Above him, the security camera blinked red, watching his terror.

"No, no, no!" Bacchus hollered as his fear turned to rage.

He tried the buttons again, pushing them all to no effect. He spat and fumed, cursing God and man. Never since he was a boy and his father took the belt to him for not polishing his shoes had Bacchus ever felt more powerless. It was a feeling he'd been running from all his life, fortifying himself with money's influence and a callous disregard for those he deemed weak. The losers. Recalling the belt's lash, Bacchus buckled to his knees, whimpering as the elevator whistled down through the shaft in the center of the building.

"Fuck, fuck, fuck!" he moaned, the air squeezed out of him, his body heaving upward as if he might float.

The next instant, the lights went out, and in absolute darkness, Bacchus crashed to his death, his legs shattered beneath him, his arms torn from their sockets and dangling like a rag doll's, his spine pushed up through the back of his neck as the floor rose to split his skull against the ceiling, dislodging his eyes, shattering his cheekbones, and scattering his teeth.

Having just gotten out of the shower, Atan was dressing in his room when Maybel called out to him from downstairs. Descending to the kitchen, he found her at the table, a half-eaten bowl of oatmeal at her elbow, her eyes fixed on the small television that sat atop the counter across from her.

"It's awful," Maybel said. "Awful. Look at those poor people."

On the screen, Atan saw live footage from 432 Park Avenue. According to witnesses, an elevator in freefall had slammed into the third sublevel beneath the lobby with a ghastly thud, rocking the building and sending pulverized cement and metal shooting upward through the vents in the first floors. Panicked residents had fled through the hallways and stairwells to congregate in the street, uncertain whether to linger or keep running, the obscene collapses of Nine-Eleven still vivid. Now, amid the flashing lights of fire trucks and ambulances, the police were tying off the area with yellow tape and pushing onlookers onto the sidewalks across the intersection while a ruddy-cheeked, cherub-like field reporter, the picture of the American boy next door, stood in the foreground expounding on the latest details.

"What we know for sure is an elevator here at fabled 432 Park Avenue has fallen," he said. "The elevator may have been descending from the penthouse, on the eighty-fifth floor of this incredible skyscraper, but that is still to be confirmed. As you can see behind me, the FBI is on the scene. We don't know if this was an accident or something worse, but because so many of the residents who live here are among New York's wealthiest and most influential citizens, a thorough investigation is underway."

The reporter touched his earpiece.

"One second," he said. "I may have an update." After a moment, he looked into the camera, stricken. "Two more elevators have fallen in Chicago and Boston." He fiddled with his earpiece again. "Wait—make that three. Another one has just gone down in Philadelphia."

"Somewhere, the horses are eating each other," Atan muttered.

"What?" Maybel asked.

Atan shook his head, too anxious to explain.

Within a span of twenty minutes, as the pair looked on, a skin forming on Maybel's oatmeal, elevators fell in eight more cities across the country, from Detroit to Seattle, repeating the nightmare and carnage seen in New York. With fourteen dead in twelve attacks, the nation on high alert, all elevators across the land were shut down until further notice.

At 9:20 a.m., when security footage from the fallen elevator in New York confirmed the death of billionaire Bacchus Altwied, son of nineteenth-century sugar baron Lloyd Altwied II, Atan was certain what had happened. Even if he hadn't seen Nash leaving 432 Park Avenue a month before, Atan would have known. He didn't need to wait for an investigation to find out. The notoriously rich targeted in the other attacks, their names reported across the morning, filled in the blanks, making palpable what had been mere banter in his Washington apartment months ago.

Dead in the fallen elevators were an arms dealer pardoned by the last president, an oil magnate poisoning rivers with arsenic, two CEOs of pharmaceutical companies hiding deaths in clinical trials, three war profiteers heading companies contracted by the feds, two couples using their charitable foundations to hide genocidal dealings in undeveloped countries, and two deep-state players whose money had bought murder again and again.

On the television, Atan watched burly men in black gear, FBI emblazoned across their chests, exit the shattered lobby carrying evidence bags. Maybe they'd found a hard drive with some sort of incriminating code left behind, Atan thought, feeling sick. He wondered if the FBI had been keeping tabs on others in his Washington circle. Had they been watching Nash too? Did they know he'd made a delivery to 432 Park Avenue in January? If they did, would they catch him? Would he talk? They would ask him whose idea it was to hack elevators, wouldn't they? Well, it was Atan's idea, Nash might say. Atan was there when the decision was made. He knew about the plan and did nothing to stop it.

Atan hadn't taken the talk of hacking elevators seriously. He'd blamed it on shock and grief—also Wheeler's drinking—in the hours after Brooklyn Willy was gunned down. But Atan couldn't prove that. Directly or indirectly, he was involved. What if Nash named him along with the others? The government would declare them terrorists, freeze their bank accounts, and hunt them down. Atan needed to run before anyone implicated him.

Leaving Maybel at the kitchen table, he went upstairs to his room and logged into his bank account. After transferring as much money as he could to the accounts of his sisters and parents, he wrote to say he would let them know where to wire him cash in India. To avoid a risky stopover in Toronto, he booked the next direct flight to New Delhi. He still had to wait a day before he could leave, and he wouldn't land in India until the day after that, but it was the best he could do.

Meanwhile, as all the papers would later report in detailed timelines, the investigation was unfolding just as Atan feared. Even before attempting to recover the hard drive of the fallen elevator, the FBI scanned the security footage from the lobby of 432 Park Avenue and spotted Nash. With facial recognition software, its technicians could see anyone of interest in their database who had passed that way, including all the people photographed commiserating with Atan and Wheeler at the Turn Your Back protests.

By noon, Nash had been identified, the delivery logs showing that on January 25 he'd dropped off an envelope addressed to the chef of the restaurant on the twelfth floor. Inside the envelope, the chef told the FBI, he'd found a brand-new smartphone. Oddly, upon opening it, he'd found it powered on. Seeing no note, he'd concluded that the phone was a gift from one of the restaurant's many wealthy patrons, and he'd given it to his son.

When FBI agents examined the phone, they discovered it had sent a software update to the elevator's hard drive on the day it was delivered to the restaurant's reservation desk, likely while the building's concierge ascended in the elevator with his deliveries. Only three hours after the death of Bacchus Altwied, the FBI was already close to figuring out Nash's part in the scheme—how the update had caused the elevator carrying Bacchus to go into freefall at a time chosen by the attackers according to his habits, easy to track once they'd cracked the building's Wi-Fi network card and hacked into its security cameras, enabling them to find out everything they needed to know about his comings and goings.

Just after 2:00 p.m., even though the hard drive in Bacchus Altwied's elevator turned out to be unreadable after the fall, the FBI found a record of the fatal software update sent by the smartphone Nash had delivered. It was on the building's mainframe computer, logged there during a virus sweep. Nash went from a person of interest to a prime suspect, and the FBI's search for him intensified.

By the next morning, with the help of airport security footage, the FBI had tracked Nash to Seattle, where he had left the airport in a taxi. Locating the driver, the FBI got an address for an apartment on Avalon Way in the name of a woman the agents couldn't identify until they realized she was—"Ready for it?" the lead investigator asked his colleagues—Wheeler's ex-wife. He had lived there with her after moving to Seattle from Vancouver when they were first married, and apparently, he'd acquired the apartment in their divorce but had never changed the name on the deed of ownership.

On the West Coast since December, where he'd set up the crews that took down the elevators in Portland, Los Angeles, and San Francisco, Wheeler had played the role of the bicycle courier in the Seattle attack.

At midday on February 23, Wheeler and Nash were together at the Avalon apartment. Seated on the couch in front of the television in the living room, they watched their handiwork on the news and debated what to do next. Wheeler thought they should release the footage from inside the falling elevators.

"It would be no different than watching the towers go down," he said.

Nash didn't like the idea. He tried to explain to Wheeler that until the elevators fell, he'd been able to disconnect his role in the plot from its gory end. Now, feeling like he was going to suffocate, he didn't want to watch the video of Bacchus Altwied's descent.

As Wheeler reached for a can of beer on the coffee table, the front door splintered with a deafening bang, and a dozen SWAT agents crashed into the room with a battering ram.

"FBI," they hollered, their semi-automatic rifles at the ready.

One of the agents, mistaking the beer for a gun—or so he would claim at trial—swung his rifle around like a nunchuck and struck Wheeler with the butt end, splitting his face from ear to mouth. About to get the same, Nash threw himself on the floor, his hands behind his head. Cuffing them, the agents dragged the pair down three flights of stairs like bags of garbage destined for the curb and chained them to the wall in the back of a van—Wheeler bleeding and furious, Nash white as a ghost. It was treatment reserved for blue-collar terrorists, Wheeler thought. The motherfuckers!

Early in the afternoon, satisfied with Wheeler's assurances that no further attacks were planned, his interrogators turned to the task of identifying the other players. Wheeler could avoid execution, they told him, if he ratted out his friends. The only question was who would crack first and be spared the death penalty—Wheeler or Nash?

By seven o'clock the next morning, in alcohol withdrawal and getting the tremors, his swollen cheek throbbing through a jagged row of forty hasty stitches, Wheeler had nearly reached his limit. But no matter what the interrogators promised him, he refused to talk.

Not until the trial would Wheeler find out that Nash had already given the FBI the whole story, his tears and snot streaking the tabletop as he recalled the meeting in Atan's Washington apartment and how the idea to hack the elevators had come up. He named everyone there. The only thing he couldn't tell the FBI were the names of the Outliers who'd delivered the phones to the other targeted buildings because Wheeler had kept them a secret.

After launching a nationwide manhunt for Atan, Kara, Terrence, and Marcus, the FBI listed their names with Interpol and conducted a search of travel records to see if any of them had left the country. At nightfall, Kara would be arrested trying to enter Canada at a rural border crossing outside Quebec, and a month later, Terrence and Marcus, who had fled to Mexico in January, would be arrested in Cancun and finally extradited.

Flagging Atan's purchase of a ticket to India, the FBI alerted authorities in New Delhi, and airport police rushed to the baggage claim area to intercept the passengers on his twelve-hour flight from LaGuardia Airport, which had already touched down.

Traveling light, as he always did, Atan carried only a single backpack and had no luggage to claim. Clearing security, he glanced behind him to see police accosting the male passengers on his flight, spinning them this way and that to get a good look at their faces. Without stopping to buy a taxi chit, he hurried toward the exit, passing the office of airport security as an Interpol bulletin with his picture came up on a computer screen behind a bank of windows. Scanning the faces of the male passengers now emerging with their retrieved luggage, the agent behind the glass didn't seem to notice Atan as he reached the doors and stepped out into the hazy morning, the air acrid with the smoke of garbage burning in small piles along a nearby road.

As Atan approached the edge of the parking lot, a camel went by pulling a wagon piled with green grapes, and he fell in behind it, walking on amid the sputtering three-wheeled tuk-tuks and rumbling lorries, their cabs brightly painted to look like Hindu gods.

"Horn please!" cried the stickers on the back bumpers of the tuk-tuks as the lorries bore down on them.

Relieved to be out of sight of the airport—grateful to have escaped New York—Atan let the current carry him along, uncertain where he was going.

TWENTY

2042

It has been almost seven weeks since I arrived in Washington and was sequestered in this safe house. The soldiers are becoming convinced there may be something to the Chinese threat after all, which has made the possibility of a general strike seem more unlikely since they don't want to go AWOL at a time when the country may need defending. At my insistence, the young woman who brings my food convinced one of the soldiers to visit me so I could see for myself that the military is not entirely against us. I also wanted to ask what the generals really think about the chances of a war with China.

The mid-career soldier, a man pushing forty, came yesterday. Born not long after Nine-Eleven, he grew up during the War on Terror and went straight into the army after high school.

"It was my duty," he said.

He hadn't known the wars against Iraq and Afghanistan were part of a bigger plan to outflank Iran by positioning military bases on its western and eastern borders as the United States pivoted toward China. And he'd never heard of the Axis of Evil, which counts not just Iraq and Iran among the targets of the United States but also North Korea.

"Why was North Korea singled out in the War on Terror?" I asked.

He had no idea. But the answer should be obvious to anyone who looks at a map. Just as Iran is bordered by Iraq and Afghanistan, China is bordered by Afghanistan and North Korea.

"The United States has been preparing for war with China since at least the turn of the century," I explained. "It even has military bases in Central Asia north of Afghanistan, extending its presence on China's western border."

Seated on the edge of the bed, I watched the soldier squirm in the chair opposite me.

"How did China respond to this aggression?" I asked.

But again the soldier didn't have an answer.

"Did it build its own military bases in Canada and Mexico, mimicking the war footing of the United States? No, it didn't. Instead, it took a page from the playbook of the white man by getting its hands on as much land and real estate in the United States as it could. Over the past forty years, while the elites destroyed the middle class and collapsed the economy, pushing everyone into debt, China has inched closer to owning your country without firing any bullets or dropping a single bomb. Worse, most of your national debt is owed to China. How did this happen? Why does China have so much money to lend at a time when the United States has so little?"

The soldier shrugged his broad shoulders.

"The blame," I told him, "lies with your bankers—the old white men who pull the strings of your presidents and keep the engine of the deep state chugging along. Because they're privately owned, Western central banks profit only the very rich. They are the most pervasive form of organized crime the world has ever seen. In contrast, most of China's banks are owned by the state and serve the public good. That's why China's economy is thriving while yours is in shreds.

"You should've gotten rid of the bankers and issued your own currency back when John F. Kennedy first attempted it. If you had, you wouldn't have lost your middle class. Your cities wouldn't have been allowed to degrade so badly that your water pipes are poisoning people and your trains are jumping from their tracks. You wouldn't have failed so miserably to end your reliance on oil and warfare to stay afloat.

"The truth is that China has no need to start a war with the United States. The bankers have already defeated you. And why would China bomb a country it owns so much of already? More than that, how would China be able to collect on the debt the United States owes it if your country was in ruins? As far as I can tell, the threat of an attack from China is a lie meant to keep you all scared at a time when you should be running your government out of office. If you have reason to believe otherwise, I'd like to hear it so I can get out of here while I still have a chance."

The soldier stroked his clean-shaven chin and looked at me as if I was the first person who had ever told him how the world works.

"I don't know what to believe anymore," he said.

I asked him what the generals are saying, and he told me about one who was arrested while recruiting for the underground—but not before assuring the soldiers that he supports a strike. "Come hell or high water," the man had insisted, "the generals are going to force the president to stand trial for her crimes."

"Is that why you joined the underground?" I asked him. "Was it a vendetta against the president?"

He shook his head. "One president is the same as the next, I figure. I didn't see that before, but you wise up, you know. Nah, it was because of the new directives."

"What are those?"

"Orders from the top. Now strikers are supposed to be treated like domestic terrorists. They want us to shoot them."

"Shoot them?"

"Yeah. Live bullets. I can't do it. If that makes me unpatriotic, okay."

I admire his courage. By joining the underground, he is at risk of cutting himself off from an idea that has defined him for half his life. If he is not a soldier, he must ask himself, then who is he?

"It takes patriotism to make good people do bad things," I told him.

He nodded. "Yeah, I'm starting to get that."

"How about the soldiers? Do they see things the way you do?"

"Some, but most need convincing. That's why I was hoping, well, maybe you could talk to them."

"How would I do that?"

He took his phone out of his breast pocket and turned to the young woman, who was behind him at the window, her eye on the street.

"You could record something, and maybe we could get it out there."

"That's risky, but it would help," she said. "It could be the right time."

"More than anything I've told you today, there is one thing everyone has to accept," I said.

The soldier leaned back and scratched his stomach.

"The white man's days of piracy and war are over. He doesn't own this century. The United States is not a superpower anymore, and the other white nations can do nothing to prop it up. If the white man wants a place in this new world, he can't make this standoff with China about race. He can save himself only by helping to change the rules of the game. To do that, he has to wake up from a long trance induced by the lies of madmen. He has to see with the eyes of spirit, not ego. Spirit is the only authority we should answer to."

Now, as I sit here alone listening to the creaks and groans of this aging house, I wonder if I was wise to have made the recording. By this time tomorrow, it will no longer be a secret I'm here.

TWENTY-ONE

2023

Come mid-morning, the sun growing hot in a smog-filled sky, Atan sat down to rest at an underpass beneath a six-lane stretch of the Golden Quadrilateral, a network of highways connecting New Delhi in the north to Mumbai in the west, Chennai in the south, and Kolkata in the east. Watching a roadside tea wallah spread cardamom pods atop a flat stone and crush them with a rock, Atan felt the whole of India's history swirling by with the traffic overhead.

More than five millennia ago, the emergence of Hinduism among a hunter-gatherer people had furnished the country with a rich parade of gods whose names stood in for a single animating force. Then had come the grandeur of civilization 2,500 years later, with India's withdrawal from nature and the resulting proliferation of evils like hierarchy and exclusion by caste. Finally, Islam had taken hold in the north, its one god descended from the god of Christianity and Judaism before it, a male figure detached from creation and residing somewhere beyond anyone's reach.

As the tea wallah gathered up bits of black seed from among the split cardamom pods and crushed them into powder, Atan contemplated the collisions of history rippling all around him, the past and the present tugging against each other. He recalled the trading rivalries that had broken out as capitalism came to occupy the moral center of Christianity, the European powers storming India's shores—the Dutch in 1605, the British in 1612, the Danish in 1620, and the French in 1668.

The British had already been colonizing the Indian subcontinent for more than half a century when, on the other side of the world, the Hudson's Bay Company extended the British colonization of Canada westward in 1670. And just as the British and the French would fight over North America, they were battling each other for control of India by the late 1700s.

With the end of the British Raj in 1947 came independence, and India was partitioned to create Pakistan, culminating in the debasement of both Hinduism and Islam as hundreds of thousands were murdered in the name of their opposed religions. Like a dull, brutal machete, the white man's meddling in brown people's lives had cut a ragged, gruesome swath across the planet.

After tossing the cardamom powder into a pot of goat's milk, the tea wallah sprinkled in some ground cinnamon and anise seeds, followed by a handful of dark tea and two spoonfuls of whitish sugar. When the milk came to a boil, he took the pot by the handle and swirled the mixture around before pouring the contents through a sieve, creating a long stream in the air as it splashed into a stainless-steel cistern. Picking up another cistern, he poured the mixture back and forth between them until the tea was frothy, the long streams appearing to resist gravity. At last, the man tipped the piping-hot chai into eight glasses arranged on a rusty Coca-Cola tray and offered them to the customers. The last one he presented to Atan, whose long beard, he figured, must have made him look just like any other spiritual pilgrim from the West.

As the chai passed Atan's lips and slid across his parched tongue, he remembered the word Brad Wheeler had used to describe avocado—"ambrosia." Food of the gods. That's what he was tasting now. Never had he known anything more wholesome. The rich goat's milk, likely gathered at dawn, made him think of the grasses and flowers that the animals had nibbled in the fresh air of the field. And in the spices, he found the mysteries of the earth itself, the secret molecules of her minerals, tannins, and resins. Above all, he felt nourished by the tea wallah's devotion to his task and by the apparent gentleness of the man's heart. All this before the first sip had reached Atan's throat.

And in the eyes of the men and women crouched beside him with their glasses of chai at the tea wallah's stall, Atan saw the same pleasure he was experiencing—a deep contentment that denied the poverty visible in their sunken frames and weathered skin, in the men's layers of ill-fitting dress shirts and suit vests, in the women's dusty headscarves and threadbare saris in hues of pink and orange.

At the corner, two young boys hawked bootlegged copies of American bestsellers at the windows of stopped cars. Seeing Atan with his glass of tea, they pressed in beside him, followed by a wild-haired girl with the most radiant and honest eyes Atan had ever seen. As the tallest of the boys fanned out his John Grisham thrillers and Dan Brown mysteries for Atan to see, the young girl bunched up the fingers of one hand and gestured toward her lips.

She wanted food, Atan thought. Getting up from the curb, he fished some crisp rupees from his pocket, courtesy of a Brooklyn currency exchange, as a woman appeared with a tray of sticky buns balanced atop her head. After paying the tea wallah for the chai, Atan got a bun for the girl and another for himself. But the boys wanted a bun as well, so Atan bought two more. Before he could pay the woman, a gaggle of passersby had encircled him, all wanting a bun too. Soon the woman's tray was empty, and several people went away with long faces, two old men bickering because one had gotten a bun and the other hadn't.

"Keep that up, and you'll be broke by dinnertime," said a voice at Atan's shoulder.

He turned to see a broad-chested man, his gray eyes sparkling on either side of a large nose, his brow knitted. A good three inches taller than Atan, who stood almost six feet himself, the man seemed like a gentle giant, his words shaped by a German accent familiar to Atan from his days growing up in Kitchener, once called Berlin—at least until the First World War erased its former name, if not its history.

"It's hard to say no," Atan replied.

"It gets easier," the man said, extending his hand. "Gunter," he declared.

Atan shook the man's thick hand, its broad fingers encircling his.

"Atan," he said, forgetting just then that he was a wanted man and a halfway famous one at that.

But his name seemed to mean nothing to Gunter, who simply nodded, possessing a carefree ease that Atan liked.

"You haven't been in New Delhi long, I guess," Gunter said.

"Just got here."

"Where from?"

"New York."

"Ah, yes. Like Germany, America is better at hiding its poor than India is. But don't let your shock get the better of you. One way or another, most will eat today without your charity. And when the beggars get tired of begging, they will remember that Mother India takes care of her own, and they will go back to their villages, where fat mangoes hang from the trees waiting for them."

"I hope you're right."

"I am," Gunter said, showing not the slightest self-doubt but no trace of arrogance either.

"What do you play?" Atan asked, looking at the large case slung across Gunter's back.

"The tambura."

"I've never seen one."

"Like a guitar but with a much longer neck and no frets. I'm giving a concert today if you want to come with me."

"Now?"

"Yes, I'm just returning from a lesson. That's my taxi."

Gunter pointed at a stubby white Hindustan Ambassador waiting at the curb, its back seat big enough for Gunter and Atan, the tambura, too, with space left over.

"Where's the concert?" Atan asked, not that it really mattered. He was keen to go.

"At the ashram where I live," Gunter said. "Get in."

As the taxi careened east across the city, fighting for every inch of road, the sides of the cars dented and gouged, no doubt from rubbing against each other like bulls in a chute, Atan saw dogs and cows strolling freely and clusters of people lounging under the trees. Through the cracks in New Delhi's modern facade, he glimpsed the skeletons of old buildings—destitution amid luxury—and spied headstones peeking out of alleyways strung with flapping clotheslines. People with happy faces crouched at the edge of the road, eating colorful food from small tins, their tasks, their tools, their baskets set aside. Elated, Atan found himself back among the sand eaters, so scorned by his mother in his childhood, people caught on the wrong side of money with their hands still in the earth. These were the people he'd always liked best.

More than that, Atan felt the presence of something he hadn't experienced since his boyhood in the north—spirits. As old as the world, they sighed and whispered, infusing the scene with reverberations of the sacred as soothing as the fragrant incense permeating the strings of gold and ruby tassels hanging between the front seat and the back. Hoping the spirits had plans for him, Atan let himself relax as he surrendered to their pull. He even dozed off for a bit as Gunter recounted tales of his youth and his own journey to India, where he now spent half the year studying with his teacher before returning to Europe each spring for a season of concerts.

When he was young, Gunter told Atan, he'd often run away from home—not because he disliked his parents but on account of his curiosity. He wanted to understand how the world worked, and to do that, he needed to experience it directly, not in a classroom. Sometimes that meant camping out in the bushes of a roundabout as the traffic whizzed by for hours on end. Or he would board trains to distant towns, where the local police captains became his chums as they drove him home. Most of all, he liked walking deep into the forest, where he passed the day listening for the perfect note in the flutter of leaves, the gurgle of water, the song of an unseen bird.

At thirteen, recognizing the worry his wanderlust caused his mother, Gunter mended his ways and promised not to stray again, vowing to stay in school until he was sixteen and never to miss a day. With the arrival of that long-awaited milestone, which fell in the middle of June, just two weeks before the end of term, Gunter gathered up his textbooks and returned them to the headmaster's office. He no longer needed them, he said, because he wouldn't be taking his exams. That very morning, he left school and home for good, roaming where he wished. After finding a banjo in the trash and teaching himself to play, he earned money by busking while living on the streets and sleeping on overnight trains.

For several years, he lodged at a center for transcendental meditation, where a visiting musician taught him to play the tambura. He read many books of Eastern theology there but mostly studied the people who came to the center in search of something none of them would ever grasp because, he insisted, it was wrapped in so many layers of nonsense that only the adept could understand it. In disgust, he finally proclaimed one day that everyone there was full of shit, and he went back out into the world, eventually making his way to India, first Mumbai and then New Delhi, in search of a tambura teacher. At fifty-seven, only a few years older than Atan, he'd been living there off and on for almost thirty years.

"The concert is in the meditation hall," Gunter said, pointing out the window as the taxi stopped at the end of the ashram's long driveway, its tires crunching in the gravel. Getting out of the back seat,

Atan saw a simple square building standing alone in the front garden, its roof sloped, an entrance on either side. Gunter paid the fare and set his tambura down on the lawn. In front of them, a path led to an octagon-shaped building three floors high with rooms that opened onto balconies overlooking an inner courtyard.

"There are four buildings like that," he said. "Also a dining hall, a library, a medical clinic, and even classrooms for lectures by visiting gurus. Take a look around."

Atan followed Gunter as far as the courtyard, where brightly colored saris draped the railings that ringed the upstairs hallways, the sky a blue jewel overhead, the slabs of white stone at Atan's feet bathed in sunlight.

"I need to go shower and dress," Gunter said. "If anyone asks, tell them you're with me."

As he climbed the stairs to the second floor, guests of all ages emerged from rooms along the halls—women in headscarves and chunky necklaces, barefoot beneath diaphanous skirts, men with wise beards on their chins and ornate rings on their fingers, most of the people not Indian but white like Atan. Descending to the courtyard, they flowed past him and went into the front garden.

Following them to the meditation hall, Atan left his sandals in the pile of footwear at the entrance and stepped into a cozy room, its low ceiling pocked with dimmed lights, the air thick with the perfume of resinous incense burning in alcoves along the walls. He found a cushion on the floor among the other guests and waited for the concert to start, filled with a sense of well-being. The room was like a reservoir of peace, as if saturated, he thought, with the energy of a thousand resting minds—the calm palpable.

On a low stage at the front of the room sat two Indian musicians. One had a pair of leather-skinned tablas that made Atan think of Winnie the Pooh's honey pots, the larger pot double the size of the smaller. The other musician cradled a sitar in his lap, its countless golden frets glinting beneath a long row of black pegs stretching so far up its neck that Atan was staggered just thinking of all the sounds it might make.

Shortly, Gunter entered by the far door dressed in a knee-length blue shirt of fine cloth embroidered with gray thread. Sitting down cross-legged on a tasseled pillow between the other players, he began at once to pluck the strings of his tambura, its rose-tinted neck as long as the sitar's but free of frets and pegs. No melody was formed, only a harmonic hum that seemed to Atan to hover visibly in the air as Gunter's hands drew out the sounds, the effect haunting.

After a time, the tabla player added a rhythm, his fingers fluttering against the skins of his pots. Soon the sitar player joined in, the first traces of a tune emerging as one of his hands caressed the frets and the other plucked the most peculiar—the most exhilarating—notes Atan had ever heard. The sounds filling the room carried more meaning than all his lyrics together. And how different this concert was from his gigs at Café Wha?—with their drunk patrons and all the waitresses dressed for tips.

Here was music as prayer, he thought, and for the first time, he understood what old Ataninnuaq had meant when he'd appeared to Atan in a time of despair and said, "This is the medicine." Like prayer, music vibrated into the unseen, shaping reality.

Later, Atan sat over a tray of dahl and rice in the dining hall with the other guests and the ashram's staff—the chambermaids and gardeners, the clinic nurses and cooks—all perched on benches before tables as long as the room, apparently amiable, peaceful, and openhearted. He could grow to like their company, he thought. There was some love in the place.

"Where are you staying?" Gunter asked, dipping a chunk of buttery naan into his dahl. "Do you need a taxi?"

"Maybe. I don't know. I don't have any plans."

"You didn't get a room anywhere?"

"No."

Gunter smiled.

"I see. Most people aren't so fearless. India terrifies them. They need their itineraries and tour guides."

He chased his naan with a sip of milky tea.

"You can stay in my room then, at least for tonight. But you'll have to take your passport to the office."

"My passport? Is that normal?"

"Yes. At the hotels too. You can't get a room—or even stay with another guest—unless you sign in. It's a holdover from British rule. Everyone has to be enumerated and tabulated."

Atan didn't know what to say. Having seen his face come up on the computer screen in the office of airport security, he knew the FBI had connected him to Wheeler and the Outliers. His passport would surely set off alarms, and the police would be there to arrest him in no time.

"I don't think that's a good idea," he said.

"No?" Gunter asked. "Why not? I don't snore. Well, maybe I do. How would I know?" He laughed heartily. "So why not?"

Certain he had nothing to fear from Gunter, Atan leaned across the table.

"Interpol," he said.

"Interpol? As in—the police?"

"Yeah."

"What about them?"

"They're looking for me."

Gunter put down his spoon.

"Are you serious?"

"Yes."

"What happened?"

"Nothing I was part of. I kept the wrong company. That's all."

"I can maybe help, but I should know why they're after you."

Atan decided to take a risk. "Elevators," he said.

Gunter sat up.

"The attacks—the elevators in the United States?"

"Yeah."

"Ah, I saw that on the television at the barber shop."

Atan looked at Gunter's neatly trimmed mop of hair.

"Did they say anything about me?"

"Yes. I realize it now. They showed your face but without the beard."

Atan was filled with a terrible sinking feeling. The ceiling seemed to be pressing down on him as the dining hall grew small and dim.

"So that's it," he mumbled.

"No," Gunter said with a wry smile. "You're in luck. The computers here are used only for email and Google. Guests have to register in a big leather book like in the days of the Raj, everything written out in pen."

Laughing, he picked up his spoon again and went back to eating.

"What if the police come looking for me?"

"Why would they start here when there are so many hotels for them to check? It's easy to disappear in India. Just stick to places like this or go stay in a *khanqah*."

"A what?"

"*Khanqah*. Where the Sufis live—the wild Sufis. I'll take you sometime. They always have great hash."

For now, Atan decided, it would be best if he stayed at the ashram. So, after washing their dishes in the sinks along the far wall of the dining hall and replacing their trays on a trolley by the exit, he and Gunter went to the office. The clerk, a plump woman in her sixties with gentle eyes the burnished brown of chestnuts, let Atan fill in the guestbook himself, glancing at what he wrote only long enough to assign him a room number. For fifteen dollars a day, he could take his meals there and make use of the meditation hall. Classes and workshops were extra, with sign-up sheets posted each morning.

Over the coming days, Atan would attend a lecture on the wheel of karma and how it linked cause and effect in inevitable chains, another on the illusions of maya, with its deceits and seductions, and one more on the many faces of Brahman, the unchanged changer. The Eastern frame of explanation for reality, with its holistic orientation, was not unlike the tribal one. He saw that the people who came to the ashram were all seeking the same thing—a way back to the indivisible god, the ground of all being, the light that was their own.

As Atan had once done, they talked of wanting to kill off their egos as if the self served no purpose. Indeed, many of the guests at the ashram acted as if they had already succeeded, affecting a lightness of being and nonchalance that struck Atan as false. He wondered why it was necessary to post signs above the sinks in the dining hall that reminded guests to wash, dry, and stack their own dishes, as well as signs in the shared washrooms outside the library that reminded them to clean up after themselves for the good of others. Why did people who had transcended the ego need to be reminded not to be selfish?

No, as Atan had learned in the desert, pretending to have killed one's ego did nothing. Instead, the ego needed to be brought into a complementary relationship with spirit. It could not be transcended so one might exist as spirit alone but needed to become the face of spirit. When he discussed this idea with Gunter one morning over breakfast, his friend chuckled and patted Atan's arm.

"This place is a kindergarten," he said. "It is because the people who come here don't know what you're talking about that they need to come here. Don't go to the classes. They're not for you."

If that was true, Atan wondered, why didn't he feel light and nonchalant for real? Why was he burdened by the nagging sense he'd run from a fight and should be doing more? In New York, he'd seen for the first time that there was a spiritual battle afoot in the world. Part of him wanted to confront the liars and hypnotists of the deep state, powerful people who meddled with the unconscious of the masses for wicked ends, the ones Leonard Cohen called the "killers in high places who say their prayers out loud." But he was done with all that, Atan told himself. In his meditations at Maybel's house, he'd tried to locate the person who'd sent a gunman to kill him in Lafayette Square, and it had led to nothing but the street number of the elevator attack in New York, 432 Park Avenue, a clue to the doings of the Outliers but a dead end for him.

As Atan's stay at the ashram stretched into months, he spent hours in the meditation hall, slipping farther and farther beyond the edges of the material world. Alone very early one morning, he went so deep into the unseen that he vanished from the hall, body and soul—or perhaps it was a dream—and found himself in the street outside 432 Park Avenue in New York. Leaves skittered along in a fall breeze as pedestrians hurried past, pushing him aside. Barefoot in a T-shirt and shivering, Atan heard a bang—the one that had pushed its way into his thoughts the day Larry Smiles had interviewed him. As Atan lifted his gaze to the sky, his vision became binocular until, hundreds of feet in the air, he sighted a crow sitting on the sill outside a window of the penthouse suite, its beak chipped, a nickel-sized hole in the glass. As the bird screeched, Atan saw reflected in its eyes an old man in a royal blue housecoat scrambling across the floor on his knees. Reaching an alcove in the opposite wall, the man pulled himself to his feet and hastily blew out a black candle on an altar.

With a jolt, Atan's eyes flew open, and he was back at the ashram in New Delhi, now certain the person he'd been looking for in the unseen was the Washington puppeteer Bacchus Altwied, the penthouse occupant killed in New York. Atan had only meant to find Brooklyn Willy's killer. He hadn't gone so far as to wish the man dead. But as he sat there in the hall, the birds chirping with the day's first light, his stomach was filled with knots, for he feared that in looking for Bacchus, he'd helped Brad Wheeler and the Outliers after all, leading them right to him. In an inspirited reality, where all was intermeshed and all were in communion, wasn't it possible? Hadn't Atan spotted Wheeler in the unseen, content in his beer satori, lurking where the spirit of each man overlapped with the other's?

Perhaps the reason Atan had thought of hacking elevators in the first place, the idea surfacing in his Washington apartment after Brooklyn's murder, was that he unconsciously knew where the bang had come from as Bacchus was casting the spell that had brought the crow to his windowsill. Lacking knowledge of his abilities as an *angakkuq*, had Atan misused his power? Had the ego's need for revenge and the catharsis of blood gotten the better of him?

Afterward, when Atan told Gunter about his discovery in the meditation hall, it came out like a confession.

"I'm not as wise as you might think," he said. "I haven't mastered my ego. I don't even know half the time what drives me."

"That doesn't make you a killer," Gunter said.

More than Atan's sense of guilt, it was his story of turning the assassin's bullet to stone that intrigued Gunter, just now hearing the details of what had transpired in Lafayette Square.

"You might be a sadhu, though."

"A sadhu?" Atan asked.

"One of those holy men who can materialize objects out of thin air."

"It wasn't on purpose. I mean—you know, I couldn't do it again."

"Maybe not without training, but you were in nature's laboratory messing with the raw materials. That's what the sadhus do. It's a neat trick, especially if it saves your life, but I don't see the point of it. How does impressing people with miracles help anybody?"

"It doesn't."

They were riding together in another Hindustan Ambassador, Gunter's tambura beside them on the back seat, the driver muttering under his breath as he struggled to get into the lane he wanted.

"*Maan kameene*!" he shouted, his frantic eyes turned in their direction as a lorry with the face of the elephant god Ganesh thundered down on them. "Sorry, sir. Sorry," the driver said to Gunter, giving up the attempt. "Must go around again."

"What did he say?" Atan asked.

"Motherfucker," Gunter laughed.

On their left sprawled the centuries-old Muslim neighborhood of Nizamuddin, home to a famous mosque and the shrines of Sufi saints, a pool of sacred waters at its center, Gunter had explained to Atan. They had to get out at Baoli Gate Road near the shrine of Inayat Khan, the man who'd brought Sufism to the West when he'd traveled to England in 1914 as an Indian classical musician on tour, staying on to start a Sufi order there. Gunter was to give a concert at the shrine that evening, and he'd invited Atan along. Inayat Khan, he told Atan, had spread the message of divine unity found in all mystical teachings, but more than that, he'd argued that music itself was the thread that could unite the world in harmony.

As the taxi continued along Lohdi Road—passing the same auto shop and guest house as before, the same crowded food stalls and oil-slick grills arrayed with sizzling lamb kabobs, the same parade of jostled, hungry humanity waiting to be fed—it felt to Atan like it was his life itself that was going in circles, spiraling around and around without getting anywhere. If only he had used his own music as medicine like old Ataninnuaq had done, instead of trying to become someone, he might have done a little good.

The taxi in the correct lane at last, Gunter told the driver to forget about circling back to Baoli Gate Road. Instead, they got out at the nearest alleyway that would take them to the heart of Nizamuddin. With the concert about to start and no time to spare, Atan had to struggle to keep up as Gunter led them through a maze of cramped streets lined with vendors hawking everything a pilgrim to a Sufi shrine might need. He saw destemmed roses for them to strew upon the altars, printed shroud cloths to lay atop the tombs, white skullcaps to cover their heads. Everything was arrayed amid shops and shanty homes, the pavement occupied by flea-bitten dogs nipping at flies in the waning heat, the gutters taken over by goats picking through garbage.

As the sun set and the day's fourth call to prayer rang out from all the minarets in the neighborhood, the dying light appeared to transform the whole into a sacred place in its own right. Those who struck Atan as the most holy were the men and women crouched together sorting paper, plastic, and metal into piles in a large dirt field a block from the shrine of Inayat Khan, toddlers at their knees and babies in their arms, sleeping mats beside them, the gulls swooping overhead as the first stars came out.

When Atan and Gunter reached the shrine, a smiling young boy of no more than ten ushered Gunter into the music hall, Atan trailing behind. Taking Gunter's hand as if they were brothers, the boy led him along the rows of guests, who were seated on pillows that seemed to float upon the stone floor.

"This way, sir," he said, following a path to the stage at the other end of the room.

Beckoned by a middle-aged white couple dressed in Indian garb and adorned with jewels and scarves, Atan squeezed into a spot beside them in the back row. At once, without ceremony, the ethereal notes of the fretful, crying sarangi brought the audience to rapturous attention as bow met string. Next came the patter of the tabla, like small feet stepping lightly between puddles on a muddy road. By the time Gunter joined in on the tambura, slipping wisps of vibration into the silences between the notes of the sarangi, the audience seemed to have entered into a collective bond of love that grew only more tangible as the concert went on.

But Atan could not surrender to the experience, his ennui only deepening as he listened to the ethereal music and beheld the peaceful demeanor of the players flanking Gunter. Even the cheerful poise of the boy who'd led Gunter to the stage had filled Atan with regret that he'd never cultivated the same characteristics. In comparison to both the musicians and the boy, he felt inferior. What had he done with his life? What if he hadn't listened to old Ataninnuaq and become a musician?

More to the point, what if he hadn't been named after the old man in the first place? Who would Atan be then? The scene before him brought all these questions to mind as he sat at the back of the hall next to the tomb of the great mystic and musician Inayat Khan.

Right then, giving up his struggle, Atan denounced his namesake and stopped striving to be anything at all. In his lap lay a notebook where he still scribbled song lyrics and kept track of thoughts that seemed important. Slipping a pen from its spine, he tore out a page and wrote, "Don't wait for me." He handed the note to the woman next to him, bringing her back to the world of the mundane just long enough to say, "For the tambura player."

Taking the paper, she nodded and closed her eyes again, her blonde hair dropping about her face as Atan stood up and gingerly made his way between the back rows of the audience to the door where he'd entered.

Outside, Atan found the sky full of stars, a thin crescent moon floating among them like a cup adrift. He crossed the courtyard of Inayat Khan's shrine and went out onto Baoli Gate Road. Opposite him, on a stone wall bordering the street hung a mirror, and atop a thin mat on the ground next to a chair slept a barber, his combs and scissors folded inside a piece of cloth protruding from his vest pocket. In the morning, he would rise with the sun, Atan thought, and bathe at the community pump he'd seen nearby. The man would sip chai with his neighbors at a tea stall before returning to this spot of earth he'd claimed as his own. Here, he would pass his day cutting hair and shaving chins in the open air, the breeze scattering the locks he snipped so the birds could carry them away and weave them into their nests.

That was what Atan wanted—a simple life honestly lived and infused with the rhythms of nature. He slipped in among the pedestrians jostling with scooters for space in the narrow road, their faces framed by white skullcaps and bright scarves as their heads bobbed along beside him, his heart lighter already.

TWENTY-TWO

2042

The sick woman across the hall remains silent, her mind in a stupor. The captain doesn't visit her anymore, and whatever connection she had with the world of the past has been severed. Nor has she entered my dreams again to reveal what she needed to tell me. I want to believe that if it was truly important, old Ataninnuaq would come to me as he once did and explain everything. But I renounced his hold on me years ago, and he has never returned.

Mid-morning now, a helicopter has been circling overhead since daybreak. Something is amiss, and I'm worried it has to do with the message I recorded. As the helicopter swoops low over the front yard, rattling my windows and shaking the walls, I hear the boyfriend of the student who lives above me descending the staircase in the hall, his gait unmistakable as he leaps to the bottom. It is Saturday, so the postman next door is home. All morning, he has been muttering on his phone. Now his door opens and he goes out to meet the boyfriend. Through my peephole, I can almost see them off to the left near the front door. They are talking in animated whispers when the actress comes out of her room to join them, her cat slinking along behind her. Their conversation continues for several minutes, and I surmise they are talking about the helicopter, as the actress keeps pointing above them—except when she is glancing at my door! Eventually, the old man who lives upstairs comes down into the hall dressed in a neat black suit and a fedora. Spryer than usual, he orders them all back to their rooms and continues outside onto the porch.

I cross to the window, watching him pass on the walkway. I've never seen him move so fast. At the curb in front of the boyfriend's van waits a car as neat and black as the man's suit. With an ease clearly born of habit, he ducks into the back seat and exchanges words with the driver before the car speeds off, quietly disappearing around the bend at the end of the street.

I don't know what to make of it all. I've never known the postman to talk to anyone else in the house, the actress either. But they all seemed so familiar with each other! I can't help but think I've been misreading the goings-on here all along.

Compelled to find out what my schizophrenic neighbor was doing in my dream, I go out into the hall and rap on her door. After the third knock, I hear her shuffling across her room to look at me through the peephole. She undoes the chain lock, and the door swings open.

"Hi," I say cautiously, worried she'll be afraid of me after what happened with the men who came to take her away.

She smiles, her eyes eerily calm. "Oh, yes. Come in."

Curls of tangled hair bounce against the shoulders of her soiled housecoat as she turns and walks to an armchair pushed into the far corner by the back window, its worn seat sunken by years of use. I follow her into the room and sit down at her kitchen table.

"Did you get my note?" she asks.

"Your—? Yes, yes, I did." She seems to think I should know she wrote it, so I play along.

She nods, her eyes on me, as if she expects me to say more. After a pause filled with the racket of the helicopter, a kettle whistles behind me and she hoists herself back up.

"Tea?" she asks.

"Okay. Thank you."

She brings two mugs to the table, the strings of the teabags meticulously wound around their handles to keep the tags from slipping into the water.

"I don't have any milk," she says. "It went sour. And the doctor won't let me have sugar."

"This is perfect. Just how I like it."

"It's mint."

She takes her tea to the armchair and sits down again, cradling the mug with both hands as the steam fogs up her thick glasses.

"How do you know who I am?" I ask at last.

She thinks for a second and then says, "The captain told me."

"The whaling captain?"

"Yeah. He used to know a man with a long name that I can't remember now, someone who is important to you."

"Ataninnuaq?"

"Yeah. That Ataninnuaq guy used to give the captain fox hides for oil."

She sips her tea and falls silent for a long time, seeming to forget I'm there.

"What did the captain want?"

At once, she becomes alarmed and shoots me a terrified glance, the hot tea slopping into her lap. "Oh," she cries out.

I jump to my feet. "Here," I say, reaching for her mug.

"It's okay. I'm okay."

She sets the mug down on a side table.

"You have to go," she says.

"What do you mean?"

"North! You have to go north before it's too late."

"North?"

"Yes, yes." She gets up and pushes me toward the door. "Now! You have to go!"

Shaken, I return to my room and pass the afternoon watching the street, uncertain what to do. Old Ataninnuaq has found a way to reach me after all, and I can't ignore his warning, but without help, I may have no way out of here.

Just before dark, the helicopter veers off over the top of the oak tree next door and is gone at last. An odd quiet envelops the house. We all seem to be hunkered down in our rooms, holding our breath.

TWENTY-THREE

2024

The morning after the concert in Nizamuddin, shortly before nine o'clock, his tambura on his back, Gunter headed out to meet the taxi that would soon arrive to take him across town for his weekly lesson. As he neared the ashram's office, a white Jeep appeared in the driveway, a tear in its gray canvas top flapping urgently, its wheels spitting stones into the grass. Large red letters on its hood cried, "POLICE," and through the front window Gunter could see two grim-faced officers in ball caps and khakis. When the Jeep came to a halt and the men emerged from its cab, an intrepid peacock strutted across the lawn to greet them but was shooed away by the polished toe of a black boot.

Watching the policemen enter the office, Gunter immediately thought of Atan. His friend had missed breakfast in the dining hall, and Gunter hadn't seen him since yesterday, when he'd left the concert early. Atan must be in his room, still fast asleep after getting in late, Gunter thought. Wasting no time, he went back into the courtyard and bounded up the stairs to the third floor. As he reached Atan's door, he heard shouting below.

"Close the front gates! Close them! Close them!"

Looking over the railing, Gunter saw the two officers at the foot of the stairs.

"Go now!" the older one shouted as he frantically pointed at someone out of sight near the office.

Gunter pounded on Atan's door as guests, summoned by the commotion, came out into the hall. An elderly man dressed all in white went to the railing and stared down at the officers with stricken eyes, as if to condemn them for their noisy intrusion.

At that moment, the officers were joined by the plump clerk who had admitted Atan to the ashram months ago.

"There is another gate for the workers," she said, pointing toward the dining hall. "It's that way."

"Go!" the older officer said to his colleague, who immediately ran off, the clerk plodding along behind him.

Gunter again pounded on Atan's door, but no sound came from inside his friend's room.

"Damn it!" he muttered.

When some of the guests started down the stairs to the courtyard, the older officer waved a stern finger at them and bellowed, "Back to your rooms! No one is to be leaving!"

Stone-faced and resolute, he remained where he was, ready to thwart anyone's attempt to escape. Suddenly, the air was pierced by a horn honking outside the main gate, sending a roost of squawking parrots skyward in alarm.

Realizing it must be his taxi come to fetch him, Gunter descended to the courtyard and stood before the officer, disregarding the man's wagging finger and repeated demands that he go back upstairs.

"Are you here for me?" Gunter asked, towering above him.

"That doesn't matter," the officer said. "No one is to be leaving."

"That honking you hear is my taxi," Gunter explained. "An esteemed pandit is waiting for me, and I don't dare be late."

Having evoked his teacher's wisdom and learning with the gravity of the word "pandit," which the officer could hardly ignore, Gunter smiled benignly.

"Pandit?" the officer asked.

"Yes," Gunter said, indicating the tambura on his back. "If I'm delayed, he will surely hear of your part in it."

"Who is it, then, this pandit?" the officer asked, clearly concerned his superiors might reprimand him for overextending his authority if it meant insulting a personage of importance.

"Only Suresh Nadu," Gunter said.

Hearing this name, the officer nearly choaked, and his eyes grew fearful.

"The musician?" the officer asked in disbelief.

"The pride of India," Gunter said calmly, knowing he'd won the battle.

At this point, the younger officer returned to say the workers' gate was now locked and guarded by a member of the ashram staff.

"Very well," the older man said. "Escort this one to the front and let him out. See that no one else leaves!"

Gunter went off with the officer at his side and was soon outside on Begumpur Road, where his taxi waited at the curb. Before the attendant could close the gate, three police cars, lights flashing and sirens wailing, came to a screeching halt in the driveway. Leaving Gunter where he was, the officer who'd escorted him jumped into the back seat of the lead car, and the cavalcade sped inside.

As Gunter watched from the road, he could only hope that Atan hadn't come back to the ashram after all. He wanted to warn his friend not to return, but the damn fool didn't have a phone and couldn't be reached. Reluctantly, Gunter climbed into the taxi and instructed the driver to go.

The night before, upon leaving the concert at the shrine of Inayat Khan, Atan had walked only as far as the water pump where the neighborhood's homeless residents bathed and washed their clothes when he was greeted warmly by an Indian man his age dressed in a white lungi and a collared, button-up shirt the color of sand, his head covered with a turban fashioned out of a checkered scarf. Bearded and smiling, he was perched before an open fire that burned in the bottom of a rusted-out, sawed-off oil drum. In one hand, he held a small pipe, and sweetly scented smoke billowed above his head.

"Come, come," he said to Atan, who must have looked like he was headed nowhere in particular. "Come sit."

Curious, Atan crouched beside the fire. Across the street stood a mosque with light bulbs strung along its roofline. As the minarets in Nizamuddin sounded the day's last call to prayer, a crowd of men and boys pressed toward the mosque's entrance, a pile of shoes and sandals forming behind them as they went inside.

"Prayer time," said the man.

"Are you going?" Atan asked.

The man shook his head and touched the ground with his hand and the pipe, his eyes rolling back in his head.

"Always praying, always, always."

He handed the pipe to Atan and tossed a scrap of wood into the oil drum.

"Pull, pull," he said, gesturing toward the pipe.

"What is it?"

"Hashish and tobacco, little tobacco."

Atan put the cone-shaped pipe to his mouth, struggling to hold it upright.

"Like this?"

"Yes, very good."

As they sat together in the flickering light of the fire, a flash of lightning tore open the sky, and a torrent of rain fell.

"Come," the man said, jumping to his feet. "This way."

Taking Atan by the elbow, the man led him past the water pump to a cement patio covered by a tin roof and strewn with thin carpets. Before ducking under the roof, the man took off his sandals, and Atan did the same. Beyond the patio stood a little cement room with a closed steel door, light seeping out through the gap at the bottom. The man pulled the door open and ushered Atan inside.

Crammed into the room, shoulder to shoulder on more thin carpets, sat nearly twenty brown-faced men and boys in motley garb and turbans, some with hand drums in their laps, others holding rattles or palm-size copper castanets. Arrayed in rows, their backs to the door, they listened to the words of an older man with ebony skin and small white teeth that sparkled in his smiling face.

"That's Babah," whispered Atan's new friend, nodding at the man speaking as they sat down on the floor just inside the room.

When Babah had said his piece, all in Hindi and incomprehensible to Atan, one of the men presented Babah with a pipe like the one Atan had smoked outside. Striking a wooden match, Babah inhaled deeply again and again as fire flared in the wide end of the pipe until at last he emitted the longest stream of smoke Atan had ever seen issue from a person's mouth. Finally, placing a hand on his heart, Babah gave the pipe back to the man who'd prepared it.

As the pipe was passed among the men, one of them sang in Arabic, his tone pure and melodic. Atan couldn't tell where the voice was coming from until he saw that the singer, who was blessed with the face of a Bollywood star, sat a foot lower than the others because he had no legs. All the men bobbed and swayed, vibrant sounds rising from their throats as they joined in, chanting what Atan would learn was a litany of names for Allah. The percussionists picked up the rhythm on their various instruments, filling the room with joyous, raucous song.

Unlike the classical Hindi music Atan had encountered since arriving in India, this music was tribal, the chanting and the drums reminding him of what he'd heard among the people of the desert. More than that, the performers were not set apart. No one could be construed as claiming the status of a musician above the others. Exhilarated, Atan joined in, doing his best to imitate the sounds of the words he was hearing.

When the pipe reached him, Atan took the smoke into his lungs and held it. Like the others, he placed his hand on his heart—the path of Sufi devotion, he would learn—and passed the pipe to the man seated next to him. As the chanting became hypnotic, Atan released the smoke, his mind spinning, but at his center, all was still. His deepest self had opened into the larger self that is God, and he was back in the unseen. This time, however, he wasn't searching for anything. Merely happy to be there, he felt something like peace.

At midnight, when the evening drew to an end, about half the men left for home, and those who lived in that little shelter by the water pump—the orphaned and the homeless—prepared themselves for sleep, each finding a space on the floor and wrapping himself in a blanket.

Babah, who must have seen that Atan was reluctant to go, opened a trunk and pulled out a new blanket, still wrapped in plastic.

"Take," he said, extending the gift to his guest.

"*Shukriya*," Atan said, using an Urdu expression of gratitude he'd learned from a guest at the ashram, and Babah smiled broadly.

"Here," Babah said, pointing to a spot on the floor next to the man who'd brought Atan in out of the rain.

As Atan squeezed in beside the others, trying to get comfortable on the thin carpet that cushioned them from the cement floor, one of the men went to the door and looped a chain through the handles, securing it with a padlock. Gunter had warned Atan about bandits who disguised themselves as Sufis and duped foreigners into spending the night. While the gullible visitors slept, the impostors slit their throats, fleeing with anything of value—cash, jewelry, phones. As Atan watched the man at the door, their eyes met, and the fellow frowned.

"Bad man coming," he said, pointing outside.

But Atan wasn't worried. He could see he'd fallen into a den of devotees, not a den of thieves.

The next morning, sipping chai as flies darted to and fro above the water pump, his face turned to the sun, Atan wondered if Gunter had missed him at breakfast. Set on staying with the Sufis, he thought about returning to the ashram to say farewell and get his clothes—a pair of jeans, a week's worth of T-shirts, a sweater—but Gunter had his tambura lesson that day, didn't he? In fact, he was probably about to leave and wouldn't be back until late afternoon. At that moment, there flashed through Atan's thoughts the image of a screeching peacock fleeing the kick of a polished boot—the ashram's peacock! Struck by a powerful sense that returning was a bad idea, Atan clutched the leather satchel that hung at his hip with his passport, wallet, and notebook inside. Everything he needed. His clothing unimportant, he resolved not to go back. He would phone the ashram from one of the yellow booths that dotted Nizamuddin and let the office know to rent out his room, his bill already paid. Gunter would understand.

Living with the Sufis, Atan cherished the lack of urgency that marked their days, the men and boys in Babah's care passing the mornings stringing together semiprecious stones donated to them for the necklaces and bracelets they sold in the street. That task done, they swept the floors and washed their clothing at the water pump before preparing meals for the people of the neighborhood who came to visit.

A resident of Nizamuddin all his life, Babah was widely sought out by couples for advice, families in need of prayer and money during times of illness, and Westerners longing for a taste of the mystical. Sufis from across Northern India made frequent pilgrimages to Nizamuddin's shrines to commemorate the births or deaths of fabled saints like Inayat Khan, always stopping to stay a night, a week, or a month at Babah's *khanqah*, filling the evenings with music and chanting, the hash abundant and the good cheer endless, Atan mused, despite the abject poverty of all.

During the long afternoons, with Atan at his side, Babah walked the neighborhood's winding streets to drop in on the elderly, congratulate new parents, or share a cigarette and a laugh over the latest goings-on in their vibrant, tumultuous world. This was the real work of an *angakkuq*, Atan realized. Babah was a mystic—a bridge between the seen and the unseen for those who needed it—but he was also in service to the people in his midst.

Not for the first time, Atan wished he was such a man. But as a teenager, when he'd set his sights on becoming a minister, the idea hadn't survived his inability to reconcile what he saw as a contradiction in Christianity between Jesus as a mediating savior and the Holy Spirit as a force that resides in everyone.

He wondered if Babah had the same misgivings about the contradictions between Sufism and Islam, the first one ancient and tribal in its direct experience of spirit, the second one fraught with the same barriers between oneself and Allah that the deification of Jesus had erected between people and God. But as Babah didn't speak English, Atan couldn't ask him.

The tensions Atan saw between Sufism and Islam—the latter religion having absorbed the former—came to a head one evening when Atan ventured out of Nizamuddin to attend a performance by a harmonium player and a group of qawwali singers. As he approached the large tent erected for the event, he was accosted by a devout Muslim dressed in a white skullcap and knee-length shirt.

"What are you doing with these fellows?" he asked Atan, there with three of the Sufis who lived at the *khanqah*.

"What do you mean?" Atan asked.

"Look at you."

Since abandoning his jeans and T-shirts, Atan had taken to wearing an ankle-length lungi and a collared, button-up shirt like the Sufis. On his head, he wore a red scarf wrapped like a turban.

"These are not proper Muslims," the man declared. "If you want to follow Islam, you cannot be going about like this."

"Why not?" Atan asked.

"They're—well, they're beggars. Heathens."

"Heathens," Atan repeated, impressed by the man's English but a little angered by the insult directed toward his friends.

"They ignore the five pillars of Islam," the man protested, raising a finger. "They make hashish their god, when there is no god but Allah." He raised another finger. "They do not pray five times each day." Up went a third finger. "The only charity they give comes from others, not from their own wealth." He unfolded yet another finger. "They do not fast for Ramadan." He held his hand in Atan's face, all five fingers raised. "None of them will ever make the pilgrimage to Mecca to visit the house that Ibrahim built for Allah. At least once in your life, you must go! Do these five things, and you will be a good Muslim."

Faced with the man's contempt, so different from the cheerful love emanating from the eyes of his friends, Atan felt sorry for his interrogator.

"But will that make me a good person?" he asked.

"Of course!"

"I doubt it," Atan said, pushing past the man and continuing toward the entrance to the tent.

"No, no," the man hollered. "You cannot doubt!"

Stopping, Atan turned back.

"These men are closer to Allah than you think," he said. "Their love is proof of that."

"Come," said one of the Sufis with Atan, taking him by the elbow. "No need to argue, yes?"

And they all disappeared into the tent together, leaving the devout man fuming.

Despite what Atan had said to the man outside the qawwali concert, he knew that for many of Babah's devotees, Sufism was a way of life, a cultural affectation, more than a means to pursue the mystical. If anything, the Muslim idea of Allah as separate from creation held as much sway with them as not, and in his exchanges with the Sufis about their beliefs, inevitably conducted in fractured, barely coherent English, it was the inner idea of Allah that Atan tried to impress upon them.

"One Allah," the Sufis often pronounced, asserting the first tenant of Islam.

"Yes, one Allah, but many faces," Atan once responded as he pointed to each of the men, causing them to look to Babah for clarification, the idea perhaps too much to grasp.

Babah smiled. "Atan babah," he said, provoking the others to kind laughter and closing the discussion.

Babah knew better than to belabor the mysterious, Atan thought.

One day, the boy who directed the men in their cooking and cleaning tasks—a sixteen-year-old orphan who'd lived with Babah since he was nine—insisted on washing Atan's clothing for him. When Atan refused, the boy became haughty.

"No good. I wash," he said, marching off to the water pump with Atan's soiled lungis and shirts balled up under his arm.

Following him, Atan attempted to take the clothing away from the boy, and a tug-of-war ensued.

"Give me!" the boy cried.

"Why?" Atan asked.

"You are important."

"I'm not important."

"Yes, important. Only white man who stay with Babah."

Ah, there it was, Atan thought, disturbed by the internalized inferiority he'd so often detected among residents of New Delhi. He thinks I'm important because I'm white.

"No, we're the same," Atan said, pointing at the boy and himself.

The boy yanked the clothing away from Atan.

"Not same."

"Yes, same," Atan said gently. "One spirit."

Kneeling side by side, the water splashing around them, the boy and Atan washed his clothes together.

Several times a year, Babah and some of his household would leave Nizamuddin on pilgrimage to the shrines of Sufi saints west and north of New Delhi, boarding a bus on Baoli Gate Road long after dark and traveling through the night hundreds of miles to reach their destinations. Arriving tired and hungry, they would be ferried in tuk-tuks to the shelters of other babahs, where they were fed and accommodated for days.

Atan had been living with Babah for almost a year when he joined the annual pilgrimage to a shrine on the outskirts of Mussoorie in the northern state of Uttarakhand, paying for all the bus tickets himself so most of Babah's acolytes could go too. There, they would celebrate the life of the Sufi poet Bulleh Shah, whose verse, Atan learned online at an Internet kiosk, had been put to music by a popular rock band in Pakistan and by a revered musician in India. Some of his poems had even been adapted for the soundtracks of Bollywood films. Intrigued by this fusion of spiritual and pop culture, Atan felt an affinity with Bulleh Shah even before leaving New Delhi for the five-hour bus trip and taxi ride high into the foothills of the Himalayas, where a symbolic tomb had been erected in honor of the eighteenth-century poet on a forested mountainside.

Bulleh Shah's actual tomb was in Kasur, Pakistan, but as the Sufis of India had been cut off from his shrine since India's partition, the Mussoorie site had been created as a stand-in. Moreover, upon his death in 1757, some of the mullahs of Kasur had declared Bulleh Shah a non-Muslim, denying him funeral prayers because he had denounced Islamic orthodoxy for its worldly corruption. The mullahs, he said, had forsaken the true teachings of the faith. Snubbed by Bulleh Shah's excommunication, the Sufis of India wouldn't have set foot in the shrine at Kasur even if they'd been welcome there.

Above all, Bulleh Shah insisted that violence was not the answer to violence, his poetry professing love, compassion, and oneness with the divine. Here was a man after his own heart, Atan thought. Indeed, the tensions between the worldliness of Islam and the transcendence of Sufism had begun to chafe, and Atan was growing weary of the strictness over trivialities that he'd observed among the men he lived with, one of whom had recently chastised Atan upon his return from the washroom in the middle of the night because he'd forgotten to take a cistern of water with him to wash his privates so he would be clean for Allah. Calling Atan out in front of the others, the man had caused a scene meant to embarrass, and Atan had resented it.

By the time they reached Mussoorie, the hazy mountain ranges stretching out above them, one layered atop the other like strips of torn tissue paper, grays and blues merging with mauves, the air thick with the scent of pines, Atan had decided it was time for him and the Sufis to part ways. Feeling the pull of nature—the sublime—more strongly than he had since his youth, he told himself that when the gathering at Bulleh Shah's tomb was over and Babah departed with the other Sufis who'd traveled with them from Nizamuddin, he would stay behind.

Admittedly, the idea seemed foolhardy. Unlike when he'd wandered away from the shrine of Inayat Khan, he was far from any populated area and would likely be forced to fend for himself. But as Atan's spiritual questing had shown him time and again, there was nothing to fear but fear itself. Jump, he reminded himself, and the net will appear.

So, when the ten-day gathering came to an end, Atan jumped, waving goodbye, a hand on his heart, as Babah turned to gaze at him through the window of the Hindustan Ambassador that had come to take the Nizamuddin contingent back down the mountain. Throughout the day, the last of the men and boys who'd come north for the occasion left, too, until only Atan remained, along with an elderly caretaker who would spend days cleaning up the site. The task required sweeping away the destemmed roses strewn about and removing the hundreds of printed shroud cloths now layered three feet high atop Bulleh Shah's symbolic tomb so they could be laundered and sold again to next year's pilgrims.

Unsure where to go, Atan stayed on to help with the work. October turning cold, he donned jeans again, as well as a pair of boots and socks, all purchased for the trip. Like the Indians, to stay warm, he wore his shirts in layers under a wool vest—a gift from the caretaker, who'd reluctantly accepted as payment some of the money from Atan's most recent visit to Western Union, where his family had been sending him funds, first addressed to Gunter and later to Babah. Sitting together to watch the sunset, Atan and the caretaker smoked the last of the hashish Atan had brought from Nizamuddin, grateful for the calm that had descended now that the multitudes were gone, the woods filling with the sounds of insects as the stars came out.

On the morning of the fifth day since everyone else had left, Atan heard a car stop in the dirt parking lot outside the shrine as he lay dozing. Stretched out next to him on the carpeted floor, the caretaker snored softly. A door slammed, and footsteps crunched along the forest path.

"Hello?" the visitor called out. "Is anyone there?"

Atan sat up, surprised to hear English, but just as startled by the soft lilt of a woman's voice, so different from the gruff male cadences that had filled his ears while living with the Sufis.

The space heater broken, Atan had slept in his clothes. He threw off his blanket and went outside.

"Hi," he called back, catching sight of a white woman who looked to be in her mid-forties.

"Oh, hello!" the woman cried happily, a row of earrings glinting in the sun as she pulled her tussled hair away from her face and knotted it at the back. "I wasn't sure anyone was here."

"Just me and the caretaker."

"Can you tell me if this is the road to Chail? My driver doesn't seem to have a clue where we are, and my Hindi is terrible."

Atan had seen Chail on a map of the foothills that he'd brought along. It was 125 miles to the west in the state of Himachal Pradesh and farther north.

"Yeah, this is it," Atan said. "It should take you about, oh, six hours to get there."

"Six hours?" she asked. "Ouch."

"It gets narrower the higher you go, or so I hear."

"Oh, is it safe?"

"I think so. I'm heading that way, too, so I guess I'll find out."

"Okay. Thanks." The woman seemed hesitant to go. "You're sure it's safe?" she asked again, laughing at herself.

"Yeah. I mean, it must be." Atan laughed too. "If you want, we could share the ride," he said. "I was planning to leave soon."

The woman smiled, the sunlight dappling her cheeks as it shone through the leaves of the branches overhead. "Yeah?"

"Yeah, sure."

"Okay. I'd love it if you came along. I've been living at a hostel in Rishikesh for weeks with no one but twenty-somethings for company."

"Let me get my things," Atan said.

"Oh, I'm Jessie," she said, offering her hand.

"Atan," he said, surprised at how warm her fingers were.

As the taxi climbed north past dense virgin forests and thick drifts of white clouds that had settled between the snow-peaked mountain ranges overnight, Atan talked so much—glad to be speaking in full sentences again after months of broken English—that he feared he was boring Jessie. Or maybe he just felt self-conscious because she was the only woman he'd really talked to since leaving the ashram in New Delhi.

He shouldn't worry, he told himself. Jessie seemed to be as grateful for Atan's company as he was for hers. Alone on sabbatical from her job at a community college in Boston, where she taught architecture, her children nearly grown, her divorce from their father long behind her, she was on a long overdue adventure and eager to hear about Sufi life.

"Why Chail?" Atan asked, his tales exhausted.

"The buildings," she said, pushing her hair back from her face. "I've been fascinated by the Indo-Western style since I was a student, but I never made it to India before now."

Jessie fished a guidebook out of a woven bag beside her on the seat and opened it to a page with a folded corner.

"Did you know Chail was deliberately made to resemble Shimla, the summer capital of British India during the Raj, which is only thirty miles to the north? The story goes that when the British banned one of Shimla's maharaja for life, he created a summer retreat of his own at Chail, spending his fortune to ensure that Chail's opulence and modern comforts surpassed Shimla's in every way."

"Why was he banned?"

"He had outraged the British viceroy of Shimla, one Lord Henry Kitchener—"

"Kitchener? The city where I grew up in Canada is named after Lord Herbert Kitchener. I bet they're related."

"I think I read something—" Jessie checked the book, flipping back a page. "Here it is. You're right. They were brothers."

It occurred to Atan that if the British had remained in India, with Shimla's name changed to Kitchener, he would be on a symbolic trip home, just miles from India's Kitchener, the name meaning the same thing there as it did in Canada. No matter how far Atan had run, he hadn't escaped history. It still confronted him.

"So, tell me the rest," he said. "What was the Maharaja's offense?"

"Oh, it's juicy," Jessie said. "The Maharaja had eloped with Lord Kitchener's daughter, who'd just arrived from England for a visit."

"The Maharaja and the Lord's daughter," Atan laughed. "It sounds like a parable."

As the trip wore on, the road winding more sharply the higher they went, the steep cliffs below them grew menacing. Instead of slowing, the driver blasted his horn as they careened around the bends, unable to see if anyone was coming the other way.

"Sir!" Atan scolded, raising his voice. "Careful, please."

"No problem," the driver said. "Everyone is honking."

Jessie turned from gazing out the window and looked at Atan in surprise.

"What?" he asked.

She stared at him, her eyes flashing with curiosity.

"Are you Ataninnuaq?" she asked. "The singer?"

Atan's heart sank, and a nervous silence filled the taxi. Even the driver slowed down and let up on the horn as they continued around the next turn. Atan smiled weakly, wary of what would come next.

"Yeah," he said. "That's me."

"I didn't make the connection because of your beard, but when you raised your voice, I recognized it. My kids are big fans. Just wait till I tell them."

Atan was surprised.

"But I'm a wanted man. What will they think?"

"Nobody believes what they say about you. I don't believe it. People hear your lyrics, and they know who you are. My students still watch your speeches on YouTube—from the Turn Your Back protests."

Jessie continued to stare at Atan, her words a balm to his soul.

"When you told me your name, I didn't make the connection because people call you Ataninnuaq now," she said.

"How did that start?"

"I don't know. Maybe they wanted to reclaim you after your name was dragged through the mud. I like it. It's strong. It's a powerful name. Like Leonard Cohen instead of, you know, Leo."

"You like Cohen?"

"I love Cohen. But I only discovered him thanks to that song you wrote. My youngest played it for me. What's it called again?"

"The River of the Baptist," Atan said.

He hummed the tune to the last song on his self-released album.

"Yes, yes," Jessie said in recognition. "How does it go?"

"I was just a wondering Jesus no more than the age of sixteen," Atan sang. "Down on King Street with a friend hanging round the record store when I found my John the Baptist, the one singer to bend my ear."

"And the chorus? I remember liking the chorus a lot."

"In the river of the Baptist," Atan sang softly, "each song has a sacred chord. That's where I hear the angels. That's where I see the Lord."

Jessie smiled.

High overhead now, the sun sparkled off the snowy mountain peaks. Above the forested valley, seven eagles circled silently as they descended on the breeze, a mesmerizing sight that seemed to Atan like a good omen.

"Did you really stop that bullet?" Jessie asked as the taxi rounded another curve, the valley lost from view.

"Yes."

"How?"

"It's a long story."

"That's okay," Jessie said, pulling her feet up onto the seat and tucking her knees under her chin. "We have miles to go."

TWENTY-FOUR

2025

Atan and Jessie arrived in Chail late in the afternoon, their bottoms numb and knees aching after hours in the taxi. Wanting nothing more than to nap before dinner, they headed to a palace-turned-hotel that Jessie had spoken of, pushing through the crowds of a flea market full of bustle, its tables of electronics and kitchen utensils, sweets and spices, clothing and purses shielded from the sun by colorful, flapping canvases. Tangles of power lines crossed overhead as they passed a row of two-story buildings with high roofs and gabled windows that, Jessie pointed out, wouldn't have looked out of place in the Swiss Alps.

At last, they arrived at the palace, which sat in the middle of a sprawling green lawn, its guest cottages tucked into the surrounding forest. Passing under the colonnade and through the massive wooden front doors, they continued along a carpeted hallway lined with glittering chandeliers until they reached the reception desk.

"Good afternoon," said a smiling clerk in a pressed white shirt with silver cuff links, a ruby tie knotted at his throat.

"Hi," Jessie said, handing him her passport. "I have a reservation."

The clerk turned to the computer console at his elbow. "Yes, here it is."

"There will be two of us," Jessie said.

"No problem, madam," the clerk said. "May I have your passport, sir?"

"No registration book?" Atan asked.

"Oh no, sir," the clerk said proudly. "Only the computer. Here, we are fully modern."

Atan made a show of looking for his passport in his satchel, where it lay between his wallet and his notebook. Then, pretending it wasn't there, he turned to Jessie.

"I must have left it in the car."

"The taxi?"

"No, no. The rental car. I put it in the glove compartment," he said, retreating toward the entrance.

"Sorry," Jessie said to the clerk, retrieving her passport. "We'll be right back."

Outside, Atan explained his predicament with Interpol.

"Maybe the Buddhist monastery outside of town will take me in," he said, half-serious.

"That's at least a half-hour drive from here," Jessie told him.

"We passed a campground a little ways back. And I think I saw a store that sells gear. I may end up needing a tent anyway."

"I'll come with you."

"No, you should stay. Enjoy the hotel."

"I can see it tomorrow. A night under the stars sounds good."

"And cold," Atan warned.

"I'm not worried. They must sell winter sleeping bags at this altitude."

Retracing their steps through the flea market, they located the camping goods store.

"There it is. Patel Wildcraft," Atan said, pointing at a squat building on the other side of the street, its windows bursting with nested pots, battery-powered lanterns, fishing tackle, gas stoves, and folding chairs.

Before long, they had bought a tent and sleeping bags and all the cookware they might need, everything stuffed into a new backpack.

In the street again, they stopped for butter and cream at one stall and found garlic, ginger, and onions at another before following a trail to the campground on the edge of the forest. Never mind a computer, there wasn't even a registration book in the little wooden hut where they paid for a campsite. Atan bought a bundle of logs and kindling from the attendant, a wiry little man with swollen feet that bulged through the sides of his sandals, and before the sun set, Atan and Jessie had settled in.

Having learned from the Sufis how to make a tasty dahl over an open fire, Atan had a bag of black lentils with him and some treasured spices—fenugreek, cinnamon, and turmeric, cayenne, cardamom, and cumin, Himalayan salt, coriander seeds, and peppercorns—all stowed in small tins that he carried in an old wooden box given to him by the sixteen-year-old orphan who had battled with Atan about washing his clothes at the *khanqah* in Nizamuddin. As the sky grew dark and the pot of food bubbled, filling the air with aromas that Jessie said were more delicious than anything she'd ever smelled, the Little Dipper appeared above the horizon, with the tail of Draco, the dragon, curled around it.

"Here, tell me what you think," Atan said, scooping some of the dahl from the pot with a wooden spoon and passing it to her.

Atan watched her face as the flavors tripped across her tongue.

"Oh, my god. It's so good."

"Are the lentils soft enough?"

"Yeah."

"Not too spicy?"

"No, they're perfect."

After they'd eaten dinner and washed their dishes together at a tap near the entrance to the campground, they sat on a blanket in the waning light of the fire. The night cold beneath a sea of stars, Jessie got up to put another log on the fire, slipping under Atan's arm for warmth when she returned. It was the first time he'd held a woman since Samara over thirteen years before.

"I could get used to this," he said.

"Me too," Jessie agreed, a hint of hesitancy in her voice.

"You don't sound so sure."

"In seven weeks, I have to go back to my job and my kids."

"Seven, huh?" Atan mused. "That's one week for each of the eagles we saw today. A good omen."

Jessie sat up to face him, her eyes meeting his. "Yeah?"

"Why not?"

"I like how you think."

Leaning closer, Jessie kissed Atan, her lips full and warm, as he marveled at their chance encounter, the grace of it all. He'd jumped, and here was the net he'd trusted would appear.

In the morning, waking to the chatter of birds, the air chilly, Atan and Jessie returned to the flea market in search of chai to warm themselves. Approaching a tea wallah's stall, they passed a newsstand, where a short, balding man bustled about, arranging the day's papers for view, his stomach bulging beneath a white *kurta* unbuttoned at the collar to expose a nest of kinky chest hair. Glancing his way, Atan caught sight of what looked like a familiar face on the cover of the *Times of India*.

"Trial in Elevator Terror Case Concludes—All Fifteen to Die," said the headline above five rows of mugshots. In the first tier, Atan saw Brad Wheeler, "the ring leader," jagged stitches from ear to mouth, and beside him Nash and Kara, "the couriers," one haunted and the other resigned. In the second tier, Terrence and Marcus, "the hackers," stared out at him, solemn and defiant, along with a woman unknown to Atan, the courier caught in the Chicago attack, the caption said. Below them glared the faces of nine more couriers, all Outliers. Atan grabbed a copy of the paper and pulled some coins from the front pocket of his jeans, his hand shaking as he counted out sixty-five rupees and dropped them into the news vendor's eagerly outstretched palm.

At the tea stall, Atan read through the article, summarizing the details for Jessie as they sat on the curb with their chai. Nash's confession had been declared inadmissible since it was made under duress. And gone with the confession was the promise to spare him the death penalty, reinstated in the United States for federal crimes in 2019 after a sixteen-year hiatus. Since the attacks occurred in separate states, the defense lawyers had asked for state trials so the accused could be tried in jurisdictions that forbid executions, but the prosecutors had convinced the court the elevators were used as weapons of mass destruction, bringing the case into the purview of the federal government. Bent on making an example of the Outliers, the feds had located the trial in Washington, DC, where no elevators fell, claiming an impartial jury could best be assured on "neutral ground."

Reading between the lines, Atan knew there had been nothing neutral about the jury of twelve white men and women selected from a pool of fifty candidates. The prosecutors, whose first criteria had clearly been a juror's entitlement born of wealth, had dismissed anyone for cause who was blue collar and lower class. And when they had no cause for dismissal, they used peremptory challenges to keep the poor off the jury, most of whom were Black men and women in a city where whites, Atan knew, earned three dollars for every dollar Blacks earned, the gap between the haves and the have-nots being so great that there was almost no middle class to bridge it. Time and again, the defense lawyers had felt compelled to remind the judge that peremptory challenges couldn't be used to discriminate based on race, and each time, he had overruled their objections.

A prominent figure in the trial, Wheeler had pushed the Outliers' lawyers to mount a necessity defense on the grounds that the average citizen was in danger of murder by wealthy elites with unbridled power to direct the actions of the federal government. Targeting men and women like Bacchus Altwied for death was a justifiable response, Wheeler said, to the heinous murder of thousands in crimes like Nine-Eleven. But the defense lawyers, adamant they could make no connection between the victims of the elevator attacks and the perpetrators of the Nine-Eleven attacks, had refused to employ this strategy.

Nevertheless, the Outliers' lawyers had allowed Nine-Eleven to bear on the trial as an explanation for the mindset and motives of the accused. Castigating the government for having left too many questions unanswered, they tabled well-known published evidence suggesting the Twin Towers were destroyed with explosives. The Nine-Eleven Commission's report, they pointed out, did not explain the total collapse of the towers but only everything up to the moment of collapse. The defense lawyers concluded the government had exposed itself to conspiracist speculation, leading directly to the retribution, even if misguided, that the Outliers had inflicted. This tactic was the only hope the defense lawyers had of generating sympathy for the accused and avoiding death sentences for all of them, whose crimes were indisputable.

The jurors hadn't been swayed. In their deliberations, as interviews revealed, they pooh-poohed the claim that investigators hadn't looked for explosives, chuckling at the idea that anything other than fire could have caused the destruction of the Twin Towers, the event too fearsome, Atan knew, to permit further reflection on anomalies they'd all seen with their own eyes. They were bewildered, too, by the idea that men like Bacchus Altwied did not deserve to wield influence in the halls of power—not that this power had in any way ever been used to direct the murders of American citizens, they insisted, just that it was theirs to wield by virtue of their enormous success—or at least, Atan thought, that was the unspoken implication. If not money, what else could be said to separate the wheat from the chaff? Surely, no one believed the poor should have the same influence. To the jury, that was a laughable idea.

As the headline said, all the accused had been sentenced to death. It would be an eye for an eye. Atan felt sick, as if the chai had turned rancid in his gut. Wheeler was going to be executed—Wheeler, who'd taught him to play the guitar, who'd believed in his songwriting, who'd been more than a roommate. Why hadn't Atan talked him out of it? Why had he let things go so far? Was it because, if he was honest, Atan had always seen Wheeler as a bit of a slob, overweight, working class, the unredeemed son of a struggling, insecure actor who'd robbed his children of confidence? Was Atan any better than the jurors, their class blinding them to the lifelong frustrations of Wheeler, of Terrence and Marcus, of Nash and Kara? His friends hadn't been born with the advantages Atan enjoyed in a world where the people most valued were the ones who rose high enough to leave the sand eaters behind or crawled over each other to get there.

Sitting by the tea stall, the street teeming with people who'd been crawled over in this way, Atan voiced his self-doubts to Jessie.

"You've done more than most to stand up for others," she told him, taking his face in her hands, his thick beard between her fingers. "Your music has inspired so many."

Atan wasn't convinced.

"Has it?"

"Of course. You just haven't been around to see it."

"And whose fault is that?"

"Don't do this to yourself. You aren't to blame." As tears ran down Atan's cheeks, Jessie brushed them away. "You're strong, but you're just one man."

Atan wiped his eyes and drank his chai. Reading on, he shared with Jessie the final words of Wheeler to the court before the jury began its deliberations—taken from a dissenting judgment in a 1928 case that Wheeler said he'd come across in the library of the prison where he'd been held in Seattle for over two years while awaiting trial. "If the government becomes a lawbreaker, it breeds contempt for law; it invites every man to become a law unto himself; it invites anarchy. Our government is the potent, the omnipresent teacher. For good or for ill, it teaches the whole people by its example." With that, Wheeler had turned to face the judge. "That's all I have," he'd said.

"If he's right about the government's part in Nine-Eleven, he has a point," Jessie told Atan.

"Right or not, the government never investigated the most obvious cause. That's on them. Wheeler's mistake was letting himself become what he condemned."

Atan stood up and tossed the newspaper into a box of trash behind the tea stall before helping Jessie to her feet.

"If you ask me, the lawyers were as blind to the truth of Nine-Eleven as the jurors," he said, returning their empty glasses. "That kind of blindness is like a mental illness. They all need to visit the shrine of the Sufi saint Mira Datar in Unava so they can be saved from the afflictions of black magic. That was Datar's thing—healing the insane."

"What do you mean by insane?"

"People have been hypnotized by the fear inflicted on Nine-Eleven and by the years of lies. They literally can't see the truth. Their subconscious won't let them."

"Are we all hypnotized?" she asked, pausing to watch the tea wallah as he passed an impressive arc of frothy milk back and forth between two small pots.

"How else can we explain the ills of the world?" Atan asked. "We've been hypnotized by black magicians, and we don't even know it."

"What do you mean, hypnotized?"

"With fear. Brooklyn Willy once told me that scared people do bad things. It's true. Our fears are hypnotic. They allow unreasonable ideas to skew our moral compass. And powerful people use that against us. We all need to be dehypnotized."

"How do you do that?"

"I don't know," Atan admitted.

Leaving the tea stall behind, they started off along the road. "To the palace?" Jessie asked, stepping aside as a donkey loaded with pots and pans trotted toward them.

"To the palace," Atan said.

In the coming days, Atan and Jessie visited as many temples and remarkable buildings as they could find, Jessie filling his head with more architectural history than he would ever recall. She was a passionate teacher, he thought, her students lucky to have her. Yet more than Chail, it was the Himalayas that most seduced them, and they treasured their return to camp each night above all else. There, under the star-bejeweled sky, the forest had a presence so resonant with time that the architecture of the town appeared flimsy by comparison, the stuff of a child's pop-up book, destined to fray and tear with each viewing.

Instead of traveling north to Shimla in search of more buildings to admire, as Jessie had originally intended, they passed their days in the wildlife sanctuary on Chail's eastern edge, happy that it seemed impossible to exhaust the trails that meandered through its seventy square miles of towering evergreens, rugged oaks, and lush grassland, the limbs of the trees resplendent with a marvelous array of birds. Here, a grey-headed flycatcher took to the air, its yellow belly gleaming in the sunlight. There, a cinnamon-colored russet sparrow alighted on a branch with a pine nut in its thick bill. Strutting out from behind a stand of trees, a pair of red-faced pheasants announced themselves with a cacophony of clucking, the male's regal-blue plumage lending the bird an air of nobility.

Eventually, Atan and Jessie decided to break camp in Chail and venture deeper into the wild, carrying their gear with them, the nights growing colder as mid-November brought winter air down from the mountaintops. With their tent set up on the outskirts of the sanctuary, they often heard wild boars foraging after dark in their compost, and each morning a pair of red deer greeted them through their screened windows. Walking alone one day, Jessie saw a goral on the trail, which she told Atan had looked to her like a goat crossed with an antelope.

"It made me think of something you might see in Narnia," she said.

Another time, as Atan gathered kindling, he was so startled by a flying squirrel that he cried out, causing Jessie to come running, certain he'd met his end. How they laughed! Most delightful of all, everywhere they went, gray langurs swept through the branches overhead, their pitch-black faces encircled by a fluffy white mane that made Atan think of Inuit parkas trimmed with fox fur.

Atan and Jessie became so immersed in nature's temple and so in tune with its rhythms that returning to Chail, even just to buy groceries, felt jarring. Overrun with the downtrodden and misshapen, the town now seemed utterly divorced from all instincts that could otherwise have alleviated many of its residents' poverty and want. No one escaped the emptiness that Atan saw in the eyes of those harried by their daily efforts to profit from the tourist trade, so abject did they appear in their obsequious utterances of "Yes, madam" and "Yes, sir" as an endless flow of entitled Westerners darkened their doors—Atan and Jessie among them.

Resolved to leave Chail behind, they bought a second backpack at Patel Wildcraft and stocked it with rice, split peas, and beans.

"Here, sir. This one is most important," the owner said, handing Atan a large bag of dried moringa leaves. "Very many vitamins, sir, and much protein."

The man then placed a pouch of ground moringa seeds on the counter.

"Even more important, sir. Only two spoonfuls you are needing to purify a big pot of water. Just follow the instructions, yes?"

To the pile, Jessie added a hiker's guide detailing all the edible foods they might find in the valleys and on the mountain slopes. And since Atan intended for them to stay close to the rivers and streams, he picked out a fishing rod and a box of tackle.

Ready at last to leave civilization behind, they started north en route to Shimla Airport at Jubbarhatti, a trek of almost thirty miles that they could easily complete in the two weeks remaining before Jessie had to fly home to Boston. To avoid the roads where possible, they stuck to the hiking trails that crisscrossed the rugged terrain, growing bolder and more sure-footed by the day. There didn't seem to be an obstacle they couldn't find their way past—not a fallen tree, the shards of a rockslide, or the loss of a trail swallowed up by the undergrowth of the forest.

Ten days into the trip, not far from the tiny village of Badoh, Jessie went off to fish early in the morning while Atan struck camp and built a fire, hoping to cook her catch for breakfast. She had just left when he heard her scream. Running along the path she'd taken, Atan emerged above the river to find Jessie standing frozen at the water's edge, the fishing rod at her feet where she'd dropped it, along with the tackle box, its lures and hooks now strewn among the smooth, round stones that lined the bank.

"Jessie?" Atan called as he descended toward her.

"Shh!" She held up a hand.

Atan stopped at her side.

"What is it?"

Jessie pointed, and just feet away, Atan saw a full-grown male lynx skulking toward them, its tufted ears flat against its head, its back arched, its stubby tail pointed skyward.

"Into the water," Atan urged Jessie, grabbing her by the arm.

"No, I can't!" she cried, pushing against him.

The lynx bared its long, sharp fangs, and a horrible screech issued from its throat.

"We have to!"

"I can't!"

Snarling, the lynx crouched down and inched closer.

"It's shallow. Look, you can see the bottom." Atan pulled her into the river.

"I can't!" she shouted, pulling free.

"Why not?"

"I got—when I was a kid, I almost—I was pulled under. I could've drowned."

The lynx prowled around a large rock, close enough now to leap upon them.

"But the water's calm."

"No!"

Seeing the terror in Jessie's eyes, Atan understood what he had to do. There was no point reasoning with her. Reason was the stuff of the ego, and no matter how safe the river was, Jessie's fear of it had been shaped by trauma, locking her into dread.

"We are more than our childhood fears," he said. "We are more than our egos. We are also spirit. Close your eyes and breathe. Spirit is wiser than we are. Breathe and trust it."

After a deep breath, Jessie shut her eyes and became still for what seemed like forever, the lynx drawing nearer. At last, her eyes flashing open in surprise, she pushed Atan ahead of her into the river, no more than waist deep, as the lynx pounced, cracking the lid of the tackle box in two.

"Is it gone?" Jessie asked as they reached the other side.

Atan could see the lynx's grayish-brown coat flashing between the trunks of the pines that lined the shore.

"It's gone."

Jessie looked at Atan in amazement.

"What did you do to me?"

"I didn't do anything," he said.

"I was hovering above the river for a second. I could see everything—how deep the water was, how slowly it was moving, even the small striped fish swimming lazily along the riverbed. I felt fearless."

Shivering in her wet jeans, Jessie took Atan by the hand. "Come on. Let's build a fire before we freeze," she said, surprising him as she started back into the water.

Warmed by the leaping flames, their wet clothes drying on a branch in the sun, they sat in silence as the events of the morning sunk in. Although their brush with the lynx could have ended in disaster, Atan felt elated. He'd stumbled upon an answer to the question Jessie had asked weeks before. "How do you dehypnotize people?" If her near drowning had entranced Jessie, allowing for the hypnotic induction of the lie that every river was deadly, her fear of the lynx had entranced her again. Only this time, she'd seen the truth of the situation, letting a new idea take hold. She'd dehypnotized herself.

"Not that people need to be scared for that to happen," Atan said, explaining the idea to her. "They just have to be entranced, I think. And lots of things can be entrancing. Like music and beauty. Anything that fills us with awe or stirs the spirit. That must be why shamans use chanting, like the Sufis, or fearsome masks, or the dark itself. It alters consciousness. It makes self-transformation easier."

"Are you a shaman?" Jessie asked.

"I don't think so. My music isn't like that."

"But you dehypnotized me."

"No. That was you."

Atan had spent years imagining what a decolonized world might look like without ever realizing that people needed to be decolonized too. Hypnosis, he now saw, was colonization of the mind. Shamans had known how to resist it, but most people didn't. Even the minds of the settlers and marauders who'd come to India and the Americas had been colonized by a story about money and wealth long before they'd arrived. How else could anyone explain slaughters of the kind Atan had watched the Spanish enact in the desert in pursuit of silver?

At nightfall, still on the trail after walking through the afternoon, Atan and Jessie looked for a clearing to set up camp, but nothing showed itself. As they rounded a bend, fat raindrops pocking the dirt at their feet, the ground gave way to stone where the mountain face broke the forest floor. It would be impossible to get a tent stake into the dirt there, Atan despaired as he looked around. Just then, in the dying light, he spied the opening to a cave high above them. Struggling up the steep incline, they scrambled inside as the raindrops turned to sleet.

Casting the beam of his flashlight across the floor, Atan could see no bones scattered about or other signs of an animal's den. Satisfied they weren't intruding, he used the last of the morning's kindling, lashed to his backpack and carried with them, to build a small fire. Settled into their sleeping bags, now zipped into one, they watched big, fluffy snowflakes drift down like in a storybook, curtaining the mouth of the cave as they made love, the call of a pygmy owl echoing off the walls—whoo wup-wup-wup whoo, whoo wup-wup-wup whoo.

With only three days left before Jessie would board her plane in Jubbarhatti, Atan woke early, his thoughts preoccupied with her departure. He imagined them standing on the tarmac. He would tell her he was going to figure out a way to return to the United States if he could and then come find her.

"Not if I come find you first," she might say.

They would have to pull themselves apart. He would try not to cry, he knew, but his heart would be heavy. And when she was gone, he would ache to love, as he had when he and Samara parted, but once more he would be alone.

Crawling out of the sleeping bag, he left Jessie to doze, her hair tousled on the pillow like a stormy sea, and went outside. He wondered where he would go after he'd picked up some money at the Western Union in Jubbarhatti, addressed this time to Jessie, and they'd said their dreaded goodbyes. Taking in the valley below, where snow melted in patches on the limbs of the trees, Atan decided he would stay there when she was gone. This place had everything—the cave for shelter, a stream not too far distant, nearby villages where he could restock his food, and a vista as majestic as any they'd seen along the way. Also, Jessie would know where to find him if she ever did come back.

Atan had to laugh at the idea of holing up inside a cave in the Himalayas, the proverbial recluse withdrawn from the world. But as it happened, he would never be alone for long in the years ahead. From time to time, after discovering him at the stream as he fished or spotting him on the trail as he foraged for mushrooms, hikers would spend a night or two visiting. Most of his guests were on a spiritual journey as they trekked between the temples that dotted the plateaus of the Shimla district. Coming to the cave like pilgrims to a *khanqah*, they fell into conversation with Atan about the most pressing questions.

Atan did not pretend to have the answers. He could speak only from experience, and he always pointed out that his retreat from the affairs of life was born of necessity. If possible, one should stay in the world, he said, and alter it for the better. Revolutionaries, he insisted, were people who used whatever they were doing, whether driving a bus, baking bread, or selling real estate, to be who they truly were.

"And who is that?" the visitor might ask.

Atan's answer was always the same. "You are not your ego," he would say. "The ego has only as much wisdom as you've been able to gain in your lifetime. Rather, you are spirit made flesh so it might know itself in the relations that arise between us—so it might look through your eyes into the eyes of another and see itself there and experience love, its highest expression. The wisdom of the ages is carried by spirit, not ego."

"But how do you know when the voice you hear is spirit?" the initiate might ask.

"I used to wonder the same thing," Atan would say. "But it's not that difficult to tell the difference after all."

Here, he would pause, taking in a raised eyebrow or an expectant smile.

"Do you ever argue with yourself?" he would ask.

"Yeah, sometimes—of course."

"And in those conversations, there is always one of you who is behaving like a child and one of you who is the parent, yes? One voice whines like a child for more dessert while the parent voice scolds it for a lack of restraint. Or the child voice always expects the worst, no matter how much the parent voice tells it otherwise. In those conversations, all you want is for the child, the ego, to submit to the parent."

"Yeah, I guess so."

"Well, just as your ego has a child-parent relationship with the self, so too does the self have a child-parent relationship with spirit. When the self comes face to face with spirit, it acts like the child, resisting intuition, crying out for free will, refusing to submit. So, when the self behaves like a child, you know the voice you're responding to is spirit. You should submit to that voice."

With those visitors who suffered life more than others, as Atan once had, the desire for death often at hand, the conversations entered a different terrain.

"I never liked conflict," Atan would explain. "As a child, either I kept to myself or I was the peacemaker. When I got older, I prided myself that there was wisdom in this stance. I didn't see that life itself is oppositional. Spirit divides itself into the many, creating opposed selves. Only in opposition is life possible. To say I didn't like conflict was to say I didn't like life. All love is about overcoming opposition—the gulf between us—by recognizing spirit in another. So, cherish life."

As the years passed and word spread far and wide of the white guru who lived like a monk high in the mountains north of Delhi, sixty miles west of India's border with Tibet, many people came to see Atan. But instead of merely talking to them about spirit, he enabled his visitors to experience spirit firsthand. As he had done with Jessie the day they'd encountered the lynx, Atan showed the seekers who stayed with him in the cave how to induce a trance that bypassed the ego and brought them into the unseen, where the lies that had bent them to the misguided ways of the world could not withstand the presence of their timeless authority. Empowered by spirit, they were ready at last to be true revolutionaries.

TWENTY-FIVE

2042

Yesterday, not long after the helicopter left, the young woman who brings my groceries came to visit unexpectedly.

"Did you talk to anyone today?" she asked as soon as she'd come up from the tunnel. "Well, did you?"

"Yes, the woman they took to the hospital. I went to her room—"

"Damn!"

"Why?"

"After we posted your message, they matched your voice to a recording of you at the checkpoint the night you came here. If they recorded you again today—"

"How could they have done that?"

"How low was the helicopter?"

"Low, very low."

"Yeah, they use directed sonics. Like a super-powerful microphone. Okay, okay—um."

She ran to the front window and looked out through a crack in the curtains. Turning around, she stared at me, panicked.

"Come here," I said, motioning for her to join me on the edge of the bed.

Tugging at the cuffs of her sleeves, she sat down.

"Whatever happens, I'm okay," I told her.

"This is my fault."

"No, I chose this, all of this, a long time ago."

"But you were safe in India. You should have stayed there."

"I was planning to leave anyway."

"How were you going to do that?"

"My sisters hired a lawyer and got me a trial in absentia. Nothing material links me to the attacks, only a confession that was ruled inadmissible. So they dismissed the charges. I'm no longer a wanted terrorist."

"When?"

"I found out a month before I got here. But I'm still banned from the United States, which is why I agreed to be hidden."

"You could have gone home, but you came here?"

"Yes."

"That's because of me."

"No, it isn't. After visiting me in the cave where I was living in India, the young man who brought me here suggested I return with him. He's the one who arranged for the chip implant in New Delhi and bribed security at the airport to let me out of the country despite my expired travel visa, not you."

"I sent him to the cave."

"You—? But you couldn't have known where to find me."

"My mother told me."

"I don't understand."

"I was conceived in that cave. It was snowing, right? It was one of her last nights in India."

I couldn't believe what I was hearing.

"My mother was Jessie."

"Your—?"

"I'm your daughter."

I looked at her, and for the first time in my life, I felt like I'd done something right. If nothing remains of me when I'm gone, there will be her, brave, poised, inspirited. We hugged, the bristles of her cropped hair tickling my cheek. Now things made sense—why she seemed so familiar, why she so desperately needed me to be what she'd always imagined.

"My name is Rachel," she said, releasing me from her arms.

"Rachel?" I sang out, unable to contain my delight.

"Mom said you once knew an Inuit girl named Rachel who was important to you. She hoped some Inuit wisdom might rub off on me."

"I think it did," I said. "And where's your mother now?"

Rachel shook her head. "The police killed her."

My heart nearly stopped.

"We were protesting the new laws. They shot her in the eye with a rubber bullet, and she bled into her brain. I couldn't help her."

"You were there?"

"Yeah."

"I'm so sorry, Rachel."

I would've wept or thrown a pot against the wall, but some fatherly instinct wouldn't let me. Neither of us said anything for a long time. Finally, I asked Rachel to come to Canada with me. I told her the woman across the hall had warned me to go north before it was too late.

When I was young, I explained, I'd gone west to study, and when I was forty-two, I'd gone south to the desert. After the elevator attacks, I'd gone east to India. But I'd never gone north. I needed to complete the medicine wheel that the ancient people of the desert had shown me. The west is the seat of the intellect, I told her, which was why I'd gone there for school. The south is the seat of emotions, so I'd gone there to heal. The east is the seat of the spirit, so I'd gone there in search of my true self. "And the north, the seat of the physical, is where I will give up my body," I said. "I'm not going to die in Washington."

I insisted she come with me, but she refused. For her, the trenches are here. Running away now would be a betrayal of her mother.

When she left me, it was late, long after curfew, and I was worried she wouldn't make it home. But she assured me she knew which checkpoints to avoid and which ones were manned by soldiers on our side. She promised to come back today by four o'clock with any news about the helicopter.

Now, as the day wears on—the house still burrowed into a silence that worries me—I can only wait and hope. I have laced up my boots and put them on. My few belongings are in my backpack. The notebook where I record my thoughts is the only thing I haven't stowed away. If I don't leave today, I may never be free again.

The old plastic clock on the wall above the sink, its face cracked, didn't work when I got here, but last night before Rachel left, I replaced the batteries with the ones from my flashlight and asked her to set the time. All day, I've had to listen to its relentless ticking. Almost 3:30 now, the sound is starting to drive me mad—whir-tuck, whir-tuck, whir-tuck. In a few hours, the sun will set. I'm thinking about trying to get to the nearest metro stop before the streets are empty. The one at L'Enfant Plaza is only three blocks away. I would have to go four stops to reach Union Station, and from there I could catch the next Amtrak train north. Would I make it? How much longer should I wait?

There is a commotion under my feet, followed by a loud bang as the cast-iron plate that covers the fireplace falls into the room with a thud. Rachel comes out of the tunnel behind it, wild-eyed and frantic. Jumping up from the edge of the bed, I grab my bag and start toward her, ready to duck into the fireplace and get out of here at last, but she pushes me to the door instead and yanks it open. As we flee into the hallway, a man's voice rises from the tunnel.

"Stop!"

I realize Rachel is being chased. The postman's door opens, and I catch sight of stacks of pamphlets printed in purple ink, like on a mimeograph machine, a whiff of alcohol-like vapors wafting out behind him as he enters the hall and slams my door, barricading it with his body. At that moment, the student's boyfriend arrives from upstairs and pushes us toward the side porch.

Outside, I'm hustled along the walkway to the curb, where the chauffeured car that was here before waits for us. In the back seat, I find the old man from upstairs dressed in his neat black suit and fedora. I get in beside him, and Rachel closes the door.

"I love you," she mouths through the glass, before running off along the sidewalk.

I can't bear to let her go, but what choice do I have? As I watch her disappear into a nearby house, a military transport climbs toward us from the bottom of the street. The boyfriend hurries into his Volkswagen bus and starts up the engine just in time to pull out, blocking the transport's path. His bus abandoned, he runs up beside the car and leaps into the front seat beside the driver.

"Go!" he hollers as the driver pulls the car away from the curb.

Looking back, I see my room's window shatter, and the muzzle of a rifle appears through the curtains, brandished by a soldier in riot gear. A bullet pierces the trunk, just missing me, as soldiers scramble out of the transport, ready to shoot too. We round the bend and turn onto the next street, slipping into the late afternoon traffic. The boyfriend turns around and smiles at me, no one in pursuit.

How wrong I was about the people in the other rooms of the safe house. When I saw the stacks of pamphlets on the floor of the postman's room, I realized I'd mistaken the fumes of the mimeograph ink for alcohol. He isn't a drunk after all, the boyfriend tells me, and he's not just a postman; he's a writer for the underground. Going low tech to avoid interception, he uses his day job to deliver his words.

The man beside me in the back seat is a retired general. Every morning, he fetches the postman's latest writings from our mailbox, stashed there when he goes out for his morning cigarette. The general takes the pages to be typed up and printed while his wife shops for food. Returning home, he carries the pamphlets in the bottom of his grocery bag, the odor of the ink masked by bushels of dill and mint. Lilacs, the pamphlets are called, or lacs, because of the ink, the boyfriend explains.

As for the actress across the hall, although she does get parts in plays put on by a local theatre, she is not a professional actress but a press secretary embedded in the White House, where she helps sympathetic politicians craft coded media messages directed at the mules. She and the others have been living in the safe house for me.

"But why?" I ask.

"You're Ataninnuaq," the boyfriend says. "The wise counselor."

The general removes his fedora and looks at me.

"Many of us are revolutionaries, thanks to you."

"And there are plenty of us. We're everywhere," the boyfriend assures me.

Before we reach the city limits, the boyfriend and the general get out at a metro stop, thanking me when I should be thanking them, so humbled am I by what I've learned. They've shown me the fruit of my life, and for the first time, I'm not ashamed to be Ataninnuaq. If there are enough of them, I say, a general strike will force the government to resign, and the system will come crashing down, billionaires be damned! And if they are truly inspirited, they will not replicate what they topple but break the mold of the colonizers and forge something timeless and right. Departing, they promise not to fail, and I'm almost hopeful.

Hitting all the safe checkpoints, the driver continues north toward Niagara Falls, where I will have no trouble crossing into Canada. My escape has left me shaken, but as the hours pass, the rhythm of the wheels against the road lulls me into a deep repose, and my agitation abates. After more than forty years, I'm ready to go home.

Sources

CHAPTER ONE

failed to spark anything like excitement in their passive faces. / Heather E. McGregor, *Inuit Education and Schools in the Eastern Arctic* (Vancouver: UBC Press, 2010), 75–76.

A name is one of our spirits. / Jean Malaurie, *Hummocks: Journeys and Inquiries among the Canadian Inuit* (Montreal and Kingston: McGill-Queen's University Press, 2007), 234.

When we had let the leaders pass. / Elisabeth Padilla and Gary P. Kofinas, "Letting the Leaders Pass: Barriers to Using Traditional Ecological Knowledge in Co-management as the Basis of Formal Hunting Regulations," in *When the Caribou Do Not Come: Indigenous Knowledge and Adaptive Management in the Western Arctic*, ed. Brenda L. Parlee and Ken J. Caine, 190–227 (Vancouver: UBC Press, 2018).

the government was trying to move our people to villages. / Frank James Tester and Peter Kulchyski, *Tammarniit (Mistakes): Inuit Relocation in the Eastern Arctic, 1939–63* (Vancouver: UBC Press, 1994).

I used its ribs to make runners for a small sled. / Wade Davis, *Shadows in the Sun: Travels to Landscapes of Spirit and Desire* (Washington, DC: Island Press; Covelo, CA: Shearwater Books, 1998), 20.

CHAPTER THREE

in a letter home to her parents. / Letter from Patricia Dian Lewis (né Naish), Frobisher Bay, to Ralph and Jessie Naish, Calgary, 22 August 1966, copy in possession of the author.

In her second letter home. / Letter from Patricia Dian Lewis (né Naish), Frobisher Bay, to Ralph and Jessie Naish, Calgary, 4 September 1966, copy in possession of the author.

the people took the wicks out of their stone lamps. / John R. Bennett and Susan Rowley, eds., *Uqalurait: An Oral History of Nunavut* (Montreal and Kingston: McGill-Queen's University Press, 2004), 387.

the amulets were for decoration. / John R. Bennett and Susan Rowley, eds., *Uqalurait: An Oral History of Nunavut* (Montreal and Kingston: McGill-Queen's University Press, 2004), 317.

all the students were taught the same things. / Helen Raptis, "Tsimshian Education versus Western-Style Schooling," in *What We Learned: Two Generations Reflect on Tsimshian Education and the Day Schools*, 35–55 (Vancouver: UBC Press, 2016).

known to tear one another to shreds for a bone or scrap of sealskin. / Jean Malaurie, *Hummocks: Journeys and Inquiries among the Canadian Inuit* (Montreal and Kingston: McGill-Queen's University Press, 2007), 3.

CHAPTER FOUR

paved over paradise just to make a parking lot. / Joni Mitchell, "Big Yellow Taxi," *Ladies of the Canyon* (Reprise Records, 1970).

kicked over the moneylenders' tables in the temple. / John 2: 13–16.

Jesus traveled the same road into the city. / Matthew 21: 1–11.

CHAPTER EIGHT

a fiction created to force human meaning upon an inhospitable reality. / Nicholas Davey, "An Introduction," in Friedrich Nietzsche, *Thus Spake Zarathustra*, trans. Thomas Common, ix–xxx (Ware, UK: Wordsworth Classics, 1997), xiii.

Baruch Spinoza imagined something similar to animism. / Roger Scruton, *Spinoza* (New York: Routledge, 1999).

So foul and fair a day I have not yet seen. / William Shakespeare, *Macbeth*, act 1, scene 3.

a dark comedy by Christopher Durang. / Christopher Durang, *The Marriage of Bette and Boo* (New York: Grove Press, 1985).

When the battle's lost and won. / William Shakespeare, *Macbeth*, act 1, scene 1.

and the horses eat each other. / William Shakespeare, *Macbeth*, act 2, scene 4.

Hamlet's "to be or not to be" monologue. / William Shakespeare, *Hamlet*, act 3, scene 1.

Fill your bowl to the brim and it will overflow. / Lao Tzu, *Tao Te Ching*, trans. Stephen Mitchell (New York: Harper Perennial, 1994), ch. 9.

ripped into a wild cover of "Psycho Killer." / Talking Heads, "Psycho Killer," *Talking Heads: 77* (Sire Records, 1977).

CHAPTER NINE

the trees in Anton Chekhov's The Cherry Orchard. / Anton Chekhov, *The Cherry Orchard*, trans. Stephen Mulrine (London: Nick Hern, 1998).

a paper about Albert Camus and suicide. / Albert Camus, "An Absurd Reasoning," in *The Myth of Sisyphus and Other Essays*, 3–65 (1955; reprint, New York: Vintage Books, 1991).

Janis Joplin's "Me and Bobby McGee." / Janis Joplin, "Me and Bobby McGee," *Pearl* (Columbia Records, 1971)

The Guess Who's "American Woman." / The Guess Who, *American Woman* (RCA Victor, 1970).

Johnny Cash's "Folsom Prison Blues." / Johnny Cash, *With His Hot and Blue Guitar* (Sun Records, 1955).

Cohen's song "Dress Rehearsal Rag" was playing. / Leonard Cohen, "Dress Rehearsal Rag," *Songs of Love and Hate* (Columbia Records, 1971).

Long Day's Journey into Night. / Eugene O'Neill, *Long Day's Journey into Night* (1956; reprint, New Haven, CT: Yale University Press, 2002).

CHAPTER ELEVEN

Among this lot was Isaac. / Rafiq, *Be Smile: The Stories of Two Urban Inuit*, documentary (Hay River Films, 2006), https://vimeo.com/103911360.

Leonard Cohen's song about Janis Joplin. / Leonard Cohen, "Chelsea Hotel #2," *New Skin for the Old Ceremony* (Columbia Records, 1974).

CHAPTER THIRTEEN

Dan Rather was as startled by the events of the day. / "9/11: Dan Rather Commentary," *YouTube*, 12 September 2010, https://www.youtube.com/watch?v=idokOg_Nf_k.

At least three dozen reporters on the ground said the same thing. / Ted Walter and Graeme MacQueen, "9/11 News Coverage: How 36 Reporters Brought Us the Twin Towers' Explosive Demolition on 9/11," *Global*

Research, 15 September 2020. https://www.globalresearch.ca /how-36-reporters-brought-us-twin-towers-explosive-demolition-911/5718119; Graeme MacQueen and Ted Walter, "The Triumph of the Official Narrative: How the TV Networks Hid the Twin Towers' Explosive Demolition on 9/11," *Global Research*, 9 September 2022, https://www.globalresearch.ca/triumph-official-narrative-how-tv-networks-hid-twin-towers-explosive-demolition-911/5792911.

a copy of The Miracle of Mindfulness. / Thich Nhat Hanh, *The Miracle of Mindfulness: An Introduction to the Practice of Meditation* (Boston: Beacon Press, 1999).

this evidence was the smoking gun. / Neils H. Harrit, Jeffrey Farrer, Steven E. Jones, Kevin R. Ryan, Frank M. Legge, Daniel Farnsworth, Gregg Roberts, James R. Gourley, and Bradley R. Larsen, "Active Thermitic Material Discovered in Dust from the 9/11 World Trade Center Catastrophe," *Open Chemical Physics Journal* 2, no. 1 (2009): 7–31, https://benthamopen.com/contents/pdf/TOCPJ/TOCPJ-2-7.pdf.

CHAPTER FOURTEEN

They don't let a woman kill you, not in the Tower of Song. / Leonard Cohen, "Tower of Song," *I'm Your Man* (Columbia Records, 1988).

CHAPTER FIFTEEN

Come senators, congressmen, please heed the call. / Bob Dylan, "The Times They Are A-Changin'," *The Times They Are A-Changin'* (Warner Bros., 1963).

CHAPTER SIXTEEN

"This visitation," Ataninnuaq said gravely, "is but to whet thy almost blunted purpose." / William Shakespeare, *Hamlet*, act 3, scene 4.

CHAPTER SEVENTEEN

The book is a Western. / Zane Grey, *The Fugitive Trail* (1957; reprint, New York: Pocket Books, 1963).

CHAPTER EIGHTEEN

What does it profit us to gain the whole world but forfeit our souls? / Mark 8: 36.

CHAPTER NINETEEN

the title of Chuck Berry's first hit song. / Chuck Berry, "Maybellene," *Chuck Berry Is on Top* (Chess Records, 1955).

CHAPTER TWENTY-ONE

killers in high places who say their prayers out loud. / Leonard Cohen, "Anthem," *The Future* (Columbia Records, 1992).

CHAPTER TWENTY-THREE

"That's Babah," whispered Atan's new friend. / Rafiq, *Khanqah: A Sufi Place*, documentary (Hay River Films, 2011), https://vimeo.com/105021255.

CHAPTER TWENTY-FOUR

the Twin Towers were destroyed with explosives. / Neils H. Harrit, Jeffrey Farrer, Steven E. Jones, Kevin R. Ryan, Frank M. Legge, Daniel Farnsworth, Gregg Roberts, James R. Gourley, and Bradley R. Larsen, "Active Thermitic Material Discovered in Dust from the 9/11 World Trade Center Catastrophe," *Open Chemical Physics Journal* 2, no. 1 (2009): 7–31, https://benthamopen.com/contents/pdf/TOCPJ/TOCPJ-2-7.pdf.

did not explain the total collapse of the towers. / Steven E. Jones, Frank M. Legge, Kevin R. Ryan, Anthony F. Szamboti, and James R. Gourley, "Fourteen Points of Agreement with Official Government Reports on the World Trade Center Destruction," *Open Civil Engineering Journal*, no. 2 (2008): 39, http://benthamopen.com/contents/pdf/TOCIEJ/TOCIEJ-2-35.pdf.

a dissenting judgment in a 1928 case. / *Olmstead v. United States*, 277 US 438 (1928), https://en.wikipedia.org/wiki/Olmstead_v._United_States.

Wheeler had turned to face the judge. "That's all I have." / Wendy S. Painting, *Aberration in the Heartland of the Real: The Secret Lives of Timothy McVeigh* (Waterville, OR: Trine Day, 2016), 210.

We all need to be dehypnotized. / Four Arrows, *Point of Departure: Returning to Our More Authentic Worldview for Education and Survival* (Charlotte,

NC: Information Age Publishing, 2016); Rafiq, "Indigenous Perspective on Four Arrows' Book Point of Departure," *International Journal of Fear Studies* 1, 2 (2019): 71–75, https://prism.ucalgary.ca/handle/1880/111133; Rafiq, "Indigenous Worldview and the Dehypnosis of the West," *Journal of the Canadian Association for Curriculum Studies* 17, 2 (2020): 125–30, https://jcacs.journals.yorku.ca/index.php/jcacs/article/view/40385.

About the Author

ROBERT SEAN LEWIS (aka RAFIQ) wrote his first book, *Gaj: The End of Religion*, to counter the idea of God or Allah as an individual who could take sides in the War on Terror. His memoir, *Days of Shock, Days of Wonder*, chronicles his disillusionment with the religious and political models of our times. Among his online documentaries are *Be Smile: The Stories of Two Urban Inuit* and *Khanqah: A Sufi Place*. *Atan the Revolutionary* is his first novel.

www.ingramcontent.com/pod-product-compliance
Lightning Source LLC
Chambersburg PA
CBHW030625310726
48979CB00003B/880
* 9 7 8 1 9 5 5 0 1 8 3 6 4 *